A SEASON OF PERFECT HAPPINESS

A SEASON OF PERFECT HAPPINESS

A Novel

MARIBETH FISCHER

DUTTON

DUTTON

An imprint of Penguin Random House LLC
penguinrandomhouse.com

LIBRARY OF CONGRESS CATALOGING-IN-PUBLICATION DATA

Names: Fischer, Maribeth, author.
Title: A season of perfect happiness: a novel / Maribeth Fischer.
Description: [New York]: Dutton, 2024.
Identifiers: LCCN 2023054078 (print) | LCCN 2023054079 (ebook) |
ISBN 9780593474679 (hardcover) | ISBN 9780593474686 (ebook)
Subjects: LCGFT: Novels.
Classification: LCC PS3556.I7628 S43 2024 (print) |
LCC PS3556.I7628 (ebook) | DDC 813/.54—dc23/eng/20240112
LC record available at https://lccn.loc.gov/2023054078
LC ebook record available at https://lccn.loc.gov/2023054079

Printed in the United States of America

1st Printing

BOOK DESIGN BY SHANNON NICOLE PLUNKETT

A SEASON OF PERFECT HAPPINESS

PART I

For, unless we perform, we do not live.

—Serafin (played by Alfred Lunt)
to Pedro (played by Alan Reed),
in S. N. Behrman's *The Pirate,* act 1, scene 3

CHAPTER 1

If you could live an entire season of your life in perfect happiness, knowing that once the season ended, you'd remember nothing at all of that time, would you still take the chance?

A question I read in a book called *What If,* and I remember thinking, *Of course I'd take the chance.* Who wouldn't choose a season of perfect happiness? And the part about forgetting? I didn't believe it possible to live an entire summer or autumn in perfect happiness and *not* have those memories be part of you. If sadness can alter the chemicals in one's brain, alter how a woman loves, how she grieves, how she thinks—and I know all too well sadness does do this—then why not happiness?

Why do we assume happiness is benign, that it doesn't leave scars?

I read that archaeologists can determine—from a fragment of bone buried for centuries—a man's age and height, what he typically ate, what his job might have been. I like to believe that happiness, even at the level of bones, marks us similarly. A slight softening, a pale discoloration, and the archaeologist hundreds, even thousands, of years into the future will know: Once upon a time, there was a season, perhaps more, of perfect happiness.

It's hard to believe I've been living in Wisconsin for over a decade, this state I chose based only on its shape. Shortly before moving here, browsing magazines in the library in the Delaware beach town where I lived, I'd happened upon a map of the United States that depicted the states in pastel colors according to annual rainfall or snowfall or maybe population density. All I noticed was Michigan and Wisconsin, like a pair of child's mittens, pale pink, with their thumbs of land around a Great Lake. Were these the only pink states? The only pink states surrounded by yellow or blue or green, that minty green that for thirteen months was the dominant color of my life?

It was the green of new plants, the green of a fading bruise, and the green of the walls in the hospital that became, when I was twenty-five and twenty-six, the place I felt safest.

A child's pink mittens.

I didn't move to the Midwest right away after seeing the map. I didn't yet understand that I'd have to leave Delaware if I ever wanted to retrieve my life from the place I'd lost it, without ever meaning to, which is how we almost always lose the things that matter most. If I learned anything in the hospital, I learned that sometimes, maybe most of the time, it happens just that quickly: You can lose a part of your life as easily as you can lose an earring or a pair of sunglasses or a mitten. And you don't realize until it's gone.

I'd been living in Wisconsin for six years the summer I met Erik. We met at the Y. I'd noticed him before because I couldn't *not* notice him. He's so tall, at six foot three tall enough that when standing beside him, I have to tilt my head back to meet his eyes, which are a beautiful startling blue.

Thick dark hair without the gray he has now; a lanky athletic body. When we saw each other, we'd nod in recognition, but that was it. I liked him for this. I didn't go to the Y to flirt or make friends. I went because I needed to, especially that summer, ten years since the accident. Exercise and work were the only things keeping the glacier-like depression from advancing once more across the surface of my life. Still, I did notice Erik wasn't wearing a wedding ring; later, he confessed he'd noticed the same thing about me.

By August, I was in the gym sometimes twice a day, and it was on one of those days when I saw Erik was also in for the second time. "Uh-oh," he said. We were both leaving, walking across the lobby. "You too?"

"Me too *what*?" I laughed.

"Twice in one day." He shifted his gym bag on his shoulder. "It's never a good sign."

He was right, and I wondered what in his life was troubling him. He seemed like one of those guys at ease with himself and at ease in the world. But isn't this what we often imagine? Everyone else is doing okay, we think. They look good, they're functioning, and we forget: We are too.

"Maybe I'm just disciplined," I teased as Erik and I stepped into the sticky midsummer night. Even the sky looked sunburned, a hot fiery pink.

"Disciplined, huh?" It was a Sunday. Only a few cars in the parking lot. "I wish that's what I was." He squinted past me, and I felt a pang of regret. Who was I kidding? I wasn't disciplined either.

But then he shifted his blue eyes back to me and grinned. "So, are you too disciplined to get a frozen custard with me?"

"Are you kidding?" I smiled. "Half the reason I come here is so I can eat stuff like that." This wasn't true either. But

Kopp's Frozen Custard was down the road, and the sky was still light, and the thought of spending another night eating salad while I watched TV felt beyond lonely.

We didn't talk about anything personal that night. In fact, he made a point of it. "Let's have a moratorium on families, exes—especially exes—serious illness, therapy. . . ." He handed me a paper cup of custard. "My last date covered all that and more in the first ten minutes."

"No tattoo descriptions either," I laughed. I didn't think he had any. I glanced at his tanned, ropey arms.

"Tattoos? You've had tattoo confessions? On first dates?"

"You haven't?" I dipped my spoon into the custard. "Well, okay, only once, but still. He thought I should know up front where his ex-girlfriend's name was tattooed. Talk about too much information."

"Jesus," he laughed. "No kidding."

We were sitting outside at one of a dozen picnic tables, the place loud with staticky music played from speakers, the crunch of tires over gravel, zigzagging strings of multicolored Christmas lights. It felt like a scene from the 1950s. *Laverne and Shirley*; *Happy Days.* We were both in workout clothes—running shorts and a tank top for me, my long brown hair in a ponytail; basketball shorts, Nikes, and a T-shirt for him.

We talked mostly about our jobs. The year before, he'd become project manager of the Ten Chimneys restoration. *Ten Chimneys.* The name was vaguely familiar. He told me it was the summer retreat built in the 1920s by Alfred Lunt and Lynn Fontanne, the most critically acclaimed American stage actors of the twentieth century.

"Does it really have ten chimneys?"

He cast a bemused look my way. *Bemused.* Had I ever used that word? But already I was different. Relaxed; happy.

"You have heard of Lunt and Fontanne, right?" he asked. And then, "Are you a theater person at all?" He arched an eyebrow, because no, I wasn't a theater person, though in that moment I wanted to be.

The sky was nearly dark, fireflies flashing, the murmur of conversation filling the air. "My closest friend growing up was—is—an actress." I was surprised at how easily the words slipped out, though as soon as I said them, I felt the night shift, memories kaleidoscoping: Kelly sitting on the beach, knees to her chest, practicing lines for Ophelia, or Kelly waving a pair of Broadway tickets, a Christmas gift from her parents, and *of course* she was taking me! Kelly in Audrey Hepburn sunglasses and red lipstick; Kelly flopping dramatically onto her bed, clutching the acceptance letter from Yale to her chest. No wonder Ten Chimneys had sounded familiar. She would have known who Lunt and Fontanne were, had probably mentioned them, mentioned Ten Chimneys. In another life, I would have phoned her the minute I got home and told her, *I met this guy and you'll never guess where he works.* Except that made no sense because in the life where Kelly had been my friend, I was married to her older brother.

"I need a moratorium on my job, don't I?" Erik said. "I'm sorry. I start talking about Ten Chimneys and—"

"No, no. It's fascinating." And it was. Noël Coward was such good friends with Alfred and Lynn, he'd had his own bedroom at Ten Chimneys; Katharine Hepburn used to visit, Helen Hayes, Laurence Olivier.

"We call him Larry around the office." Erik leaned forward and stage-whispered, "Vivien used to visit him during breaks in the filming of *Gone with the Wind.* He was still married."

"Vivien Leigh?" I whispered back. "Here?"

"It's wild, isn't it? All those people in this little town no one's heard of."

Is that when he asked how I'd ended up here? I told him I'd seen a map and liked that Wisconsin was shaped like a mitten.

"Seriously? You liked the *shape* of the state?" Lights from passing cars moved in a straight line along the rise of Interstate 94 to the south. A breeze riffled the leaves.

"Well, there might be a little more to it." I felt my pulse in my throat. "But we do have that moratorium."

"Ah, yes. We do, don't we?"

He asked about my job then, and I told him what I did as a graphic designer, how my real love was making collages that I sold in a local gallery.

"Collages? Like scraps of paper?"

"Photos, wallpaper, snippets of cloth, anything really."

"So, what do you love about it?" I could no longer see his face in the darkness.

"It's hard to explain. It's . . ." *Healing,* I wanted to say, or *redemptive,* but I wasn't sure if this was true or if I just wanted it to be. "The collages are like puzzles," I said. "There's all these random fragments, and if I can just figure out how to arrange them, I can make a completely different story." Of course, I was talking about my life. Trying to arrange the broken pieces into something whole. I wasn't sure it was possible, but sitting there with Erik, I felt such longing to believe it was.

We were silent then, but it was a good silence. Across the parking lot, an impossible number of teenagers—nine? Ten?—tumbled, laughing and shrieking, from their tiny car.

"What were you like as a kid?" Erik asked. "Goody Two-shoes? Nerd? Bad girl?"

"Pure Goody Two-shoes," I said. "And you were a bad boy, I can tell."

"Oh, bless you." He put his hand on his heart, grinning. "No one has accused me of that, *ever.*" He shrugged. "I'm a rule follower. Always have been."

"Me too."

"You? The woman who chose where to live based on the shape of the state?" He shook his head, but there was this look in his eyes—I felt how much he liked me, and I liked him too, and for a second, I wished so much that I could tell him the truth. I never had a reason to move to Wisconsin so much as I had a thousand reasons to leave Delaware.

Or maybe not a thousand.

Maybe only three: My best friend, Kelly. My ex-husband, Nick. And Lucy, our daughter.

Erik asked me out for the following weekend, and I said yes, though it terrified me, the spike of joy when I saw him at the gym, the rush of adrenaline when I heard his voice on the phone. I'd been on a few dates since moving to the Midwest; I'd even been in a brief relationship, but I hadn't, not since Nick, felt that *whoosh!* of hope plunging through me.

Shortly before I moved here, I'd joined a monthly outpatient group at the hospital for women like me, and one of the things we discussed was how we would talk about our children when we met someone new. Dr. Fasnacht had us role-play situations where we tried to explain. But no matter who acted as the friend or potential spouse or lover, the responses were the same: "How do you live with yourself?" or "How do you ever get over something like that?" It didn't matter that we were pretending to be someone else, some imaginary character from our unimaginable futures. We couldn't fathom that anyone would understand what we had done because we didn't understand it ourselves. "This isn't helping," I remember weeping in the middle of role-play. "Why would anyone decent want us?"

"Because what you did is not who you are," Dr. Fasnacht said.

I thought of that a lot that summer of 2000, the summer I met Erik. It seems so long ago, but in that time before iPhones and Facebook and YouTube, second chances still felt possible.

CHAPTER 2

"You've lived here five years and never been to the state fair?" he asked me over the phone two days later. "That's unacceptable! Where else can you see a thousand-pound pig?"

"Exaggerating, are we?" I'd just come in from a run and was lying on my living room carpet in front of the window AC. I felt like a giddy teenager.

"Scout's honor," Erik said.

"You were a Boy Scout?"

"Hell no."

I closed my eyes. His laughter swirled through me.

And he wasn't exaggerating. We strolled through the 4-H barns filled with Holsteins and Clydesdales and, yes, a thousand-pound pig. We breathed through our mouths, the air pungent with the smell of manure, thick with dust. When he casually laced his fingers through mine, I felt as if silver coins were falling through my insides.

"So, what's next?" he asked when we exited Agriculture Hall, squinting into white sunlight. "We could get a bite to eat or . . . There's always monkeys racing on greyhounds."

I laughed. "You're joking."

"Come on." He grinned. "They're my daughters' favorite."

Daughters.

A feeling of ice in my lungs.

"What?" he asked. And then, "Oh, crap. You didn't know I had kids. Three. They're amazing. Exhausting, sometimes terrifying, but amazing." Everything about him—his eyes, face, voice—lit up with love for those kids. Nick used to look like that.

I glanced away, trying to compose my face. I'd never seen him with kids at the Y, and when he hadn't mentioned them the other night, I had thought . . . had let myself think . . . My face burned. I couldn't go out with him again. It would be unbearable to be around children, and even if I could let myself love a child again . . .

"Hey." He stooped to meet my gaze. "You okay?"

"Just surprised. Three, wow!" My voice sounded cartoonlike and as fake as my smile. "What about their mom? Is she . . . Are you . . ." I wasn't sure why I was asking, especially when I had already decided I couldn't see him after this.

"Are we divorced? Yes. Thoroughly. Completely. Happily. Well, I don't mean I'm happy that we—actually, I am. We were a mess; the marriage was a mess." He looked at me helplessly. "And now this conversation is a mess. Were you ever married?"

I'd always said no to this question because it shut down the other question, which was unanswerable: *Do you have kids?* But this time, the lie I'd told a dozen times before, that tiny inconsequential *no,* dissolved in my throat, and a sad flickering *yes* came out instead, the neon green of Nick's name flashing meteor-like across my thoughts. I didn't know what else to say, though, how to joke or indicate with a rueful smile that it no longer hurt. It did. It always would.

Whatever Erik saw in my face, he abruptly, thankfully,

switched gears. "Come on, let's get a drink. I'll show you a picture of my kids."

We found a table in a German-themed beer garden beneath a blue-and-white-striped umbrella. He handed me his wallet, the plastic picture sleeve open to a photo of three children, dark-haired like Erik. "The best things in my life." He pointed. "Spencer, Hazel, and Phoebe."

"Your daughters are twins?"

He nodded.

It was a studio portrait. The girls, infants in red velvet dresses, chubby legs in white lace tights, sat together in a plush armchair. The boy, Spencer, stood beside them. A Christmas tree in the background. "They're beautiful," I said. My face felt rubbery. After a moment, I handed the wallet back.

He stared at the picture before folding the wallet shut and sticking it in his pocket. I think I asked how old the kids were, but my voice was polite and as faraway as the silver speck of an airplane moving across the sky. I didn't hear what he said. And then we were quiet, but it wasn't the comfortable silence we'd shared at the custard stand. Everything felt wrong.

"I guess the kids were part of my wanting a moratorium the other night," Erik finally said. "It's not that I don't love talking about them, but things are . . . complicated." He stared off toward the fairgrounds. The Ferris wheel turned against the endless blue sky. "I just wanted simple for one night, you know?" He raked his hand through his unruly hair. "You must think I'm a lousy dad."

"I don't think that at all."

"Really?" Relief flooded his eyes. "I'm glad." And then, "So, what about you? Any kids you accidentally forgot to mention?"

Accident.

A word from another life.

It took most of my thirteen months in the hospital to say that word, *accident,* without faltering. I wanted more than anything in my life for that afternoon to have been an *accident,* but I wasn't sure. Once I'd looked up the word, as if my confusion were a matter of definition. *Accident: sudden and unexpected event.*

The definition had stopped me. Hadn't there been warnings?

Could it be an accident if it *wasn't* unexpected?

I couldn't meet Erik's eyes, gluing mine instead to the bright circle of the Ferris wheel. It had stopped, the small carts swaying against the sky.

The night before the *accident,* Nick and I had gone to the boardwalk and ridden the Ferris wheel. The boardwalk was packed, and it was impossible to maneuver the stroller through the crowds. All I did was apologize and say "Excuse me" until I wanted to scream. Mostly what I remembered, though, was how I had stared at the ocean from atop that Ferris wheel, the waves endlessly rushing forward, then retreating.

It was how motherhood felt.

Something I both longed for and wanted to run from.

I didn't know that that view, from atop the Ferris wheel, would be the last view I'd have of the ocean for months. The last view of my life as it had been. I still see it sometimes when I think of home. Not the house a block from the ocean where I grew up or Kelly's house near the country club, her bedroom plastered with posters—*Cats, The Phantom of the Opera;* Nick's bedroom down the hall. Nor was it the little bungalow Nick and I had on Fourth Street near the bay or even my parents' restaurant on the main avenue in town. It was the view from atop the Ferris wheel my last night with Lucy and Nick. As if I somehow knew I needed to see as much as possible. That the view would have to last me for years.

"Hey, where'd you go?" Erik said. From the arcades lining the midway came the bells and buzzers and the *rat-a-tat-tat* of fake machine-gun fire.

"I was thinking about the town where I grew up," I said. "It was a resort, so we had all this. . . ." I nodded toward the midway. "A boardwalk, arcades, a Ferris wheel."

"Seriously?" He looked at me curiously. "We used to vacation at a resort up in Door County, and we'd drive by a high school or . . . I don't know, a Jiffy Lube, something non-resort-like, and it would surprise me to realize regular people who went to school and got their oil changed actually lived there. I always wondered what that would be like."

"To live in a place people dream about visiting all year? It's magical."

"Do you get back there much?"

"I wish, but . . ." I lifted one shoulder in a shrug. "It's complicated."

"Ahh, yes. *Complicated.*" He smiled knowingly, and I felt how already the word had become ours. *Complicated*—an IOU, a promise: *I'll tell you, just not yet.* I'd forgotten about this shorthand between couples, ordinary words packed with layers and history. I wanted that again.

For a moment we were quiet, and then, because I needed to say something, I said, "I'm surprised your girls are so young."

He nodded. "Two years on Sunday."

"So, you and your wife . . . How long have you been divorced?"

"Is there a limit on how many *complicated*s we get?"

"Bad question?"

"More like bad answer." He sighed. "We've been divorced two years. We were separated when the twins were conceived."

I felt my stomach knot with jealousy at the red flag of his ex-wife and their perhaps unfinished relationship. For a moment I forgot: After today, I wouldn't be seeing Erik again unless it was in passing at the Y.

"Yeah, I know how it sounds," he was saying. "I was at the house helping her with Spencer, and it got late. . . ."

"So, did you try to work things out?"

"We were done. Had been." He glanced at me. "We became very different people after Spencer was . . . I'm not sure *diagnosed* is the right word because there have been half a dozen diagnoses."

"For what?"

He didn't answer, just shifted his arm on the small plastic table so that his knuckles grazed mine. He stared at our hands for a long moment, then said, "Spencer's got a lot of learning and behavioral issues. And like I said, a lot of diagnoses, which aren't necessarily wrong, but I'm not always convinced they're right either. Maybe I just don't like the labels or . . . maybe I don't like the assumptions people make about the labels."

"Is this why you didn't mention your kids?"

"Because of Spencer? Jesus. I hope not. . . ." His eyes met mine. "But maybe." Something forlorn crossed his expression. "I don't want to scare you off, Claire. At least not before you get to know us." He moved his hand from mine. "Though I guess if you're going to be scared, I might as well get it over with."

A breath of sadness swept through me. No matter what I said, he would assume this was why I didn't want to see him again. "You're not going to scare me off," I said quietly. "Believe me." *Him* scare *me* off? It was more like the other way around: *I* would scare *him* away. "So, what kind of issues?" I said.

He explained that even as an infant Spencer hadn't liked to be touched or held, that he hadn't spoken until he was four. "Annabelle and I learned sign language for basic words—*mama* and *daddy* and the most important word of all." He grinned. "*More.*" He showed me the sign, then said, "Spencer's still 'delayed' with speech"—he put air quotes around the word *delayed*—"although that's one of those things I don't always trust. He's such a watcher and a thinker—why isn't that enough? Plus, he's smart as hell. He's fascinated by science and the weather—God, just ask him about the types of clouds or what causes storms. . . ." He exhaled slowly. "I just think the world comes at him too fast."

"Ha! I feel like that myself some days."

"Exactly, right? Only for Spence, that too-muchness is exaggerated exponentially, and it's not just some days. It's constant. The most ordinary stimuli—lights, sounds, colors, textures—ambush him in ways I imagine feel threatening. Any change in routine, anything unpredictable . . . it's a struggle for him."

I know, I wanted to say, though of course I didn't. But I thought of the years since I'd left the hospital, years when I craved routine and certainty, years when I confided in no one, years when I found my own ways to push the too-muchness of the world away. It was exhausting, though, and sitting there in that hot sun, our arms leaving lines of sweat where our skin lay against the plastic table, it seemed impossible that I could keep being this alone.

I liked Erik. A lot. He was kind and fun and good-looking and smart. But *he had children.* There was nothing beyond this. And yet when his knee grazed mine as we sat on makeshift bleachers watching a cream puff–eating contest; when he brushed my hair from my eyes as we waited in line for beer, his fingers callused against my cheek; when we aimed only for each other on the bumper cars, laughing and ruthless as we rammed into each other, I kept forgetting that I had to walk away from him. *He has children.* Each time I remembered, I felt a splintering of panic in my chest and then anger: I didn't want to walk away. And why, why, did I have to? It had been ten years. *Ten.*

We were strolling down the midway, Erik's fingers laced through mine. The sky was russet with sunset, heat unraveling from the day. I was silent, my grief and guilt and love for Lucy pushing against my ridiculous hope that maybe one day I could tell Erik the whole story and maybe once he'd gotten to know me, he'd understand. I pulled in a deep breath as a dozen more *maybe*s scattered themselves through me: Maybe he was the reason I'd moved here; maybe he was my second chance. Because why meet him at all, why go on this date, why feel everything I was feeling, unless . . . *Maybe,* I thought again, the word a kind of prayer tattooed on the night, hundreds of pricks of pain that could *maybe maybe maybe* turn into something beautiful.

I tasted my first bratwurst that day. Another thing he was appalled I'd lived here six years and never tried. I wanted to dislike it, find a thousand differences I could stack like bricks between this man and the way my heart was pounding. But even as I was thinking this, he was cupping his hand beneath my chin as I leaned forward and took a bite, and in the next instant, he was straining across the little table to kiss me, tasting of mustard and beer, and I was half laughing, butter dripping on my hands from the corn on the cob I'd just set down. We kept kissing, soft quick kisses, as if we couldn't bear to have our mouths apart, and everything went quiet around us.

"Wow," he said thickly when we pulled away from each other finally. He took a sip of beer, then handed the plastic cup to me. My hands were shaking.

Until that moment, I'd thought I'd made peace with the fact that I probably wouldn't feel this way again.

Of course, we had frozen custard that night. Already it was *our* thing. We got cones and walked, the air cooler, the sky the color of roses, a smoky pink that reminded me of the color Nick and I had painted her bedroom.

"Penny for your thoughts," Erik said.

"The sky is so amazing here." I was staring up. "It's not like this back east."

"Do you miss it?"

"No."

The answer came out too sharply, and I saw a flicker of something in his eyes. But he just put his arm around me and said, "You and I have a bunch of complications, don't we?" Before I could answer, he said, "Wait, come here," and when I turned to him, he wiped a dot of custard from the tip of my nose. The gesture made me ache; it was so simple and so tender. Longing and happiness and something else—hope maybe, gratitude?—moved against the edges of my lungs, then expanded.

"I like that," Erik said gently.

"What?"

"The look in your eyes."

And I liked the look in his. I thought of those missiles projected from across an ocean to explode in one specific spot, an exact target, and I thought of how his gaze ignited into mine that night, obliterating everything that came before.

CHAPTER 3

I loved mornings, something I inherited from my mother. I could count on one hand those rare times, growing up, when I came downstairs and she was *not* already up, often before it was light out, sitting on our screened-in front porch. In the winter, she'd wrap herself in a blanket, wear mittens and a hat over her pj's. A mug of coffee on the wicker table next to her, a novel in her lap, though mostly, she'd be staring out across the street, the houses empty in the off-season. She'd be so still, so lost in thought, it worried me. Where did she go? Was she unhappy? "Your mom's just charging her batteries," my dad would say, and it's true that if she didn't get her time in the mornings, she'd seem out of sorts, something clipped in her movements as if she were hoarding her energy.

I was the same way now, setting the alarm for four thirty, though I wouldn't run or go to the Y until later. I liked watching the swerve of daylight across the lawn, igniting the maple tree out back, the faded siding of the house behind mine. I liked sitting in bed, drinking coffee, paging through magazines I found at thrift stores, looking for words or images to use in collages.

When the phone rang just after five, I knew it would be

my mother. We usually talked in the morning, though not as often in the summer, when she was at the restaurant late every night with my dad.

"So?" she said. "How'd it go?" I'd told her Erik and I were going out again. The fourth time in two weeks. That he had children.

"It scares me, Mom," I said. "I haven't felt like this since . . ."

"I know," she said. "Since Nicky." *Nicky.* Only my mother had gotten away with calling him that. It surprised me to hear her say it. She'd been so angry at him. For a long time, he'd been just Nick, that hard *K* of his name sounding like something she wanted to snap in half.

I nodded, unsure why I'd hesitated to mention him. Maybe the anniversary, a week away. Ten years. It felt impossible. Or maybe I hesitated because being with Erik was bringing up the past in ways I hadn't anticipated. You don't expect the good memories to hurt more than the terrible ones, but they do. For years I'd revisited all those last scenes with Nick: the few times in the hospital when everything about him was shuttered against me, and the brief, difficult visits after, which were worse. But in the past week I'd remembered other things: Kissing Nick for the first time in his parents' kitchen when Kelly was out of the room, then trying to act normal once she returned. *Why are you guys being so weird?* Or driving down Coastal Highway in his ancient blue pickup to go surfing at the inlet, my hair blowing in my eyes and him telling me, "You should see how beautiful you look."

I glanced at the magazine in my lap. *Respiratory Medicine.* Margaret, who lived in the other half of the duplex I rented, was a respiratory therapist at Waukesha Memorial. I was working on a collage about breath and air, which had started with, of all things, a map of the 1913 Great Lakes shipwrecks. The collage was really about drowning, though I'm not sure

I knew this until later and then it stunned me that I hadn't known it all along.

"Part of me thinks it's stupid to keep going out with him," I told my mother, setting down the magazine and sliding out of bed. I needed more coffee. "Eventually I'm going to have to tell him, and I can't imagine—"

"You're putting the cart way ahead of the horse," my mother interrupted. "A step at a time, sweetie."

"I know." I set my mug on the counter and opened the blinds over the sink. The sky looked heavy and close, the neighborhood still but for a guy walking his dog. He was tall, like Erik, and I smiled, thinking of how, when we were driving home the night before, Erik and I had started kissing at a red light and didn't realize the light had turned green until the driver behind us laid on the horn. "This is crazy," I said, pulling away from him.

"I'm thinking it's kind of nice."

"Well, that too."

And then, ahead of us, the traffic light turned yellow and he slammed on the brakes.

"You could have made that," I said. "Easily!"

"But why?" he said, and pulled me into his arms.

"You know what's weird?" I said to my mom as I refilled my mug. I didn't wait for her to answer. "I didn't think anything could ever hurt me again. After what happened, it just seemed . . ." I blew out a long breath. "But he could. He probably will."

"You don't know that."

I took a sip of my coffee, then moved into the living room, opening the blinds in there too. Light fell in stripes across the carpet. "I've known him less than two weeks, Mom. This is nuts."

She laughed quietly. "Actually, I think it's called falling in love."

"I barely know him." I'd known Nick almost my whole life before I felt even close to what I felt for Erik after four dates—barely four, because the custard stand wasn't actually a date, was it?

"Just enjoy this time," my mom said. "Let Erik get to know all your wonderful qualities." In the background I could hear the squawk of seagulls and knew she was sitting on one of the wooden benches facing the ocean. I liked picturing her there, eyes closed, face lifted to the sun, but it made me ache too. She no longer had her porch. Our house had been sold to pay the hospital bills. She and my dad lived in a one-bedroom condo outside of town now. Most mornings she rode her bike the mile and a half to the boardwalk. She never complained, but how could she not have mourned the loss? The ease of walking barefoot onto her own porch, the ocean a block away, the boom of the surf?

"I've been thinking about Kelly a lot," I said. "Probably because of Erik's connection to the theater, but it's also that whenever I imagine telling someone . . ."

"Of course you'd think of her."

"It's not that I thought we'd stay friends, but if *she* couldn't understand . . ."

"I know. She's the most difficult for me too."

But the truth was my mother hadn't understood either. Not really. Even now, there was so much pain in her.

"She had a lot of guilt, Claire. A lot. Which I understand all too well. Don't underestimate what that did to her."

"I hate that you feel guilty." I leaned my forehead against the window. "You saved my life."

"I don't know about that. But I know you tried many,

many times to tell both me *and* Kelly what was going on and neither of us took you seriously. Or not seriously enough. That's not easy to live with."

"Is it weird that I miss her?"

I could hear the wistfulness in my mom's voice. "She was one of a kind."

"Remember that rhinestone-studded jean jacket she bought Lucy?"

My mother chuckled. "For a three-month-old!"

I smiled. "Nick was appalled."

"You sound different," my mother said.

"I feel different. And I know it's crazy, but I keep thinking maybe Erik's the reason I moved here. Maybe he's my reward—" I stopped. "I didn't mean that." *Reward?* No. No way. My throat tightened. "God, Mom, what am I doing?"

"Claire, it's okay."

"Except it's not. I want it to be so badly, but it's not, and it's never going to be."

"If you really believed that, you wouldn't have gone out with him again."

She was right. And wasn't this why I'd moved here to begin with? I wanted another chance. And I'd been given one. I had a good job, a home, a life I mostly loved. And yes, it was lonely. I didn't have any real friends, by my own choosing, and I missed my family, I missed Delaware, but some mornings, running through my quiet neighborhood of 1930s bungalows, the broad Midwestern sky beginning to lighten, I felt, if not happy, then at least content. *This is enough,* I told myself. *It's more than enough.*

And it was, until I met Erik.

From next door, I heard Margaret leaving the house, and then there she was in her maroon scrubs and clogs, blond hair in a bun, unlocking her car. She glanced up at my window before she got in and gave a little wave. We'd long ago agreed we were perfect neighbors. Now and then we'd sit on our shared porch and have a glass of wine, but we were both extremely private. She knew the basics about me: graphic designer, from Delaware, liked to work out. We often left the house at the same time in the morning, she heading to the hospital, me to go running. And I knew she was one of nine kids, from Minneapolis, and the man she was involved with was a pilot for American Airlines. Because he was around so infrequently, I assumed he was married, but I never asked. Once, after he left her house, I heard her wailing with such terrible grief it scared me.

After I got off the phone, I sat on the porch and laced up my running shoes. The low sun had burned through the clouds, the air thick with humidity. I stared down the street, named after a tree, as all the streets in this neighborhood were—Elm Avenue, Maple Lane, Spruce Street, which was mine, though there were no spruce trees at all. Someone told me once that housing developments were often named after what was destroyed in order to build them, so Willow Run was once a grove of weeping willows and Marsh Estates was once a beautiful marsh with long grasses that caught the falling light each afternoon. *Do we always name our absences?* I wondered as I eased into a jog. I thought of my collages, which I signed with her name and mine: Lucy Claire. Sometimes I thought the whole reason I created the collages at all was so I could write her name next to mine, attach them both to something beautiful. Or maybe I just wanted someone to ask "Why Lucy?" as Erik had the previous night, so that I could have that moment of sounding so nonchalant as I answered, "Oh, I've always loved that name!" It was what I used to say in my other life, the one where I had been her mother.

CHAPTER 4

Erik's ex-wife phoned as we were driving into Milwaukee for dinner. "Crap," he said, relinquishing my hand. "Let me make sure everything's okay with the kids."

"Of course." I leaned against the seat back, taking in the tiny details I already loved: his strong hands and laugh lines, the openness of his face. It was our sixth date, and I wondered when I would stop counting. Was there a magic number—ten dates, twenty?—when I would finally believe that what we both felt was . . . *what*? Lasting? Real? Already I could see glimpses of how our lives fit together: running after work, cooking dinner, making love.

The traffic had slowed, four lanes merging into two. "We're downtown," Erik was saying to Annabelle. A crane dangled a block of concrete overhead, the blue sky radiant. "The Mexican place by the lake."

I glanced at him as he talked. The conversations I'd heard him have with Annabelle always seemed perfunctory: How was everyone? Could she put the kids on? Or when was he taking the girls to McDonald's? Could he pick up Spencer from school? Still, he ate dinner at her house a few times a week. It was easier for the kids, he said. Breaking Spencer's routine caused him so much distress—and why do that to him?—plus, the girls were so young. It made sense, though I felt a pang on the nights he was there. I imagined the five of them siting around the table, a family.

The first time I spent the night with Erik, she phoned, and I could hear her crying. She couldn't calm Spencer; could Erik come over? He apologized profusely to me—*I can't believe, of all the nights*—but he didn't hesitate, and again, though I understood, it scared me. "I don't want to be a fool," I told him when he returned. "If there's unfinished stuff with you and Annabelle . . ."

"Her timing sucks, Claire, but it's not like she knew you were here."

"Was Spencer okay?"

The bed creaked as he turned to face me. "Sometimes when he gets agitated . . . it's hard to describe, but he doesn't just bounce back. I guess Phoebe accidentally turned off the TV when he was watching and it just—Annabelle put it right back on, but he was inconsolable. And the poor kid, he was trying to explain why—I think he felt like he was restarting in the middle of the show, and he can't. He really and truly can't. His brain isn't wired that way and it . . . it breaks my heart." He paused. "Annabelle really did need help." He leaned up on one elbow, his eyes dark pockets. "Please don't be jealous." He brushed his thumb along my lip. "I promise you there's no reason."

I thought of this now as I watched him on the phone. "No, you can't talk to her! Jesus, we're on a date." He let out an exasperated breath, eyes flicking to the rearview as he switched lanes, but he looked happy.

I leaned forward to close the vent, the air-conditioning suddenly too cold, then reached for Spencer's book of maps tucked into the door pocket. *Road Atlas of Waukesha County.* Erik had told me how, even if they were just driving from

Annabelle's to his house or to school, Spencer traced the route on his map. I flipped through the pages, aware of Erik's eyes on me. I'd read that after the bombing of Pearl Harbor, and again after the attack on Normandy, Americans bought in a matter of hours as many maps as they would have bought in an entire year during peacetime. Europe felt too close, and they needed to see where they were in relation to it. I felt like that about Annabelle. She was near in a way I didn't yet understand.

By the time the traffic started moving and we exited at Wisconsin Avenue, the sun had dipped behind the buildings, bathing everything—sky, park, lake—in a soft impressionistic light. I felt sad and out of sorts, though I knew some of it stemmed from the anniversary of the accident the day before. It always set me back. I had told Erik I'd be busy and might not talk to him—back-to-back meetings, an after-work party, none of it true, but I knew if we spoke, he'd hear things in my voice I wasn't ready to explain.

At the lakefront, the water was crowded with sailboats, cyclists whizzing by on the bike path, a group of shirtless guys playing Frisbee on the lawn.

"Sorry about that," Erik said when he hung up.

I nodded without looking at him. Annabelle seemed like the kind of mom I'd imagined I would be. Practical and organized and matter-of-fact, juggling a thousand details for her kids—schedules, logistics, concerns—but making it seem easy.

Erik put his hand on my knee. "Talk to me."

But I could feel myself shutting down. I stared at the lake, remembering how, when I first moved here, people told me it was so vast that it would feel like the ocean, but it never did. Although I loved running here, which I did most weekends, the first time I saw it, I felt bereft. It was a flat desolate gray, so completely not the ocean in the same way that my life was so completely not my life. I felt that way again now. I wished I were more confident, more relaxed, more sure of who I was, but I'd lost that surety ten years ago.

After a moment, Erik lifted his hand from my knee. "I feel like a jerk," he said. "Talking to her when I have this gorgeous woman whom I'm absolutely smitten with sitting beside me."

I shifted in my seat to look at him. "I'm smitten with you too," I said. "And I'm not upset you were talking to her. You're a good dad, Erik."

"I'm not so sure about that." He sighed. "She's having a rough day, I guess, and wanted to know if we could stop by and have dessert with her and the kids. And the invite was for us *both*." He lifted his hand from the steering wheel in a gesture of helplessness.

I reached for his hand. "Do you want to have dessert with them?"

"Actually, no, I don't. I've been looking forward to this dinner all day."

"How often do they stay with you?" I'd asked Erik the first time I went to his house and he showed me the kids' rooms. *Beauty and the Beast* wallpaper in the girls' room, matching cribs, sheets patterned with dancing teapots. In Spencer's room, a lighted globe, a map of the United States on one wall, a huge atlas on his dresser.

"They don't stay here," he said. "We tried it. Once. It was a disaster." He glanced around Spencer's bedroom, which smelled of new carpet. "Spencer couldn't sleep. And Hazel woke from a bad dream and wanted Annabelle, and there wasn't one thing I could do to comfort her, which set Phoebe off. I ended up driving them home at three in the morning."

He scrubbed his face with his hand. "I felt like an ass. Why do that to them just because I want them here?" He flicked off the light in Spencer's room and shrugged as if it were no big deal.

"Does she want them to stay with you?" I'd asked.

"Trust me, she'd love a break," he said.

I believed him; I knew how hard it was to be with a young child all day, and she had three kids, one of them with special needs. Only a saint wouldn't have wanted a break. But I also knew—all too well—that motherhood and fear often go hand in hand, and I would come to learn that Annabelle was terrified of not being there for her kids, even if that meant something as simple as letting them stay with their dad for the night.

Erik found a parking space a block from the restaurant. He turned off the car but didn't move to open the door. "I feel like I'm screwing this up." He reached across the gearshift for my hand. "Maybe I'm rushing things. I want you to meet my kids, but that means meeting Annabelle. I wish that weren't the case, but with the girls so young and the complications with Spence . . ."

"Meeting Annabelle makes me nervous," I said.

"Why?" He looked surprised. "She's going to love you."

But I didn't want her to love me. I didn't want him to want that. I was getting the impression that Annabelle was a package deal with him, the way the kids were, and it felt odd, vaguely incestuous, to be friends with his ex-wife. *I already have friends,* I told myself. *My mom and Margaret.* I didn't need more. "What if she doesn't like me?"

"She will. I know her. And she's not trying to interfere, Claire. It probably seems that way, but once you meet her, you'll realize she means well."

And she did. I would learn this too: What Annabelle wanted more than anything was to have her family around her, and if that meant including me—so be it. Later, we would laugh about the beginnings of our friendship, when she had no choice but to put up with me and I had no choice but to put up with her. Still, I often think of that night, out to dinner with Erik, when the possibility of being friends with Annabelle first arose, and I resisted so fervently. Long before Annabelle and I met, long before she became my closest friend, long before that last summer together, did I somehow intuit that history was already repeating itself?

CHAPTER 5

I met Annabelle and Erik's kids on Labor Day weekend. Six years later, our summer of perfect happiness would end on that weekend as well. Our story like one of the perfectly structured plays I'd one day watch at Ten Chimneys, though I wouldn't understand this until long after it was over.

The twins were out front running through the sprinkler when we arrived, naked except for their red galoshes and red harlequin sunglasses. Every part of me was tense—back straight, hands clutched in my lap—as we pulled up behind Annabelle's SUV, its bumper covered with stickers: *Experience Wildlife: Have Twins; What If the Hokey Pokey Really Is What It's All About?*

As soon as the girls saw Erik, they were shrieking and racing toward him, one of them slipping in the wet grass, then erupting into loud sobs. Erik scooped her up and swung her around until she was giggling and the other twin was reaching up, begging, "Me too, me too!" Erik's shirt and the front of his shorts were soaked.

I stood by the car smiling a huge, nervous I'm-so-glad-to-be-here smile that I wished were real. The look on Erik's face when those girls came running was so joyful, a wave rising up and curling over in his eyes, but all I felt was fear bordering on panic. I hadn't been around a little girl in seven years.

The twins were beautiful. Nut-brown from the sun, they had dark hair, Erik's blue eyes, sturdy little bodies. Lucy had had Nick's coloring, blond and brown-eyed with pale, almost translucent skin, and she was tiny. I used to marvel at her little wrists, her knees. "Your bee's knees," I'd coo, kissing one, then the other, back and forth, as she giggled and blew spit bubbles. Later, in the hospital library I found *Etymologies of Sayings, Clichés, and Aphorisms,* and when that phrase, *the bee's knees,* swarmed out from the page, I'd felt as if I were being stung by wasps.

The meaning dated to the 1920s: One of many silly phrases coined to mean "outstanding": *You're the flea's eyebrows, the canary's tusks, the cat's whiskers.*

The bee's knees.

At first, I didn't notice Spencer, a skinny boy with a crew cut, standing against the porch wall. Erik had told me to go slowly, that Spencer probably wouldn't talk to me the first few times we met, that something as minor as a stranger staring at Spencer could send him into a meltdown. I understood this: how painful it sometimes is simply to have someone look at you. Even a glance can feel too close.

Although I avoided looking in Spencer's direction, I felt his eyes on me. And though Erik had described Spencer's tendency to "shut down" around new people and in new situations, I sensed that whatever was going on with this little boy was the *opposite* of shutting down, almost as if he were seeing too much. Not the details of my life or who I was to his dad. Just me. My aloneness. Erik had told me that Spencer saw the days of the week and certain sounds or voices in colors—Mondays were yellow, and my voice, I would learn, had silver splashes in it, like raindrops. Later, I would wonder if my aloneness that day had had a color too.

Erik was walking across the lawn, soaking wet, the girls giggling and half hiding behind him. "Come on, you two," he was saying. He grinned at me, and I held his eyes for a second, felt that look go through me like fire as I crouched down to meet his soaked and squirming daughters, who were peering from behind his legs. I was shaking. It felt impossible to smile or say hello.

"This is Claire," Erik said, tugging one of the girls from behind him. "And, Claire, this is Hazel."

My breath caught. I could see Lucy so clearly. In a white fur hat that made her look like a little bear. And in an expensive crocheted thing like an old-fashioned bathing cap she wore with a matching sweater. Nick's mom had loved hats and bought Lucy dozens of them—velvet berets, wool beanies, floppy sun hats. Once Lucy was older, she would throw her hat onto the floor and Nick would retrieve it and say in a booming voice: "Who threw this hat on the floor?" Lucy would bob in her bouncy swing, cooing her big toothless smile and placing her hands on her head, until Nick put the hat back on, and then she'd throw it again and he'd retrieve it: *Who threw this hat on the floor?*

"You like pink cupcakes too?" Hazel asked shyly.

"I love pink cupcakes," I said, just as the other twin, Phoebe, toppled into me, her wet hand on my chest. "Mommy breasts!" she shrieked, and then they were both giggling and running back to the sprinkler.

Erik held out his hand and pulled me up. "She's been fixated on breasts."

I smiled shakily, and he tugged me close. "I think it's sweet that you're nervous meeting my kids," he whispered.

"What about you?" he'd asked the night before. "Did you ever want children?" We were lying in his bed, and I'd been asking a zillion questions about his kids: Had he been there for the girls' birth? Was being the father of a son different from being the father of daughters? Had he felt like a dad right away?

That's when Erik asked, "I know you were pretty young when you got married, but were kids ever on the radar?" Early evening, and although the curtains were closed, it was still light enough outside that the room was shadowy.

"Oh my God, I wanted kids more than anything," I blurted. It made me smile. No matter how confusing everything became later, wanting Lucy had been pure and unequivocal.

"So, did you try or . . . you were married three years, right?" We were curled on our sides, my knees against his, the sheet draped over us.

I wanted to tell him how we had planned for her, prayed for her. And the day she was born—how do I even begin to describe that moment when Nick put her in my arms, red and wrinkled with that pale thatch of blond hair, and I burst into tears because I couldn't fathom, almost couldn't bear, what it felt like to already love someone *this* much?

"I can't have kids," I said instead, and felt as if a stone were lodged in my throat. I'd had a tubal ligation in the hospital, so it was true that I wasn't able to have children, though not exactly accurate. Tears burned my eyes.

"Oh, Claire. Jesus, I'm sorry."

"No, I've wanted to tell you," I said. "I figured you wondered."

Spencer was walking toe to heel, toe to heel, around the perimeter of the porch. Head bowed, he wouldn't look up when Erik called his name, wouldn't look up when Erik walked onto the porch, speaking gently—"Hey, Spence, it's Dad, I came to say hi; it's okay, buddy"—wouldn't look up even when Erik gently touched Spencer's shoulder.

Wouldn't look up.

He began twisting the bottom of his T-shirt around his fist, staring at the ground and repeating: "Winds out of the north-northeast at sixteen miles per hour; eighty-three degrees for your high, and we start out with sunny skies." Erik had told me Spencer loved the Weather Channel and that on nights he couldn't sleep, he would stare at it for hours, often with the sound off, watching the colored movement of storms and high-pressure systems across the map. When he was anxious, he'd repeat forecasts to calm himself.

I understood this, all the ways we make the world safe when it's not. After the accident, I became hypervigilant in ways I'd never been before, never needed to be. If I could control all the little things, could I maybe, *maybe,* control the bigger ones? How desperately I'd wanted to believe that. I walked the same number of laps each day around the hospital courtyard no matter the weather, and I sat at the same table in the cafeteria, and I became rigid about my food in ways I'd never been, counting calories not because I cared about my weight but because whatever the goal was—1,200 calories a day, 1,400—it was something solid and achievable. Even now, though I was a long way from those days, I woke at the same time every morning, ran the same premeasured routes, moved through the weight machines at the Y in the same order. Driving to meet clients in an unfamiliar part of town, I'd check and recheck the route the night before, my anxiety over getting there far greater than my worry about the actual meeting. I was early for everything because to be late was to be hurried and to be hurried was to possibly make a mistake, and I was terrified of this most of all.

"This is my friend Claire," Erik said.

"Winds out of the north-northeast at sixteen miles per hour . . ."

"Hi, Spencer," I said softly.

Abruptly, he stopped talking.

"I've been looking forward to meeting you."

He didn't look at me, just started walking again, toe to heel, toe to heel, twisting his shirt, which was inside out, and then abruptly, he picked up where he'd left off: "Eighty-three degrees for your high, and we start out with sunny skies. . . ."

He stopped again when he returned to where I stood, but this time, almost inaudibly, he whispered my name before continuing: "Winds out of the north-northeast at sixteen miles . . ."

And just like that my heart blasted into space, gravity, weight, and sound all falling away.

Annabelle was wearing jean overalls and orange running shoes, her hair in a ponytail. Her back was to us when we entered the kitchen, sunlight falling over her as she stood, one hand on her hip, the other cradling a phone to her ear. She laughed and said, "He's going to kill me, but who cares?" Her hair was a zillion shades of gold, brown, and red, and when she turned, the dust motes streaming in the air behind her glittered with light. As soon as she saw us, she said a hurried goodbye, hung up the phone, and said, "Claire?" with such surprise it caught me off guard. Who did she think I was? But then she said, "I'm sorry, it's just the way he's kept you hidden, I thought you'd have a birthmark the size of Texas across your face."

"For God's sake, Annabelle," Erik said.

She ignored him. "Did you meet Spencer?"

I nodded. "He's beautiful."

"Isn't he?" She beamed.

"He called Claire by name," Erik said.

She stopped. "He did?" She looked from Erik to me, back to Erik, her eyes full of questions I didn't understand. I glanced at Erik and felt as if I were walking over broken glass, something long-ago shattered between them that hadn't been swept away. Maybe she saw my uncertainty, because suddenly, she was grabbing me in an excited hug. She was tiny, maybe five feet tall, no more than a hundred pounds. "I told you, didn't I?" she said to Erik after she pulled away.

"Annabelle, come on, you just met—"

"Oh hush," she said. "I told him I had a feeling about you. And I was right. You're perfect. You're absolutely perfect."

I didn't know what to say, and when I looked at Erik, he just shrugged: *Now do you see what I mean about her?*

I did.

"It looks like the wild ones got hold of you," Annabelle said to Erik. "I'll grab a towel." As she was walking away, she called over her shoulder, "Did Phoebe grab your boobs yet, Claire?"

I couldn't help it. I liked her. I liked her a lot.

CHAPTER 6

Three days after we met, Annabelle phoned me at work as I was finishing for the day. "I just made a pitcher of margaritas," she said. "And Erik took the twins to *The Emperor's New Groove,* so it's just me and Spence. Please say you'll stop by." She sounded nervous.

I hit save and closed the document I'd been working on: a brochure for an assisted-living facility. All day my memories of the hospital had been too close. "A margarita sounds great."

"Hooray!" she said. "I was afraid you'd think it was weird, but this way, you can get to know Spencer a little more."

As soon as I rapped on the screen door, she yelled at me to come in. "Salt or no salt on your margarita?"

"No salt," I said as I walked into the kitchen.

She wrinkled her nose. "Yuck, really?" She was wearing cutoff jeans, running shoes, and a plain white T-shirt, and when she glanced up, all freckles and curly hair and the glint of a silver cross at her neck, I was struck by how naturally beautiful she was. Next to her, I felt matronly in my khaki skirt, cardigan, and ballet flats. I wished I'd gone home and changed.

I looked around the kitchen as Annabelle rinsed the blender, noticing things I hadn't the other day: the "It's all about me!" magnet on the fridge, the old-fashioned teapots atop the cabinets, the whiteboard on the wall by the table. "That's Spencer's," she said. It was a day chart with squares for each hour, some filled with rudimentary drawings, some smudged. "If I can show him ahead of time what's going to happen, our lives are much easier." She handed me my drink and took a sip of hers. "That's you." She pointed to a stick figure with long brown hair. "As soon as we got off the phone, I drew you in, then showed Spencer." She licked the salt from her lips, then nodded to the crooked numbers written next to each hour. "The temperature. It's the first thing he does in the morning." She stared at the board, something sad in the shape of her mouth. "He checks constantly, if he's having a bad night. I'll find out it was seventy-one degrees at three in the morning, sixty-nine at four. It's his way of preparing for the day."

She glanced at the ceiling. "We're painting his room, so we've had a few rough nights lately. It's a major change, and any change, for Spencer, is traumatic." She took another sip of her drink, and I noticed the bruised shadows beneath her eyes.

"Is there a reason you're painting it?" I pictured his empty bedroom at Erik's.

"A couple weeks ago he started saying the colors in his room hurt. It's always been blue and yellow, so I have no idea what's changed, and he can't explain beyond telling me that much, but he starts crying when he goes in there, which he now refuses to do." She cocked her head at the sliding glass door. "He's outside. Do you mind sitting out there?"

"I'd love it," I said. "I've been in a cubicle all day."

"Hey, Spence!" she yelled to the boy jumping on the trampoline. His arms were spread straight out, as if he were flying.

"So what color are you painting his room?" I asked once we settled on chaise longues.

"It's pretty, sort of chocolate brown." She smiled. "And speaking of pretty, you should see my painter." Her face grew animated. "I should be shot for thinking the stuff I'm thinking because he's just a kid—well, not really, but in his twenties. I want him to paint my whole house." She laughed at herself, and I thought how easy she was, how real.

I laid my head against the chair back. The grass was lavender colored with dusk, the trees limned in sunlight. Spencer hadn't stopped jumping, doing so in such an even rhythm, those arms spread wide. It was mesmerizing. "Doesn't he get tired?"

"It calms him."

And her too, I thought, something sweet in her expression as she watched him.

Without turning, she said, "He'll love your sweater, by the way. Wednesdays are green—actually blue-green, but you're close enough." She pulled a cigarette from the pocket of her T-shirt, then turned from the trampoline to light it. "The kids don't know I smoke," she said as she sat back, and blew out two smoke rings. She held the cigarette low between inhales. "It's my last vice. One drink and I'm done, chocolate isn't a vice, and sex? I don't remember what that is. Well, except in my mind." She laughed again. "My painter and I have been having quite the torrid romance."

The second mention of her painter, and I wondered if she was trying to reassure me about her and Erik.

"So, what does that mean exactly, Wednesdays are blue-green?" I asked. "Is it some kind of synesthesia?"

She looked surprised, then said, "I forgot. You're an artist. Of course you'd know. But yeah, that's exactly what it is. Sounds, colors, textures—they're entangled in Spence's brain. He hates red, for example, because it's too fast, he says. Other colors are too sharp, which is what I assume is happening with his room." She sighed. "Hopefully the brown will take care of it. He told me yesterday it's the same color as silence."

"I have a quote over my desk at work that says 'Colors exert a direct influence on the soul.' Kandinsky. It sounds like that's what colors do to Spencer."

Annabelle looked at me, then nodded. After a minute, she said, "Thank you for that."

"For what?"

"You get it, Claire. Which means you get him. Most people don't. Or can't. Or won't."

I didn't say anything, but I sensed she didn't need me to. We both just watched Spencer as he jumped, a steady rhythm, arms at his sides now.

"Our voices have colors too," Annabelle was saying. "Mine is dark blue, with a thin line of purple at the edge. Unless I yell, and then my voice gets purple with black bars across it."

"And he's only six?"

"I know."

He was just a dark silhouette, a blur rising and falling against the backdrop of pine trees. A dog started barking next door, racing along the fence where I couldn't see it. The light was fading—it occurred to me that the dark blue sky was now the color of Annabelle's voice, the horizon just a thin strip of purple. "So, what color is Erik's voice?"

"Rust-colored," she said. "The same color as Sundays."

"It fits."

"Doesn't it?" She glanced at her watch. "They should be back soon. Wait till he sees your car. He'll be surprised."

"Wait." I sat up. "He doesn't know I'm here?"

"Oh, don't look like that. He gave me your number. I just wasn't sure what I was doing until after he'd left. I needed to see how Spencer was. I never know until . . ." Her voice trailed off. "It's hard," she said quietly.

I nodded, though I felt tricked, my face burning. What was I doing here? I was sleeping with her ex-husband. I was falling in love with him.

"The girls will be thrilled to see you. It's been nonstop Claire for three days. 'Claire's pretty. Claire's hair is longer than yours, Mommy. Where is Claire's house?'" She glanced at me, then turned back to Spencer. He was a black shape against the navy-blue sky. "I need to get him in," she said, but she didn't move, just fingered the silver crucifix at her neck. "It's important that my kids like whoever Erik is with." Her voice sounded wistful, and I wondered what color Spencer would say it was now. "It's scary, having to share your kids with another woman." She was staring straight ahead. When she held a newly lit cigarette to her lips, her hand trembled.

So, this was why she'd invited me over.

She swung her legs over the side of the chair and called, "Five minutes, Spence!"

When he didn't answer, she stood. "Spencer. How many minutes?"

"Five minutes, then four, then three, then two, then one," he called between jumps.

She sat back down. "Erik probably told you I didn't want Spencer at first."

"No." I pulled my cardigan tight. Why would she tell me this?

"Four minutes, Spence!" she called, then said, "We do the countdown a lot. Any abrupt change, mostly between activities, freaks him out." She glanced at me. "I didn't mean to shock you. Saying I didn't want him. Erik says I have no filter."

"It's fine," I said, but my skin felt prickly. The conversation was too close.

"I guess I just want you to know I understand how you might have times when the last thing you want is my kids in your life. I mean, if I'm their mom and I've felt that . . ." She sighed. "Everybody thinks a baby will bring you closer. But I resented Spencer for coming between me and Erik. Suddenly, all we were was parents. All I was was a mom. Not a wife or Erik's best friend or . . . or anything! I loved Spencer so so much, and obviously, I was depressed, but he was born, and I felt like my life was over." She looked at me, then laughed sadly. "Oh my God, you're thinking, *No wonder Erik divorced this horrible woman—*"

"No." I shook my head. My heart was pounding with fear and recognition and grief. How could this woman I barely knew be speaking so casually of these feelings that had always filled me with such shame?

"Three minutes, buddy!" she called to Spencer. The darkness was complete now. All I could see was the glint of her cross. "I know what I'm saying sounds awful," she said. "And I can only say it because I love that boy more than life itself." She bent to retrieve our empty glasses and stood. I did too. "But it's a struggle. This isn't how I pictured my life." She glanced at her watch. "Two more minutes!" she called into the blackness. She handed me the glasses. "Will you take these in, while I get him?" Before I could answer, she said, "I have a feeling you'll be spending a lot of time with my children, and I want you to know it's okay if you don't always like them. Believe me, those little girls of mine will run you ragged. And you haven't met stubborn until you've met

Phoebe." She laughed that plaintive laugh again. "In fact, any parent who *doesn't* admit to not liking her kids now and then is full of it."

From the front of the house, I heard the slam of car doors and the shrieks of the girls. "Oh good, they're back," Annabelle said, and then, "Don't get me wrong, Claire. When it comes to my kids, I wouldn't change a thing, but you're lucky, in a way, that you didn't have any."

CHAPTER 7

"This is unexpected," Erik said, walking around the house to the patio, the girls hiding behind him. A motion-sensor light flicked on as they passed the sliding glass door, and the yard was suddenly flooded with brightness. "Jesus, what watt bulb is that?" he asked Annabelle, shielding his eyes. He gave me a quick kiss, hand on my back. "What are you guys up to?" But his casual tone didn't match his stony expression. Clearly, my being there was not, as Annabelle had promised, a good surprise. I felt foolish for letting her talk me into thinking it was. I'd never liked surprises either.

"I had a pitcher of margaritas in need of drinkers," Annabelle laughed. "Claire was kind enough to oblige."

"A whole pitcher," Erik said. "Imagine that."

Annabelle's face fell. "Seriously?" she said. "You're upset?" And then, "Don't worry. I didn't reveal any state secrets." She crouched down, arms open wide to the girls. "I missed you *so* much! Come give me big hugs!" She sniffed their hair and necks and said, "Yum! You smell like butter."

"Popcorn!" one of them yelled. The other was staring at me. I couldn't tell them apart yet, though in time, I'd learn that Phoebe was the yeller; Hazel was the watcher. I smiled at her, and she smiled shyly back. How was I ever going to get used to this? I wondered helplessly. Lucy had been only ten months older than these girls the last time . . . I pulled in a jagged breath. The girls looked like bumblebees—black-and-white-striped tights, yellow T-shirts.

Look at your bee's knees!

Annabelle was still crouched down, hand shading her eyes as she squinted in the too-bright light. "Okay, maybe I do have the wrong wattage. I might be blind." To the girls, she said, "Did you say hello to Claire?" but they just giggled, then burst into peals of laughter. Slowly, she pushed herself up, a twin on each hip. "Holy moly," she said, "you guys are getting way too heavy." To Erik, she said, "Spencer just went inside. You want to tuck him in? He's sleeping in my room until we finish painting."

"I should get going," I said.

"Oh, not yet!" Annabelle said. "It won't take us long to get the kids—" She stopped, looking at Erik, her jaw tensed. "Oh, Lord, what now?" She lowered the girls back down. "What great faux pas have I committed this time?" Before Erik could respond, she added, "We aren't Hasidic Jews, Erik."

"What?"

"You don't have to keep us separate. Honestly. It's okay to mix the meat and the dairy."

Despite himself he grinned. "Jesus, where do you come up with this stuff?"

"Well, you're acting like—"

"Annabelle, stop, okay?" He held up his hand. "I'm not acting like anything. I'm tired; it's been a long day."

"Was I supposed to get your permission?" she asked. "You gave me her number."

"Yes, I did."

"What, then? You're practically shooting sparks, you're so irritated. And you're making Claire feel badly."

"I'm fine," I lied. "But I am going to go."

She leaned forward to hug me—not one of those polite hugs women give one another, but a real hug. And then she spun around and, nudging the girls ahead of her, went inside, not bothering to pull the sliding door shut after her. Immediately, the twins started howling, "But Daddy said he'd read to us," and I heard her answer tersely, "He will, he will, but only if you stop fussing. He's just saying good night to Claire."

"Claire too!" one of them sobbed.

"Come on, I'll walk you to your car," Erik said.

"What was that all about?" I asked as we picked our way across the shaggy grass. "When she said you'd given her my number, I assumed this was what you wanted."

"I do. Or I did. I just had no idea she meant tonight."

We were standing at my car, parked at the curb. The dog from next door was barking again. "I really do think she meant well."

"Oh, I'm sure she did."

"But?"

When he didn't answer I said, "I'm confused, Erik. Do you *not* want me to become friendly with her?"

"Of course I want you to be friendly. It just caught me off guard." He was staring past me. The street was filled with two-story tract houses, each with a bay window and manicured lawn, lights glowing from front porches. *This was Erik's street for over a decade,* I thought. *His house.*

"Hey." I reached for his hand.

"Hey, back." He gave my fingers a quick squeeze, his expression softening. "It just annoys me," he said. "She can't stand being left out."

"That's sad, though."

"Do not feel sorry for her."

In the distance, the sky flashed with lightning, and we both turned and looked. "Did you know it was going to rain?" I asked.

"Just thunderstorms." He smiled. "You're worried about your run tomorrow, aren't you?" He tucked a strand of hair behind my ear. "Do you have a big day?"

I shook my head. I liked that he knew this about me: that I needed to run every morning, especially if I had something important at work. "I just . . . This unsettles me." I nodded toward her house, though it wasn't really Annabelle I was worried about, but his changing reactions—one minute wanting me to like her and in the next breath, almost resenting it. *Do not feel sorry for her.* I scanned his eyes.

"There's nothing to be unsettled about," he said. "I promise." Another flash of lightning, and this time the growl of thunder. From across the street, we heard someone wheeling their trash can down the drive.

"This has to be hard for her, Erik." I swallowed. "Seeing the girls excited about a new woman." *Seeing you excited about a new woman.*

He nodded, then leaned against the car, arms crossed. He was still staring up at the sky. "I know you're right," he said. "I'm probably not being very sensitive." He turned his gaze back to me. "She just always has to control everything." He sounded tired more than angry, and I thought of Spencer saying Erik's voice was the same color as Sundays.

"She told me about not wanting Spencer at first."

"She did?"

"She wanted to reassure me it was okay if I had a hard time with him. I can't imagine it, though. I'm falling for your boy already." How could I explain that he was so much easier for me than the girls, who reminded me too much of Lucy, too much of everything I had lost?

He smiled, but it was what my mom called a Cheshire cat smile, sort of floating separate from his face. "Annabelle blames herself for a lot of Spencer's issues."

"*What?* Why?"

"Because she didn't bond with him right away."

"But she knows that's not how it works, right?"

"Intellectually, yeah. She'd be the first to tell you it's bullshit. But emotionally . . ."

"That's awful, Erik."

"It is." He was staring up again, head tilted back as if searching for one particular star. A breeze moved through the trees, the leaves making a swishing sound. "I should go tuck the kids in. Apologize to her, I guess." He sighed. "Can I call you in a bit, or will you be asleep?" He looked at his watch and smiled. "You do realize it's almost your bedtime?" He was appalled that I was usually asleep by nine thirty.

"You're a funny man." I pushed up on my toes to kiss him. "And yes, you should call, and yes, I will be asleep, but I don't care."

By the time I got home, the rain was coming down in sheets. An SUV with Arizona plates, a rental, was parked in our drive. Margaret's pilot. Inside my house, drenched and cold, I moved through the rooms, toweling off my hair, checking that the alarm was set for morning, then wandering down the long hall to the kitchen. I hadn't eaten dinner and stared into the refrigerator, suddenly ravenous. I ate a yogurt standing up, a handful of Triscuits from the box.

Later, waiting for water to boil for hot chocolate, I felt how bare the room looked, the counters gleaming, no photographs or magnets on the refrigerator. I pictured Annabelle's kitchen with its drawings taped to the fridge, the whiteboard by the table, laundry piled on a chair. In the doorway to my living room, I took in the vacuumed rug and carefully arranged throw pillows, the wicker basket filled with magazines, the coffee table empty, and I felt how unlived-in my home looked, like something from a furniture showroom.

After Erik called, I lay awake, listening to the patter of rain against the windows, now and then hearing Margaret's laugh, a man's deep baritone through the thin connecting wall.

CHAPTER 8

I was immensely curious about Eva and Gabe. They were not only Erik's closest friends but Annabelle's as well. They'd all met freshman year at UWM. Erik and Gabe had been roommates all four years, Eva living with them senior year. Annabelle commuted from home so she could care for her mom, who was dying. That last autumn, Erik told me, the three of them took turns staying with Annabelle. They bought groceries, did laundry, and sat with Annabelle's mom while Annabelle slept or took a shower.

A year after graduation, first Erik and Annabelle got married, then Eva and Gabe. They house-hunted together when Annabelle and Erik decided they'd use the inheritance from Annabelle's mom to buy the house Annabelle still lived in; commiserated when Gabe didn't pass the bar the first time and celebrated when he did; attended opening nights for Eva's plays; celebrated Annabelle's promotions in the PR firm where she still worked part-time. Eva was the first person, after Erik, to hold Spencer. She and Gabe were his godparents.

"Who met who first?" I asked Erik. We were sitting on Annabelle's leather sofa, staying with the kids while she was out with Scott, her painter. A school night, and we'd planned to bring the kids to Erik's, but Spencer had panicked, and it was easier to just stay at Annabelle's. It felt strange watching Erik there, his familiarity as he opened the right cabinet to get a beer mug or went into the laundry to flick on the outdoor garage lights.

"I met Eva during registration. She was—well, still is—gorgeous. I thought I'd died and gone to heaven."

"So, you were attracted to her?"

"Everyone's attracted to Eva. Just wait. You will be too." He lifted my hand and kissed the tips of my fingers.

"Not so fast, mister." I tugged my hand back. "How long did this attraction last?" I pretended to glare.

"About two hours. Until she met Gabe. It was like an eclipse, those two. You went blind looking at them. They were perfect." Something dark flashed across his face, but it was so fleeting I wasn't sure. I cocked my head at him. "What?" he asked sheepishly.

"I don't know." I waited for him to say more. When he didn't, I asked, "Was it difficult for them, your divorce?"

Again, a flicker of something I couldn't read. "I think they saw it coming before we did." He leaned his head against the couch back and closed his eyes, lifting his arm for me to curl against him. "Come here," he said.

The leather squeaked as I shifted close. "Does it bother you to talk about this?"

"Not really."

"Why don't I believe you?"

He opened one eye to look at me. "You don't? Seriously?"

"Not a bit." I kissed a spot beneath his jaw. "It's refreshing, you being the vague one."

"*Moi?* Vague?" But then he smiled and closed his eyes again.

"So, there's more to the story?"

"Isn't there always?"

"Are you going to tell me?"

"One day. I want you to meet them first."

I nestled against him, and we were quiet, just the ticking of the paddle fan. The far wall was covered with mirrors: small ones with tarnished glass in wooden frames, a full-length art deco one, another surrounded by hand-painted Mexican tiles, even a silver hand mirror. It was eclectic and charming, and I thought of my own bare-bones home. "Is this how the room looked when you lived here? I'm trying to picture it as your house."

He lifted his head and surveyed the room, then said, "Yeah, it's basically the same." He sighed. "This place never felt like mine, though. It was whatever Annabelle wanted." He swept his arm toward the mirrors. "I never got that. Why not hang a painting that actually means something? Or hell, leave the wall blank." He laughed. "Of course, she would have painted it some wacked-out color. I'd go to work and when I came home, the kitchen would be sage or the bedroom thistle, what other people call purple. Jesus. I used to beg her, can we please *please* have one wall in this fucking house that's white?"

"Is it weird for you, being here?"

"A little." He patted the couch. "I spent a lot of nights here. Things got pretty ugly at the end."

"You seem to get along now, though."

"We do." He glanced at me. "Eva was great about not choosing sides, which helped. I remember whining about Annabelle once, and she told me flat out that Annabelle was her best friend and she didn't want to hear it. End of story."

"Yikes. Is she always that direct?"

"No. She's sweet. To a fault. We called her Grandma in college. She bakes casseroles for people when they're sick.

Who does that?" He set his hand on my leg, and I felt the warmth of his palm through my jeans. "I can't wait for you to meet her."

"You don't think it will be strange? Because she and Annabelle are so close?"

"Please. Annabelle thinks you're great." He reached for his beer, took a swig, then sat back, long legs propped on the coffee table. He looked boyish, closer to thirty than forty. "I know she appreciated you being here tonight."

"It wasn't as strange as I thought. She really likes this guy."

"He seems nice. Though it might have been a little unnerving for him to have the ex greet him at the door."

"You think?"

Erik pulled me against him, his lips grazing my hair. "Have I told you how much *I* appreciate you being here?"

I could have fallen asleep right there, feeling the pulse in his throat against my forehead. The room had grown chilly, and he stood to close the windows. When he sat down, his arm around me again, I picked up his free hand and held it in my lap.

"I love how you always touch me," he whispered.

I smiled, thinking of how often we said the word *love* to each other. Not *I love you,* but *I love that you touch me.* Or *I love that you just go with the flow on all this Annabelle stuff.* I was the same: *I love that you run with me. I love watching you with your kids. Love.* The word like fire and we were kids circling it, poking the flames with sticks, afraid to get too close.

"I know this whole setup is strange," Erik said after a minute. "And I wish I could tell you it'll change, but she gets the respite-care nurse only once a month and beyond that . . . It's not like we're ever going to be able to just hire some teenage girl down the street to babysit. You saw Spencer tonight."

"I'm fine with it, Erik. I really am."

And I was. Which surprised me. I'd been wary of how entrenched in each other's lives he and Annabelle were, but she was so open and welcoming, it was impossible not to just accept the situation for what it was. And she was so unpretentious. I thought of how, earlier, the minute we walked in the door, she grabbed my arm and said, "Thank goodness. I need wardrobe advice."

"Oh God, not from me." I'd glanced helplessly at Erik, who just grinned and lifted his hands in a don't-look-at-me gesture.

I'd been upstairs at Annabelle's before, to peek at Spencer's newly painted room, but it was strange to be in her bedroom, knowing it had once been Erik's too. Nights undressing and talking through their days—had he set his loose change in a glass jar atop the bureau as he did now? Had they spent mornings in bed, their kids piled in with them?

In truth, it was almost impossible to imagine him in that room with its lavender ("thistle") walls, the small crucifix over the bureau, and stuff everywhere—the bed unmade; dirty coffee mugs on one night table; a box of Ritz crackers, books, and magazines piled on the other. And not an inch of carpet to be seen under the clothes strewn everywhere. "It's not usually this bad," Annabelle apologized as she ushered me inside and closed the door. "I'm a wreck. I haven't been on a date since—" She glanced at me. "Since forever." She scooped a pile of stuff off an armchair and dumped it onto the bed. "Sit here," she said. "I've whittled it down to two options and you have to be brutally honest with me, Claire. I mean it."

She swept some hanging clothes from the closet door and disappeared into the bathroom while I glanced around. The last time I'd sat in a friend's bedroom, weighing in on clothing choices, was with Kelly. I skimmed the titles of the books on the night table closest to me: *Daily Devotions for*

Moms; Advocating for Your Special Needs Child; Codependent No More—and felt a pang of remorse for being jealous of Annabelle.

But then she was stepping out of the bathroom in skinny jeans and boots and a sleeveless shimmery gold blouse that brought out the gold in her hair. "So, here's option one." She bit her lip. "Maybe the gold is too . . . I don't know. Does it make me look like a grandmother?"

I burst out laughing. "A grandmother? No. You look gorgeous."

"Okay, well . . ." She exhaled slowly, turning this way and that in front of the full-length mirror on the back of the closet door. "Here comes option two," she said, and disappeared back into the bathroom.

Option two was the same jeans, black stilettos, and a long black sweater that hugged her body. "I think this one makes me look younger," she said, "but I don't want to look . . . you know, like I'm trying too hard, which of course I am." Her face crumpled and she abruptly plopped down on the bed. "Oh God. Am I making a fool of myself?"

"Not at all," I told her. "And go with the black."

I liked her so much. How vulnerable she let herself be, how honest.

A minute later, as she was debating between two pairs of black shoes, I noticed the tattoo on her ankle—a single word in blue cursive. I pointed to it. "What does it say?"

She glanced down. "Stasia. It's my mom's signature." She rolled her eyes. "My grief tattoo. There's a reason they tell you to wait a year before making any important decisions."

"You don't like it?"

"I've just never been a tattoo person. That was my mom's thing—full sleeves on both arms, her shoulders, her calves—God, I hated her for being different. 'Why can't you be a normal mother?' I used to scream at her all the time. She was only sixteen when she had me, so she was more older sister than mom, and I wanted a mom." She moved around the bed to the bookshelf next to me. It was cluttered with knickknacks—photos, angel figurines, a Rubik's Cube, Julia Cameron's *The Artist's Way* next to a row of books on PR. "This is her," she said, handing me a framed photo of a woman who looked like a younger Annabelle in cutoffs and a halter top, arms covered in ink. She was crouched next to Annabelle, who couldn't have been more than five. They were holding lollipops in their fingers the way you'd hold a cigarette. "We were pretending to smoke," Annabelle said, "which isn't exactly mom behavior either."

"You look like her," I said.

"Yeah, which is another reason I didn't need the tattoo. All I have to do is glance in the mirror and there she is." Annabelle took the photo back and stared at it before returning it to the shelf. "If you had told me when I was a teenager that I'd miss her as much as I do . . ." She shrugged. "Are you close to your mom?"

I nodded. "She's my best friend."

"You're lucky," Annabelle said. "I wish I'd had that chance with mine." And then she was holding up two pairs of earrings and asking which I preferred. "I bet you never imagined this is what you'd be doing tonight, is it?"

"Helping my boyfriend's ex-wife get ready for a date?" I laughed. "That would be a no."

"It's so crazy." She exhaled a long breath. "I'm glad he's found you, though."

CHAPTER 9

Annabelle wanted Erik and me, Eva, and Gabe to accompany her to Hattie Magee's, a bar in Milwaukee where Scott had a weekly gig, playing guitar. "She has the respite-care nurse that night, so we can all go," Erik explained. We were running through my neighborhood after work, the streetlamps casting orange circles onto the pavement. Though we wore shorts, the air smelled like fall, lawns blanketed with leaves. Already the sky was dark, the houses silhouettes. I'd always loved autumn. More than spring, it filled me with hope, maybe as a result of growing up in a beach town, where the fall meant a return to our normal lives.

"Of course, we don't have to go." Erik's breathing was getting ragged. "You can meet Eva and Gabe another time."

"But it's usual for the four of you to do stuff together?"

I felt him glance at me. "I know it seems odd, and I guess it is, but yeah, we see each other pretty regularly. It's habit as much as anything. We've been friends for so long." A pause as he caught his breath. Our footsteps were perfectly synced. "You like Annabelle, right?"

"I do. It just feels a little . . . tangled, maybe? Messy." A part of me liked that mess, though. I wasn't the only one with a complicated past. But I also liked the whole world that came with Erik—children, friends, ex-wife. It felt nuanced and textured, full of contradictions and problems, but joy too. Showing up with Erik to pick up the kids and Annabelle shouting from upstairs for me to see if Phoebe's purple socks were in the dryer. Or having dinner in her kitchen, cutting hot dogs, pouring milk, Spencer saying grace. Afterward, Annabelle gesturing for me to come out back with her while she smoked.

At the end of our run, Erik and I wordlessly picked up our pace until we were all-out sprinting to my driveway. I beat him by a couple of feet, raising my arms and letting out a whoop.

"Do you have pictures of them?" I asked a few nights later. Erik was boiling water for pasta, the windows steamed, both of us in workout gear.

"Of Eva and Gabe? Probably. But Annabelle and I are in them too."

"Then I *definitely* want to see them," I said, and insisted he get them.

"I've got more somewhere," Erik said when he came back downstairs, "but these are a start." He handed me two.

The first was from a cross-country-skiing trip to Door County. They were all so bundled up—down jackets, wool hats and scarves—I could barely tell them apart. Eva wore a parka with a fur-trimmed hood and movie-star sunglasses. The second picture was from Eva and Gabe's wedding. Outside somewhere. Eva was facing Gabe, head thrown back in laughter, her veil, long blond hair, and dress billowing around her as an impossibly young Erik and Annabelle, with 1980s haircuts, stood to the side, holding hands, eyes glued to each other, also laughing. The photo was filled with so much joy, so much palpable, breathtaking, devastating joy. "She really is beautiful," I said, pretending to stare at Eva. but I was spinning inside, feeling stupid and naïve not to have realized how in love Annabelle and Erik had once been. And in the next breath I was back to my own wedding, to the silver-framed photo I'd kept on the bureau in our bedroom, Nick and me in the surf, his tuxedo pants rolled up and bow tie askew. I stood beside him, gathering my dress in handfuls and lifting it from the water, the two of us laughing so hard, you could see the cords in our necks. We had literally been bursting with happiness, with pure, exhilarated, exuberant, uncontainable happiness. The memory sideswiped me, the last two months with Erik rushing away and that awful hopeless feeling rushing in.

"You okay?" Erik turned from the stove. And then he lowered the flame and took the photo from my hands and set it face down on the table. "I knew this wasn't a good idea. Jesus, I'm an idiot."

"No, it's fine." I tried to smile.

"Bullshit. It's not fine."

"No, it is. Honestly. I just . . . it's hard to see it, you know?"

"So don't say you're fine." An edge to his voice.

"You were so in love," I said quietly.

"And you and your husband weren't?"

I glanced down. What happened to me and Nick was so cataclysmic, I wanted to say, of course our love died when Lucy . . . after the accident. *Of course.* But you and Annabelle, how could you have felt what you felt in that picture and . . . *What happened?* "It just surprised me," I said. And I felt not only stupid but arrogant too, because I'd assumed he'd loved Annabelle but hadn't been *in* love, that awful cliché.

"I'm confused, Claire. I get it. I probably don't want to see pictures of you and Nick, although . . . actually, I take that back. I'd *love* to see a picture of you from before. I feel like I'm in a black hole when it comes to your life before Wisconsin."

"That makes two of us," I tried to joke.

"Except it wasn't a black hole." Again, that edge.

"You're right." My chest felt tight. "I don't mean to be so mysterious."

"Then don't be. Tell me something. Jesus, anything."

"Okay." I took a deep breath. "Seeing that photo made me think of my wedding and how happy I was, how in love I was." I was shaking. "It makes me sad, that's all."

"Did you have a big wedding? Did you . . . I don't know, did you wear a white dress? Do you have pictures?"

"Not anymore." I couldn't look at him. "We got married on the beach at sunset, sixty or seventy people, and I wore a white dress with a ridiculously long train that ended up so weighted with sand I felt like I was in a tractor pull." Grief slammed over me.

I felt Erik waiting for me to say more. After a few seconds, his voice gentle, he said, "I want to know you, Claire. Is that so terrible?"

I shook my head, not trusting myself to speak. I felt like more of a liar than ever, not because I'd said anything false, but because he thought I'd opened up by talking about my wedding. Those were easy details, though, crumbs I'd offered in place of the truth he needed and deserved to know and that I needed to tell him. But how? I would lose him. And yet if I didn't open up, I'd lose him that way too. "It scares me." I nodded toward the photos. "That it can disappear. All that happiness."

"It scares me too," he said.

My mother picked up right away. "Just the person I want to talk to." She laughed. "Actually, the only person."

I'd left Erik's before it was light, telling him I wanted to do a long run. It was only six, seven my mom's time. I forced myself to take a deep breath. "Are you already on the boardwalk?"

"I am. The sun just popped over the horizon." I heard her sip her coffee. "So, what's up?"

I leaned my head against my bedroom window, feeling the panic ratchet up again.

"Claire?"

"I'm falling down the rabbit hole," I whispered. "I don't know what to do."

"Why?" Her voice was immediately on alert.

"I'm going to lose him, Mom. I know it." I told her about the photos of Gabe and Eva, and Erik's anger because I never spoke about my past, and how I'd tried to talk about Nick, but it was fake, and this was all too good to be true, and maybe I should just call it quits before—

"Claire, stop," she said. "Take a breath."

In the background, I could hear gulls cawing, the sound plaintive, and I felt such homesickness for her and the beach and our old house and who I'd once been. But even if I could have gone home, that world was gone. "I'm already so mixed up in his life and his kids' lives, and I'm becoming friends with Annabelle, and . . . it's gotten so complicated. I feel like I should have told him before I got this involved." My lungs felt waterlogged, and I thought of how in one of Margaret's respiratory magazines, I'd read that although asthma sufferers felt they couldn't get enough breath, in truth, their lungs couldn't expel it. They were actually drowning in air.

"His life is so normal," I said. "And I'm supposed to meet his friends, and they'll think I'm just this nice woman, and it's all a lie."

"No, it's not."

"It is! I'm not who he thinks I am, and I know you love me and want to believe the best, but I imagine how I would feel if he were the one telling me this awful thing. There's no way I could just *accept* it." I spat the word at her.

"Claire, I need you to listen to me," my mother said calmly.

"I can't!" I cried. "You're going to tell me it will be okay, and it's not, Mom, no matter how much we want it to be!"

She didn't say anything for a second, then quietly she asked, "Are you finished beating yourself up?"

I didn't say anything. My eyes felt scratchy from not sleeping.

"You have done absolutely nothing wrong when it comes to Erik," she said slowly. "You've done nothing wrong, period. And yes, you need to talk about Lucy, but you were right to get to know him first, to figure out if there's a future. And this panic attack—because that's what this is, Claire—is your body's way of telling you it's time; you've gotten to the point where *not* telling Erik is more harmful than telling. It's not a bad thing."

"I'm so afraid."

"Of course you are. And he might have a hard time, but all the things he loves about you will still be there."

"How am I going to do this with his friends, though?"

"What's there to do? This isn't about them. You go out and you have a good time."

CHAPTER 10

Hattie Magee's was a typical sports bar: muted TVs tuned to ESPN, the waitstaff in football jerseys, Scott's band in jeans and cowboy boots. Erik had had a fundraising event nearby, so I'd driven over with Annabelle and Eva, whose family was from Philly and had vacationed in Rehoboth every summer when she was growing up.

"You lived there? It's one of my favorite places in the world," she told me.

"Mine too," I said.

When she learned that my parents owned the restaurant her family had made a point of frequenting each year, she squeezed my arm and said, "It's almost like we already know each other."

As soon as we walked into Hattie's, Scott, in the middle of "Brown-Eyed Girl," broke into a huge grin, eyes laser-focused on Annabelle. Two older women at the bar swiveled to look at us, then said, "He certainly didn't respond like that when *we* walked in the door."

Erik and Gabe were already at a booth, and as we approached, they stood and started singing "Mrs. Robinson," just loud enough for Annabelle to hear. A reference to her being eight years older than Scott.

"Shut up," she laughed.

Eva kissed Gabe, then reached up to wipe the smudge of lipstick off his lip. "You're not being very nice."

"That's why you love me. Nice is boring."

"I love you because you're smart and kind," Eva said as she settled into the booth.

"What? Not good-looking?"

She rolled her eyes. "Yes, my love. Good-looking too." He was, though not the kind of good-looking Scott was—chiseled features, dimpled smile, bodybuilder arms. Gabe was more handsome than good-looking: wrinkled oxford, wire-rimmed glasses, close-cropped gray hair. And a great smile. As soon as I sat down, he said, "So, Erik says you aren't a theater person either, thank God!" He grinned. "Give us the dirt: He talks about Ten Chimneys in his sleep, doesn't he?"

"He whispers Lynn Fontanne's name," I teased.

"Traitor." Erik squeezed my leg.

"Even I whisper Lynn Fontanne's name in my sleep," Eva said. "God, that woman could act!"

"What you should all be whispering about is a new name for that place," Annabelle said. "It's a PR nightmare."

"Ten Chimneys is what Alfred and Lynn called it," Erik said.

"Who cares?" Annabelle retorted. "Why not just call it Ten Drain Spouts, Fifteen Gutters?"

"Thirteen Toilets," Eva laughed.

"That's low," Erik said, but he was smiling.

The whole night was like that: banter and jokes and such gentle affection between them. "You still with us?" Eva asked Annabelle as she gazed at Scott. "How many fingers do you see?" She held up two.

Annabelle smiled and, without turning, said, "How many do you see?" and flashed Eva her own finger. We all laughed.

What surprised me most was how much I not only liked them but liked who I was with them. Relaxed, funny, happy. I had been serious for so long, had wondered for years if I'd ever be able to enjoy myself again without feeling guilty.

We talked about Gabe and Eva's recent vacation to Door County, grilled Annabelle about Scott, talked about the kids. Eva and I chatted about Wallace Stegner's Wisconsin novel, *Crossing to Safety,* a favorite for us both, and then we were all discussing our shared addiction to *The Sopranos.* We shifted from teasing to serious, then back again effortlessly. I thought of a performance I'd once seen where a dozen dancers moved about the stage in complicated, intricate ways, all while holding the edges of a huge swath of fiery orange fabric so that the rippling and folding and twisting and unfurling of the cloth became its own performance. Our conversation was like that, a bright billowing thing, each of them holding an edge.

During the break between sets, when Scott pulled up a chair, I watched how they folded him into the group as naturally as they had me. Despite their incessant Mrs. Robinson references to Annabelle or the way they referred to Scott as "your painter boy" or made fun of his looks—"You could fall into that dimple and never find your way home again!"—I loved how genuine and welcoming they were, Erik buying Scott a beer, Gabe asking what kind of guitar he was using, and Eva, the nurturer in the group, nudging her plate of nachos toward him and urging him to eat. It was obvious they liked him not only because Scott was immensely likable but also because they loved Annabelle, and if this was what she wanted, then they did too.

Or should I say *we*? Because by the time Scott joined our table, I felt like I was a part of them, like I had been for years.

CHAPTER 11

Two months.

Sometimes it felt like two weeks.

Sometimes it felt like two decades. How else could I know so much about Erik if we'd been dating only two months, two pages on a calendar? How could all I'd learned about him fit into that impossibly minuscule time frame?

Sixty-one days.

All the little things I discovered by watching him: Whenever he drank more than two beers, his language became oddly formal. *Did I not tell you,* he'd say, or *Shall we think about . . .* "Oh no, you're getting British," I'd tease. He sat at tables or bars sideways because of his too-long legs. People often asked if he'd played basketball. "When you're this tall you don't have much choice," he'd say.

He'd been close with his dad, who died of bladder cancer two days after Spencer was born. Erik brought Spencer to his dad's hospital room, and though his dad was barely conscious, he reached for Spencer. "When I took Spencer back, my dad had tears rolling down his cheeks. Spence was the last person he held." Erik paused. "I feel like Spencer has my dad's soul."

We emailed constantly, spoke on the phone nights we weren't together, went running and to the Y after work, brought the kids to his house on Saturdays, had dinner with them at Annabelle's. He gave me a tour of Ten Chimneys, and we visited the gallery that sold my collages. I introduced him to Margaret one night, and we had Gabe and Eva to dinner at his place. In the kitchen, as I was making coffee, Eva told me, "I've never seen Erik this relaxed."

I nodded, picturing that photo of Erik and Annabelle, their happiness so real it felt like you could cup it in your hands. Eva regarded me, then said, "I'm not saying he wasn't happy before, but there's an ease in him now." Before I could answer, she said, "Wait. Don't move," and reached to fix my earring. "There. You were about to lose it." I must have looked stricken—it's how I felt—because she asked, "What? What did I do?" but I could only shake my head.

How could I explain? That casual gesture. That intimacy between women. Fixing an earring, adjusting a collar. Kelly licking her index finger and smoothing my eyebrow into place. I could have that again, I thought: friends and laughter, drinks at Hattie Magee's; my footsteps in sync with Erik's as we ran, the crunch of leaves underfoot, the smell of woodsmoke in the air. All his nicknames for me—"Sunbeam" and "Pea," and "Carl Lewis," after the Olympic runner—as if I were multiple people instead of the single thing that had defined me for so long.

And there was Annabelle, giving me grief whenever I gave her wardrobe advice, because if the choice was between something black and something with a color, I always chose black. The way she'd cock an eyebrow and nod to her back deck, which meant "I need a cigarette." We'd sit outside, teeth chattering as the nights grew colder, and she'd talk about Scott, her face animated and happy. When I stopped by, mostly with Erik but a few times by myself when Erik worked late, the girls would race to the door, fighting over whose turn it was to open it. Their solid weight as I carried them on my hip, their sticky hands on my neck and face. Wanting me to tuck them in, wanting me to read them a story. And Spencer shyly launching into a recitation of weather facts.

How could I have guessed all the ways I would learn to love Erik and Annabelle's children? All the ways loving them—and being loved by them—would begin to heal me? I think of the night I'd been coloring with the twins while Annabelle was doing something with Spencer, and Hazel reached over and set her warm hand atop mine.

"What's up, bunny?" I asked. "You getting tired?"

"I just want to hold your hand," she said.

I'm not sure why it was that moment of all the dozens just like it when I realized: I would have been a good mom. If I'd only had more time.

It happened again the night we were all at Annabelle's watching *The Wizard of Oz* and Spencer wedged himself between me and Erik on the couch, then leaned his head on my shoulder. The thought was there then too—*I would have been a good mom,* the realization moving through me like an electrical current.

I could have this life, I would think as I stood in front of the bathroom mirror after Erik left for work some mornings. My makeup worn off, skin flushed, eyes tired because we never got enough sleep. I'd stare at that woman and realize how much I wanted to be her, wanted to hold a child's hand or sit at a picnic table eating frozen custard with a man who, after kissing me, would grin and say, "Oh, your mouth is so cold, I better warm it up." Then kiss me again.

And I *was* her, wasn't I?

That was the part I wasn't sure of: Could I be her *and* me all at once?

Our favorite place was Kopp's. On Friday nights, packs of teenagers arrived after football games, shouting to each other across the parking lot, but during the week, now that night fell earlier, it was sometimes just us and an older couple who always sat in their pickup with the windows down. "Good evening!" the guy would call, his wife waving through the windshield.

"That'll be us in twenty years," Erik whispered.

Something in me soared: *us in twenty years.*

We called them "the farmers" because of the truck and the John Deere cap the guy wore, and then it became "our farmers."

"You realize he's probably an executive," I said.

Kopp's was closing on November first, and as the days ticked down, I felt almost sad. It had become our place. We talked differently there, ended up in conversations we didn't have on the phone or in his kitchen or even in bed.

It was there that Erik told me he was estranged from his mother, who had remarried and moved to Arizona only five months after his dad died. I told him about my parents having to sell their house, though I didn't say why. It was the house my dad grew up in, I told Erik, and losing it broke something in him. He used to come home from the restaurant at night and sit on our back deck with a scotch and a cigar, but in the condo, the small balcony overlooked a parking lot, and the neighbors complained about the smoke, so he quit. It was the only time I heard my mother cry about the loss of the house. It broke something in *me,* I told Erik.

It was also at Kopp's that I told him about Kelly. She'd landed the role of Belle in the Broadway version of *Beauty and the Beast* at the Lunt-Fontanne Theatre. My mom had sent the article from the *Cape Gazette*: "Local Star Shines on Broadway." A grainy photo of seventeen-year-old Kelly in our high school production of *The Scarlet Letter.* I stared at that photo for a long time, feeling unmoored.

"This is *your* Kelly?" Erik said when I showed him the clipping.

"She probably told me about Alfred and Lynn years ago," I said. "I know Shakespeare because of her."

"Your face lights up when you mention her," he said. "Do you ever think about getting in touch? Mending whatever happened?"

"I can't." A chalky taste in my mouth. I had tried. Only once, but it was enough. I'd been out of the hospital for just a few weeks, but already too much had happened that I'd been shielded from. My mom told me that, at first, Kelly made the hour-long drive every week to visit me, but I'd been too drugged, too numb, too afraid, too *everything,* to respond. Eventually she stopped coming.

I came home after eight months, though it wasn't really home, wasn't the bungalow on Fourth Street I'd shared with Nick, but my parents' house, the house I'd grown up in and the one they would lose paying for the private hospital I'd end up returning to. The day I saw Kelly again, I was in Browseabout Books with my mom. I was like a child in those first weeks, terrified of being alone, shadowing my mom everywhere. She was looking at books and I wandered over to the cards, and there was Kelly. "Kel?" I said quietly. And then, "Oh my God! I can't believe it's you!" I blurted it without thinking, without considering how stupidly cheerful I sounded—as if the last eight months had never happened.

The look on her face when she turned to me: confusion, hurt, anger. *"I can't believe it's you*?" she said incredulously. "Are you kidding?" Tears filled her eyes. "You don't call me *Kel;* you don't call me anything." And then she left. I wouldn't see her for over a year. And that time would be even worse.

I stirred my plastic spoon through the melted custard, grateful for the darkness, grateful Erik couldn't see my face. My heart felt huge inside my chest. Kelly was Lucy's godmother. She'd been in the delivery room. She used to hold Lucy for hours, marveling at her tiny fingernails, her spiky eyelashes.

I glanced at Erik. There was so much I needed to tell him, but Kelly was a start, wasn't she? The Christmas lights swayed, colors washing across his face. He knew Kelly had been my best friend since preschool, knew we'd had a terrible falling-out connected to the end of my marriage. But I hadn't told him Kelly was my sister-in-law, afraid to get too close to the black ice of talking about Nick. As a result of the omission, though, I'm pretty sure Erik jumped to the conclusion that Nick had cheated on me *with* Kelly, that this was why I'd left Rehoboth. He never said this, but I saw the scenario flit across his face, and I thought of how we often create the stories we need out of the fragmented information we have.

"What I didn't tell you about Kelly," I said hesitantly, "is that she was also my sister-in-law."

"What?" Erik set down his custard. "Kelly was . . . Nick's her brother?"

I nodded.

He exhaled slowly. "Okay." He glanced sharply at me and then away, across the narrow road toward the empty cornfields. "That kind of changes everything, doesn't it?"

"What do you mean?"

"What do I *mean*? You knew this fucker your whole life, Claire. You were kids together." He shook his head as if to clear it. "I assumed he was some jerk and you made a mistake, but that's not the case, is it?"

I was shivering, and it wasn't from the cold. I hadn't expected Erik to feel so deceived. I pushed my hands between my legs, trying to keep from trembling. "I never said he was a jerk." I forced myself not to look away.

"It's what you don't say, Claire." His voice was hard. "I thought he and your friend . . ." He sighed heavily. "I'm glad it's not that. It's just . . . Did *you* cheat on him? Is that what you're so afraid to tell me?"

"No." The question stung, not because he'd asked but because it was the worst thing he could imagine. Before Lucy, I might have thought this too.

In the lighted window of the custard shack, a ponytailed girl was wiping down counters, getting ready to close. "I know I've asked before," Erik said, "but you are divorced, right?"

"We're very divorced. Nick's remarried. He has a child." *Another* child, I almost said. I forget how I knew this. Nick didn't live in Rehoboth anymore. He'd moved, maybe for the same reasons I had—to try to start over.

A breeze swayed the lights overhead, and a wash of green spilled across Erik's features. "Does your mom send you articles about him?" His question like a sharpened point.

"No," I said quietly, my mouth dry, my heart hammering a mile a minute. *Tell him,* I thought. *Tell him about Lucy.* I had to. I wanted to. And there would never be a good time, a right time. I could feel him waiting, willing me with his eyes to speak, and . . .

"I can't," I said helplessly. Disappointment swept over me.

He held my gaze for a moment, then reached for my hand.

Our last night before Kopp's closed for the season, Erik told me his own secret, about what had happened in his marriage. We'd been talking about Spencer, and he said quietly, "I was the one who blamed Annabelle for Spencer's problems."

I remembered he'd said she blamed herself, and I thought again of how complex every story is, a prism reflecting different things depending on how you turn it. "You actually said that?"

"Oh, I said it, all right. It was unforgivable. I was just so pissed off about—" He stopped, raked a hand through his thick hair. Our farmers were the only other customers, sitting in their idling truck, a plume of smoke trailing from the exhaust.

"She was taking all these vitamins when she was pregnant," Erik continued, "not because her doctor suggested it, mind you, but because *she'd* done the research. But whatever, I didn't think it was a big deal, until after Spencer got diagnosis number three or four or whatever it was and we learned folic acid had been linked to some of the disorders we kept hearing about."

"You didn't."

"Oh, but I did." They'd been arguing, he said, not about Spencer, but about Annabelle being reckless. "Although it doesn't really matter what we were fighting about. The truth is I wanted to hurt her, and the bottle of vitamins was there. I was so angry. I told her that her carelessness with our son was unconscionable." He let out a long breath. "The second the words left my mouth, I wanted to take them back, but . . . you can't. I've told her a hundred times I didn't mean it, and I didn't. . . ." His voice trailed off.

It explained a lot, I thought. His guilt, his capitulation to Annabelle. But it scared me too. *This?* I thought. This *is your biggest sin? Who hasn't said the awful thing?* "Why did you want to hurt her so badly?"

"Why did I know you would ask?" He glanced past me, beyond the cornfield to the line of lights in the distance that was the interstate. After a minute, he said, "I've debated telling you. I want to because . . . well, because I want to tell you everything. But I don't want it to change how you feel."

"I promise I will still like Annabelle." I held up my hand as if swearing an oath. I honestly couldn't imagine anything she'd done that would make me not like her. She was fun and zany and kind, and mostly, she was so honest about being a mom that it made me wonder how my life would have been different if *she'd* been my friend ten years ago. She had no qualms talking about how lonely motherhood often was and how, some days, when she was at her PR job, dressed in a suit and heels with people paying her ridiculous amounts of money to help them strategize about problems, it was all she could do to get in the car and come home to toddler tantrums and macaroni and cheese and Spencer repeating the same phrase three hundred times.

"It's also Gabe I'm worried you'll change your mind about," Erik said.

"Oh." I dropped my hand. "Okay."

"He and Annabelle had an affair."

"*What?* Does Eva know?"

He shook his head.

I had so many competing thoughts. That he could forgive this mistake, because clearly he had; that was the first thing. If he could forgive something this damaging . . . I felt as if a bell were ringing in the center of my chest. He got it, I thought. He understood. *What you did is not who you are.* But right on the heels of this was the realization that they were all keeping this secret from Eva. It seemed a horrible betrayal, as horrible as the affair itself, maybe worse. And I would now be part of it. I wondered if it meant I could never truly be Eva's friend. "Don't you worry she'll find out?"

"I used to."

"But that you all know—"

"It's fucked up. Believe me, I am well aware."

"And you're really okay with Gabe?"

"What's the choice? He and Annabelle both swore it was a huge mistake and if they could do it over . . . and they never meant . . ." He shrugged.

"You don't believe them?"

"No, I do. Which is why it's complicated. Because how do I let one mistake—and granted, it's a big one—but am I really going to let it destroy two *decades* of friendship? Gabe's been there for me. Big-time. When my dad died, when we were going through all this hell trying to figure out what was going on with Spence. The day of my interview with Ten Chimneys he came over to make sure my tie looked good." He laughed, but it was serrated and sharp. "And then there's Eva. I'm going to let a stupid regrettable mistake destroy what she has with Gabe? Gabe's her world. She's his."

How was that possible? I wondered. But wasn't this the same logic people had used with me? How could I have loved Lucy? Even though loving her was the only thing I knew for sure.

Scratchy music—*Mr. Sandman, bring me a dream*—came through the speakers mounted to poles. Our farmers were leaving and we waved, watching the red taillights of their truck until it disappeared.

"Should I not have told you?" Erik asked.

"Of course you should have."

"I've made you complicit, though." His voice was quiet. "I hate lying, I especially hate it with Eva, because like I said, she's one of the best people I know. But I just can't see how telling her the truth helps in this situation."

Of course I would think of this later that week when I finally told Erik my own truth.

CHAPTER 12

Every time I tried to tell Erik about Lucy, my throat would close, my heart would race, and I'd back away, thinking, *Not yet, not yet, not yet*. Again and again. Finally, driving home from Kopp's the night Erik confided in me about Annabelle and Gabe, I said, "I think the only way I'm going to be able to tell you about my past is to just pick a date and do it."

Erik glanced at me. "How about Friday? We'll go out to dinner, then come home and talk all night if that's what it takes. All weekend."

I nodded, teeth chattering. I couldn't get warm. Friday was only four days away. *But he forgave Gabe,* I kept thinking. One mistake does not undo an entire friendship, an entire life. *He forgave Gabe.* Three words. Tiny stones I turned over and over, comforted by their shape and solidity. *He forgave Gabe.*

Three days.

Then two.

He forgave Gabe.

Headed downtown on our way to dinner, the sun almost setting behind us, I stared from the passenger window at an autumn sky that was all fiery color and the urgency that comes with one season's end and another's beginning. We'd already begun talking about Thanksgiving. We'd have it at Annabelle's. Eva and Gabe would come. Soon it would be winter. Christmas. Would we still be together? I pulled in a breath, inhaling lavender from the bath soap Annabelle had given me the week before. "One of the moms at Spencer's school makes it," she said, handing me the tissue-paper-filled bag. "You're so good with my kids." She smiled. *"And* you put up with me."

Erik and I ate in a restaurant overlooking the lake. He was talking about Claggett Wilson, the famous set designer who had decorated Ten Chimneys during Alfred and Lynn's heyday, painting the walls with fleur-de-lis to resemble wallpaper, painting a proscenium arch over the entranceway. Their entire house an elaborate stage set. I know I nodded and asked questions—I loved when Erik talked about his work; he was so animated and erudite and funny—but none of it made sense that night. I wanted to believe in the kind of world Erik was describing, one where you could orchestrate your life like a play, emphasize only the most beautiful details, but how was this possible?

Didn't I owe Erik the truth?

I was in love with him, had fallen in love that first night outside the Y when he touched my elbow and goose bumps rose along my arm as if I'd been shocked. I loved that moment when I jerked my eyes up to see if he too had felt that spark of electricity, and he blew on his fingers as if they'd been burned.

I love you, I thought, as I regarded Erik across the table from me. Neither of us had spoken it out loud. But wasn't this why I needed to tell him about Lucy? *Because* I loved him and I believed he loved me, *because* I wanted a life with him, *because* I wanted us to be able to talk about my daughter?

And *because* wasn't this what love was?

Letting someone in, letting someone love you despite your mistakes?

I pushed my salad around my plate: Blue cheese, cranberries, vinaigrette—I couldn't taste it. Adrenaline was pumping through me, my feet and hands bloodless, my heart siphoning every bit of energy. Fight or flight. I knew that once I told Erik, even if he understood and accepted what had happened, he wouldn't see me in the same way. Which meant it wasn't just Erik I would lose but the woman I was when he looked at me: a happy, spontaneous woman who he admired and trusted and was falling in love with; a woman his friends liked, a woman his kids—his kids!—loved and trusted too. It felt like a miracle every single time the twins hurtled themselves at my legs or grabbed my hand, or Spencer tapped my wrist to tell me something. But the minute I told Erik the truth, that woman would disappear and the person I'd see in his eyes would be the last person I wanted to be.

I looked at him across the table, this handsome, kind, *good* man. His shirt, a blue oxford, was missing a button in the collar, and a space opened inside me as I remembered the night nearly two months ago—our third date? Fourth?—when he stood from my sofa to leave, both of us flushed, my hair tangled. As he reached for his keys, the edge of his collar poked his face. He started to button it, then said, "Oops, I seem to have lost something."

"Your mind?" I teased. "Your heart?"

"Oh, definitely my heart, but a button too."

I turned to stare out at the lake, but all I could see was our reflection, the white-cloth-covered table and candlelight, Erik lifting his fork to his mouth. Why had I agreed to come here? Had I really thought I'd be able to eat? I watched Erik in the window and felt my stomach clench. *Don't,* I thought. *Please.* But I wasn't sure to whom the plea was addressed. To Erik? *Please don't leave, please don't stop loving me*? Or was it to myself? *Please don't say anything, Claire. Don't ruin this. He doesn't have to know.*

Except he did.

CHAPTER 13

We were sitting on my couch. I couldn't get warm. Was still wearing my coat. Erik reached for my hand, but I shook my head. "I can't." I felt my smile wobble. "I wish I didn't have to tell you this."

"If it means I get to know—"

"Please. This isn't something you'll be glad to know." I swallowed. "It's about my marriage." I glanced at him. "We had a child."

"You—*what*? My God, Claire."

"She's ten, and she lives with . . . with Nick. I lost—" But I couldn't say it. Once I did, nothing would be the same. "I lost—" I needed to say *I lost my parental rights,* but all I could get out was, "I lost her."

"What do you . . . You mean you lost custody?"

I nodded. It was a start.

"Lucy, right? That's why you sign your collages that way?"

I nodded again. I kept staring at the tip of his collar. The missing button was probably here, I thought, beneath the couch cushions or under the rug, and I had the crazy longing to find it, to fix this one small thing. Instead, I forced myself to meet his eyes. "I relinquished my parental rights, Erik. She was almost three." I felt as if I was going to get sick, though I knew not to come up for air. *Keep going, keep going, don't take a breath.* "There was an accident," I continued. "I—I spent time, over two years, in a psychiatric hospital."

"What do you . . . I don't understand." He looked pale, eyes dark with shock and confusion. "What do you mean 'accident'?"

"I'm sorry. I know you don't want to hear this. She . . . she almost drowned, and it was my fault."

"Oh, Claire, no. No, honey." *Honey.* It's what he called Spencer when Spencer was upset.

"Nick saved her, but I . . . I let it . . . We didn't know if she would . . . it was touch and go for months." I clenched my teeth to keep my jaw from trembling, but my whole body was shaking. I pressed the tips of my fingers together until they turned white.

"Hey. Come here." His voice a candle flame lit against darkness.

I stared at the collar of his shirt. The missing button. His chin moving as he spoke.

"Claire, honey, look at me." But I couldn't. I knew what he was thinking. Maybe she fell into a pool. Was pulled away by a wave. A freak tragedy, the sort of thing no one could predict or prevent.

His knee, his khaki pants, his hands, his long fingers, fingers that had touched every part of my body.

"It's called postpartum psychosis," I said thickly, and something in his gaze crumbled.

"What?" he said. "Wait. *What?*"

I started with before. She was born in January and I was fine, happy—God, I was so happy! I was a mother! I had a daughter. I loved saying that word. "Our *daughter* slept six whole hours," I would tell Nick. Or "Is that our *daughter* crying?" And he'd laugh and say, "I believe it is our *daughter*."

We had such a good life, I told Erik. We lived at the beach, close to our parents; our mothers were over the moon about their granddaughter, Kelly was my sister-in-law now, and Lucy, Lucy was beautiful. "I loved being a mom," I said. "And I was good at it."

"I have no doubt." He brushed a strand of hair from my face.

"And then, when she was five months old, everything changed."

I started having panic attacks, though I didn't know that's what they were at first. But every second she wasn't near me, I imagined awful things happening: She'd stop breathing or . . . I don't know, carrying her across the room, I'd see myself tripping and she'd go flying. I could barely drive when she was with me; I pictured gruesome crashes, or not even that, just my car swerving for no reason into oncoming traffic. I was terrified of everything, every minute. "It's like I became afraid of her," I told Erik. "She was so little and fragile and it seemed impossible that I could protect her." I never thought I would hurt her; I just was afraid someone or something would.

"Everyone said it was 'the baby blues.' 'All mothers go through this,' my mom and Nick's mom kept insisting. 'It *is* overwhelming! *Of course!* To be so responsible for another life!'" I paused, struggling to keep the tremor from my voice. "I wanted to believe them, but it was devastating. To be failing so horribly at being a mother? It felt like failing as a human being." I told him how my mom phoned every afternoon and she'd ask all these little things: *What did you dress her in today? What book did you read at nap time? Did you notice her hair is getting a little curl to it?* All these years later, I could still hear the pleading in my mom's voice, how desperate she was to help me fall back in love with my baby, because the fear was ruining that too. I was so tense around her, afraid to just play or be silly or take her places.

I took another deep breath. "The day it happened—"

"It?"

"The accident." I swallowed. Except for my lawyer, I'd never told this story to anyone outside the hospital. I'm not sure I believed I'd ever find someone I would trust enough. I looked at Erik's kind eyes, worry lines creasing his forehead. *Please understand,* I willed him. *Please.* I thought of that night Spencer had uncharacteristically squished next to me on the couch, head on my shoulder, and the expression I'd seen on Erik's face: wonder and gratitude and love.

"Do you have any clue what that means to me?" he asked later. "To know my son feels safe with you?"

"The day it happened, I thought I was doing better," I said softly. I told him about taking Lucy to the boardwalk the night before, riding the Ferris wheel. The fact that I could do that at all! But it was okay, more than okay! The three of us in our own little basket, away from the noise and heat, the lights of Cape May shimmering in the distance.

The next morning Nick got up with Lucy, brought me coffee in bed. We talked about how we'd gotten so caught up in being new parents we'd forgotten each other. "We'll make more time," Nick promised. "We'll go on dates!" I felt such hope. Later, I left to run errands, and even that felt great. *I'm getting out,* I thought, *I'm leaving her with Nick, I'm not panicking, I'm doing ordinary things. Ordinary.* I told Erik how my mind still snagged on those first two letters—*or*—and I think of how many alternatives, options, *ors*, were stacked up next to that day, and how I couldn't imagine any of them.

Until later.

After Lucy and Nick were gone.

"I always wondered if, because it was such an ordinary morning, I let my guard down," I told Erik. "But honestly, there was no reason to have my guard up. Even in the worst panic attacks, the things I imagined hurting Lucy were always things *I* needed to protect her from: my own clumsiness or a lousy driver or a sharp object left within reach. The idea that *I* might hurt her—it never crossed my mind. Not once. Not ever."

I told him how, when I got home from my errands, I felt like a switch had been flipped: Suddenly I was terrified again. "I don't know what's happening," I sobbed to my mom on the phone. She said she'd be right over, but I told her Nick was there—he was mowing the lawn and Lucy was asleep. And then . . ." I stopped. More than any other moment, this was the one place where I could have changed everything. "My mom asked if I was worried I'd hurt myself or Lucy."

If I had just said yes.

I will never not be haunted by that.

"But I wasn't worried," I told Erik. "I was devastated my mom could think this. 'I can't believe you,' I told her. 'Have I ever said or done *anything* to make you think I'd harm my own child?'

"'No, sweetie, but I'm asking. That's all. You're taking the antianxiety meds, right?'

"'Yeah, Mom, and they're helping about as much as this conversation.' And then I was full-on furious, which years of therapy taught me was probably terror at how close to the truth my mom actually was."

I hated remembering that conversation. My mom is devastated to think she might have put the idea of hurting Lucy in my head, something she admitted to me only once. "I thought I was doing the responsible thing by asking," she had sobbed, and though I promised her that her words had nothing to do with what happened, I can't ever really know, and neither can she. I can only remind her that none of the usual signs were there. For most women the psychosis occurs weeks after their child is born, not months. For most women there's a family history of bipolar illness or a difficult birth, a difficult pregnancy, and for me there weren't any of those things. For most women there are dark thoughts of hurting their babies, and I never had any. So, my mom's questions felt far-fetched, insulting even. And in another version of that day, that's all they would have been.

"I don't remember much after that," I said. "Lucy woke with diarrhea, covered with it. There was nothing to do except get her in the tub. . . ."

The rest was a blur: the scissoring drone of the lawn mower interspersed with her crying the minute I lifted her into the tub. I'd checked the water, terrified it was too hot, but it wasn't. "I was careful," I said, a pleading tone creeping into my voice. "I was trying." I paused. "She wouldn't stop screaming. That's all I remember. What was I doing wrong?" Even in memory the sounds are amplified, deafening, as they were that day, so that I felt as if I were being smashed apart in the same way a wineglass can be shattered by a high frequency. The bathroom was white—white walls, floors, towels—and the white was unrelenting, suffocating. I felt blinded, as if the whole world were reduced to her screams and that constant roar of the lawn mower, and I remember thinking that if I just let her go for a second, let her sounds go underwater—one second—it would fix whatever was wrong.

Erik's eyes were closed. He'd brought his steepled hands to his mouth. I waited for him to look at me, but he didn't, and I realized he couldn't, that he was bracing himself.

There were only fragments after that. Nick slamming me

sideways into the toilet and shouting and calling 911. I thought he'd hurt himself with the lawn mower, and I kept trying to take Lucy, but he wouldn't let me and I didn't understand and then Kelly was there and the EMTs and the police and then my mom. . . . "I never meant to hurt her," I said quietly.

Nothing. Erik didn't move or open his eyes. It seemed he was barely breathing.

She was underwater for two and a half minutes, I learned later. "I don't remember," I said again. "It's a medical . . . I still . . . It's called a fugue state. Nick came in and she wasn't . . . He called 911." I knew I was repeating myself.

I didn't look at Erik, but at my hands, his shoes. I could feel his retreat, and the metal ball of the word *over* pinging through my insides, knocking against my ribs, slamming into my heart. Erik hadn't moved, but an awful thrumming radiated from him. Finally, I saw his eyes: bewildered, hurt, stunned. Like watching a TV screen scramble into static, the confusion of too many emotions all competing with one another. And then the picture cleared. "I don't know what to say," he said. His skin was blotchy, as if he'd been slapped. "You said . . . Is she okay now?"

"I think so. Everyone thought . . . they said she'd have a full recovery. I know that doesn't undo anything, but I wasn't in my right mind, Erik. You have to know that. It's like being in a coma. You wake up and weeks have passed."

"You told me you couldn't have kids."

"I can't. I had a tubal ligation."

"And after the hospital? You said you were there two years? Did you see her? Did you *want* to give her up?"

"I wanted her to be okay," I said quietly. "That's all I wanted. And—and I wasn't sure she would be with me." Even more than the accident, this was the part that still filled me with a shame so strong I could taste it. I told him how Nick would bring Lucy to my mom's or I'd go to his parents' house, where he was living, but Lucy didn't know me, or maybe she did and was frightened, and, of course, I was anxious too, afraid to be alone with her. It was awful. Awful for her, awful for Nick, awful for my poor mother, who fought me tooth and nail to not relinquish my rights, actually got down on her knees in the kitchen one day and begged me. Nick was already involved with Andrea, Lucy's physical therapist, and Andrea loved Lucy. "I felt like giving her up was the only way I could even begin to . . . to make it up to her. To give her a chance at a normal life."

"And she has that now? A normal life?"

"I hope so, but . . . we have no contact with Nick. I think my mom tried. And at one point, we thought maybe Kelly—but I don't know."

He nodded, eyes closed.

I glanced at the manila folder on the dining room table: medical articles about postpartum psychosis; etiology, prognosis. *Occurs in one out of a thousand births . . . commonly misdiagnosed . . . I should have given him the articles first,* I thought. And now it was too late. A memory rose of watching a surfing movie, Nick explaining how the moment the wave climbs into its perfect curl is already past the moment when you have to make a decision whether or not you're going to surf it.

"I printed out some information." I could hear my own breathing. Waves rising and falling. "I know you have questions."

"Claire." His voice was so far away.

"I'm not saying it isn't awful, but it can't happen—"

"Claire." His voice was gentle. "I understand everything you're saying, and I'm sorry you went through this, but it's so far beyond anything . . ." His voice cracked, and he bowed his head again, elbows on his knees. When he glanced up, his eyes were glassy. "I don't know what I think right now beyond feeling like a fool."

"Why?"

"*Why?* Because the past three months . . . I've been living in fucking la-la land. Everything I thought . . ." He inhaled a shuddering breath. "It's all been pretend."

"Please don't say that." My voice felt impossibly small. A straight pin trying to hold up a painting. "Maybe it was stupid to think you would understand, but it doesn't nullify . . ." I was holding myself by the elbows, trying to stop from shaking. "It doesn't nullify how we felt. And I know you love your children—you're an amazing dad—and it must seem . . . I don't even know what it seems, but I loved my daughter too, Erik. I still do."

"How, Claire? *How?* I'm not trying to be a jerk, but you don't even know where she is!"

"Because I can't!" I cried. "How would that help?"

He looked at me blankly, then lowered his face to his hands. I stared at the curved line of his back, the knobs of his spine against his shirt. Hesitantly, I touched him, just my hand on his shoulder blade, feeling his warmth and the rise and fall of his breathing.

"I need to go," he said. "I'm sorry." He stood, reached for his jacket on the arm of the couch, and walked to the door. "I know you're in pain, and there are things you probably need me to say, and I wish I could." He paused. "I need time. I . . . I just need time."

"I know." My heart was pounding. "But will you . . . if you can't, if you . . ." *Please don't go,* I wanted to say. *Please don't leave me.*

"I won't just disappear," he said. "I'll call. I just—I don't know when."

After he left, I lifted the pillows from the sofa, reached into corners, searching for that button from Erik's shirt. I looked under the edges of the rug, felt under the skirt of the couch. Dust, a pen, a plastic cap from a water bottle, and then, the thumbtack-sized button. I clutched it in my fist; lay down on the couch, still in my coat; and closed my eyes. I was exhausted. I felt the blood rushing back into my arms and legs, a tingling prickly feeling. Beneath my eyelids a bright burning color. Red. Or orange. Something painful. I felt the sting of tears but couldn't cry.

I woke later, the lights on, the button making a small indent in my palm. I pushed myself up, my stomach growling. I hadn't eaten much dinner, the leftovers in a Styrofoam box in the refrigerator. How could I feel hungry now? The earlier adrenaline was gone, leaving behind a dull sadness. I walked into the kitchen, then sat with the box at the table.

I stayed there for a long time, feeling the grief pour through me, over me, as if I were standing in a rain shower. What hurt as much as anything was his accusation that I'd been pretending, that I wasn't who I said I was, as if I could only be one thing: the woman who hurt her child. It was my greatest fear.

I had loved Lucy. All those months I carried her, and the five and a half months before the psychosis set in, I was a good mom. Proud of my girl, delighted with her every blink and expression and gurgle. The shape of her ears and toes. Her furrowed brow and wispy flyaway hair. Her bee's knees. I had loved her.

As I had the rainy March morning I sat in my lawyer's office in Georgetown, Delaware, and completed the parental rights termination form. My dad came with me because my mother wouldn't, railing at me that they hadn't lost everything—everything! their house, for God's sake!—for me to throw it all away. But I wasn't. What I believed was that I didn't deserve to be a mom, or maybe something had broken in me and I wasn't capable anymore, but at least I was giving Lucy the best chance I could. Maybe that was wrong, maybe I should have tried harder—I will never know, but I was trying to do what was right for my child. How, *how,* could that not count for something? I gave her the only thing I thought I had left to give her. And coming here, starting my life over, what other choice did Erik think I had?

I pushed my chair from the table and walked to the window. My reflection was transposed onto the dark glass like an image from one of my collages, and I thought of how the collages themselves were really about her. All the layers of paper and cloth and tissue and paint, as many as ten layers on some canvases. In the end, wasn't every piece a metaphor for drowning, for what lies beneath the surface? And even then, not a single collage felt complete until I signed my name with hers: *Lucy Claire.*

That's not pretending, I wanted to tell Erik.

It's surviving.

PART II

CHARLOTTE: *It's no use.*

HERBERT: *What is no use?*

CHARLOTTE: *Pretending.*

HERBERT: *Pretending what?*

CHARLOTTE: *That we are happy . . .*

—Noël Coward, *Quadrille,* act 2, scene 1

CHAPTER 14

When my phone rang Saturday morning, I leaped for it, then felt my heart deflate: It was my mother. "Well?" she asked, and I could hear how eager she was.

"He left," I said. "He thinks I've been pretending, that I'm not who I said I was."

She didn't answer for a beat. And then, "Oh, Claire. When you didn't call last night, I thought maybe—" She stopped. "Do you want me to come out there?"

I want to come home, I thought. It didn't matter that I was thirty-four years old. I wanted to crawl into my childhood bed and have my mom bring me chicken broth and saltines and orange Jell-O. And I wanted to sleep. For days. I felt exhausted by everything, by the last ten years, by my rigid routine: running, working out, going to my job, and trying to have a normal life. How would I keep doing it? "I'll be okay," I said. "I just want to sleep."

"Will you call me later?" she asked. "We can talk about the weather, but I want to hear your voice."

I promised her I would.

I slept until midafternoon and still felt exhausted. In the sunlight-filled kitchen, the brightness was overwhelming.

My eyes ached, my throat ached, and as I stood at the sink, gulping a glass of water, I felt blasted apart with sadness. *I can't do this,* I thought, whatever this was, whatever I'd done before Erik.

For the past two months, we'd spent Saturdays with the kids at his house. We built forts in the dining room with blankets draped across chairs, baked and decorated cookies in fun shapes: a cactus, a star, a rocket. I loved being with them, loved helping Erik make his house into their home. Buying plastic place mats with fun facts about the universe, all of us taking turns and reading out a fact—Erik and I reading for the girls. I'd painted a little table and chairs for them with giraffes and elephants having a tea party. We had a movie blanket, which was *only* for watching movies, Erik declared, and the five of us would snuggle in a row under it. I wondered if Erik had taken them to his house that morning, wondered what he'd told Annabelle about why I wasn't with him. I closed my eyes, feeling dizzy and scared. Would he tell Annabelle about Lucy? They still had that married-couple habit of sharing everything.

I curled up on the sofa by the window, willing him to come over. Every time a car drove by, my heart beat erratically. I sat there all afternoon, wrapped in a blanket, hugging a throw pillow. The sky turned lavender, then purple, and I watched lights come on in the houses across the street. Once it got dark, I phoned my mom, then slept another twelve hours.

Sunday was the same.

I didn't run on Monday, didn't go to the Y. Midafternoon, I pleaded sickness, left work early, and crawled into bed again. "I'm so tired," I told my mom.

"You're depressed, sweetie. Can you go for a run? This much sleep isn't good."

I did run the next day, and it helped. It always does. I'd started running in the second hospital, the one in Pennsylvania with the private rooms and real flowers in the dining hall, a view of rolling hills. It was the hospital my parents sold their house to afford, the hospital that let me believe I was worth something. Dr. Fasnacht was there, and she suggested I try running to help with the depression. At first, I couldn't go a half mile without my lungs being on fire, my legs wobbly. It felt pointless, but I kept doing it. *Just go to the fence,* I'd tell myself; *make it to the oak tree.* And this breaking the distance into doable increments became the way I lived my life. *All you have to do is get dressed,* I used to tell myself, and then, *All you have to do is make coffee.* Step by step, until I'd gotten through the day. And so Tuesday, I told myself, *Just go to work—you don't have to stay.* And then, *Try to last until lunch. . . .*

I ended up working all afternoon. *You've done this before,* I kept telling myself. *You can do this.* And underneath that, *He said he would call.*

I was sitting on the porch counting stars, as Spencer sometimes did. He couldn't articulate why he did this but one of his teachers had suggested that reducing the world to numbers was a way to make it less confusing. At Erik's, he had a collection of measuring cups and spoons, a butcher's scale, a tape measure, thermometers. As if what he could measure, he could contain. I'd wanted to explain that the problem wasn't the things you could measure but all the things you couldn't: the weight of a secret, the velocity of shame.

Still, he measured our heights and weights, then weighed ordinary objects and recorded the measurements: Claire's coffee cup, 7.3 ounces; Dad's MP3 player, 4 ounces. He wanted to measure the wind, and I told him about the Beaufort scale. At one point, he wanted to measure the weight of songs, the temperature of colors. I made the mistake of telling him how people had once tried to measure sadness by collecting tears in a cup. He wanted to measure *our* sadness then. "But we don't have any!" I told him.

I couldn't think about this, though. It was all I could do to get through the next hour, the next day. I made myself eat dinner, laid out clothes for work. But even these tasks reminded me of Spencer, all the rituals that consumed such large chunks of his time.

I counted 131 stars, my neck aching from staring up, my face cold. I thought of the night Erik told me about Annabelle and Gabe, how driving home from Kopp's, I'd felt him wanting to say he loved me, but I'd steered the conversation away. Until he knew about Lucy, what could those words really mean? Now, as I stared up at the trees, the stars spinning, I regretted this. Wouldn't the words have made it more difficult for him to walk away?

And then his SUV turned onto my road.

He pulled into the drive, turned off the engine and headlights, then sat there, head bowed as if in defeat. Is this what coming back to me felt like?

Was he coming back?

He was almost to the porch when he stopped. "I didn't see you," he said, then held out his arms. "Come here."

In the next second, I was off the porch and he was holding me so tightly I could feel his heartbeat. He smelled like him, a clean earthy Erik smell I wanted to inhale. "I missed you," he said into my hair.

"I missed you too," I whispered.

When he finally stepped back, he exhaled slowly, his breath pluming in the chilly air. "It's hard to believe it's November," he said quietly. He was staring up, as if mesmerized by the sky. I thought of my mom saying, *We can talk about the weather, but I want to hear your voice,* and I felt how much I'd needed to hear Erik's gravelly, rust-colored voice. But I also knew talking about weather was safe, and I thought again of Spencer, of his fascination with the Weather Channel. Was this part of what attracted him? Not just the patterns, but that you could predict those patterns, that you could chart something so vast and uncontrollable: the beginning of a storm hundreds of miles away, a cold front days into the future.

Erik's Adam's apple was pronounced because of the way he was leaning his head back. It made him seem boyish. "A hundred thirty-one so far," I said.

"What?"

"A hundred thirty-one stars. I was counting."

He smiled. "Spencer would be happy to know that."

"I missed them this weekend."

"They missed you too." He sighed. "My kids love you, Claire."

"I love them too." I hadn't said that to him before and it felt good.

"I know you do." He looked at me, and I saw the confusion in his eyes. "I've had so many conversations with you in my head the last few days."

"I've had a lot of those too." I glanced at him. I'd forgotten how tall he was, how I had to tilt my head back to stare up at him. "Do you want to come in?"

"I'm not sure what I want." A breeze moved across the lawn, and the magnolia leaves clicked like castanets. "I had this whole speech. . . ." He was staring at the ground, toeing a crack in the cement. I glanced at my own feet. I was wearing fuzzy slippers and leggings and a ratty sweater of my dad's, and I had the crazy thought that if I didn't look up, Erik couldn't say whatever he was trying to.

"I'm not sure I can do this," he said finally. He spread his hands. "Us."

I think I nodded. *I understand,* I almost said, but I didn't. How do you decide to stop loving someone? "I'm not sure what you're saying," I said. "I'm sorry. I don't mean to be dense." I took a step back and sat on the stairs, my legs feeling as if they would buckle.

He shoved his hands into the pockets of his leather jacket. "I don't know what I'm saying either," he said, and sat next to me, his shoulder touching mine. "I know it took a lot of guts for you to tell me what you did. And a part of me—a big part, Claire—wishes I could tell you it doesn't change anything."

"But it does."

"Yeah. It does."

I forced myself to inhale slowly, to exhale. "I knew you wouldn't see me the same," I said, "and I wanted so much for that not to happen." I hugged my knees to my chest as I spoke, wrapping my arms around them, as if I were literally holding myself together. I felt Erik's gaze on me, but I couldn't look at him.

He reached for my hand, but I couldn't let go of my legs and so he linked his pinky in mine. "Hey," he said gently. "It's not that I don't see all your good qualities, Claire. I do. It's just . . . I don't know how to reconcile what you told me with the woman I thought I was falling in love with."

Thought I was falling in love with.

The phrase was a snowball packed around ice. I tugged my finger from his and closed my eyes, feeling the cold cement through my leggings.

"I'm not trying to hurt you," he said.

"I know," I said again. It seemed all I could say: I know I know I know. And I did. I'd imagined this conversation a hundred times. Nothing was a surprise. But that didn't mean he'd always feel this way, did it? I looked at him. "You forgave Gabe," I said. "I know it's not the same—"

"I've thought about that too."

"It's just, you knew his cheating didn't make him into an awful person or change who he was." My voice cracked. "I thought . . . I hoped you would know that about me." I was pleading and I hated it, but I couldn't stop. "What happened was out of my control, Erik."

"But was it, Claire? Giving her up was a choice, wasn't it?"

"It didn't feel like it."

He nodded, elbows on his knees. Moonlight pooled in the leather of his jacket. "You mentioned . . . she had a physical therapist?"

"And speech. And vision." I inhaled sharply. "I won't candy-coat it. Once she got into school, there might have been issues with learning." My voice cracked. I felt as if I were made of glass, everything in me trying not to shatter.

"I guess that's what I can't . . . that this child's whole life . . ." He shook his head. "I look at my girls and—isn't it hard for you?"

What could I say? What could I possibly say? There would never, for the rest of my life, be a time when I didn't feel Lucy's absence, never be a time I didn't see girls her age and wonder where she was and if she was happy and if she was healthy. How could Erik ask me this? *What do you think?* I wanted to cry. *It's never* not *hard!*

But I also understood: It was a question most people would ask, if only because most people couldn't fathom—and why should they—how their lives could be upended in a heartbeat.

How every day, every single day, some parent somewhere was glancing away from her child for one second, and in that space a tragedy was unfurling: Suddenly that child is running toward a busy highway, or there's a truck or a train or a wave crashing down as she is playing in the ocean and that child's hand slips from yours—one second. Or she tumbles down a staircase or falls from a jungle gym—one second—or is stung by a bee and you don't have the epinephrine pen, *you* forgot. One second, one mistake, and the world careens to a halt. *You aren't exempt or special or better than me,* I wanted to tell Erik. *You're just lucky.* I had been too. The luckiest woman in the world. I had had everything.

I felt exhausted all over again. How could I keep doing this—sitting upright, nodding, explaining—when those two and a half minutes, with all the repercussions and loss, were all I would ever be to most people, to Kelly and Nick and now Erik? I wished I'd never gone on a second date, never set myself up for this. I had been okay before him; my life had been fine.

But I also told myself he'd had only four days to absorb what I'd struggled with for ten years. Not that I forgave myself—that was impossible. I would forever question why I hadn't been able to bond with Lucy after. But the day of the accident? Time and therapy and a thousand conversations with my mom had helped me understand that I hadn't been a careless person or a bad person or even a bad mother. I'd been very sick. And that wasn't an excuse. It just was.

Overhead the sky was such a deep black and the stars were so bright it seemed impossible they were millions of years away. A car turned down the street, and we both followed it with our eyes. "I don't want to end things," Erik said.

"I don't want you to." My voice hitched. The glossy magnolia leaves were like teacups full of moonlight.

Erik reached for my hand, and this time I gave it to him. He was so warm.

He sandwiched my fingers between his palms. "Driving over here, I was sure I was going to say I couldn't continue," he said. "But there's this other part of me that has woken up so happy these past few months and has felt so grateful to have met you, Claire, so grateful for the joy you've brought into my life, my kids' lives. And that part of me thinks maybe I can get to a better place with all this."

"I will tell you anything," I said.

"I can't make any promises."

"I know."

"I'm all over the map. I can't stand the thought of you hurting, and I'm pissed you didn't tell me sooner, though I get why you didn't." He looked at me, a tug-of-war in his eyes, sadness and worry, but love too, and compassion.

I touched his jaw with my fingers, aware that I was trembling.

"I'll need to take a few steps back," he said. "Maybe not do as much with the kids."

I dropped my hand from his face as if I'd been burned. "Are you worried about my being around them?"

"No! Jesus. That came out wrong."

"Because if you are—"

"I'm not, Claire. I wouldn't be here if I was. It's just, until we figure us out, I don't want them getting more attached." He scrubbed his hand over his face. "It was a crappy weekend. Spencer had a meltdown, and the twins wouldn't stop asking where you were. . . . Annabelle was full of opinions."

"I'm sorry." I touched his arm. "Did you tell her?"

"God, no. Annabelle's the last person I'd talk to about this."

That surprised me. She'd been so depressed after Spencer's

birth. If anyone could understand, I thought, it would be her. In fact, in some ways, without our ever talking about it, I felt like she already did.

But in that moment, nothing mattered except Erik. He had come back.

CHAPTER 15

Thanksgiving with Erik felt like a gift I'd hoped for but had been afraid to want, as if the wanting itself might jinx me. The day dawned luminescent beneath a glaze of sleet that would melt by midmorning. I woke to the jingle of car keys and the rustle of Erik's down jacket. "I'm running the turkey over to Annabelle's," he whispered. "I'll be right back."

In that moment, we felt normal again, and lying in his rumpled bed, coffee mug balanced on my breastbone as I waited for him to come home, I felt happy for the first time since I'd told him about Lucy.

"I didn't know it would be this hard," I had told my mother on the phone a few days earlier. "I guess I never imagined anything beyond telling him."

"Would it help to see a therapist?" my mother asked.

"I don't know. I'm not sure what a therapist can say that you haven't already said: Erik needs time. I get it. It's just hard. I'm not sure he wants to be close to me."

"He might not be capable, sweetie. At least not yet. But he hasn't walked away. That's what you need to hold on to."

I was trying, but more and more it seemed I was clinging to air.

It's not that Erik and I didn't talk. He had a ton of questions. About the state hospital, and what happened when I finally understood what I had done (I wanted to die), and about my decision after coming home to go to the second hospital, where I'd stay for another year. He wanted to know when I'd last seen Nick (the day I relinquished my rights; a dingy courthouse, and he was weeping, Andrea sobbing and thanking me and telling me she'd love Lucy). Did I want to see Lucy again? (Of course!) And did I think I would, maybe once she was eighteen? (No. She had a mother.) Did I think I'd ever go back to Rehoboth? That was the hardest question because it wasn't only about my past but my future. My parents would have loved for me to come home, but I wasn't sure what it would do to me, seeing all the places where I'd been who I was before the accident.

"And who was that?" he'd asked.

"Not this." My voice was bitter. I gestured around my spotless kitchen. "I wasn't so obsessive, so afraid." I flashed to the kitchen of the house with Nick: his surfboard leaning against the exposed brick wall by the refrigerator, newspapers and library books crowded on the table, a jumbo pack of diapers on the washing machine. How disorganized and unscripted our lives had been, how full. I glanced at my running shoes on the mat by the door. "Until the hospital, I was the most unathletic person you could imagine. I was probably overweight, and I didn't care." I tried to smile, but thinking about it made me ache. "I miss who I was," I said. "I never counted a calorie, never worried that I wasn't good enough." I pushed a pile of rice to the side of my plate. "I realize some of that's just youth, and I like a lot of who I am now—"

"So do I," he said.

I looked up. "Really?"

He reached for my hand. "I'm struggling to fit all these pieces together, but yeah, Claire. Really."

"Do you think you can? Put the pieces together?"

"I'm trying."

But trying was part of the problem. At least for me. All I did was try, desperate to make every second perfect, always appearing upbeat, some cheerful Stepford wife asking about his day, practically fetching his pipe and slippers, if he'd only had a pipe and slippers to fetch! I never complained when he left after dinner, which he'd never done before, never expressed disappointment, always *always* understanding, kissing him goodbye at my door, urging him to drive safely, my voice pitched too high, my smile stretched thin. And poor Erik, every time he so much as sighed, I was asking, "What's wrong? Talk to me," until finally he set down his fork one night, closed his eyes, and said, "Please stop. Please let me just be tired because I'm tired."

Of course I started to apologize, stopped myself, then heard myself apologize for apologizing. "I'm scared," I said. "I don't want to lose you."

"I'm right here," he said.

But he wasn't. Not really.

"How about a moratorium for the weekend?" I'd said to him the night before Thanksgiving. "No discussion about what happened." I was peeling potatoes; he was rinsing the turkey. Outside it was sleeting, a steady tapping at the windows.

"Ahh, a moratorium." He smiled, and it was his old Erik smile. "A moratorium would be good. Great actually." For a moment, the sadness in his eyes retreated. Or maybe I just wanted to believe this.

After Erik returned from Annabelle's, we lay in bed talking and drinking coffee like we used to, hopscotching from one topic to another. Had the kids been up yet at Annabelle's? Were they excited? He laughed, arms crossed behind his head. "Spencer has the day planned to the minute."

"Of course he does."

He laughed again, and I was struck by how unguarded his expression was and how much I'd missed these daily anecdotes about the kids: what new tidbit of information Spencer had discovered or something one of the twins had said. I'd skipped the last Saturday, Erik saying he needed some one-on-one time with them. "Of course!" I chirped, and told him to give them a big hug from me, but all day, I'd felt as if I couldn't pull in a full breath, a punctured feeling in my lungs. Now I realized how little Erik had talked about the kids lately, just parceling out a detail here and there. The phrase *throw a dog a bone* flashed to mind, and I felt my face get hot, even as I pushed the thought down, told myself no, this wasn't fair. Erik had been clear about wanting more distance between his kids and me until we figured things out, and I had agreed.

Still, the thought lingered, even when we skipped to the next subject. By then the sun was fully up, ice melting in silver rivulets down the windows. My turn for coffee refills, and I found his robe in the closet. "Seriously?" I teased. Burgundy velour, a black velvet collar. "Please tell me you didn't buy this for yourself."

"I absolutely bought it for myself," he said indignantly. "One of my first purchases as a bachelor."

"Oh, you poor man. This is something Hugh Hefner would wear."

"What are you talking about?" he sputtered. "That robe is pure Andrew Carnegie!"

I was halfway down the stairs when he yelled, "Warren Beatty!"

"Here you go, Hugh," I said, handing him his mug a minute later.

"Fine," he said mock-grudgingly. "The robe is yours. It looks better on you anyway."

The robe is yours. Happiness ballooned in me. I pictured mornings of me wearing that robe as we ate breakfast, opened Christmas presents with the kids.

"Okay." I settled back into the bed. "So, when did this start, the four of you doing Thanksgiving?"

They'd cooked for Annabelle's mom the last year she was alive, and the next year, Annabelle wanted to stay in her mom's house, so they repeated the whole thing. "I guess we decided it then, that we'd always do the holiday together."

"And you never missed?" We were leaning against the headboard, his fingers trawling lazily up and down my arm.

"Never. The year Annabelle and I separated, I sure as hell thought about it, but . . ." He shrugged. "I wanted to be with Spence, and honestly, I didn't have anywhere else to go. Maybe if my dad had been alive . . . but yeah, this will be fourteen years."

He asked about Thanksgiving for me growing up—what my best Thanksgiving was and where I had celebrated last year. I lied about my best Thanksgiving. I'd been seven months pregnant, and my life felt perfect. I loved being Nick's wife; I couldn't wait to be a mom. I lied because I didn't want to break the spell Erik and I were under. And I lied about where I'd been last year, as well. I told him I'd had dinner with the family of someone at work, which I *had* done, only it was the year before. Last year I'd stayed home, but I didn't want Erik pitying me or thinking about why I hadn't been with my family. Instead, I made him laugh by telling him about the Jell-O salad my coworker had served: cherry Jell-O with chopped-up celery and miniature marshmallows. I'd been baffled: Celery in Jell-O? We were supposed to eat this?

"Welcome to the Midwest," Erik said. "My mom put diced ham in Jell-O."

I snorted coffee up my nose. *"Why?"*

Even though we were laughing, I felt how hard I was working to keep things light and how much I couldn't talk about. The moratorium on Lucy, which I'd asked for, was actually a moratorium on my life.

By midmorning, we were in the kitchen, mashing potatoes, chopping pecans. I was wearing his robe over my sweats. Annabelle had called three times.

"It's like she's planning D-Day," I said. For weeks, she'd been debating recipes, writing up checklists, doling out jobs. "Does she do this every year?" I'd asked Eva. We'd been at Hattie Magee's. Erik and Annabelle were arguing about stuffing.

"Oyster dressing?" Erik said. "We live in the Midwest, Annabelle. We don't do bivalves here."

"'*We don't do bivalves here*'?" Eva hooted. "Did you really just say that?"

It became our punch line.

All night, apropos of nothing, someone would say *No bivalves! We live in the Midwest.* At one point, Scott told Annabelle, "Hey, babe, I love your bivalves," and Eva sprayed us with her appletini as she burst into laughter. That week, I ordered long-sleeved T-shirts with the phrase *We don't do bivalves* printed on the back. I chose an orangey-gold color, the color of Thursday, according to Spencer. Perfect for Thanksgiving.

I gave Erik his shirt that morning, and when he pulled it from the bag, he burst out laughing, put it on immediately, and swept me into a bear hug. "And it's the right color for Spence." I showed him the shirts for the kids. A flash of something in his eyes—grief about Spencer? About all the ways the world would be difficult for his boy? Or tenderness, maybe, that I'd thought to get the shirts in the right color? I couldn't name it, and didn't consider until later that it was sorrow about me.

We wore our shirts to Annabelle's, and she put hers on right over her sweater, all of us wearing them for dinner, and someone—Gabe, maybe?—raised his glass and declared the shirts an official part of Thanksgiving. We'd wear them every year.

I glanced at Erik, but although he was smiling, it was that awful half smile I'd seen too much of in the past few weeks, that smile like a placeholder for something else, that smile that was only there to soften whatever blow was coming.

CHAPTER 16

We drove to Ten Chimneys the next afternoon. "I can't believe we're doing this again tonight," I said. "I'm still full from yesterday." We were reconvening later at Annabelle's for leftovers. I'd suggested we have everyone at Erik's to give Annabelle a break, but he'd just rolled his eyes and said, "Good luck with that."

"Why? The kids love being at your house."

"Which she probably hates."

"You don't think that." He didn't, but I understood his frustration. He thought Annabelle was a great mom—everything in her life was secondary to the kids' needs and schedules, and she was a pit bull when it came to advocating for Spencer—but it was almost like she forgot sometimes that Erik was also their parent, that he was perfectly capable of taking care of his son when he had a cold or getting the twins ready for a birthday party. "I can put cute barrettes in their hair too," he would gripe. "I'm not a moron."

He glanced at me as we made the turn into Ten Chimneys. "It'd just be nice to have one damn holiday in my house, you know? And not even the holiday. Leftovers." He shrugged. "Maybe I'm being selfish. It probably is easier for Spencer this way."

"You're not selfish at all," I told him. "It's just the kids are her whole life."

We'd woken to another day that couldn't have been more beautiful: frost silvering the grass, the sky such a clear blue it looked shellacked. Erik had on sunglasses and a heavy red-and-gray flannel shirt over his turtleneck and jeans. Work boots; a down vest. He looked sexy and rugged. "Like the *Playgirl* version of Wisconsin," I laughed. "Studly lumberjack."

He lifted his sunglasses, shot me an amused glance, then lowered them again. "I like when you laugh. I've missed it."

I've missed it too, I wanted to tell him. *I've missed you. I miss us.*

"What? You've got a look on your face." Erik pulled into the lot and turned off the car.

"Do I?" I put my hands to my cheeks. "It's not a bad look, is it?" It couldn't have been. I was happy. I loved this man.

"Actually, it's rather fetching."

"Fetching." I laughed again. "I don't believe I've ever been called fetching." I stepped out into the biting cold.

Erik came around the front of the car and crooked his arm at the elbow. "Shall we?"

"We shall." I looped my arm through his. In the distance, a pair of hawks circled over the trees. "So, what does *fetching* even mean?" I asked. "I always thought of it as connected to milkmaids. Or shepherdesses."

"Excuse me?" Erik said. "Have you ever seen a milkmaid? Or a shepherdess? Do they have shepherdesses in Delaware? Do they even have sheep?"

"Of course they have sheep in Delaware!"

We walked for nearly two hours, holding hands, the sun warm despite the below-freezing temperature. The land dipped and curved, then lifted into rolling hills covered with leaves that we scuffled through like kids. Shadows stretched out from the trees surrounding the buildings: the Swedish-style main house, the barn and creamery, the guest cottage, where, on the eve of the Second World War, Robert Sherwood, who had been FDR's speechwriter, wrote the Pulitzer Prize–winning *There Shall Be No Night*.

By the time we headed back to his car, the shadows were taking on a purple tint, the trees black silhouettes. Our breath plumed in the metallic-scented air, our mouths so frozen, our words slurred. "We sound like we're drunk," Erik laughed. We were debriefing about Thanksgiving again: We loved Scott, and Spencer had been amazing, despite his routines being obliterated.

"The T-shirts helped," Erik said. "Everyone in the same color, and the *right* color." He squeezed my hand, though my fingers were so cold, I could barely feel them.

I glanced at him, though I couldn't see his eyes behind his mirrored sunglasses. I was holding my free hand over my mouth, trying to warm myself. "I was worried you thought I was being pushy." I had been. I knew this. I'd been trying too hard.

"Gabe's toast threw me a little, and I'm sorry, because the shirts really were sweet." He paused. "I just need more time."

More time for what? I wanted to ask, and took a deep breath, my lungs aching with the cold, sadness creeping in with the falling light. Overhead a line of geese flew by, black marks against the gold sky, and I turned to watch as they disappeared over the trees. Why wasn't this enough? I wondered. It had been such a perfect afternoon, a nearly perfect two days. But I did what we'd both become so adept at doing and changed the subject. "So, tell me about tonight." I swung his hand in mine as we resumed walking. "Is this part of the tradition?"

"Leftovers? Of course. Annabelle turns everything into a tradition."

"Is it because she didn't have a lot of traditions growing up?" She'd never known her dad, and her grandparents had died before she was born.

"I guess that's part of it. If you call something a tradition, it ensures that whatever it is stays the same." His voice softened. "She's had a ton of loss, so I get it, the need to hold on."

I'd done the opposite, held on to nothing, so there'd be nothing for me to ever lose again. Except that hadn't worked either. I glanced at Erik, the last of the light draining from the afternoon. *This should be our tradition,* I wanted to say, *walking at Ten Chimneys the day after Thanksgiving. And going to Kopp's for frozen custard and eating brats at the state fair.* I wanted my whole life with him to be a tradition. How could he not want to hold on to this?

But he is, another part of me whispered. *He's trying.*

We were quiet driving home, the heater on high, a Lucinda Williams CD playing. My feet felt like blocks of wood, they were so frozen. Many of the houses we passed—squat 1940s bungalows—already had Christmas lights up.

"What's Christmas like for you?" I laid my head against the seat back. "Do you put up lights? Do you hang stockings?" How could I not know this?

"Yikes! I haven't even thought about Christmas." Light from an oncoming car washed over his face, and I saw the tightness around his mouth.

"You realize it's less than a month away? Do you get a real tree?" Nick and I had had a Christmas tree in our living room *and* bedroom. "We should get one with the kids next weekend.

We'll bake cookies, watch a Christmas movie." The last remnant of light lingered at the horizon.

"That sounds nice."

"*Nice*? What kind of word is that?" I pretended to glare. "Don't tell me. You hate Christmas trees, don't you?" I wanted to make him smile, wanted to cajole us back on track, but my voice sounded as fake as I felt. I hated it, and hated myself for trying to joke around the fact that Erik clearly didn't want to talk about Christmas. And the only reason was that he wasn't sure we'd be together. I closed my eyes against the sting of that truth.

Lucinda was singing "Sweet Old World," and listening to her croon, *"See what you lost when you left this world,"* I felt broken suddenly. I thought about Lucy and the world I'd wanted with her and never had, and I thought of the world I'd left six years before and still missed with a sharpness I felt in my spine, and mostly, I was thinking of this sweet world I had found with Erik and his kids and his friends and how much I wanted to stay in it and what lengths I'd gone to to try. It was all there then, the tremendous hurt of the past month: All the times Erik left after dinner with that cheery "I think I'll head on home," as if it were no big deal, even though he used to always stay the night. And all the times I asked about the kids, and he gave me those terse answers; all the times I mentioned something—anything—about the future, and he brushed it aside: "You'll like my dad," I'd commented the week before, and instead of "I bet I will," or "I'm looking forward to meeting him," Erik had said, "He sounds like a nice man," as if we'd been talking about some clerk in a store. Every time, I'd push the hurt down. Even that day, driving home from Ten Chimneys, I wanted to make it okay, but I was emptied out. *I can't do this anymore,* I thought. *I don't want to.*

I stared out the window, the song lyrics hitting too close

to home: *"Didn't you think you were worth anything?"* The sky was black, empty fields in either direction. When the song ended, I leaned forward and turned off the CD. "You're not sure we're spending Christmas together, are you?"

Erik glanced at me. "I don't know that we're *not* spending it together."

"But you can't say we are."

He paused a beat too long. "How about just one holiday at a time?" And then, "Didn't we have a moratorium in here somewhere?"

We did. Of course. Tears burned my eyes, and I turned to stare outside so he wouldn't see.

"Hey." He touched my shoulder. "You okay?"

There was a cemetery to our left, and in another mile we'd pass Kopp's, boarded up for the winter. "I think I want to go home," I said. "To my house."

"Okay . . . Are you . . . What's going on? I thought we were having a good afternoon."

I leaned my forehead against the passenger window. Our relationship had become a fun house hall of mirrors where every time I thought I was getting close to Erik again, every time I thought we were finding our way back to one another, I bumped against the cold glass of my own reflection. I was tired: of the wrong turns, the surprises, the way light glinted off surfaces.

"You're jumping to conclusions," he said softly, hand on my knee.

"Am I?"

"You're assuming I've decided things that I haven't."

"I think you have, Erik. You just haven't said it out loud."

"That's not fair. Do you want me to pretend I know how I'll feel in a month? Because I don't. I wish I did." He retracted his hand. "Jesus. You really think I've decided *anything*? You dropped a huge fucking bomb, and I'm sorry if I can't absorb it as quickly as you need me to."

"I know you're trying." I shifted in my seat to face him. "And I'm grateful—"

"I'm not asking you to be grateful. I'm asking for time—"

"Time for what?" I cried. "What do you think's going to happen, Erik? The facts aren't going to change! And I wish everything else you knew about me was enough, but I don't think it is." That's what it came down to, didn't it? A simple equation: All that he knew about me, maybe even loved about me, wasn't enough. And the big disconnect was that I'd assumed it would be. I felt myself crumble. I made him laugh. I loved his children. I loved *him*.

But it wasn't enough.

He was staring straight ahead, the lines of his face set and hard, though when he finally spoke, there was only bewilderment. "So, what are you saying? We're done? That's it?"

"I think we have been." I paused. "This probably sounds ridiculous to you, but I deserve better." I'd said those words to myself, but I'd never spoken them out loud. I wasn't even sure I believed them, though I wanted to.

"I know you deserve better."

"I'm not sure you do."

"I would really *really* love for you to stop telling me what I think."

"I'm not judging you, Erik. Most people probably don't think I deserve a second chance." Kelly certainly didn't. Oh, sure, maybe I got credit for "doing the right thing" and giving Lucy up, but to fall in love again? To be happy? No way.

The last time I saw Kelly was the summer after I'd terminated my rights. Nick and Andrea had moved away. I'd heard Andrea was pregnant. I'd been on the boardwalk eating ice cream while my mom ducked into one of the shops. Eyes closed, head tilted up to the sun. And then Kelly was in front of me, screaming. *Are you freaking serious? How dare you?* The guy she was with was strong-arming her away as she kept shouting, *How dare you! How dare you!* Over and over. It shattered me. I wasn't allowed to enjoy a beautiful day? Treat myself to an indulgence? Why, *why,* would she begrudge me? Hadn't I lost more than any of them?

I thought of that now and wondered if some part of me still believed, as Kelly clearly had, that there *was* something shameful or wrong about a mother who'd done what I had enjoying *anything*—even a stupid ice cream cone. Was that why I was ending things with Erik? Because deep down, *I* didn't think I deserved happiness? Or was I ending it because he didn't? I wanted to backtrack, wanted to go back to coffee in bed and shepherdesses and talking about traditions. But before I could say anything, Erik said quietly, "Maybe you're right. Maybe I did decide." He let out a ragged breath and clicked on the turn signal, taking me to my house instead of his.

CHAPTER 17

Walking through my house and flicking on lights, I felt as if I were returning home after a long absence. *This is my life,* I thought, and maybe it wasn't as joyous as the life I'd hoped for with Erik, but it was mine. I felt oddly comforted by the most ordinary things: my orange teakettle, the bag of Epsom salts by the tub, the clip-on reading light on my night table. I'd bought the light so I wouldn't wake Erik when I woke early to read. Heaviness settled over me. I wouldn't need it anymore.

I picked up the phone to call my mom, then set it down. Her well-meant questions would undo me: Was I sure about this? No. What if Erik just needed more time?

By then he was already at Annabelle's. I wanted to be there, wanted to be folded into the warmth of their chaos and affection. Abruptly I sat at the dining room table. I'd lose Annabelle too, wouldn't I? And then I pictured Spencer clapping with delight yesterday when he realized we were all wearing the same T-shirt: "*Everyone's* wearing the color of Thursday?" he'd shouted. "*Everyone?*" That wild bright giggle that was his happy laugh. It took my breath away, the realization that I wouldn't see him or the girls again, wouldn't be spending Christmas with Erik. What would I do on Christmas? Where would I go?

On the table were leaves ironed between sheets of wax paper that the twins had decorated our Thanksgiving table with. Annabelle had given them to me to use in a collage. I'd dropped them off last night on our way to Erik's. The leaves looked frozen in ice, submerged beneath water. Idly, I began moving them around, ideas for a collage coalescing. This was often how I began, starting with an item and juxtaposing this and that, until a title popped into mind. It usually took weeks, but that night, the title rose up immediately: *Leavings.* I pictured doorways and goodbyes, things left behind.

I worked on it all night. My table spread with photos, magazine articles, scraps of fabric, and ribbon. *This is my life,* I kept thinking. The smell of gesso and the howl of wind outside, the creak of the floors as I walked around the table. *This is my life.* It felt so still; *I* felt so still. I promised myself I'd get back to my routines; maybe I'd meet my parents in Chicago for Christmas. Or I could go somewhere new, somewhere warm, near the ocean. The thought surprised me. I wasn't a traveler. I'd been on an airplane only once, a trip to Disney when I was ten, and until I moved here, I'd never been farther west than Pittsburgh.

But I liked the image of myself wheeling a suitcase through a vast terminal, boarding an airplane, checking into a hotel, sitting on a minuscule balcony with my coffee, watching the sunrise. St. Augustine, maybe? Tybee Island? I'd run on the beach, eat on patios surrounded by palm trees. I wasn't brave enough to go to another country—I didn't even have a passport—but I could do this, I thought, and felt a tiny beat of excitement.

Even as I imagined this, though, another part of me wondered what they were doing at Annabelle's, what Erik had told them. I glanced at the answering machine, hoping Annabelle or Eva would call. Of course they didn't, and I thought of how Erik would eventually meet someone else and she would become the new woman the girls idolized and Annabelle confided in. Someone athletic and smart: the curly-haired spin instructor at the Y or the drama teacher from Waukesha West who'd flirted with him at a donor dinner. My stomach clenched, and though I had chosen this, I realized how much I'd wanted him to talk me out of it.

I kept telling myself, *You deserve better,* but the words were hollow, and as the hours passed, all I thought about were the good moments: The two of us racing at the end of a run—first one to reach my driveway! His nodding to the farmers at Kopp's and saying, *That'll be us in twenty years.* My opening his silverware drawer and finding two long-handled iced tea spoons to eat my yogurt with. "You bought these for me?"

"I figure if you have everything you need here, you'll never go home."

On Saturday morning, I drove to the lake to run. The water was choppy, the wind gusting so hard it made my eyes water. My face felt windburned and raw, but I kept going, not wanting to return to my empty house. The minute I pulled into the drive, I saw the red canvas bag I'd kept at Erik's house on the porch, and I felt as if it were my heart he'd left there. I sat in my car and thought of how Spencer hated the color red. He said it was too "speedy," meaning, Annabelle thought, that the intensity made it feel as if the color were moving. He cried if we wore red. "Red is goodbye," he would sob. "Why are you wearing goodbye?"

The weekend passed. I grocery shopped, went to the Y, and scoured thrift stores, looking for things to use in the collage. *Leavings.* At home, I paced around the dining room table, adding things in, taking things out—blueprints of beach houses torn from an architectural magazine, a Post-it from Erik: *I miss you.* A xeroxed photo of the house I'd grown up in; a map of Czechoslovakia from 1990, the year Lucy was born; three years later, the country no longer existed. (How does an entire country disappear?) I added a pencil sketch of a little girl that I quickly erased, only faint lines remaining—leavings, traces. A strip of film negatives, the button from Erik's shirt, the manifest of the SS *Carl D. Bradley,* which broke in two during a storm on Lake Michigan in November 1958.

I finished the collage on Sunday night after tucking into the layers tiny things that were red: a feather, beads, Christmas wrapping paper, yarn from a child's sweater. The color of goodbye. I'd never completed a collage this quickly, and I wanted to tell Erik. I loved how he'd asked about my work: *Why did you include . . . ? What made you decide . . . ?* He'd note even the smallest changes. He'd been like that about my whole life. On the mornings we weren't together, he'd ask me on the phone how many miles I ran, what I ate for breakfast. Once he asked if my hair was in a ponytail, and when I laughed and said, "Seriously?" he said, "Yes, seriously. I want to picture you." That attention, that care with the minutiae of someone's days, what else was that but love? And what if I'd squandered it?

I finished three more collages that December. I stood at the dining room table as my coffee brewed, the windows dark and glazed with ice. After work, I hurried home, loving that moment when I flipped on the chandelier and instantly saw where I needed more color or text or layers. I thought about the collages as I ran during my lunch hour, miles disappearing without my noticing. Sky, road, lake, trees. I'd look up and be at my turnaround point. I thought of the collages as I drove to and from work. As I fell asleep.

Beneath my focus, the grief was right there, a swollen and rising river against which I was piling sandbags as fast as I could. What I had feared most had happened: I'd told Erik about Lucy and he'd walked away. And no matter what he had said about my deserving love, he clearly didn't think I deserved his. There wasn't a single hour when I didn't feel the blow of that truth.

I missed talking to him, missed seeing him. I missed the fact of him in my life. Driving by Annabelle's one Saturday night—it was stupid; of course, their cars were all there—I was devastated. "It's like I was never part of their lives," I told my mom. I knew I was being ridiculous: Erik was the father of Annabelle's children, he'd been friends with Gabe and Eva for twenty years, and I'd known him for, what? Four months? But I'd hoped Annabelle would at least reach out, tell me she was sorry it hadn't worked. We'd been friends.

Unless he'd told her about Lucy.

And why wouldn't he? He had no allegiance to me. It would have explained our breakup, how hard he'd tried. Would anyone blame him? *She harmed her own child, then gave her away. Who does that?*

As soon as my mom picked up the phone, my voice broke. "I'm pretty sure he told Annabelle." It was past midnight in Delaware.

"Hold on." She sounded groggy. "I'm walking to the kitchen."

"I'm sorry to call so late," I said.

"What happened? How do you know?"

"I just do. It's been three weeks and not a word." I closed my eyes against the glare of my lighted bedroom. "We were becoming friends, Mom."

"You're assuming, Claire. For all you know, Annabelle feels hurt that *you* haven't called. Maybe *she* feels betrayed. You're the one who just disappeared."

I laid my head on my knees, feeling stupid. This hadn't occurred to me. "Do you really think that?"

"I think it's as likely as anything else."

"I hate this," I said. "I just want to be normal." I tried to steady my voice. "I'm sorry I woke you." I felt like a teenager. I didn't want to be this way.

"You're hurt, sweetie," my mom said, "and that's very normal. For what it's worth, though, I don't think this is just about Annabelle."

"I liked having friends, Mom. She was fun, and kind, and . . . we talked about stuff that matters." I sighed. "What do you mean it's not just about—" But my mother was right about this too.

She waited, giving me that silence, then said, "Sometimes I think Kelly hurt you far more than Nick ever did."

"Sometimes?" I said bitterly. "Nick didn't . . . I've never blamed him." I shook my head vehemently, then added, "And I can't blame Kelly either."

"I'm not saying you should. But that doesn't mean you weren't terribly hurt by her, and getting close to Annabelle probably triggered that."

I squeezed shut my eyes, head still on my upraised knees. "I liked who I was with them, Mom, not just Erik, but all of them."

"Which is huge, Claire: That you know this now; that you want friends in your life again. And children. That's wonderful. It's more than wonderful."

The next afternoon I bought an artificial Christmas tree for my bedroom. I hadn't had one in ten years. Later, in bed, I kept glancing up from my novel to stare at the lights and the shimmer of ornaments, and for the first time in a decade I let myself remember that last Christmas with Nick. We couldn't stop talking about how the next year we'd have a child, and she was going to be the most loved child in the world!

For a while, she was.

Other memories crept in, things I hadn't thought of in years, hadn't let myself think of: The solid weight of her on my hip as I moved around the kitchen, getting coffee, pouring cereal. How when the sunlight streamed in the window, she'd reach out and try to grab the beam of light, then look at me with a baffled expression. "Who knew babies could furrow their brows?" I'd laughed to Nick. Or Nick balancing her on his palm high overhead and the way she'd kick her arms and legs like she was paddling a surfboard.

Talking about her to Erik had somehow given her back to me, given me back to myself. For ten years my heart had felt like an island on the other side of the world from where I lived, a remote and impossible-to-reach place. And then I told Erik the story of what had happened, and as awful as that had been, it had healed some small part of me. I wasn't ready to travel alone yet and I couldn't bear the idea of dating anyone else, but for the first time in years, I felt what it was like for my heart and my life to live in the same time zone, share the same weather.

CHAPTER 18

Winter in Wisconsin is always bleak, but it felt more so that year, the days truncated, light seeping from the sky by midday. It was too cold for snow, something I'd never heard of until I moved to the Midwest. *How can it be too cold to snow?* I wondered, and remembered thinking maybe it was similar to how you can be too sad to cry.

My parents met me in Chicago on Christmas Eve and stayed for three days. Neither mentioned Erik, though my dad told me, "I'm proud of you, Claire."

"For what?" I asked.

"For staying in the game. Not giving up."

A few times that January, Erik's SUV was still at the Y when I arrived. I went to Starbucks on those nights, hoping he'd have left when I returned. Once, I saw him walking to his car with the people from his spin class, calling something over his shoulder, laughing. There was something so easy and unencumbered in his movements. No scanning the parking lot for my car, as I always did for his. *He's moved on,* I thought, and felt as if I'd been cupping my hands around a match flame, and in that moment, a gust of wind had blown it out.

When it finally snowed, nearly fifteen inches, it was her birthday.

She was eleven.

I woke to a world that had been transformed into a silent moonscape with every tree and leaf, mailbox and car, outlined in white. Everything was closed. Schools, work, the Y. I stood at my living room window, feet cold on the wood floor, my coffee mug warm against my breastbone, thinking about snow days as a kid, all the hope and exuberance, how the days always felt like an unasked-for forgiveness. *I want that,* I thought, and understood, as I hadn't two months before, that it had never been up to Erik to forgive me. I needed to forgive myself, though I wasn't sure I could. The autumn with his kids had taught me that with time, I would have been a good mom to Lucy, and I wanted that knowledge to bring comfort—shouldn't it have?—but if anything, it did the opposite, filling me with so much grief and regret and anger that I felt some days it would topple me. Why hadn't I fought harder for my child? Why hadn't I fought harder for myself?

I watched the guy across the street shoveling his drive, the rasp of metal against cement echoing. His kids were building a snowman. I remembered how, when I was her age, eleven, I'd wanted to be a cashier. Kelly and I spent hours pretending to scan food items across a place mat on the kitchen table. My mom used to joke about it. "Other kids wanted to be astronauts, veterinarians, movie stars, and my girl wanted to be . . . drumroll, please . . . a cashier."

"Do you remember that?" I asked when I called her.

"How could I forget? I used to wonder: What am I doing wrong that this is all she aspires to? But it's one of your best qualities."

"My lack of ambition?"

"Your ability to find joy in the ordinary. It's why your collages are so good: You take the most mundane objects and find possibility in them." She was quiet. "What else do you remember from that age? Eleven's kind of magical, isn't it? Right on the cusp before everything changes." There wasn't anything specific I remembered, so we talked instead about my mom's tradition of baking cinnamon rolls from scratch on snow days. We'd eat them for dinner. "I always thought I'd be that kind of mom," I told her.

After we hung up, I dressed in so many layers I couldn't bend my arms, then clomped to the Kwik Mart a mile away to get yeast. The morning sparkled with snow and light, the hill near Madison crowded with kids on sleds, their shouts echoing. I spent the afternoon baking, and when Margaret came home just after dark, I brought her a tinfoil-wrapped square of the still-warm rolls.

"God, I could smell these from the car." She was in her scrubs. "I have whiskey for Irish coffees, but you've got to come in. No way are we sitting on the porch."

Inside, I wandered around her living room while she made coffee. Everywhere—on bookshelves, end tables, the fireplace mantel—were photographs of her and her pilot: the two of them in leather jackets on a motorcycle; at a pool flanked by palms; at a formal event, he in a tux, Margaret in a shimmery sleeveless gown. There were photos of him water-skiing one-handed, in his American Airlines uniform, squatting between two little boys with his curly dark hair and eyes.

I hadn't known he had children.

"They're seven and nine." Margaret handed me my coffee. "Teddy and Owen."

"You've met them?"

"Oh God, no." She laughed self-consciously. "He's got a wife too."

"Isn't that hard?"

Margaret kicked off her clogs and plunked down on the sofa. "It's impossible, but we've both tried to walk away more times than I can count." She'd set the plate of cinnamon rolls on the coffee table, and she reached for one as she spoke. "I guess I'd rather have twenty percent of him than nothing." She shrugged. "Did you know air contains only twenty-one percent oxygen, yet that's all we need to breathe?"

The line sounded rehearsed, and I wondered who she'd said it to before.

Later, I kept thinking about Margaret telling me, *I'd rather have twenty percent of him than nothing.* Shouldn't she have wanted more? Was this why she had so many photos? Proof that her pilot was real. Proof that he loved her. I thought of how, after I terminated my rights, it felt wrong to keep Lucy's photo, as if I'd relinquished my right to that too. But I wanted one, I realized, and promised myself I'd ask my mom to send some.

The following weekend, I showed the new collages to Colleen, who owned the gallery in Waukesha. We leaned the canvases against the wall, and I watched as she squatted in front of *Leavings*. "Will you at least think about doing a show?" She looked up at me. "These are beautiful." She'd asked before and I'd always said no, afraid of the publicity, afraid someone might find out about Lucy. This time, though, I said yes. It terrified me, but in a good way. I didn't want to *not* say Lucy's name. Our story was more complex than what had happened the afternoon of the accident or the awful months after. And the collages were part of that, weren't they? Not that I felt healed in making them, but repaired, maybe? Less broken?

Repair. Already I was imagining a new collage: photographs torn in half and taped together, letters with words crossed out and rewritten, bandages, a needle and thread . . .

That night, I sat in bed with a glass of wine and the *Dictionary of Word Origins. Repair* once meant "to make ready." Maybe this was what I'd been doing for the past six years. Trying to make my life ready again: for friends and laughter and love.

CHAPTER 19

R*epairs* opened the last Friday in March. And like the afternoon I married Nick, like the day Lucy was born, it was perfect.

"Why do I get to have all this?" I asked my mom as we drove to the gallery. She'd flown in that morning.

"Why do you get to have all what?"

"This whole night." My voice hitched. "Everything."

"Don't you dare question your right to this," she said. "You've worked hard for every bit of it, Claire."

Outside the gallery, a narrow storefront between a yoga studio and a bar called the Fox's Den, we could see Colleen setting out wineglasses. "Breathe," my mom reminded me as we picked our way carefully in our heels over the salt-crusted sidewalk.

The minute we walked inside, my mom stopped, hand over her mouth, eyes darting from one collage to the next.

"It's really something to see all the work in one room, isn't it?" Colleen asked.

My mom looked at me, eyes brimming. "Oh, my sweet girl. How did I not know you were this good?"

The night itself was a collage.

Mazzy Star on the stereo; a vase of pink roses from my dad; Margaret introducing me to her pilot, her neck flushed. People came from work and the Y; Colleen introduced me to buyers, and my mom bustled around in full-on hostess mode, chatting with strangers, then circling back with whispered reports: "The woman in turquoise teaches art at Carroll College; you should introduce yourself." Or: "I just met Ron—Don, maybe?—from the Y." Eyebrows bobbing suggestively. "He seems nice."

"Ron," I said. "And he's gay."

More people crowded into the little space. "I had no idea!" people kept saying. A woman from a Chicago gallery pressed her card into my hand. Colleen brushed past to put a Sold sticker on another collage. Margaret took my empty wineglass and handed me a full one. "Are you pinching yourself?" she asked.

"I'm black and blue," I laughed. It was surreal to see my work on the walls, to be surrounded by so many people congratulating me. I felt giddy and happy, and yet beneath the giddiness was a deep well of sadness: I'd started making the collages at the hospital. How could I reconcile my joy with *that*?

"I'm not sure you do," my mom had said when I'd mentioned it. "I'm not sure you can."

We'd been stretched out on either end of my couch after I picked her up from the airport. It was too early to check in to her hotel. "So where are you with tonight?" she asked, cradling her teacup in both hands. "Are you worried or excited or . . . you seem amazingly calm." She had her coat draped across her chest and she looked old in a way I hadn't noticed three months ago in Chicago. Deep lines at the corners of her mouth, more gray in her thick shoulder-length brown hair. She'd had to get up at three to make her flight.

"I'm weirdly calm," I said. "If anything . . . I almost don't know how to feel. I'm proud of the show, but I wouldn't even be living here if I hadn't gotten sick or if . . . if I'd been able to be her mother." I smiled sadly. "I wouldn't be making collages, I wouldn't be a runner, I wouldn't know Margaret or . . . I basically wouldn't exist as this person I am now." I kept staring down, but I felt my mom's unwavering eyes on mine. "I don't know what to do with that. I feel guilty."

"I wish you didn't." She reached forward and squeezed my ankle. Neither of us spoke for a moment, and then she said, "When we were first married, one of your dad's favorite pieces of music was this odd, very haunting piece by Mahler called *Songs on the Death of Children*."

I glanced sharply at her.

"It's based on poems written by a father after losing his children to scarlet fever. I'm not sure your dad knew this; he just loved the music. But I don't imagine the poems or the song cycle would have been written if those children hadn't died. That doesn't make the poetry or the music based on them perverse. Have you ever heard that piece?"

"No, and I don't want to."

She nodded. "Your dad doesn't listen to it anymore either. But a lot of art comes out of tragedy, Claire."

"I've thought about her so much lately," I said.

"Telling Erik about her probably opened doors you didn't realize were shut. And there was a lot of good behind those doors."

Erik didn't come to the show—and I hadn't expected him to—but Annabelle and Eva did. I turned, and suddenly

Annabelle was wrapping me in a hug, her wild curly hair in my face. "Holy moly, Claire," she whispered. "When you mentioned collages, I pictured, I don't know, scrapbook shit."

I smiled. I'd forgotten how blunt she was. "It is so good to see you!" I glanced at Eva over her shoulder. "You too." I reached for her hand.

She squeezed it. "Annabelle's right. I'm embarrassed we never talked about your work."

I asked about the kids then, and Gabe and Scott. And then Colleen was introducing me to a buyer and Margaret was leaving, and I didn't get back to them until the end of the night. "I'm glad we came," Annabelle said.

"Me too." I hugged her.

"And I know you broke up with him and you've got your reasons, but he's miserable without you, Claire."

CHAPTER 20

The secret to performances, Charlie Chaplin said, is "entrances and exits." I think of this when remembering that first year with Erik. *Entrances and exits.* They are the secret to our lives, as well. How we leave rooms, jobs, people's hearts.

And how we return.

In mid-April, in the grocery store after work, I heard my name, and suddenly Spencer was loping toward me. "Claire's here!" he shouted. And then again, "Claire's here!" He looked like he'd grown two inches; he'd lost a tooth.

"Spencer!" I held out both hands for him to fist-bump just as Erik came around the corner with the girls standing in the cart. "Claire! Claire!" Erik's eyes met mine, and there was such gladness in his expression, it took my breath away, and the five months of trying to get over him came crashing down like a pyramid of carefully stacked cans, days tumbling off one another, rolling in all directions.

I fussed over the girls. Hazel was wearing her shiny Easter shoes and she could count to ten now; Phoebe wanted to know if I knew how to somersault and then informed me, "My daddy misses you."

Erik blushed and said, "Thanks, Phoebs," then asked about my running—was I loving the warmer weather?

I mentioned the recent article about Ten Chimneys I'd seen in the *Journal Sentinel*. I couldn't breathe right. His eyes were bluer than I remembered. After a pause, I said, "So, you have them on a school night?"

Erik rolled his eyes. "Scott's parents are in town."

"Oh no."

"Oh yes. Eva's over there now helping her figure out what to wear to dinner."

I thought of the night I'd done that—Annabelle's first date with Scott, how scared she'd been—and I wished so much I were still a part of their lives. Something pained in Erik's expression told me he was remembering too. "Can I call you later?" he asked hesitantly.

He phoned on his way home from Annabelle's. I could hear the rush of air from his open window. "It knocked me out, seeing you tonight," he said.

I lay back against the pillows, my heart pounding so slowly, I thought it would burst. "It surprised me too. I left all my groceries and just walked out."

"You did?" He laughed, and I remembered how much I loved his laugh. "Look, can we do dinner tomorrow? Or coffee or . . . what's your schedule?"

"Let's do coffee." I would have loved dinner, but I was afraid to let it feel too much like a date.

I woke before the alarm to the sound of rain and was instantly alert. *It knocked me out, seeing you tonight.* Walking back to my bedroom, holding my coffee mug in both hands, I was already talking with him in my head, asking about his holidays, telling him about my show, confessing that I'd hoped he'd come. In the bathroom mirror, it surprised me, how happy I looked, eyes shining, my skin flushed. Later, when I opened the refrigerator to grab a yogurt, which I didn't have since I'd left the store without my groceries, I thought of how I'd tell him this too: *I was famished, and it was all your fault!*

Even in my imagination, I was lighter with Erik, more playful. *I'm buoyant with you,* I told him in my head, and saw how he'd cock his eyebrow. *Buoyant, huh?*

It was still raining at lunchtime, the sky dark, streetlights on. I went to the Y to run, the place loud with the churning of machines, shoes squeaking on the wet floor. *It knocked me out, seeing you tonight.*

I'd just finished three miles and was punching up my speed when I glanced at my reflection in the mirror in front of the treadmill. I was smiling even as I ran—and it startled me. What was I doing? I slowed the treadmill to a jog, then a fast walk. A five-minute *chance* conversation, and I was going to fall all over myself for him? *Why?* What had changed?

In my car, I stared at the rain sluicing down the windshield and waited for my mom to pick up.

"Claire?" She sounded breathless. "Is everything all right?" I never called her midday.

"Everything's fine, Mom. I just . . . I ran into Erik last night, and we're supposed to meet for coffee, and I'm not sure I should." I forced a laugh. "So, of course I come running to you." I wondered if she was as tired of these calls as I was.

"Well, I'm glad you come running to me, if that's what it

is. And of course you're not sure. You're protecting yourself. As you should."

"It's just . . . last November, he couldn't see past what had happened. And it's not like he didn't try. So what could possibly have changed?"

"I don't know, but it sounds like something did."

"But *how*? He just woke up one day and decided: *Oh, okay, I'll now accept Claire's not a psycho*?"

My mother didn't say anything, though I could feel her annoyance. I listened to the rain pounding on the roof. "Why are you doing this?" she asked.

"Doing what, Mom? Being truthful? Being realistic?"

"Is that what this is?" She paused. "There's a difference between protecting yourself and being unforgiving, Claire. Doesn't Erik deserve a chance to explain? And not just for his sake, but for yours?"

I stared at the curtain of water running down the windshield. "I don't want to be judged, Mom, especially by someone I—" I didn't want to say *love*.

"I don't want you to be judged either, sweetie. But I'd hate for you to not at least hear what Erik has to say."

A bus drove past, headlights sweeping over my windows. "Is it wrong to want to talk about her?"

"Of course not."

"It's the one thing I miss from the hospital. The only thing. I could talk about her there. And I know it's not healthy and she's not mine and she has a mother who loves her, but—"

"She has two mothers who love her."

"Don't, Mom."

"You carried that child in your body, Claire. And against even my wishes, when it came time to do what was right for her, you put her interests ahead of your own. If that's not a mother, I don't know what is."

"Maybe," I said. "Maybe that's part of it."

"Part of what?"

"I don't want to pretend anymore that she never existed. I don't know if I can." I hadn't realized how strongly I felt until the words came out, sounding wobbly as I struggled not to cry. I remembered how not speaking about Lucy my last weekend with Erik—our "moratorium," a word I'd come to hate—had meant not speaking about every single thing that mattered in my life: my parents and Rehoboth, my running, my collages. Lucy wasn't just a *part* of everything, she was the center of everything, how I saw the world, how I moved through the world. How could I not have known this?

"You think that's what Erik will want? To pretend she doesn't exist?"

"Wouldn't you?"

She didn't answer right away. When she spoke, she sounded melancholic in a way I hadn't heard before. "I'm not sure you know this, but your dad and I don't talk about her. He can't."

I probably did know this, although it hadn't ever been spoken. It hurt to hear. My dad had never wavered in his support of me. But he also never mentioned her name.

"I'm not complaining," my mother said. "And I'm not telling you this to make you feel badly. Your dad loves you and I know he loves me, and his silence isn't a reflection of that love. And because I love your father, I accept his limitations, Claire." She sighed. "I hope you can talk about Lucy with Erik, but if you can't, does it have to be a deal-breaker?"

"I don't know."

"Meet him for coffee, sweetie. You don't need to decide this right now."

CHAPTER 21

I stood in the doorway, folding up my umbrella. He was sitting across the café, staring outside at the rain strafing the parking lot, a manila folder on the table with his phone, his leg jiggling nervously. Everything about him felt familiar. And then he glanced up and saw me, emotions flipping like cards across his eyes: relief; joy.

He stood as I approached the table. I suddenly felt clumsy and tongue-tied, and when I pulled out a chair, I managed to bump the table hard enough that his coffee sloshed over the rim. He steadied both his cup and the one I assumed was for me. "I like that," he said.

"You like my almost dumping coffee on you?"

"I like that I can still make you flustered."

"Who, me?" I was. Completely. But when our eyes locked, I forced myself to look away. Even after I'd told him about Lucy, we had bantered and teased, made each other laugh, and I had clung to that, believing it meant we'd be okay. I didn't want to be fooled again. "Is this mine?" I nodded at the second coffee.

"Nonfat latte, no foam."

"You remembered."

"It hasn't been *that* long."

"A lot's happened, Erik." I held his stare.

"I know." He hesitated, then said, "The kids were excited to see you last night."

"I loved seeing them too." I wanted to say more, comment on how much Spencer had grown and how the twins didn't look like toddlers anymore, but I couldn't. It had hurt to see the kids. The girls especially. They were now the age Lucy had been when I last saw her. I held my cardboard coffee cup in both hands, needing the warmth, though the room was hot. I wondered if Erik understood what a big deal it had been for me to let myself love his children. I doubted it. I'm not sure I had fully allowed myself to know it either.

Laughter erupted from a table of teenagers, textbooks open in front of them, one girl lying on her arm, highlighting pages with a yellow marker. "Did Annabelle tell you she came to my show?"

"Are you kidding? I know what you wore and what kind of wine they served." He smiled sadly. "I went the next day."

"You did?"

"I did. I was so proud of you."

"I was so proud of me too." I held his eyes. "I wished you'd come on opening night."

"Me too."

He lifted his coffee cup and turned it, lifted it again and turned it. He wasn't looking at me, and it made my heart seize. What was I doing here?

Across the café was a gas fireplace, and in an armchair in front of it, a skinny woman in jeans sat with her laptop on her knees, an infant asleep in the stroller parked beside her. I'd been noticing these young mothers with their babies, watching them, studying them almost, as if trying to see what I might have looked like when I'd been a young mother. Had I kissed the top of my girl's head as I buckled her into her car seat? Had I stood in a checkout line, swaying side to side with her against my shoulder? I'd watched Annabelle similarly, I realized now, studying her easy way with her children, how she touched them constantly, hand alighting on a shoulder or back in passing, fingers straightening a collar, combing the girls' hair from their eyes. It was an ease I'd never found my way back to with Lucy, and I wished so much that I'd just touched her more in those months when I was trying to be her mom again.

"Are you thinking about Lucy?" Erik nodded toward the woman with the stroller.

I looked at him, startled. Although we'd talked around and around what had happened, he'd rarely spoken her name, as if it were taboo, which, of course, it had been. Now it sat between us like a small wrapped box. "I've been thinking of her a lot the past few months." My voice sounded reedy.

"Me too. That's what I wanted to tell you, or one of the things. Here—" He nudged the manila folder toward me. "It's the stuff I should have read last November."

"What stuff?" I sat back. I still had the articles I'd wanted him to read. I didn't know what this was. I didn't want it.

"It's okay. Just look." He opened the file so I could see the paper on top: "Postpartum Psychosis: Causes, Symptoms, and Treatment." Parts of it were underlined. Tentatively, I lifted the page, my hand shaking. Another article: "The Difference Between Postpartum Depression and Postpartum Psychosis." And then the next: "It Can Happen to Anyone." There had to be fifteen articles, underlined, highlighted.

I lifted my eyes to his. "You read all this?" I couldn't move. "Why?"

"*Why?* It's not obvious? I love you." He drew in a breath, then let it out. "I want you back, Claire. I want us back."

I pushed my tongue against my teeth to keep my jaw from trembling. *Love.* We'd danced around that word so many times. *I love being with you, I love talking to you.* But never *I love you.* "I know you wanted to love me," I said carefully. My mouth felt dry. "It's just, five months ago, love wasn't enough." I glanced again at the open file folder, underlined phrases lifting themselves up: *In the United States, research into postpartum psychosis virtually stopped around 1926. . . . Hippocrates first described postpartum depression in the fifth century BC. . . .* "I'm grateful you read all this. . . ."

"But?"

"But you didn't like me, Erik."

"No—"

"Yes. You felt disdain."

"No," he said again.

"I'm not saying you wanted to feel that way; you just did. And I'm not . . . Can these articles really change that?"

"They already have." He looked at me, his beautiful blue eyes dark with regret.

I held his gaze. Rain drummed against the windows. "What if we hadn't run into each other last night?"

He frowned. "I'm not following you."

"Would we be here?"

"Ahhh. Why didn't I phone a week ago? Is that what you're asking?"

I nodded.

"I wanted to be sure, and I was, the second I saw you. I don't just want to date you and *see what happens.*" He put air quotes around the phrase. "I don't just want to sleep with you. I want us to be a family, Claire."

I was shaking. My entire body.

He laid his hand atop mine. "You're like ice," he said. And then, "Say something."

"What if you change your mind again?"

He smiled. "Ain't gonna happen."

"Don't. I can't joke about this, Erik."

"I promise you, I am not joking. I want a life with you, Claire. I want you in my life; I want you in my kids' lives. And I'm not saying we have to decide anything right now or next month or even next year." He exhaled a long breath. "But I'm in this for the long haul."

I wasn't home more than ten minutes when he phoned. "I had all these things I wanted to tell you," he said, and we talked for another two hours. He told me the kids had started staying with him on weekends.

"Annabelle's relinquishing control?" I asked.

"Annabelle's in love and wants weekends with her boyfriend." He laughed.

He told me he'd replaced the girls' cribs with "big-girl beds," and it just about killed him. "They'll be dating soon. My hair will be white." He talked about Ten Chimneys, and he sounded happy, and I thought how just that morning I'd imagined exactly this, all the things we would tell each other.

He asked why I'd changed my mind about having a show, and I explained that telling him about Lucy had loosened something in me. I told him about starting *Leavings* the night we broke up, how I wanted to call it *Red Is the Color of Goodbye,* but I hadn't felt right using Spencer's words.

He said he'd looked for my car every time he left the Y.

"You're such a liar," I teased, and told him about the night

I'd seen him walking out with the people from spin class and how much it hurt to realize he *wasn't* looking for me.

"Oh, how wrong you are," he protested. "I know *exactly* what night you're talking about. Mid-January. You were waiting for someone to pull out of a space to the far right of the entrance. Trust me, I saw you."

"You never even looked up!"

"I didn't dare," he said. And then, "My alarm's still set for four thirty."

"It is not." I laughed. "*Why?*"

"I guess I liked thinking of you getting up and starting the day."

"You could have thought that at six."

"I'm not saying it makes sense."

I told him about meeting Margaret's pilot, about seeing "our farmers" at the craft store.

"Kopp's opens first weekend in May," Erik said. "What do you think?"

"Are you asking me on a date?"

"I'm asking for a lot more than that, but sure, we can start there."

It was nearly ten when we finally hung up. "I've got to sleep," I told him.

"Why aren't you here?"

"You think we'd be getting more sleep if I was?"

He phoned in the morning to say good morning. And on his way home after a fundraising dinner the next night. We spoke about work and the kids; Spencer was obsessed with glaciers. The twins were starting ballet. I told him about making cinnamon rolls on Lucy's birthday, about the photo I had of her in my bedroom.

"Describe it to me. How old is she?"

"She's six months." I lifted the frame from my nightstand

and held it in front of me. She was wearing a fluffy angora beret, smiling that wide toothless smile, her chin shiny with drool. You couldn't tell from the photo, but she'd been in her bouncy walker and had just learned to move around, careening into walls and crashing into furniture and emitting this little shriek of joy that sounded like a teakettle whistle.

CHAPTER 22

Well, look who's here," Annabelle said when I arrived with Erik to pick up the kids on Saturday morning. "It's about damn time."

Already the girls were tugging on my hands and asking if I was coming to ballet with them, and Spencer was bouncing on the balls of his feet as he recited facts about glaciers: "Some glaciers can travel three feet a day, and one in Greenland traveled ninety-eight feet! Ninety-eight feet is longer than our driveway! And there are glaciers in forty-seven countries and glaciers over one hundred miles long!"

Scott was standing in the kitchen doorway, smiling sleepily over the edge of his coffee cup, barefoot in low-slung jeans and a T-shirt that said "Les Paul Guitars." "Welcome back, stranger," he said. I felt like Dorothy in *The Wizard of Oz,* clicking her heels together and repeating "There's no place like home," then waking to find around her all the people she loved.

We met everyone at Hattie's the following Friday, and the next day, the kids spent the night. But mostly in those weeks, Erik and I stayed to ourselves, talking in a way we never had before, almost as if we were stitching ourselves back together with words. We talked about my choice to go back to a better, private hospital just after the one-year anniversary of the accident. I was so terrified to be with Lucy, I told him. What if I did something wrong, what if I scared her, hurt her, made another mistake? I told him about the visits, how I barely recognized her—she was almost two by then, *two!* And she was wary in a way no two-year-old ever should be, never taking her eyes off Nick or his mom, whimpering when I tried to hold her. I told Erik about arriving early to Nick's mother's house one afternoon and watching from across the street as Andrea took Lucy from her car seat. Lucy was pulling on Andrea's ponytail, and Andrea was pretending to gobble Lucy's hand and Lucy was laughing—*laughing!*—with such joy. I realized then, I told Erik, that I would have to let her go. I don't think I'd ever felt such anguish, not even when I learned what I'd done the day of the accident. This was so much worse, because although I didn't feel I had an option, I knew it was a decision I'd have to live with for the rest of my life, and I didn't think I could. Erik told me how unprepared he'd been to witness Spencer's birth, to see Annabelle in such obliterating pain, "and all I could do was offer her ice chips?" We talked about his grief over Spencer's difficulties, the numerous doctors and inconclusive tests and nebulous diagnoses that hadn't really helped, his anger at his mom, how he felt as if his father's life had been erased. I told him how much it hurt that my dad couldn't talk to my mom about Lucy.

"I don't want that to happen to us," I told him. We were in bed, only the hall light on. He held his hand up to mine, aligning our palms. "I want us to tell each other everything. No matter what. There will be times when you hate my past and maybe me."

"No—"

"My own father can't deal with it, Erik. But it's not just that. I want you to tell me when you're depressed about Spencer or you feel guilty because you wish he were different, and

I want to be able to tell you that . . . I don't know, that it scares me to be happy."

"It does?"

"Sometimes."

"Why?"

"Because I caused so much damage—mostly to Lucy, but to Nick and Kelly and their parents, and God, *my* parents. My dad lost his family's house because of me! I feel like I don't have the right to be happy."

"But you are, despite all that?" He tucked a strand of hair behind my ear.

"I am."

May. June. July. He gave me the key to his house again, made space in his closet for my clothes. My shampoo in his shower. My books by the bed.

Those months were some of my happiest. Erik and I meeting at the Y after work, cooking dinner, stretching out on his couch and watching *The West Wing* and *ER*. We attended fundraising events, had Margaret over for drinks, saw Eva play Elmire in *Tartuffe*. I forgot she was Eva during the play; I was laughing and rooting for the haughty, décolletage-revealing wife she'd become.

On Saturday mornings, while Erik took Spencer to the library—he loved that he had his own library card and would proudly showcase the books he checked out each week—I'd take the girls to ballet. Annabelle would greet me at her front door and hand over the girls' My Little Pony gym bags and whisper over their heads, "Thank you, thank you, thank you." I loved that I could give her this time to herself. I'd sit with the other moms on metal folding chairs in the hallway, watching the girls through a large window, my lap heaped with their sweaters and shoes. Sometimes Annabelle would join me for the last half of the lesson, bringing coffee in Styrofoam cups, the two of us half covering our eyes in mock horror at the spectacle of twelve toddlers, some with diapers bunched up under their leotards, trying to plié. Later, I'd watch the Weather Channel with Spencer or sit with him as he read his library books about glaciers or the constellations or the moon. He loved science, loved facts, loved sharing those facts with the rest of us.

Something healed in me that spring.

And then in June, my mom phoned midmorning when I was at work. She was crying, and I thought something had happened to my dad until she said, "Lucy," and I felt myself go still.

"What about Lucy?" I whispered.

"I saw her. With Nick." She started crying again. "I was in the car, and they were crossing the street right in front of me. She was talking and gesturing, and he was grinning. She was so animated, Claire. She's beautiful."

"You're sure it was her? Not her sister?"

"She has your horrible posture—" My mom half laughed, then started weeping again. "She walks like you did. And she's got your cheekbones."

"Did Nick see you? Did she?" I was clutching the receiver so hard my fingers cramped.

"I wasn't sure, but just as they got to the sidewalk, he looked back and lifted his hand in a wave. His eyes were so kind, Claire." She took a shaky breath. "All that hardness, that anger—it's gone. He was like the old Nicky." Her voice hitched, and she was weeping again. "She's okay. She's really okay. He wouldn't have been like that if she wasn't."

I had a sense of déjà vu that summer, the past seeping into the present, or maybe the present lifting up to reveal the past. *Pentimento.* The discovery of an original painted element the artist had covered over. Erik handing me the crust from his pizza, my favorite part, and for a flash, it was Nick setting a crust on my plate. Or Erik and me pausing in the doorway of the girls' room, listening to their rhythmic breathing, a ladybug night-light on the wall by the window, and for a second, it was Lucy's room, her crib catty-corner by the built-in bookshelves, a butterfly mobile bobbing in the draft of the heating vent. I could feel the weight of Nick's arm around my shoulder. *Can you believe she's ours?* As I pulled tiny pink or yellow T-shirts from the dryer, memories I hadn't thought of in years bloomed open. There was an unexpected joy in this, like finding things I thought I'd lost: a favorite coffee cup on a bookshelf, an earring tangled in the cuff of a sweater not worn in months. That sense of relief, of things returned.

Of me, returning.

CHAPTER 23

In July, we decided I would move in with Erik when my lease was up, and little by little, I moved bits and pieces of my home into his. Clothes, art supplies, a few boxes of kitchen things and bed linens, a beveled glass water pitcher I used for flowers, a beautiful cigar box of my dad's where I kept the photos of Lucy. My orange teapot. The dining room table with its huge claw-foot legs, where I worked on my collages. Margaret wanted my couch; everything else was getting hauled to Goodwill. It surprised me how pared down my life had been before Erik. "You never realized?" he asked. "I noticed the first time I saw your apartment. It's like you were afraid to make a mark on anything."

"I probably was." The less I had, the less there was to lose. Sometimes I wondered if this was my real attraction to collage: a way to save things no one else wanted.

We went to Kopp's on the one-year anniversary of our first time there. Our farmers had just left, and I was staring down the road, thinking of how much my life had changed, of how miraculous it all felt, when Erik set the small velvet box on the picnic table. "What—" I started to say, then stopped, eyes darting to his face.

He nodded, then said, "I want to marry you, Claire."

Behind him the sun disappeared below the tree line, the sky different shades of blue.

"Are you . . ." I'm not sure what I was asking. I was suddenly nervous. "How long have you been planning this?"

"Since the first night we came here."

"You'd just met me."

"I already loved you." He grinned. "I just didn't know it yet."

Behind us a child wailed and a woman said, "You're not going to get any custard." A breeze moved through the pines. He snapped open the lid, and the colored Christmas lights reflected in the small diamond. I felt my eyes fill, and from the next table a man called, "Hey! Congratulations!" and someone else said, "Yeah, he just gave her a ring," and then Erik was sliding it onto my finger, and tears were spilling down my face, and around us a handful of strangers was clapping.

Pentimento. I'd been here before. We both had. Nick holding out a ring on the beach during the Fourth of July fireworks. The boom of the ocean and the sky exploding with light and color. I was twenty-two. I felt my real life was just beginning.

And Erik: He'd proposed to Annabelle the year after her mom died. They'd believed their marriage would heal her, begin to soften the grief that had defined her life for so long.

Driving home, we were quiet. Neither of us believed in fairy tales or happily ever after; neither of us believed getting married would solve our problems. There was sadness in this, but hope too, immense hope, because we *did* know better, and maybe, *maybe,* we thought, that knowledge could protect us.

I phoned my mom the next morning. I was on Erik's back deck in my running stuff, the sky still dark. "Perfect timing," my mother said. "I just got my coffee." I heard her take a sip. "It's early. Is everything okay?"

"Everything's great. Erik proposed."

She didn't answer, and for a moment I thought she hadn't heard me. "Mom?" I asked, and then realized she was crying.

"Oh, Claire," she said. "I feel like the world is finally right. First our girl and now this."

Our girl. My eyes burned. "Is it weird to think they're somehow connected?" I couldn't help thinking that it was because Lucy was okay that I was allowed to be happy again.

"It's not weird at all," my mom said. "It seems connected to me too."

PART III

Grab it while you can—grab every scrap of happiness while you can.

—Noël Coward, *Shadow Play*

CHAPTER 24

Intermission begins: The audience leaves their seats to buy drinks, chat with acquaintances in the lobby, compare notes. Fifteen minutes later, the house lights blink, and the curtain rises. Years have passed.

Two years after Erik and I were married, Ten Chimneys opened to the public. May 26, 2003. The governor of Wisconsin declared it to be "Ten Chimneys Day." It would have been the Lunts' eighty-first wedding anniversary.

In the years that followed, the estate was featured in the *Chicago Tribune* and *The New York Times,* showcased on CBS's *Sunday Morning* and National Public Radio's *All Things Considered.* Tour buses from Chicago and Minneapolis regularly appeared on our narrow farm roads, their dark shapes floating past acres of corn or soybean. Stretch limousines with tinted windows waited in the gravel lot behind the Genesee Depot diner, and it wasn't unusual to see an Emmy or Tony Award–winning actor in one of the booths: Hal Holbrook, David Hyde Pierce, Bernadette Peters, the guy who played George on *Seinfeld.*

I thought of Kelly often in those years when Ten Chimneys

was in the spotlight. She would have loved the Lunts' home. Sometimes I even wondered if she was part of why *I* loved it, maybe part of why I'd ended up with Erik. Because of all the people I could have married, what were the chances it would be a man so intricately involved in the world *she* had loved? I thought of our first night at Kopp's, when Erik mentioned Alfred Lunt and Lynn Fontanne. I'd recognized those names, and a little piece of my past, a past I had never stopped grieving, had come back to me.

By then, Kelly had become a celebrity in her own right, starring in a hugely popular TV drama about a group of widows whose firefighter husbands died on 9/11. It seemed fitting that this was how she reappeared in my life, because on 9/11, when everyone kept asking, "Do you know anyone in New York?" I kept saying, "My best friend growing up."

I realized that day that although Kelly and I would probably never reconcile, I needed to know she was okay, that she was out there in the world, acting, falling in love, spoiling Lucy. In the years after 9/11, I would watch her show religiously, and on the night she won her first Emmy, I phoned my mom, who was crying and laughing. "Can you believe it?" she wept. "That she beat Glenn Close? *Our* Kelly!"

Our.

After the second Emmy, the name Kelly Jarrell was familiar. The press called her "KJ." She hosted *Saturday Night Live* and was profiled in *People* magazine, interviewed on the *Today* show: How, reporters kept asking, was she able to portray grief so well?

I ran my first, and last, marathon a few months after Ten Chimneys opened. Erik and the kids, Eva and Gabe, and Annabelle and Scott spread out along the route, cheering me on. That part was fun, if you can call running a marathon fun, but after mile twenty, I tumbled into a dark place in my head. I was weeping when I finished. I've heard this isn't unusual, the body physically and emotionally depleted, but for me it triggered something deeper: the pain and loneliness of those weeks in the hospital when I finally understood what I'd done. For days after the race, I couldn't stop crying. It scared me and Erik both, but I was also angry at myself, because running had always soothed something jagged in me, and I felt like I'd ruined it by pushing too hard, not being satisfied. Why wasn't six or eight or ten miles enough? Why did I need twenty-six? I was myself again after a week, but the experience felt like a cautionary tale I promised to heed. *I have so much,* I told myself. *Don't ask for more.*

The next year, Scott and Annabelle got married. Mine and Erik's wedding had been small—we had the ceremony at Ten Chimneys—but Scott had never been married, so they did it all: tuxedo, gown and veil, bridesmaids (Eva and me), groomsmen (Scott's bandmates). The twins were flower girls, and Spencer walked his mom down the aisle, all of us laughing when he stopped midway to turn and wave as if he were in a parade.

The day was a blur of music, dancing, and laughter, Annabelle and Scott smashing cake into each other's faces, the guests hooting and cheering. I can still picture Annabelle dancing with Spencer to "Twist and Shout," her wedding dress a froth of cream tulle shimmering around her like a cloud, sweat beading on her neck, and Spencer swinging his arms and laughing that exuberant, infectious laugh of his.

Happiness like an eclipse. So bright it hurt to look at.

It spilled into our homes and into our lives, which were

busy and chaotic and ordinary and amazing in the way most lives usually are. Erik became executive director of Ten Chimneys, Annabelle joined the board, and Eva volunteered as a docent, all of us caught in the Ten Chimneys orbit. We attended dinners and fundraising events, met actors and theater historians, and invoked the names of the Lunts so often, they felt like part of our circle.

A gallery in Chicago now represented my work, selling the collages for sums that still surprised me. This had allowed me to leave the graphic design firm, and shortly after that, Erik and I decided we wanted the kids with us half-time. The custody arrangement had always been fifty-fifty, though we never felt the need to enforce it when the kids were younger. Until the girls were in first grade, we'd had them only on weekends. But one Sunday, when it was time to go back to Annabelle and Scott's, Phoebe fell apart, begging to stay with us. Why couldn't she? she demanded. It wasn't fair! Though Erik said all the right things—*Your mommy's waiting for you,* and *She'd miss you so much,* and *I have to work all day, but I'll visit you tomorrow as soon as I'm finished*—Phoebe was having none of it. "Claire doesn't work!" she sobbed. "She can pick us up, and why don't you miss us? Why can't this be my home too?"

"How can she think I don't miss her?" Erik said after we dropped them off. "Jesus. I *never* wanted to be a weekend dad." He slowed the car at the end of Annabelle's street, as if reluctant to make the turn toward home. "I want fifty-fifty," he said after a minute. "It's time."

"I'd love nothing better," I told him, "but it will kill Annabelle, Erik. I can't even imagine." Except I could. She would feel we were taking her kids from her, and I knew exactly how that felt.

I wasn't wrong. When Erik and I sat down with her and

Scott a few nights later to talk about an arrangement whereby the kids stayed one week with us, one week with them—which would give Spencer time to adjust to the different households—Annabelle lost it. We'd been sitting at their picnic table on the back deck, the kids in bed, sharing a bottle of wine, and she immediately pushed her glass away and stood. "Absolutely not" was her first response, followed by fury—why would we even consider bringing that kind of upheaval into the kids' lives? It was selfish, it was all about what we wanted, it would be disastrous for Spencer. And it's not like we couldn't see the kids any time we wanted. "Have I ever *ever* said no when you've wanted to drop by?" she wept.

"You've been great," Erik told her. "But I don't want to ask permission to see my kids."

She refused to even have the conversation. "I can't believe you're doing this," she said, crying so hard she was choking. She ended up going inside and leaving us all sitting there, Scott looking miserable, Erik and I feeling like jerks.

I went to see her the next morning. She was in her kitchen, eyes puffy, surrounded by plastic storage tubs. "I was just going through this," she said without looking up. The tubs were filled with stuffed animals the kids had outgrown, baby clothes, board books. "This was the receiving blanket they wrapped Spencer in when I brought him home." She set it on the table, then held up a pair of knitted booties. "I can't believe he was ever this small." Her voice broke.

"You're not losing him, Annabelle," I said.

She fingered the lace edge of a sunbonnet. "It feels like it, though."

"You know you can spend as much time at our house as you want, right? And just think, the weeks they're with us, you can go to Hattie's to hear Scott, which he'd love, and you've been wanting to join a book club, and maybe . . .

maybe you can take care of yourself a little?" I reached for her hand. "You're so good at taking care of everyone else. All those years with your mom and then the kids . . ."

"They're all I have, Claire." Tears spilled down her face. "I'm nothing without them. I don't even know how I'd spend the days."

"But that's what you'll find out, and it might not be so bad."

"That's what Scott said." She sniffled. "And I want them to spend more time with Erik; I know it's healthy. Plus, there's no one on this planet I trust with my kids more than you. Not even Scott. It's just . . ." She started crying so hard she was hiccupping. "I don't want to miss anything."

My heart wrenched at her words. "I won't let you miss anything, Annabelle. I promise." And I did my best to honor that. If one of the girls got a one hundred on a spelling quiz, we called Annabelle to tell her. If Spencer and I tried a new cookie recipe—he loved loved loved to cook—we invited her over to try them with us. Eventually, I think she came to appreciate the arrangement. She took on more clients at the PR firm, spent hours in the warmer months tending her flower garden.

Which meant that finally, Erik got to be the dad he'd always wanted to be, leaving work early every Monday to take Spencer to chess club, learning how to French braid his daughters' hair for school, packing their lunch boxes. The best part of the day, he said, was pulling into our driveway, the house blazing with light and all of us inside waiting for him.

And as much as Erik loved being a dad, I loved being a stepmom, meeting the girls' bus after school, the two of them, now almost eight years old, flying down the steps with their socks around their ankles, clutching papers and art projects. The three of us would get a snack in the diner, the lunch crowd long gone. Annabelle often met us, ordering her usual peanut butter mochaccino, the girls sneaking spoonfuls of whipped cream that she pretended not to notice. We'd ask about their days, trying not to smile as the girls regaled us with stories of elementary school melodrama. And then Spencer's bus would pull into the lot out back, the girls waving and rapping on the glass to get his attention.

Twelve years old, Spencer was now as tall as I, a sweet skinny boy with rosy cheeks and long eyelashes. Although he didn't like us to touch him, he wanted to be close, sitting in the booth so that his shoulder brushed mine or Annabelle's, positioning his hand on the table so his fingers grazed ours.

After the diner, it was home and homework and getting dinner ready. When Erik walked in, the kids bombarded him with hugs and complaints and news. And then the whirlwind of dinner–TV–bath–bedtime stories, our house loud and chaotic. Sometimes, it wasn't until Erik and I were brushing our teeth, the dishwasher humming below in the darkened kitchen, that he would look at me in the mirror and say, "Hey, don't I know you?"

"You do look familiar," I'd say.

By then, I couldn't imagine my life without Annabelle, who in many ways reminded me of Kelly. Always, people had vied for Kelly's attention, competing to be her friend, to be noticed by her. Annabelle had that same effect. At Ten Chimneys events, in a crowd of flamboyant theater people, it was Annabelle's voice ringing out from across the room, and when you looked over, she'd be holding court, telling bawdy jokes and making outrageous statements.

I liked her best—and knew her best—when she wasn't putting on her one-woman show. At Hattie's, watching Scott sing, her face incandescent with pride. Or in the diner, combing the girls' hair with her fingers as they talked about school or leaning forward eagerly as Spencer regaled us with details about whatever he'd learned that day: *Did you know if you put an avocado next to a banana it will ripen faster? Can we try it, Claire?* Other than Erik, I spent more time with Annabelle than with anyone. We talked every day, even if was just her phoning to ask, "Hey, did you get Spencer's Adderall renewed?" or me asking, "Did Hazel leave her reading book there?" I kept her Diet Coke in our fridge, and she always had vanilla creamer for me. I folded her laundry; she emptied my dishwasher. We cleaned each other's houses, between which we were constantly ferrying shoes and jackets and homework assignments. We went to recitals and games and Spencer's IEP meetings. "This is Spence's other mom," she introduced me the first time. I loved her for that. I always will.

Spence's other mom.

On the weeks we had the kids, Annabelle and Scott popped by our house to see them; we did the same on their weeks. At first, I'd been annoyed when they showed up unannounced (couldn't they phone first?), but we'd just started the week-on, week-off custody arrangement, and Annabelle was raw and needed a lot of reassurance. And then on our weeks without them, I saw it was just as difficult for us. Maybe it always had been. But we wanted to see Hazel's new eyeglasses the day she got them, wanted to check out Phoebe's tooth before the Tooth Fairy claimed it, hear Spencer recite some new fact from his *Everything About the Weather* book when it was still exciting. "Cirrus clouds come from ice crystals! Even in the summer! Cirrus clouds form so high up, the sky is only ice!" His shy grin; his exuberance.

I learned to love this give-and-take, love how permeable our homes and lives became to each other. I'd always been so private, which I know now was really about fear: *Don't let anyone get too close.* I often thought of Margaret in those years, who'd moved home to Minneapolis after 9/11, her pilot ending things for good. Our friendship had been easy and unentangled and it was exactly what I'd needed, but now? I couldn't fathom not hearing Annabelle's "Hey, guys!" echoing from our foyer as we were finishing dinner. Or the way she'd saunter into my kitchen midday, plunk down the "essential oil–based" detergent she insisted we use for the kids' clothes, and say, "Here. This way you have no excuses." Or Gabe calling, "We come bearing gifts!" which meant ice cream. And how many nights had we been the ones stopping by Annabelle and Scott's unannounced? Erik would wander out back to find Spencer on his trampoline while I followed the girls' shrieks to the bathroom, where Annabelle was combing their wet tangled hair. "Oh, thank God in heaven," she'd say, and hand me the hairbrush. "They're all yours."

By this time, Annabelle and I had become friends separate from the kids. She took the train with me to Chicago to visit my gallery, accompanied me to thrift stores and yard sales, where we scavenged for things to use in my collages. We did a Zumba class together, which we both hated—she didn't have the breath (all those cigarettes), I didn't have the coordination, but we had the best time making fun of ourselves and the instructor, who was everything we weren't: cute, perky, and younger than us by a decade. "Fuck Zumba," Annabelle would laugh as we drove home. On the mornings she worked at the PR firm, while the kids were in school, she'd often show up at my house afterward, still in her suit and heels, and call up to me in my studio that she was here whenever I was ready for a break. I'd come downstairs to find her reheating samosas from the Indian place downtown or setting out a plate of stuffed grape leaves from the Greek takeout.

There was an openness to our lives that I cherished, a sense that we had nothing to hide. I know how ironic that sounds, but I believed—and despite everything, I still do—that we knew each other in the ways that mattered: In our love for our kids, our spouses, each other. Our belief in art, music, theater.

I think of all those nights when Erik was at a fundraiser and Scott at a gig, and I'd go to Annabelle's if she had the kids or she'd come to our house if I did. We'd sit out back and watch the huge Midwestern sky while she stole puffs of her cigarette and the kids cavorted around the yard, their voices seeming to echo more as night fell. Now and then she'd ask me a typical Annabelle question: *What was your favorite thing about your mom growing up? What's the nicest thing you ever did for a stranger? How come you never wanted kids of your own?* She asked that one more than once, and I always told her, "It's not that I didn't want my own, just that Erik already came with three who were wonderful. . . ."

The truth, and yet not.

Most of the time I was okay with that truth. Erik and I had decided before we got married that we wouldn't tell anyone about Lucy. He didn't think Annabelle would understand, and I didn't want to take that chance. It wasn't even a discussion, really. A few times, I'd be doing something with one of the kids, and Annabelle would see in my face the grief I didn't know I was showing, and she'd touch my arm and ask, "You okay?" I'd want so badly to tell her about Lucy then, but something always stopped me. I never thought I was being false so much as I thought I was being private. I didn't talk about the intricacies of my marriage with her either, and she never told me about the terrible final weeks of her mother's life. We all have these things, I told myself. As long as I could talk to my mom about Lucy. As long as I could talk to Erik.

But it wasn't that simple either. Even when days flashed by and I didn't think of Lucy, she was never not there. Like living near the ocean. You feel it nearby even when you can't see it. Naïvely, I'd thought that the more time I spent with our kids—and I thought of them as *ours*—the more I'd be able to relinquish my grief over Lucy. But if anything, it was the opposite: singing "Happy Birthday" and watching the twins blow out their candles; shopping for Christmas presents or teaching Spencer how to bake bread; getting the girls ready for the first day of kindergarten, the first day of elementary school—all I could think was, *I never watched Lucy blow out candles. I never bought Lucy a first-day-of-school outfit.*

I felt in those moments as if I'd replaced my daughter with these children. I kept hearing Kelly screaming *How dare you?*, a question I asked myself often: How dare I do any of these things—read bedtime stories, walk the girls to the bus stop, help Spencer study what different emotions looked like (*When someone is surprised, their mouth might make an O shape!*)—when I'd never done any of this with Lucy?

Other days, I felt grateful for this chance to love a child again. Oh, the grief was there—it always would be—and the regret and the anger, but there was forgiveness now too. I'd remember my mother's terrible rage in those weeks before and after I relinquished my rights. She was furious at Nick and Andrea for advocating it; furious at my lawyer, who felt I was mentally competent enough to make the choice (my mother didn't); furious at my dad for supporting me; furious mostly at me—for my inability to believe, as she did, that I wouldn't always be the way I was then. She had been right, and I was grateful for this too.

CHAPTER 25

And then it happens, what you have feared all your life.

I read that. Or maybe I heard it in the hospital, something a therapist said. The words came back the night Erik told me that Kelly, *my* Kelly, had been selected to lead a two-week master class at Ten Chimneys. It was part of the inaugural Lunt-Fontanne fellowship program, and for weeks, we'd been speculating about who the actor would be. Even Erik didn't know. The choice was in the hands of the advisory board, composed of theater dignitaries from around the country. We'd heard Kevin Spacey was a contender. Vanessa Redgrave.

No one mentioned Kelly.

"Are you *sure* you don't know who it is?" I asked Annabelle as she was leaving for the board meeting where the announcement would be made. It had been sleeting all afternoon; she'd picked up Spencer at the diner and dropped him off at my house so I wouldn't have to drive.

"Me? Keep a secret? You have such faith, Claire!" She hesitated at the door. "I thought it was supposed to be spring."

The sleet was coming down harder. Her headlights were the only brightness in the black and white afternoon.

After she left, I went back to the kitchen, where the girls were bickering and Spencer was agitated, flapping his arms and repeating phrases. He was upset because Annabelle had picked him up instead of me. I got the twins settled with snacks, but Spencer wouldn't sit, following me so closely that twice he stepped on the backs of my shoes. Every few minutes, he'd ask, "Am I a good boy, Claire?" and I'd tell him of course he was and try to explain: I hadn't met his bus because driving in icy weather scared me; it wasn't because he wasn't a good boy. In fact, he was the best boy ever! He'd nod, seemingly reassured, until three minutes later, he'd ask again, "Am I a good boy, Claire?"

All afternoon.

"No! You're not good!" Phoebe shouted. "Stop asking! It's annoying!"

"Phoebe," I said, warning her with my eyes. "Be kind."

Am I a good boy, Claire? Am I a good boy, Claire? Am I a good boy, Claire?

Finally, after dinner, I let him watch the Weather Channel in the TV room, the sound turned low, snowstorms moving in colorful swirls across the Doppler radar.

An hour later, muted light flickered into the hallway from that room as Erik, still in his damp overcoat, perched on the edge of the coffee table, elbows on his knees, watching me. I couldn't stop staring at the copy of the official letter the Ten Chimneys foundation would send out in the morning. All I could see was her name.

Kelly Jarrell.

"I don't understand." I looked at Erik questioningly. "Does she know I'm here? How is this—why would they choose her?

Fine, she's starred on Broadway, but her fame is for TV." Which the Lunts had famously hated.

"Even if Kelly knew you were here, the board *invites* the celebrities; they don't come to us. But honestly, she makes sense. The publicity she'd bring would be . . ." He flailed his hand, then let it drop. "It's what we need, frankly."

Of course, I thought. Of course she'd bring exactly what they needed. More than fear or panic, what I felt was fury that this was even happening. "Did *everyone* think she was the best choice? Wouldn't those other names bring great publicity?"

"The board was unanimous. If Kelly says no, they'll move on, but right now, she's it. And I guess they've made inquiries to ensure there's interest, so . . ."

"Wait." I'd been curled up on the couch, but now I sat up, pushing the throw blanket off my legs. "She *knows* she's being considered?"

"I assume so."

"But *you* had no idea?" My voice rose. "*You* have no say?" I knew he didn't. Erik handled the day-to-day stuff: budget, staffing and docent training, scheduling, fundraising. The choice of plays, hiring of actors, the Lunt-Fontanne fellowship—these were the province of the artistic director and the advisory board. I was clutching at straws. "Can't you talk to someone?"

"And say what?" He pushed himself up by the knees, then just stood there, as if he'd forgotten what he was doing. "I'm sorry," he said. "I need to eat. I'm about to drop."

I followed him into the kitchen and stood by the bay window. The sleet had stopped. There was only the clink of Erik setting a skillet on the stove, the suck of the refrigerator door opening and closing. The night felt immense. How was this happening? It was ridiculous! How could Kelly be coming *here*?

I wandered back to the counter and pulled up a stool. The room filled with the smell of sautéing onions. "So, the letter definitely goes out tomorrow?" I asked.

He nodded. "Which means if I were to say something, I'd need to do it, like, *now*." He laid his knife against the cutting board and leaned on his palms. "But what would I say, Claire? That you were married to Kelly's brother, and *what*? Your daughter is her niece, but you gave her up? There's nowhere for the conversation to go that doesn't get into our private lives."

"But isn't it a conflict of interest that she was my sister-in-law?"

"A conflict for who?" He started cutting a tomato. "Jesus, the board would be thrilled to know she'd been your sister-in-law; they'd probably want you to put in a good word for them."

"Ha! Maybe I will. That'll put an end to her coming."

"Well, there's an idea." He arched an eyebrow. "Why not contact her?"

"Very funny."

"I'm serious."

"No. No way." I stood, pulling my sweater tight around me. "I don't want her to know where I am, Erik."

"Whoa. Hold on." He turned down the burner to face me. "I'm not saying we'll do it. But can we talk about it?"

"There's nothing to say. I don't want her here. And if she comes . . ." I was shaking my head. "It would take so little for her to say something."

"But why would she?"

"Because she despised me, Erik. And sure, maybe she's

changed, especially if Lucy really is healthy like my mom said. . . ." I stopped and looked up at him. "I don't know what to tell you," I said quietly, "except that Kelly thought I should have been punished."

"And she doesn't think you were?" He spun to look at me. "Losing your child?"

"I hurt that child!" Tears burned my eyes, and I swiped them angrily. "She thought the second hospital was just a glorified—I don't know, resort or spa or—she said that to my mom once." I crossed my arms over my chest to stop from shaking. "And the idea that I'm happily married to someone like you, someone kind and successful and handsome—she would hate it, Erik; she'd find it reprehensible."

I walked back to the counter. "What if I go away when she comes? If she really doesn't know I'm here, let's just leave it that way. The fellowship's what? Two weeks? I'll go to Chicago. I'll be there for my show anyway." In August, my work would be featured alongside that of renowned collagist David Grant, who had work in MoMA.

"That's all fine," Erik said. "Except Kelly will still be talking to people who know you, Claire. And you really think Eva won't apply for a fellowship?"

My stomach dropped. Of course she would. The chance to work with Kelly Jarrell?

Erik shook his head. "And Annabelle's over the fucking moon."

Eva would be too. They loved *Widows,* loved "KJ." I felt sick. I should have told them I knew Kelly as soon as we started watching the show. But they would have had a thousand questions, and it just seemed easier not to mention her at all. Because really, in what universe would she just show up in our little town for two weeks? How was this even happening?

I watched as Erik whisked eggs in a glass bowl, then

poured them into the skillet. For a moment, the night felt almost ordinary: Erik cooking, me watching him, the flickering light in the hallway from the TV room.

"So, I guess there's no choice," I said furiously. "I have to tell them."

"Hold it. Tell who *what*?" He glanced at me over his shoulder.

"Annabelle and Eva. Tell them about Lucy. Tell them Kelly was my sister-in-law. At least if they hear it from me, up front—"

"Up front? There is no up front, Claire. We've been lying to them for years. There's—"

"We haven't *lied,* Erik! Maybe we didn't tell them everything, but—"

"Please. Every time you guys talk about *Widows* and you neglect to mention Kelly was your sister-in-law? You don't think that's a lie?"

I thought of the many times Annabelle had asked me if I ever wanted my own children, and all the moments she'd told me I would have been a great mom. I'd said nothing. I sank my head in my hands. "I hate this, Erik. God, I hate it. Of all people, why Kelly?"

"Believe me, we're on the same page." His voice was gentle. "But you cannot tell Annabelle about Lucy. You've got to trust me on this one, Claire. That you terminated your parental rights but are now raising our kids? There's no way she'll accept that."

"You always say that, even though practically every other week, she sings my praises as a parent."

"But Kelly did too, right?"

You're a natural, Claire, she used to say. *It's like this is what you were born to do.*

Erik slid his mound of scrambled eggs onto a plate and

set it in the middle of the counter. "Take some," he said. "I can't eat all this."

I shook my head, a darkness opening in me that felt awful. Outside the wind gusted, branches scraping the house. "You really think Annabelle can *never* understand?" At some level, I'd hoped I would one day tell her. I wanted to. Maybe because she was my best friend, or maybe because she saw me as a mom already. Or maybe it was just that the more I loved and cared for our children, the more I wanted to claim my own child. Was that so awful? Was it wrong? All I knew is that the thought flickered every time Annabelle told me what a great stepmom I was, every time she confided in me about her own failures as a parent or asked my advice about the kids. It was there at every dance rehearsal and chess club meeting and doctor appointment and parent-teacher conference I attended. Even when Erik missed them, I never did. The thought was there when Spencer got to be "the Big Cheese" for a day at his school (clearly a Wisconsin thing!) and was allowed to bring a special guest for show-and-tell, and he brought me. "Claire's my mom too," he said to his class, then fell all over himself laughing with delight. "Get it? Claire's my mom too and I have two moms!" Annabelle was with us that day, taking pictures: Spencer and me in our foam cheeseheads, making peace signs for the camera. How could none of these things matter? They had to. And Annabelle wasn't Kelly. She'd watched me love her children for six years.

Years.

Kelly had seen me with Lucy for seven *months*.

How perfect, I thought bitterly, how absolutely perfect that this was happening because of Ten Chimneys. A house that was all about pretense and artifice, a house that was a stage set. It's what my life felt like.

"Hey." Erik reached for my hand.

I shook my head. "What did I expect? That I wasn't going to have to pay? That I'd actually get away with this?" Because that's what it felt like sometimes—my life with Erik, the kids, my friendships—something I'd gotten away with but didn't really deserve.

"It's not that Annabelle wouldn't eventually understand." Erik smiled, but it didn't reach his eyes. "But you know her, Claire. She needs to be in control, and when she realizes we kept this from her . . . she'll lash out, and she won't think about the consequences until it's too late. What if she says something to . . . I don't know . . . the girls' teachers or another parent?"

"But why would she?" That seemed as preposterous as anything. Annabelle was my best friend. I thought of how she'd catch my eye across the conference table at an IEP meeting and I'd know *exactly* what she was thinking. Or how the two of us always "debriefed" after Ten Chimneys events, assessing who wore what and said what and did what. Now and then I'd tell her, "We're being awful, you know," and she'd laugh and say, "Of course we are, but who cares? It's just us."

"I'm not saying she *would* say anything," Erik said, "but do you really want to take that chance? Because I don't."

I didn't either. Annabelle had an awful temper. We'd seen it with Scott—the vile things she'd shout in the midst of one of their epic fights. Hours later, she'd be beside herself with remorse, scared that this time she'd gone too far. One day she probably would, and then what?

"So, what do we do? Just sit back and wait for Kelly to ruin our lives?"

"She hasn't accepted the offer yet. But even if she does

come, it's not until August. We don't have to figure it all out tonight."

I nodded. There was nothing to say. We both stood, and he set his dish in the sink and ran water over it, then flicked on the light over the stove as I turned out the overheads.

In the TV room, Spencer was asleep, storms moving across the TV in beautiful patterns.

CHAPTER 26

When I woke, Erik was gone, a pale gauzy light peeking beneath the curtains. Either I'd slept through the alarm or he had turned it off; probably the latter. We'd both spent the night tossing and turning.

It was early, the kids still asleep. I peeked into the twins' room, Phoebe on her back, arms outstretched, a strand of hair in her mouth, Hazel curled against the headboard. Even in sleep they were so much themselves, Phoebe outgoing and theatrical like her mom, Hazel more introverted. Like me. I watched them breathe, my love for them so fierce it hurt, then eased the door shut as I headed downstairs toward the smell of coffee.

Erik was at the table in his robe, his back to me, laptop open to pictures of Kelly. I wasn't surprised. It wasn't only my life Kelly would upend if she came here and blurted out my secrets, but his. It's what had kept me awake: Maybe I didn't deserve happiness, but why should the people I loved continue to be damaged? I kept thinking of how far my mom's life was from the one she'd wanted. A life of family dinners and babysitting grandchildren and mornings on the porch in the creaky glider with its faded blue-and-yellow-striped cushions. She'd called it her chariot. "My chariot awaits," she'd say as she headed outside with a mug of coffee, a novel tucked under her arm. It broke me that she had none of this. It was so little to have wanted.

I leaned against the doorframe, pulling my cardigan around myself, and watched as Erik scrolled through a slideshow of images: Kelly in a green halter dress receiving her first Emmy; Kelly with her hair dyed blond, wearing a baseball cap and ripped jeans and walking a dog on a city street; Kelly in a group hug with her costars on *Widows*. As Belle on Broadway.

"I feel you back there," Erik said without turning. I could hear the smile in his gravelly voice.

"What are you looking for?" I asked, touching his shoulder as I crossed the room to open the blinds over the sink. The sky was a pale, uncomplicated blue. "Wow," I said. "I think spring arrived."

"About time."

The lawn looked ragged and colorless, strewn with branches, and one of our trash cans had tipped over, but yellow sunlight was winking through the evergreens at the back of the yard. Forever trees, Spencer called them, because they stayed green all year. I poured a mug of coffee and inhaled a deep breath. "So, what'd you find?" I asked, pulling out the chair next to Erik.

"Not much." He took a gulp of coffee. "I'm not sure what I'm looking for. The critics practically fawn over her, but before *Beauty and the Beast* . . ." He shrugged.

"I know," I said. "There's only a handful of plays."

"And none lasted very long." He moved the cursor. "The reviews are something, though. She's tough to ignore."

I gestured toward the laptop. "It's surreal seeing her like this." Kelly on the red carpet in a silver lamé dress, eyes dark and dramatic; the night she got her second Emmy. "There was a time when I knew her better than I've ever known anyone."

"The thing is . . ." Erik scrolled back to the picture gallery. "There's not a single picture, not one, of her with a family member, boyfriend, even a friend." He glanced at me. "Doesn't that seem odd?"

"I don't know. Does it?"

"Was she a private person when you knew her?"

"Oh my God, no." She was flamboyant and outrageous, saying and doing whatever it took to get a laugh or provoke a response. Like Annabelle, I thought, not for the first time, and wondered how much of the past six years were about me trying to replicate what I'd lost.

But Kelly? Private? No way. I remembered her lying across the bar at the Bottle and Cork, T-shirt knotted beneath her breasts as some stranger did a belly button shot out of her navel while his buddies cheered. I'd been appalled, and she'd called me Sister Claire the rest of the night.

I told Erik that story. "There's a thousand incidents like it. Although . . ." My coffee had cooled enough to take a sip. "For all her . . . whatever it was . . . exhibitionism? When she hugged you, it was . . . she was so stiff, like Spencer almost, like she didn't want to touch you. 'Why is that girl so terrified to let anyone get close?' my mom used to say. She thought Kelly was shut down."

"Was she?"

"I wouldn't have said so then. I mean, she'd have no problem blurting out the thing no one else would say, and when she walked into a room, everyone sure as hell knew she was there." But my mom had been right. She rarely shared anything personal. "For years, she never told me how betrayed she felt when Nick and I began dating," I told Erik. "Not until our rehearsal dinner, when she joked about the countless times she stood in her brother's bedroom in tears, asking why, of all people, he had to take *her* friend. I was floored. I'd had no inkling. But then she turned the whole thing into a sweet anecdote about how Nick took her friend but gave her back something even better, which was a sister. . . . All night, everyone kept gushing about what a great toast it was, so, I don't know, it's like she could only be open in front of an audience. Would you call that private?"

"I'd call it sad."

"Maybe I didn't really know her." I stared at a photo of her in a flame-colored dress that looked more like sculpture, her hair pulled severely back in a high ponytail. "I used to wonder what would have happened if she'd told me she was upset when I started dating Nick. Maybe I wouldn't have gone out with him, and then . . ." I shrugged. "I'd have a very different life."

Erik paused midsip. "Well, I'm glad you have this life." He set down his mug, concern darting across his eyes. "Though I know you'd undo it all if you could change that one afternoon."

"And then I wouldn't have you." We'd had this conversation before. There was nowhere for it to go.

Light suddenly flooded the room and we both turned as the sun burst over the tree line. "Yikes." I glanced at my watch. "We need to get the girls."

"Thing One and Thing Two," Erik joked. They took forever in the morning, slumping downstairs with their tangled hair, clothes twisted or inside out, and once, in Hazel's case, with her shoes on the wrong feet. "How could she not know?" I said to Annabelle later.

She just shrugged and said, "She's your daughter, Claire."

"What the hell does that mean?"

Annabelle was laughing. "Only that she cares about clothes

as much as you do, which means she doesn't. I can totally see you doing that!"

Your daughter. I felt the familiar stab of guilt.

I began moving around the kitchen, setting out cereal for the girls, gluten-free granola for Spencer. "So, I take it you think that because Kelly's so private, she won't say anything about my past?" I was handing Erik things from the fridge.

"Exactly. Call me naïve, but to be that well-known and have *nothing* of your personal life in the media? That's not a coincidence, Claire." He clattered a bunch of spoons onto the counter. "All the times she's asked how she portrays grief so well and not once has she mentioned Lucy. Except for that one interview where she says Lucy's her favorite name."

"Wait. What interview? She said that?"

He looked at me, startled. "Yeah, it was . . ." His voice trailed off. "Hold on." He was already at the table, leaning over the computer.

I just stood there. Kelly had mentioned Lucy in an interview? "When was this?" My voice sounded faraway.

"Here." He swung the computer around to face me. "I'll go wake the girls."

CHAPTER 27

I sat in front of the computer and stared at Kelly's photo, her head thrown back in laughter, sunlight full in her face. "Kelly laughs like a guy," someone had said at a party in high school, and it shamed her. "Is it true?" she'd asked. "Do I laugh like a guy?"

"I don't even know what that means," I told her. "That you laugh loudly? Only men get to do that? What kind of asshole world is this, anyway?"

I'm not sure why, but we started saying that about everything: When she didn't get a callback, when I got a B instead of an A on an algebra test, when we couldn't find parking during the crazy summer months. *What kind of asshole world is this, anyway?* I'd forgotten that, but I wanted to say it to her now, about her possibly coming to Ten Chimneys, about how she was such an enormous absence and an enormous presence in my life, and I didn't want her to be either. *What kind of asshole world is this, anyway?*

The interview was twenty random questions posted on a theater blog called *Behind the Curtain*.

Biggest regret?

All of them, she'd answered.

Typical breakfast?

Coffee, coffee, and more coffee.

I skim-read the rest—Favorite image of your mom growing up? Your dad? Favorite holiday?—until I got to number eighteen: Favorite name for a girl?

Jeez! That really is random. But it's Lucy. It means "light." How perfect is that? What child isn't a light? Or maybe it's Lily, which is my favorite flower.

I read the words again. Lily must have been Nick's other daughter. Lucy's sister. I felt as if I were capsizing.

Lucy.

It means "light."

How perfect is that?

After Erik took the kids to school, I sat at my old dining room table in my office and read the other questions.

Go-to food when depressed:

Pizza. But do I have to be depressed? Can't it be my go-to food for everything?

Favorite room in your house:

Kitchen. It's my favorite room in any house. All the best conversations happen in kitchens.

Favorite color, favorite season, favorite role:

I know I'm supposed to say Danni from Widows, *or maybe Belle—I loved being Belle!—but it was actually K. C. in* Three Postcards. *She's so broken inside. I thought of her a lot when I started playing Danni—even when I played Belle. How we process grief—I think that's what character is.*

I stood, needing to move, trying to find a space to hold her words, but there was no room in me. My office was chilly despite the sunlight spilling into the windows we'd installed when we made the attic my workspace. We'd put in new floors, which creaked as I walked, and painted the walls a pale peach that turned orange in the late afternoon. I wanted to keep reading but needed to do it slowly, like a dehydrated person forcing herself to sip water rather than gulp it. *Kelly is coming here,* I'd think, and I'd try to let that thought settle, but it was too unwieldy, too heavy, or maybe my life wasn't stable enough to support whatever *Kelly is coming here* might mean.

On the bureau, its drawers packed with odds and ends—fabric swatches, old postcards and letters, maps, X-rays, and blueprints—was a handful of framed photos: a young woman in front of the Eiffel tower, *1964* scrawled at the bottom; the bowed back of an old man kneeling in an empty church; sepia-toned sailors standing at attention on a freighter on one of the Great Lakes—and Lucy, pulling a floppy sun hat over one eye, squinting. "Are these people you know?" Annabelle asked the first time she came up here, lifting each picture and setting it down.

"I just liked the images," I said. I didn't know how else to display Lucy's photograph except to include it with a bunch of other pictures. It's what Kelly had done with the interview, I realized. In those random answers, she had tucked the truths she had needed to say. *Lucy. It means "light."*

Perfect way to spend a morning:

Walking with a friend, people watching, making up stories for their lives. With coffee, of course!

The answer startled me. It's what we used to do.

"Woman in green sweatshirt," she'd say, "by the bandstand," and I'd locate the woman.

"Oh, her," I'd say. "Newly divorced; she and her ex came here every anniversary—"

"They got married on the beach," Kelly would interrupt.

"Six years ago," I'd jump back in. "But she left him."

"And now she regrets it."

"But she doesn't want him back either."

The entire length of the boardwalk, we'd spin the woman's story, then find someone new and start again.

"You think people ever invent stories for us?" I asked her once.

"Oh, they'd probably imagine we were best friends since age five, and the gorgeous dark-haired one is destined to become a Broadway star and the sexy brown-haired one is going to marry her high school sweetheart and have a passel of kids."

"A passel?" I said. "So, what happens when the gorgeous actress realizes she no longer has anything in common with her housewife friend?"

"Cut it out. Once the actress gets famous, she'll need her friend more than ever to remind her of what is real."

I emailed the interview to my mom, who phoned as I was sitting on the stairs, lacing up my running shoes. "She wanted you to see that," she said when I picked up.

"What?" I paced into the kitchen. "Where do you get *that*?" Light bounced off the pots and pans hanging over the counter.

"Oh, Claire." She sighed. "Mentioning Lucy, talking about how a person handles grief, making up lives for strangers, that's *all* about you."

"Then why put it in some obscure blog I'd never see?"

"Except you did."

I closed my eyes. Had Kelly been reaching out to me? Did I even want that? Once, maybe, but now? "She's coming here in August," I said. "Or I think she is." I explained the fellowship, how shocked we'd been. Light angled across the linoleum floor, and I bent to pick up a Cheerio.

"I'm sure the fellowship is very prestigious, but I'd say

Ten Chimneys needs Kelly more than Kelly needs Ten Chimneys." My mother paused. "Is it possible the real reason she's coming is to see you, Claire?"

"No." It wasn't. The thought stopped me, though. Erik and I had just assumed Kelly's coming here was purely coincidence. But finding me wouldn't have been that difficult, would it? "Why wouldn't she just reach out to me, then?"

"Oh, sweet girl," my mother laughed. "Kelly would never contact you directly; she'd never risk being rejected."

"But why now?"

"That one I can't answer, but my guess would be that despite her incredible success, Kelly has a pretty big hole in her life."

"*She* has a hole in her life?" I said thickly. "Jesus, Mom, she's not the one who gave up her child!"

"I'm not talking about Lucy, sweetie; I'm talking about you."

CHAPTER 28

What a coup for Ten Chimneys! people constantly told Erik after Kelly accepted the offer. And though I know he wished the board had chosen anyone else, he couldn't help but be pleased by the "KJ effect." She mentioned Ten Chimneys on *Entertainment Tonight*, and once the staff got over being irritated by the host's lame joke ("Ten Chimneys? That sounds like a roofing convention!"), they were ecstatic. The board had been right. Kelly was generating amazing publicity. "So, tell us about this Ten Chimneys place," Ellen DeGeneres asked her. More jokes. "Wisconsin, huh? How do you feel about cheese?" Tours of the estate were in huge demand.

As much as I might have liked to believe, as my mother did, that Kelly's coming to Ten Chimneys was about her wanting to see me, Erik didn't buy it. "Your mom just wants a happy ending," he said. "But to think Kelly orchestrated all this? How would that even work? She . . . *what*? Somehow got the entire board to unanimously choose her?"

"It's not that my mom thinks Kelly orchestrated it, just that once the board approached her, maybe she did a little intel of her own and found out I was here."

"Is that what you want?"

"What I want is for her to not come at all."

I planned to lie low during those two weeks, go to Chicago for some of it. If Kelly wanted to see me, I'd be available, but if she didn't know I was here, there wouldn't be any surprises. Erik and I decided too that I'd tell Annabelle and Eva that Kelly and I had been friends once and that we'd had a falling-out. I didn't want them to be blindsided if someone made the connection or Kelly mentioned Rehoboth. "At least we can stop pretending to be so thrilled about her visit," Erik said.

"You'll still have to pretend at work."

"I'm surrounded by theater people." He laughed. "Pretending is what we do."

There was something calm in me that spring that I loved. I ran my six miles a day, started two collages I was excited about, took the train to Chicago to meet with the gallery. The six of us attended a Ten Chimneys fundraiser with Alan Alda and went to Hattie Magee's, and on our weeks without the kids, Erik and I did what we always did: exercised, cooked, watched TV, made love. We were hungry for each other as we hadn't been since the first year of our marriage, kissing in the foyer after a night out, keys falling to the floor, coats strewn on the stairs as we laughed and groped and fumbled our way to the bedroom.

In April, the twins started T-ball, and as the days grew warm, Annabelle, Spencer, and I—sometimes Erik and Scott—spent afternoons on aluminum bleachers at the elementary school, watching games. The sky a swirl of yellow and pink, the crack of bats from the older boys in the next field, shouts of "Way to go!" or "Keep your eye on the ball." Spencer, who didn't like the crowds or the noise, paced at the edge of the field, counting his steps and anxiously repeating his phrases, or sometimes sat in the car where we could see him, head buried in a library book. "I can't imagine doing this alone," Annabelle said a few times, following him with her eyes. "Every mom should have one of you."

"A friend?" I teased.

She leaned into my shoulder. "You're way more than that, Claire."

Still, I put off telling her and Eva about my friendship with Kelly. There was always an excuse. Gabe threw Eva a lavish fortieth-birthday bash in early May, and I didn't want to spoil that. A week later, he was made senior partner, which we celebrated at Pizza Man on a rainy Friday night. And then Phoebe and Hazel came down with strep, so Spencer stayed with us for an extra week while the girls stayed with Annabelle. "You do realize Claire and I are perfectly capable of taking care of sick kids too," Erik griped to her, but she had a dozen reasons why it was better for the girls to be with her, Spencer with us. "The last thing we need is him getting sick," she insisted. True, but the changed schedule wreaked havoc with him. He was anxious and upset the entire week. And so, we got in the habit of taking long drives after I picked him up at the diner. He'd hold his spiral-bound *Maps of Waukesha County* on his lap and trace our progress.

Had I been alone, the windows would have been down, the radio cranking, but even a breeze agitated Spencer, and the radio "made the air feel bumpy." And so these were silent, almost claustrophobic, drives. But the motion soothed his anxiety, as did tracing the route, knowing exactly where he was and what was coming: a small town, a railroad crossing. It comforted me too. I wasn't aware of how lost I'd felt after

Kelly accepted the offer until Spence and I were driving and I realized the untethered feeling—as if I were floating over my own life—had disappeared.

In late May, when Eva phoned to tell me she'd made the short list of fellowship applicants, I wasn't surprised. "Was there ever any doubt?" I said to Erik when he came home.

"It's not a done deal yet. Eva's got some stiff competition." Erik bent to give me a kiss and snagged a piece of broccoli. I'd been cutting vegetables for tempura. "No one expected this level of interest." While Ten Chimneys had promised to prioritize local applicants, stage actors from across the country were vying to work with "KJ" to put on a play Alfred and Lynn had acted in.

"I feel like the crappiest friend in the world, but I don't want her to get this fellowship."

"Well, that makes two of us." He shrugged out of his blazer and stood next to me to survey the bowls of cut-up veggies.

"I'm meeting Eva and Annabelle at the diner tomorrow," I said. "I need to rip off the Band-Aid. Tell them Kelly and I were friends." I took a sip of wine. "It makes me nervous."

"Of course it does." He pulled the bottle of Maker's Mark from the freezer and got out a glass. "But the worst that will happen is Annabelle pouts for two minutes because you never told them, and then she'll have a thousand questions."

"That's what worries me." I set down my knife. "I don't want this to turn into a big deal."

"Ahh, cue up the diner." He grinned. "Have you decided what booth you'll sit in? What to wear?"

"Don't you laugh."

He held up his hands. "Have I said anything?"

He didn't have to. He'd told me a hundred times that for someone professing to know nothing about theater, I was masterful at creating scripts and orchestrating scenes. And he was right. I'd asked them to meet me at the diner because it was too small, too loud, and too public for a serious conversation, which I didn't want to have. The diner was where we waited for Spencer's bus or grabbed coffee before some event at Ten Chimneys. We were just checking in when we were there: *How was your morning?* we'd ask; *What's on your plate for the day?* It was what I wanted the conversation about Kelly to be. I'd mention that I knew her, mention that we'd grown up in the same town. Mention that we'd been friends. *Mention.*

"I know I'm overthinking this."

"How can you not?" He held my gaze and I felt an unexpected coil of sadness push against my breastbone.

"You really think Annabelle's going to be upset?" I said.

"At first. Only because you guys have talked about *Widows* so much."

"And then all this hoopla about Kelly coming and neither of us has said a word." I sidestepped Erik to rinse my knife. Outside the trees were flat shapes in the almost dark, the grass a dense glossy black. When I turned to look at him, he was at the stove, rolling up his sleeves. His tie off, collar open, he looked rumpled and handsome. I watched as he dunked a broccoli floret in batter, then dropped it into the pan of hot oil.

"So, will you mention she was your sister-in-law or just leave it at friend?"

"Friend." I leaned against the counter next to him. "I don't want them knowing we once shared a name. It's too close."

He nodded. "That's probably good."

"I figure they'll assume what you did, that Kelly's connected to my marriage ending, which will also explain why I left Rehoboth." I took a sip of wine. "Who wants to stick around and watch your best friend cheating with your husband?"

"Jesus. Talk about too close," Erik said.

"What do you mean?"

"Best friend cheating with your husband? Annabelle will shut that down in a hurry."

"Yikes! I never even thought of that." Annabelle and Gabe. It rarely crossed my mind. It had been so long ago. Ten years? Eleven?

"Well, that'll take care of Annabelle asking questions," Erik said. "And Eva won't let herself get anywhere near that."

I watched as he dunked more vegetables into the batter. The stovetop was splattered with grease. "I didn't realize how messy this would be," I said.

"The tempura?" He arched an eyebrow. "Or the conversation?"

"Both, I guess." I watched him tong a piece of cauliflower from the pan. "What did you mean, Eva won't *let* herself get anywhere near?"

"Nothing. Just . . ." He furrowed his brow. "I don't know why I said it like that."

"You don't think she knows, do you?"

"About Annabelle and Gabe? Jesus, no. But she'll also never put herself in a position where she might find out."

"So, you think she suspects?"

"I really don't."

I stared at him, unease spiraling through me. "You promise?"

"I do. Honestly. The Kelly thing's just weirding us out." He flicked off the burner. "Are you hungry? Because I think we're about ready."

CHAPTER 29

Annabelle was already at the diner, Spencer with her; his teachers had an in-service day. We'd both hoped that coming here, where Spencer normally got his bus, would help with the change in routine, but he was clearly shut down, filling in, with colored pencils, the squares on a sheet of graph paper. Red, yellow, blue, green, orange, brown. The same order, over and over. He didn't even glance up when I slid into the booth next to him, just shimmied farther away. He looked beat, purplish grooves etched beneath his eyes.

Deanna, the owner, filled our mugs, talking over her shoulder to someone else as she kept moving: "You said over easy. You never cook the yolks all the way." The room was loud with voices and clattering dishes.

I leaned toward Spencer's paper. "Those are some good colors, buddy."

He repeated, "Those are some good colors," then continued filling in the squares.

I glanced at Annabelle. She was wearing a faded green T-shirt that said "Reece Painting," Scott's company, and her hair was scraped into a ponytail. She looked washed-out, an oily sheen to her skin.

We were sitting by a window. Eva swung into the gravel parking lot in the red Jeep Gabe had bought for her fortieth birthday a month ago. "She looks like Malibu Barbie in that thing," Annabelle said.

I watched as Eva slammed the door, smiling into her phone, holding up one finger to indicate she'd be right in.

Two minutes later, she slid into our booth, green eyes flashing.

"What are you so animated about?" Annabelle asked.

"Kelly Jarrell is from Rehoboth Beach?" Eva held out her mug as Deanna swept by. "You are so busted, Claire."

"What?" Annabelle snapped her head in my direction. "Kelly Jarrell is from your hometown?" She lowered her voice. "Do you know her?"

I looked at Eva. "How did you find out?"

"Oh my God." Eva was beaming. "You *do* know her!"

"Did," I said. "*Did*. Eons ago. Another lifetime."

"Were you friends?" Annabelle asked.

Eva leaned forward, elbows on the table. "Isn't Rehoboth pretty small?"

"It is." I forced a smile, but my heart was racing. "And yes, I was friends with Kelly Jarrell for a while." It felt odd to say her full name. She was just Kelly to me. *Kel*. And *Jarrell*. Nick's name. Lucy's. It had once been mine. I'd taken my maiden name back after the divorce. It had felt unbearable—to stay a Jarrell without any of them in my life.

"I can't believe you never even hinted!" Eva said. And then, "Wait. Wait wait wait. You had something to do with getting her here, didn't you?" She turned on Annabelle. "Did you know?"

"No! Of course not." Annabelle set down her mug. "Does KJ not want anyone to know there's a connection? Is that why you haven't—"

"No." I was shaking my head. "I swear, I had nothing to do with her coming here." *This* was the conclusion they were jumping to? *This?* That I'd pulled strings to get Kelly at Ten Chimneys?

Eva took a sip of coffee, leaving a pink crescent on the rim of the mug. "You must have seen her in her high school performances, right? Was she amazing even then?"

"She was. She was our local celebrity." I heard the pride in my voice, but the grief too, which surprised me: how close to the surface it was. All those afternoons in the auditorium, watching Kelly rehearse; taking the bus to New York each January—her parents always gave her tickets to a Broadway play for Christmas. Of course, she took me.

"So, how good of friends were you?" Annabelle was still smiling, but the playfulness was gone from her voice. "Did you do stuff? Go to each other's houses?"

"Please don't be mad," I said. "I wanted to tell you."

She arched an eyebrow.

"Yes, we went to each other's houses." I pictured the pyramid of empty Mountain Dew cans atop Nick's bureau or the scratched coatrack in Kelly's room draped with fringed scarves and hats, a red feather boa from some play.

There was a brittle quality to the way Annabelle was holding her elbows and staring outside.

I don't owe you this information, I thought. *I don't owe anyone, not even Erik, every detail of my life.* But that wasn't what this was about. She was hurt, and with good reason. "I'm sorry," I said, willing her to look at me. "It's complicated, but I should have mentioned it. I know that."

Nothing.

"We met in kindergarten." I was holding my own elbows. "We were pretty close." Next to me, I felt Spencer watching his mom.

"Is she—you're not in touch anymore?" Eva asked. "Is that why you never—"

"Oh please," Annabelle said. "Like Claire's going to share anything about her past."

"Come on." Eva nudged Annabelle. "Why are you being weird?"

"Me?" Annabelle finally turned from the window and looked at me. "Two years of watching *Widows* and not once do you mention you were friends—no, excuse me, *close* friends—with Kelly Jarrell?" She shook her head. "You want to talk about weird, let's talk about that."

"Well, someone woke up on the wrong side of the bed," Eva teased, but Annabelle just shot her a vicious look, then leaned across the table to Spencer. "We're going to go soon, okay, Spence? How many more squares do you want to do?"

He didn't lift his head, just kept coloring his boxes, applying such force to the pencils, he was pushing through the paper. I leaned over and whispered, "It's okay, buddy; you don't have to press that hard."

"Don't tell my son something's okay when it's not," Annabelle hissed.

My son. I looked at her incredulously. I felt like she'd slapped me.

"Whoa!" Eva held up her hands to Annabelle. "What is wrong with you? Maybe you want to jump down Claire's throat *after* you find out what happened?"

"Claire tell us something important?" Annabelle snorted. "Good luck with that." She heaved her scratched leather purse onto the table and started digging for her keys.

My pulse was racing. "What do you want to know, Annabelle?"

"Anything! Jesus. We've known you for six years, and you've never mentioned what happened in your marriage or why you don't visit your parents, or what brought you to Wisconsin—"

I opened my mouth to protest but she held up her hand. "Yeah, we all know the story about how you saw a map and liked the shape of the state, which is bullshit."

"Annabelle, stop," Eva said.

"No, you stop, Eva. You've said it too, that it's weird how little we know Claire."

"That's not what I said."

I knew Annabelle was probably taking Eva's words out of context, but could they really think they didn't know me? Everything I was—Erik's wife; Spencer, Phoebe, and Hazel's stepmother; an artist; a runner; their *friend*—how could this not count?

I stared at my hands, cradled around my coffee mug, which had grown cold. "I don't mean to be secretive," I said quietly. "Kelly's connected to me leaving Rehoboth." I glanced at Annabelle, arms crossed over her chest, eyes full of judgment. "Talking about her isn't . . . it's not fun for me. I wish I didn't know her, and I hate that she's coming here." My voice faltered. "I don't know what else to say. I don't know what you want."

"You realize you've told us nothing, right?"

"Annabelle," Eva said.

"What? This is the same old crap, and it's all just *too* painful to talk about." She spoke in a syrupy singsong. "Do I have that right?"

She did.

"Yup. What I thought."

"Why do you need details, Annabelle? Isn't it enough to know I went through a bad time?"

"No one wants every gritty little detail, Claire. But believe it or not, friends confide in one another. I tell you everything!"

"Really?" I sat back. "You have no secrets? Because if you really want to talk about—"

"Stop it." The color had drained from Eva's face. She turned to Annabelle. "If Claire doesn't want to talk about her past, she doesn't have to." She was playing with a sugar packet, tapping it one corner at a time on the table. Bright patches of red inflamed her cheeks. *She does know about the affair,* I thought. Maybe not consciously, but Erik was right: She wouldn't let us get anywhere close to that truth. Immediately, my anger dissipated, replaced by shame. What had I just done?

Annabelle swiped her eyes over me, then leaned across the table again toward Spencer. "Five more squares," she said. Under her breath she added, "This is so fucked up."

"Five more squares," Spencer repeated. "This is so fucked up. Five more squares. This is so fucked up."

Except for us, the diner was mostly empty now. Across the room, Deanna's son, a huge bearded man in stained cook's whites, was sharing a booth with his wife. Deanna stood at the table, jiggling their infant. My mom had once held Lucy like that in my dad's restaurant. Midafternoon, chairs upside down on tables.

"All you had to do was mention that you'd known Kelly," Annabelle was saying. "And sure, we might have tried to wheedle a few details from you, but we would have respected your not wanting to talk about her, the way we've respected your not wanting to talk about . . . well, pretty much your whole life until you moved here. Obviously, though, you don't trust us."

"It wasn't personal, Annabelle."

"Lying's always personal, Claire."

"I didn't lie."

"You pretended you didn't know her. Same difference."

For a moment, none of us said a word. A jagged panicked feeling rose up in me. How could I explain that it wasn't about not trusting them? It was about shame, so much shame it would light me on fire if I ever gave it air. I'd hurt my child; I'd lost the right to be her mother. Why would I want anyone to know this?

And yet.

Weren't there times when it was just the two of us and I'd think, *Maybe*? Annabelle had suffered a terrible depression after Spencer's birth—she would understand.

But then I'd hear Erik insisting Annabelle could never comprehend what I'd done, and my mom all but pleading with me not to say anything. Because what if it changed how Annabelle felt about me? Why would I risk that? Why would I fight so hard for this second chance just to throw it away? It was the only time my mom got angry. And I understood. She'd picked up the pieces over and over when I fell apart, and all she wanted now was that I hold on to this life I had.

Annabelle was staring outside again. Eva was tearing the sugar packet into confetti.

"I don't talk about the past because I'm happy now," I said. "And a lot of that is because of you guys." It was the truest thing I could say.

Annabelle didn't blink. "I'm going to go," she said. "I'm exhausted."

"No," Eva said. "I'm not letting you out of the booth until we settle this."

Annabelle closed her eyes and said, "Move, Eva, or I'll crawl under the table."

Wordlessly, Eva got up. I stood to let Spencer out. My legs were shaking.

"Mom said five more squares and it's five more squares." His shoe was untied, and he handed me his pencils as he crouched down to tie it. They were damp from his sweaty hands. I dropped them into the baggie Annabelle was holding open. And then without looking at us, she turned, one hand on Spencer's back, guiding him toward the door. Eva and I slid back into the booth and watched as they walked across the parking lot, the air thick with sunlight.

"Give her a couple hours," Eva said.

I nodded. The diner was quiet but for the tinny sound of a radio in the kitchen. "I had no idea it bothered you guys that I didn't talk about my past," I said. "You never pushed." I was staring at the blur of cars passing by on the street out front.

"We're curious. That's all. And Annabelle adores you, Claire. She's just scared."

"Of what?"

"Losing you. I'm not sure either of us can really understand how alone she feels. We've got our families. Even if something awful happened to Gabe, I've got my older brother and my mom, and you've got your parents, but Annabelle is on her own, and she has been her whole life. Which means she works incredibly hard to make sure we need her, though the truth is that she needs us. Especially you, Claire. And not just because of the kids, though that's huge. You just get her. If I didn't like you so much, I'd be jealous." She laughed softly. "Trust me, she's not upset about Kelly. She's upset because she thinks she's not important to you. And not that this excuses her crappy behavior, but she *was* up all night with Spencer." Eva settled her purse strap over her shoulder as she slid from the booth. "Annabelle has the biggest heart of anyone I've ever known, but she's also got the biggest temper." She smiled. "Three hours, tops; she'll be at your door."

CHAPTER 30

I tried to work on *Light,* the collage I'd begun the week before. Of course it was about Lucy, and there was a ton I already loved: the canvas was a huge farmhouse window I bought at a barn sale, I'd mixed sand my mom sent from Rehoboth into the glossy white paint I was laying over the surface, and glass, through which light so often enters our lives, is made from melted sand. I loved knowing this, even if whoever looked at the finished piece never did.

But I was stuck.

I fussed with the collage after I got home from the diner, layering pages from a child's book written in Braille over paragraphs from a scientific journal on angular momentum and the ability of light waves to torque. I added shards of mirror, stepped back, laid yellow cellophane over the paragraphs, stepped back again. Nothing was right. I stared at a map of constellations, the L page torn from a book of baby names. Frustration lifted inside me. The piece was about grief—but *what* about grief?

Eva was right: Two hours later, Annabelle was at my door, sobbing and hiccupping. "I don't [*hiccup*] know [*hiccup*] what's [*hiccup*] wrong with me." With every hiccup, her body hitched, as if she were being jerked up by an invisible string.

I tugged her into our hallway as she sobbed like a kid (and she looked like one in her T-shirt, boys' jeans, and Chuck Taylors) while I kept repeating, "It's okay," and "You had every right to be upset." I felt inept. I'd watched Annabelle comfort Eva, wiping her tears with her thumb, pushing her hair from her forehead, but I wasn't affectionate like that, except with the kids and Erik. It felt like one more way I didn't know how to be a good friend, no matter what Eva had said.

We were sitting in the living room by then, side by side on the couch.

"Spencer's your son too," she hiccupped, chest juddering as she spoke. "I just get so jealous."

"*Why?*" I almost laughed. "You're an amazing mother, an amazing friend."

"Don't say that!" she wept. "I'm the last person anyone would call a good friend. And you know what I'm talking about!" Her words were choked with fury. "You can't tell her, Claire. I don't care how angry you are or how much you hate me—"

"I don't hate you!"

"I will die if she finds out." She could barely talk, she was crying so hard.

"Annabelle. Please. She's not going to."

"I knew you knew about Gabe," she said. "And I've wanted to talk to you, but I've been too afraid."

"I know," I said. But I hadn't. Just as she had no idea how often I'd considered telling her my secret. *I have a daughter.* It was such a fundamental fact of who I was. And I thought then of the afternoon a few weeks ago when Annabelle and I were at the diner waiting for Spencer, and I'd been watching the high school girls in their plaid Catholic school uniforms as they milled around waiting for their rides. One of the girls had wavy blond hair like Nick's, and she was tall and big-boned with a swimmer's broad shoulders, and I thought, *Oh. Here you are.* Everything in me went still. Was this what she would look like? Did she play a sport? *Here you are.* A crumbling feeling in my chest. And then Annabelle leaned her chin on my shoulder and asked, "Do you know her?"

I shook my head and said something about being glad we never had to go back to high school. But what if, instead, I'd told her, *I have a daughter and she's sixteen, and that girl reminds me of her*?

Annabelle had stopped crying, though tears kept leaking down her face. "Every time I imagined trying to explain to you what happened with Gabe . . ." She was staring down, twisting a Kleenex into a spiral. "It seemed selfish. All that would happen is maybe I'd feel a tiny bit better, and I don't deserve that."

"Except maybe you do," I said. "Maybe ten years is enough time to beat yourself up."

"I just want to undo it." Her face crumpled. "That's the worst part. I can never fix it. No matter how good of a friend I try to be."

"I know," I said quietly. "It's why I don't talk about my past. Not because I don't trust you, Annabelle. It's just . . . there are things I'm ashamed of."

Her eyes filled again. "Eva thinks you were raped. Or your ex-husband beat you."

"Oh God, no! It was nothing like that." And yet, hadn't I said just enough over the years to make them think *exactly* this? My marriage was too painful to talk about; I'd moved across the country to get away; I was afraid to go back. Still, hearing Annabelle say it filled me with shame. It was so far from the truth. *I* was so far from the truth.

I stared at the sunlight eddying on the floor like water and thought of how I signed my collages with Lucy's name. *It means "light," and ultimately that's what art does, focuses a light.* How many times had I said this? Enough that I almost believed it. But it was a lie too.

No wonder I was blocked. And on a piece called *Light,* no less. It served me right. Had my art, *ever,* been about shining a light on anything? It had always been about hiding. Just layer enough scraps, fragments, and half-truths over one another, and I could convince everyone, myself included, that I was actually saying something. No different from what I'd done with my friendships. Disappointment roared through me. Did I even know who I was anymore?

"I'm glad Eva was wrong about your past," Annabelle said.

"You never thought those things?"

She lifted one shoulder in a shrug. "I figured it was something you did rather than something done *to* you. That's the crap we don't talk about, right?"

I nodded. I'd underestimated Annabelle.

"Don't you get tired of it, though? Always lugging it around—whatever horrible thing you don't want us to know?" She didn't wait for me to answer. "I do."

"I do too."

"I loved Gabe," she said. "I would have done anything for him." Tears welled and she pressed a soggy tissue beneath one eye. "I made such an ass of myself."

"Because he didn't love you?" I was surprised. I'd always assumed he chased her.

"I groveled, begged, practically stalked him. Even after it

was over, I . . . I followed him on a business trip to Minneapolis. Showed up at his hotel. Sexy underwear, the whole bit."

"Oh, Annabelle."

"After Erik found out, Gabe fell apart. All he cared about, and I mean *all,* was that Eva never know. He was beside himself. Even if she found out and left him, he said, he still wouldn't want to be with me." Tears streamed unchecked down her face. She looked like a waif, tiny and miserable, her fingers, with their stubby chewed nails, clutching the Kleenex. "It's the worst thing I've ever done, Claire. I still can hardly explain it even to myself. I mean, yes, Erik and I were fighting nonstop, Spencer had just been diagnosed, and Gabe was . . . he was in a lousy place too. But I took advantage."

"Why was Gabe in a lousy place?"

"He hated being a lawyer—God, he hated it—and he felt trapped. Three years of school, another year studying for the bar, plus all the debt. It's not like Eva makes anything acting."

How could I not have known this? Not once in six years had anyone, including Gabe, *ever* hinted that he hated his career. Oh, he whined about the hours and talked about retiring while he was still young enough to do something else, but that he was doing a job he'd been miserable in from day one? "Does he still hate it?"

"With a passion."

"And Eva knows this?"

"I'm not sure."

"But he talks to *you*?" I felt as if I were on a seesaw. Outside the day felt too bright and too green; trees, grass, bushes, even the sky seemed green. I couldn't look at Annabelle. I didn't want to know even as I was asking, "But it's over with him, right? You love Scott?"

"I adore Scott." She started crying again. "And I would never—" Her voice broke. "I would never do that to Eva again, Claire. God, I can barely live with this."

"You need to forgive yourself," I said gently.

"I can't."

For a moment we didn't speak. I wished Annabelle hadn't told me any of this. It didn't make me feel closer to her, and it definitely didn't make me feel closer to Gabe. If anything, I felt like we didn't know him at all. And I considered, as I had more times than I could count, that maybe the greater act of love for another person wasn't in confiding a secret but in *not* confiding it and carrying that secret alone, no matter how burdensome, so the other person wouldn't have to. Was this what Gabe was doing by not telling Eva how much he hated the job that allowed her to pursue the career *she* loved? Could they have had the life they had without his job? Would it have been a better life?

A fresh wave of tears was streaming down Annabelle's face. "If I ever lose Eva . . ." She started crying again. "I'm not like you, Claire. You told us once that as long as you had your art and your running, you'd be okay. But you guys, Scott, and the kids—that's all I have."

"Oh my God, Annabelle. You took what I said completely wrong. Of course I need you."

"No," she said. "Maybe you wish you did, but you don't."

She was right, and I didn't know what that said about me. Sometimes I wasn't even sure I needed Erik. The second I thought it, I wanted to unthink it, but deep down, I knew it was true.

As shattered as I'd have been if something happened to him, there was a part of me I'd tucked away years ago and held in reserve, the way survivalists stored canned goods and bottled water. They did it because when the economy crashed or terrorists took over or a pandemic wiped out half the population, they—by God, *they*—would be prepared. I was no different. No matter that Erik knew about Lucy, no matter that he loved me and believed in me, and was unequivocally in my corner—no matter. I held part of myself back just in case he ever changed his mind, just in case something happened and I was alone again, just in case.

The realization was a stone falling through me. *I don't want to be this person,* I thought. There was a time when I'd needed to be her, a time when not depending on anyone was the only choice I had. Those months in the hospital, those months after I gave her up, those first years living here. But now?

I glanced at Annabelle, her face splotchy and eyes swollen, and I knew she really believed she couldn't go on living if Eva found out what she'd done. I envied her. Because wasn't it better to believe you couldn't live without someone than to believe, as I did, that you could? And it struck me that although Annabelle could be a mess—controlling, reactionary—she was also more real than anyone I knew. Watching her yank a Kleenex from the box and try to blow her stuffed-up nose, I felt such love for her. Was I capable of being so vulnerable? Had I ever been?

"I don't really know how to need people," I told Annabelle. My throat felt swollen.

"Just talk to us."

"I'll try."

"Try?"

"Okay." I smiled. "I will."

But would I really? Could I?

She left soon after. Scott was with Spencer, so she needed to get back. She'd stopped crying, though she kept hiccupping, her breath shaky. "Do you forgive me?" she asked at the door.

"Oh my God, Annabelle, there's nothing to forgive." But she insisted. Her sinuses were clogged and she kept trying to breathe through her nose, which made a sad honking sound. She was beyond exhaustion, so I told her yes, I forgave her.

Though if anyone needed forgiveness, it was me.

CHAPTER 31

I used to believe a season began on a specific day. Or maybe it started with weather, a change in the light, the blooming of flowers, the falling of leaves. Maybe with a holiday, as it did in Rehoboth, where summer began on Memorial Day weekend and ended on Labor Day, when the tourists left and the town became ours again. Now I understand seasons are like heartbeats, slowing some days so that afternoons stretch into long purple shadows, speeding up other times so that months spin by in an hour, years disappear in a night.

Perhaps if our last summer had ended differently, I would believe it had started, as it seemed to, on Memorial Day weekend. But everything that happened that summer happened because of what began back in March, when the advisory board at Ten Chimneys sent that letter to Kelly Jarrell. Afterward, our lives shifted in ways none of us apprehended until it was too late.

Annabelle's deck was ablaze with candles and pots of yellow hibiscus; white lights were strung along the railing and draped in the branches of the birch trees. I spun to look at her. "This is stunning!" It was like a stage set, shimmering against the deepening twilight and velvety green of the newly mown lawn.

"It turned out, didn't it?" She was beaming. "Scott did the picnic table."

He'd painted it a glossy periwinkle that caught the reflection of the fat candles lined up down the center. It was already set with delicate flower-patterned china plates, cloth napkins, and real silver, all of it gleaming in the flickering light. "It's beautiful," I said again, and felt a jolt of happiness leap up in me. Erik and Gabe were already manning the grill and smoking cigars, Scott was mixing martinis, and Spencer was on the trampoline, jumping straight up and down like an exclamation point.

"Hey, that's not fair!" Eva's high voice lifted across the backyard, where she was playing croquet with the girls. She was wearing a full-skirted yellow dress that caught the sunlight like a candle flame. She was barefoot, her high-heeled sandals lying in the grass. We'd all gotten dressed up at Annabelle's request.

"It's a barbecue," Erik protested when I handed him a dress shirt to wear with his Bermuda shorts.

"Well, she wants it to be special."

Compared to Annabelle and Eva, I was underdressed: black linen pants, wedge-heeled espadrilles, a sleeveless white sweater—but I'd felt excited and hopeful ever since she issued the invite. Kelly and I had always regarded Memorial Day weekend as a new start. We'd drop ten pounds, lose our virginity, save money to travel to Europe, fall in love. It never mattered how many summers didn't live up to our dreams, how many summers *we* didn't live up. Memorial Day weekend rolled around and once again, we'd imagine all the ways we would reinvent our lives.

I felt that again at Annabelle's, the sense of things starting anew. I was determined to stop being so afraid, to trust more, to eventually find the courage to tell Annabelle about Lucy. I wanted to let go, have fun, stop hiding so much; I wanted to dress up! I glanced at Eva in her poufy yellow dress and wished I'd worn something more festive, wished I were the kind of woman who owned festive clothes. *But I* could *be,* I thought. *Why not?*

It was a pretty night, the dusky sky with its quarter-moon floating over the trees, shadows stretching across the lawn. And we were all together, they knew about Kelly, and the world hadn't stopped spinning. In the falling light, swifts swooped and dove, and a cloud of white smoke drifted up from the grill. Gabe and Erik were arguing good-naturedly: *How many millions of dollars on a capital campaign? Kids coming to school without breakfast . . .* Annabelle flicked her eyes at them in mock annoyance, and I smiled. Gabe had joined the board of the Milwaukee Boys and Girls Club and was constantly needling Erik about Ten Chimneys: How could he justify all that spending on the arts, those fucking fellowships, thirty-five-dollar tours of the estate—when children fifteen miles away didn't have winter coats?

"You do realize your wife was awarded one of those fucking fellowships, right?" Erik said.

"And no one's happier for her. But this lavish spending to recapture the heyday of some privileged white actors most people never heard of. How do you sleep at night?"

"Asks the man driving a Prius," Erik laughed. "Wow. You're not just saving kids but the environment too. I'm amazed you haven't wrenched your shoulder patting yourself on the back."

Gabe's retort.

Then Erik's.

More laughter.

Verbal jousting, Erik called it, one or the other conceding a point by pretending to be mortally wounded, staggering backward, clutching his heart. Erik insisted the "debates" were fun, that he and Gabe had been doing this from the moment they met, which Annabelle and Eva affirmed, ignoring them when they started up. Mostly, I did too. But every now and then I sensed how close to the edge of real anger they had stepped. And it had nothing to do with Ten Chimneys or impoverished kids or whatever else the argument du jour was.

It was about Gabe's betrayal.

Erik forgave it, but he still couldn't fathom it—ethically, morally, even practically. "Jesus! What the hell did he think would happen when we all had Thanksgiving together?" And though I'm sure Gabe was grateful for Erik's silence, being grateful was exhausting too. Listening to them that night, though—*elitist view . . . sanctimonious horseshit!*—I felt the opposite of my usual worry. This is what friends do, I thought. Yes, you might hurt one another, maybe even badly, but you don't just throw away the friendship. There was a generosity in Gabe's and Erik's willingness to disagree, something immutable and solid about the friendship itself. I wanted that with Annabelle and Eva.

The sky was charcoal-colored now, the lawn nearly black but for Eva's dress and the white croquet wickets, the darting shapes of the girls.

"What are you thinking?" Annabelle said.

"I'm thinking how perfect this is. Like something from a magazine."

"That's exactly what I wanted." She went to grab the sliding door for Scott, who was balancing a tray of martinis. "All right, you guys," she called, taking a glass, then twirling to face us. She looked gorgeous, her hair loose, tumbling over an emerald-green sweater and sassy white skirt that flounced around her thin legs every time she moved. She was barefoot, toenails painted green to match her sweater, that tiny tattoo just above her ankle. *Stasia.* "Eva, get over here!" she called. "It's time to celebrate." Gold bangles shimmied down her arm as she lifted her glass.

Of course Eva had gotten the fellowship. She'd phoned the minute she heard. "I don't need to accept," she said. "If my working with Kelly is an issue for you."

"Oh, Eva, no. The stuff with me and Kelly, it's . . . it's so long ago."

"Are you sure?"

"Absolutely," I told her, though I wasn't at all.

After we hung up, I wandered into the living room, where I'd sat the day before with Annabelle, the Kleenex box still on the floor by the couch, and I stood at the window, a pressure in my throat that made it hurt to swallow.

The next night, Annabelle phoned to tell us Scott's band would be opening for the Spin Doctors at the Wisconsin State Fair in August. "I'm going to have to weigh him down with bricks if he doesn't return to earth soon," she said. "So anyway, we're having a barbecue on Saturday to celebrate: your show, Eva's fellowship, Scott's gig. And I want us to dress up, okay?"

Eva lifted her cosmo, and we leaned forward to clink glasses. The lights strung through the trees reflected off our arms and faces. "To our hostess," she said. A breeze rustled the leaves of the birch trees, and the wind chimes jangled softly from the corner of the deck.

"And to our chefs." I lifted my glass toward Gabe and Erik.

"Whoa. What about the bartender?" Scott asked.

"To our bartender!" someone—was it Annabelle?—said.

We laughed more, the sound of our voices crisp against the purple-black sky and the outline of the trees. Another candle sputtered out in its pool of wax. "I want to toast too!" Phoebe said.

"Sure you do, lovey." Annabelle turned to her daughter. "What do you want to toast?"

"Croquet!"

And so we toasted croquet. And then Hazel wanted to toast strawberry ice cream, so we toasted that.

"You want to make a toast, Spencer?" Erik asked.

"Why is it called toast?"

"That's a good question, lad. How about we look it up after dinner?"

He nodded solemnly. "Can I toast toasts?"

"A toast to toasts!" Scott called, and we lifted our glasses again.

The whole night was like that. We toasted Ten Chimneys, Alfred and Lynn, the beautiful weather. We talked about the fellowship, then speculated about what play—it had to be one the Lunts had done—Kelly would choose for the fellows to perform. Briefly, we talked about Kelly: "So what's your plan for when she's here?" Gabe asked. "Jackie O. glasses? A wig? A burka?"

"I was thinking all three," I laughed.

"She's gotta know you're here," Scott said. "It's too fucking weird if she doesn't."

"That's what my mom says."

"Yeah, but . . ." Gabe shrugged. "Coincidences happen all the time."

And then we were talking about coincidences. The time Gabe and Eva were in Debrecen, Hungary, and ran into their neighbors, or the time Annabelle found on the beach at Lake Michigan a ring she'd lost there the year before.

We toasted coincidences and finding lost things.

By then, the kids were flitting about with glow sticks in the black pool of the lawn, their voices echoey and sharp. Erik reached for my hand, his fingers warm. The candles had burned down to flattened discs, their minimal light low and unsteady.

At some point—was it then?—I remember watching Eva and Gabe and thinking they didn't just love each other, they *liked* each other. I watched him give a tug on her ponytail and how she swiveled to meet his eyes; I thought of how they'd slapped five at dinner and said in unison, "Go team Burns!" whenever one of them said something witty.

Go team Burns!

A year later, and the phrase echoes; it makes me ache.

Across from me, Gabe leaned back and stared up at the sky, which was glimmering with stars. Did he really hate his job? I wondered, then pushed the thought away. The night was too perfect. I didn't want anything to ruin it. I think we all felt that way. Maybe it was the fact that the deck really did feel like a stage set, the sky a velvet curtain; maybe we were all playacting a little, wanting to always be the people we were that night—generous, elegant, carefree—without secrets or damage. Maybe that was why, when Annabelle raised her martini glass yet again and said, "Here's to a season of perfect happiness!," no one made fun of the sentiment or pretended to gag because it was so sweet. We lifted our glasses.

By the time we left, we had the summer planned: We'd have picnics at the lake, go to Chicago for my show. We'd see

Scott at Hattie's on Fridays when we could get a sitter—that was a given—but Saturdays . . . Saturdays would be ours. We'd take turns hosting barbecues, dress up, make the nights elegant the way we imagined Alfred and Lynn would have. Heels and pearls, candles and croquet, cigars and old-fashioned drinks: gin rickeys, Rob Roys. "What the hell is a gin rickey?" someone laughed. "I guess we'll find out," someone else said.

I've thought a lot about that night. I suppose we all have. "Give me a break," Erik said not long ago. "Declaring a season of perfect happiness? Come on!"

"Season of perfect happiness, my ass," Gabe will scoff. "Kind of like calling the *Titanic* unsinkable right before it hit the iceberg."

I hate hindsight. I always have. Probably because I spent so many years living with the litany of everything I should have done and should have known and should have felt—and to what end? There's something smug about hindsight, something cheap.

The Lunts gave their lives to performances, made their home an elaborate stage set because they believed their lives *should* be a performance—something created with practice and care and attention to every detail. It's easy to call it false, and people did, but I think of how we arrange flowers and dinner parties and the furniture in our houses, and no one says our homes are superficial or fake for our having done this. No one pities us for trying so hard to create an ideal. What they think, instead, is that our homes matter deeply to us.

Why shouldn't it be this way with our lives?

This isn't to say that behind the scenes, things weren't fragile and messy that summer. *We* were fragile and messy.

And yet, we loved each other and fought for each other, and I will never accept, as people want to insist, that we were better off after our lives unraveled because at least everything was out in the open then, at least everything was honest.

I might have believed that once.

Sure, maybe the truth set us free. But it also broke us.

I love that Annabelle worked so hard to create that night—that magical candlelit deck and the sky ricocheting with stars and our laughter sailing out across the darkness. Even now, *especially* now, I love her determination to hold us all together despite the secrets and the betrayals. I love that she wanted so badly to salvage the best of us, to focus on what was good in our friendships. And if there was something sad in this, then it was sad in the way the string ensemble aboard the *Titanic,* who played their instruments as the ship was sliding beneath the ocean, was sad.

It was also brave.

And beautiful.

Sometimes I think our summer of perfect happiness was also a kind of requiem, and we played for as long as we could.

PART IV

EDITH: *I don't believe I should mind so very much now [dying]. You see, we could never in our whole lives be happier than we are now, could we?*

EDWARD: *Darling, there are different sorts of happiness.*

EDITH: *This is the best sort.*

—Noël Coward, *Cavalcade,* act 1, scene 1

CHAPTER 32

I've been walking the grounds at Ten Chimneys. The morning sunlight twines through the trees like yellow ribbon. Birds twitter overhead. My footsteps are quiet, the paths covered with cedar chips that are swollen and soft with dampness.

It's late October and not just chilly but cold today, thick Wisconsin clouds scudding across the sky like a school of predatory fish. Goose bumps rise along my arms. The paths twist along the bowl-shaped depressions of the kettles, then rise over the moraines to the Lunts' house. Tourist buses will pass by starting at ten and I'll see a docent standing up front, as Eva once did, telling the guests how back in the seventies Lynn and Alfred donated this land—thirty-eight acres—to the town of Genesee Depot.

Facts, I think bleakly. Like wooden sticks. People believe if they rub them together long enough, they can find the truth.

Yesterday, I sold *Weathering,* the collage I started last summer when Kelly was here. The piece wasn't really about weather but about secrets or damage or . . . maybe truth. Are secrets always true? Always damaging? Or are they only damaging when revealed?

Does any life exist without secrets?

Spencer started high school last month. His latest fascination is volcanoes. Did we know lava could travel 450 miles an hour? That 80 percent of Earth was formed by volcanoes? Or that when Mount Tambora erupted in Indonesia in 1815, the volcanic ash spewed into the atmosphere blocked the sun for so long that it was called "the year without a summer"?

The year without a summer.

That's how this past summer felt.

It's impossible not to compare it to the one before.

Yesterday I read that the summer of 2006, "our season of perfect happiness," was the second-hottest summer in 112 years. Temperatures broke records that had stood since the Dust Bowl. It surprises me, for in memory, even the weather was idyllic: skies like backdrops on stage sets, nights like a giant pinball machine, the silver ball of the moon ricocheting against the clouds.

And yet, we must have felt the press of heat on those nights sitting on each other's back decks, must have complained about the humidity, felt the heaviness in our bodies. Or did we really not notice?

The actor Peter Brooks once compared the Lunts' performances to one of Seurat's pointillist paintings: "Each little dot is not art but the whole is magnificent." A description not only of their acting but of their lives—and maybe ours too last summer.

Only in stepping back can I see the whole.

We had our Saturday nights, taking turns at each other's houses. Annabelle and I went shopping and I bought three full-skirted dresses—a black and white polka-dot with a pink sash; a sleeveless orange with matching earrings; white serge patterned with big red poppies. "Your party frocks," Erik called them. I loved the look in his eyes when I modeled them, and I loved how I felt wearing them.

One night, we attended an event for the children's theater camp Ten Chimneys ran. The party was held on the back lawn, complete with a topiary garden, of a nineteenth-century mansion overlooking Lake Michigan. Props from stage sets were scattered about: A leather armchair and ottoman beneath a maple tree. A coatrack at the entrance to the drive. A silver tea service balanced on the wooden seat of a rope swing.

The theater kids had been asked: If you could trade lives with any famous person, whose life would you want? They'd read biographies of their person, designed costumes and props, memorized mannerisms and speeches. And so, scattered about the grounds were Harry Houdinis and Abe Lincolns, Michael Jordan, Beyoncé, Georgia O'Keeffe, Serena Williams.

"Who would you guys be?" Annabelle asked that Saturday night. "Anyone in history." We were at our house, a hurricane lamp throwing light across the table. "I can't decide between Stevie Nicks and Chrissie Hynde."

"Really?" Eva knit her brows. "But you don't sing."

"I wish I could, though. I wish I had something that was wholly mine, like you guys do." She nodded at me and Eva. "Something no one could ever take."

"You have your children," I said.

"Who will be grown and gone before I can blink."

Eva chose Meryl Streep.

Erik, Alfred Lunt.

"Could you be *any* more predicable?" Eva ruffled his hair, and he swatted her away.

Scott wanted Elvis. "Skinny Elvis! Not that fat dude in the white jumpsuit."

"Neil Armstrong," Gabe said. "To stand up there . . ." He lifted his eyes to the moon, partially hidden behind clouds as thin as silk scarves. "I can't imagine anything more incredible."

"All right, Claire," Annabelle said.

Scott did a drumroll on the tabletop.

"Wait," I said. "What if I don't want any other life?"

"Nice try," Annabelle said. She was happy. This was her kind of conversation: What was your best age? What quality of your parents' do you have that you wish you didn't? If you could have one day to live again . . . "Come on. You've *never* wanted to be someone else?"

More times than I could count, I thought, but now that I had *this* life with *this* husband and *these* friends, I wouldn't have traded it for anything. There was no way I could say this, though. *Oh God, that's so sweet I'm going to be sick,* Annabelle would have said, and Scott would have suggested I hadn't drunk enough. Their teasing would have been good-natured, but I didn't want to make light of it. Maybe because I'd already had the chance to trade one life in for another, I didn't want to joke about trading it in again. "Amelia Earhart," I finally said, grabbing the first name that popped to mind, although later, it would occur to me that she too had disappeared from her own life.

"An aviatrix, huh?" Gabe teased, and then someone was asking another question—*If you could have any superpower . . .*

Days, then weeks, and suddenly it was July Fourth, the peak at the top of the roller coaster we would soon begin speeding down. We spread blankets on the hill near the elementary school to watch the fireworks (away from the crowds at the Expo Center). Other families had the same idea. Flashlights, voices, a girl's laughter lifted in the dark. And then the fireworks began, exploding over us as I hugged Hazel and Annabelle held Phoebe and Erik held Spencer, all of us gazing up, families around us oohing and ahhing.

Spencer told me that a day on Venus lasts almost as long as a year on Earth, and I recall all the times I wished that summer that our days could last so long. The six of us would be sitting out back at one of our houses, and it would be one of those perfect Wisconsin nights where we were all silent, staring up, a little drunk maybe, but content, so content, and someone would comment on how fast the days were going, and despite whatever fun we were having, despite the happiness I know was real, I sensed there was a finite number of days when we could be happy—maybe when anyone could—and ours would soon be gone.

CHAPTER 33

Kelly was everywhere that summer. Strangers chatted about her at the grocery store or the bank in the same way they'd comment on the weather or how the Brewers were doing. Union House created a drink called the "Sparkling KJ" (Ketel One vodka, Chambord, and a splash of J Vineyards sparkling wine), and in the front yard of a nondescript ranch house on Highway 83, the main road to Ten Chimneys, a hand-lettered poster counted down the days until she arrived.

Because of her, Alfred and Lynn were everywhere that summer too. "At least people know who they are!" Eva said one Saturday night. "You wouldn't believe how many times, in the middle of a tour, someone asks who the Lunts are."

"Wait." Gabe, who had been moving around their table filling wineglasses, stopped midpour. "People shell out thirty-five bucks to see Ten Chimneys without knowing who the Lunts are?"

"All the time." Eva shrugged. "It's nuts."

"Deanna says people constantly stop by the diner to ask what Ten Chimneys is, and when she tells them, they're like, *What? Who?* Apparently, that's happened a lot less since . . ."

Annabelle glanced at me apologetically. "Well, since KJ agreed to come."

I felt the covert looks they were shooting across the candlelit table, but what could I say? I dreaded her coming, and they all knew it.

"Don't you just love how every time someone mentions Kelly Jarrell, the room falls silent?" Gabe said.

"That's not true!" Annabelle turned to me. "Is it?"

"Of course it is," Gabe said.

Eva looked stricken. "I keep forgetting how difficult this must be for you, Claire."

"It's fine," I said. "The fact that Kelly's everywhere actually makes it feel almost normal."

I wanted so badly to believe this that sometimes I think I did.

And it was true I no longer felt my stomach dip every time I saw her name or heard yet another person weigh in on what play she might choose for the final performance. Gabe and Erik both wanted *There Shall Be No Night,* mostly because it was such an important play, but the rest of us were rooting for a comedy. "Kelly Jarrell is as much drama as I can take," I laughed whenever the subject came up.

"It's all I can do not to pull over and rip that sign off the lawn," I told Annabelle one morning when I stopped by after my run.

Nineteen more days until KJ!

"Ha! Let's do it," she said. "Pick a night. We'll be stealth." She grinned. "You always wear black anyway."

"I love you for offering," I said. "Even as a joke."

She arched one eyebrow. "Who's joking?"

The next day the poster was gone. Annabelle feigned

innocence, but Saturday night, she gave me a gift-wrapped box. Inside was the sign cut into pieces.

"Christ, Annabelle. That's trespassing!" Gabe exploded. "Not to mention theft."

"It's a poster board!"

"It's also a class A misdemeanor!"

Except for Gabe, we were all grinning. I couldn't believe Annabelle had done this, but I loved her for it. She stopped at absolutely nothing when it came to the people she cared about, and I felt—as I had a hundred times before—how lucky I was to be one of those people.

"You're a nut, Annabelle." Eva was laughing so hard she was crying. She looked at Scott. "Did you know about this?"

"Shit," he said. "I was the getaway driver."

Two days later, on my way to Ten Chimneys, I saw that the sign was back. *15 days!*

Erik's assistant, Christine, was leaving when I arrived, carrying her baby boy in a sling against her chest, a diaper bag over one shoulder "Well, it's happened," she said as she unlocked her car. "Your husband is officially besotted."

"We all are," I said, stroking Max's chubby ankle with my index finger. Someone had handed him to me at his christening in February. It was the first time I'd held an infant since Lucy. Afterward, despite a nasty mix of rain and snow, I went for such a long run that the sky had turned dark and Erik was about to come looking for me. I hadn't known what else to do except keep moving, as if I could outrun the memory of holding my own child.

"Oh, it's not my son your husband's besotted with." Christine placed a hand lightly on her baby's bald head, and I thought how pretty she looked, soft and rosy-cheeked, her face still carrying the roundness of pregnancy. "It's Kelly."

"Kelly?" I shook my head as if I'd heard wrong. "What do you mean?"

"I know, right? He's been totally blasé about her for months, but they had quite the tête-à-tête this morning on the phone! I guess she told him she was one hundred percent ours while she was here. Anything we wanted her to do—talk to donors, PR—all we had to do was ask."

"Wow. That's . . . it's great!" I knew Erik had been in contact with her assistant, but to actually talk with Kelly? I couldn't stop blinking. I'm not sure what else I said. Probably another comment about Max, who made me ache so much I couldn't see straight.

I'd carried Lucy against my chest in a Snugli like that.

A few minutes later, walking across the parking lot, I was aware of holding myself erect, of taking shallow breaths, as if I were injured. I felt ambushed—*They had quite the tête-à-tête this morning*—though it was hardly surprising that they'd spoken by phone. And why did it matter? In two weeks, they'd be speaking in person.

Upstairs, the offices were dark, low evening light falling in long slants through the tall windows. The sound of a vacuum echoed from below. "There you are," Erik called from his office at the end of the hallway, and rose from his desk. He turned to grab his jacket from the back of the chair, saying over his shoulder, "You still want to go to the—" *Y,* he was about to say, but stopped, his smile fading. "What's wrong?"

"Nothing. I just . . . I saw Christine."

"She told you I talked to Kelly." He came around me to shut the door.

I nodded, tears brimming. "I don't know why I'm upset."

"It's okay." Erik held my elbows, bending at the knees to meet my eyes. "Talk to me."

But before I could, my face crumpled and I was crying, hard painful sobs that seemed to erupt from my chest. "You're *besotted*?" I wept. I felt humiliated even as I was saying it and immediately plopped down into the upholstered chair behind me, unable to look at Erik. Of course he liked her. Everyone did. She was smart and funny and kind, and she made people feel good about themselves. She'd once made *me* feel good about myself. The thought only made me cry harder. I felt betrayed and hurt, but mostly, I was just so tired of holding it all in, feigning amusement and nonchalance and cracking jokes and pretending Kelly's coming here was okay.

Outside the sun was collapsing in a dramatic orange blaze, the trees cutting a jagged line against the darkening sky. I didn't know how to explain the treachery—and I knew that wasn't a fair word, but it's the one that came to mind. The treachery wasn't that Erik liked Kelly but the fact that he *could* talk with her. It felt like one more thing in a vast list of things I'd relinquished my right to without understanding how much I was giving up: Not knowing where my daughter lived, if she was healthy, happy—why couldn't I have had that much? And not being honest about my past, constantly lying to my friends because I was so terrified they'd reject me as Kelly had. Not holding a baby in my arms until I'd held Max! I knew it wasn't fair to blame Kelly, knew the only person to blame was myself, but in that moment it seemed that if only Kelly had forgiven me, my entire life would have been different.

Erik squatted in front of me. "I hate seeing you torn up like this."

I inhaled a ragged breath. The light angling through the window shone in his face, which was so marked with worry it made me start crying all over again. "I don't know why I keep crying," I sobbed.

"You've probably needed to do this since March."

But he was wrong. I'd needed to do it for thirteen years. Since the day I relinquished my child.

The letter from Kelly arrived a week later.

CHAPTER 34

Claire,

I imagine it's as shocking for you to be reading this letter as it is for me to be writing it, though I can't imagine anything more shocking than learning you are married to Erik Whitaker. Had I known I never would have accepted the position with Ten Chimneys. But you knew this, didn't you? And now it's too late to cancel.

Why do this? In what universe would the kind of chance meeting you must have imagined be okay? There is no universe, Claire. I'm not trying to be cruel—I know you've suffered too—but I will not talk to you about Lucy, which is the only reason I can imagine you'd go to all this trouble. I haven't even mentioned this to Nick. He's happy, and after all he's been through, he deserves to stay that way.

As to your husband's lack of forthrightness: It's beyond unprofessional. That's all I'll say. It's not my intention to make waves for him—or you. My therapist, who believes things happen for a reason (I don't), thinks seeing you will allow me to finally lock the door I've been trying to close for sixteen years. If so, maybe I'll be able to look at all this with a bit more generosity.

I assume we'll be seeing each other during the fellowship, and of course we'll be cordial, but I'd prefer we keep our distance as much as possible.

Kelly

Erik was sitting across from me at the kitchen table. I hadn't looked at him the entire time I was reading; I'm not sure I breathed. At first, he'd been moving around, silently unpacking the groceries I'd just brought in, although I felt his eyes on me as I read. Finally, he pulled out the chair opposite mine, his knee jiggling, and waited for me to look up.

"So, what's the verdict?" His face was ashen.

I handed him the letter, my hands shaking.

I couldn't decipher my feelings any better than I could her words. Surprise, relief, disappointment, shame—and not in that order, because there was no order—had slammed into each other, all in the space of a typed page. Not that I could have identified a single one of those emotions. I had no language for what I felt, which was the equivalent of mixing too many colors and ending up with mud.

I'd gone straight from running to the grocery store that morning and had just finished hauling everything inside when I heard Erik call from the foyer. He sounded upset. As soon as he walked into the kitchen, he handed me the letter. "This was on my desk."

"What is it?" My name was typed on the envelope; a New York return address.

"It's from Kelly," he said.

Abruptly, I sat at the table. "She knows I'm here?"

Now, as I watched him skim over the page, I couldn't remember a thing I'd read. *She knows I'm here* was as far as I could get.

When Erik finished, he blew out a big puff of air, leaned

back, and stared up at the ceiling. "Jesus," he said. "What the hell were we thinking?"

"Well, certainly not that she'd believe we set this whole thing up to . . . *what?* Lure her out here?" My heart wouldn't stop racing. "We have to explain to her," I said. "Can you?"

"I can try."

"Once she understands . . . There's nothing underhanded here. I was scared. I still am."

"I know, Claire. I do. I just feel like a jerk. I am a jerk. And don't get me wrong. I'll never understand her cruelty to you, but with me and the foundation, she's been generous and aboveboard, and I've basically been lying to her." He looked at me bleakly. "Why did we think she wouldn't find out you were here?"

"I'm not going to see her, remember?"

He nodded.

"We were never going to blindside her. I know that's how it looks, but this wasn't a setup. And once you tell her I'd planned to be gone—and I will, I'll go to Chicago—won't that help?"

"Maybe." His face was tense.

"You didn't do anything wrong, Erik."

"I know, but that's not how it looks."

"I'm sorry," I said. "You wanted me to contact her from the beginning."

He nodded again. And then, "You know what?" He slapped his hands on his knees. "We're not doing this. We're not going to beat ourselves up. It's done. We made what we thought was the best decision based on what we knew." He glanced around the room as if trying to get his bearings: the half-full coffeepot, my purse on the counter, the cutting board angled into the sink. After a minute, he reached across the table for my hand. "Maybe it's for the best. She knows you're here, she has no desire to cause trouble. What else do we want?" He searched my eyes. "Do you feel a tiny bit of relief?"

"I don't know what I feel." I paused. "Are *you* relieved?"

"Not really." He sighed. "Actually, yes. This could be a hundred times worse. She could have canceled or gone to the board." He raked his hands through his hair. "Jesus." He was jiggling his leg again. "Who knows . . . Maybe something good will come of it. Maybe seeing each other will help you too."

"What? No." I pulled my hand from his. "I definitely don't want to see her. Especially now."

He was shaking his head.

"*Why?* She doesn't want to see me either, Erik." I looked at him incredulously. "That bit about her therapist was purely to let me know how much *she's* been suffering. It's bullshit."

"You don't know that, Claire."

"Kelly's pissed, Erik."

"Fine, but she's also geared up to see you—"

"Well, too bad." I sat back against the chair. "Even if we give her the benefit of the doubt, even if she's really making the best of this, I guarantee it's going to set her off, seeing me with you or with our friends or, I don't know, laughing with Christine. . . ." I thought of that day on the boardwalk, her screaming *How dare you* over and over. "What if she causes a scene?"

"She won't."

"You don't even know her!"

"I know enough to say that the jury's still very much out on her wanting to see you, Claire. If she really didn't want to, she could have said that. But if anything, she practically handed you a script for how this will go."

After Erik left, I didn't move from the table. I felt the kind of adrenaline dump you feel after a near miss—the car swerving into your lane, the dog darting in front of you, the slam of brakes. My legs wouldn't stop trembling. I kept hearing Erik saying *what's the verdict* and *the jury's still out,* and all I could think was that Kelly had been judge and jury in my life before, and here we were again, all these years later, and I was still on trial. I knew I should feel relieved that she had no intention of "making waves," but what I felt was rage.

I kept trying to summon gratitude. She didn't have to send the letter. Erik was right: She could have canceled, could have written to the board, either of which might have cost him his job. But knowing this didn't help. I resented that this woman I hadn't seen in over thirteen years, this woman who had nothing to do with my life, still held so much power over it. Over me.

I reread the letter, slowly, and then again, and each time, the blades felt sharper: She never would have accepted the position if she'd known I was here, and her *I know you've suffered too* infuriated me. *Too?* Really? How had she suffered in the last sixteen years? What had *she* lost?

I pushed up from the table, needing to shower, to rinse off the sweat that had dried into a salty residue on my skin. I wished I could rinse off the skin itself. The kitchen was bright with midmorning sunlight, the day ticking by. But I just stood there, feeling angry and sorry for myself and panicked at the thought of seeing her again. And no, I did not feel relieved, not even a little, though why not? Wasn't this what I'd wanted? To not have to cower and hide and run from my own life as I had all those years ago? I didn't have to go to Chicago. I could see Erik in his tux at the gala, delivering the opening remarks, making the audience care about the theater and the Lunts, his voice crackling with passion as he spoke about why theater was necessary to society, had always been necessary. And I could see Eva in *Quadrille,* the play Kelly had chosen. *This is good,* I told myself. But the words felt hollow.

On the counter by the hallway, Erik had lined up items to bring upstairs: toilet paper, ponytail holders for the girls, deodorant for Spencer. Something about those ordinary items comforted me, even if it was small comfort. Knowing who needed what, keeping track of the little things that made our lives run smoothly.

Upstairs, I busied myself with mundane tasks—making beds, emptying the trash cans in the bathrooms, refolding and hanging damp towels. The house felt so still, beams of dust-laden sunlight falling into the rooms. I knew I was stalling. Anyone who's been in therapy for half a minute knows anger is about survival, a way to protect ourselves from what we can't bear to acknowledge. I knew I didn't want to feel whatever was coming.

By the time I got out of the shower, the anger was gone. In its place came the avalanche of everything else the letter had evoked: my bottomless grief about losing Lucy and my outsized disappointment that Kelly's coming to Ten Chimneys really was a coincidence. I'd wanted my mom to be right; I'd hoped Kelly wanted to reconcile. And I felt foolish for wanting something she'd never even considered, and worse, didn't want. *Seeing you will allow me to finally lock the door I've been trying to close for sixteen years.* I hadn't wanted that door closed, I realized. All my enormous pathetic hope, which I hadn't known until that moment I was holding.

I sat on the edge of the bed, wrapped in a towel, hair dripping onto my collarbone, and read the letter again. *I know you've suffered too.* The hole in the center of my chest opened wider every time I read that sentence. Had she been suffering? I thought of how there was never any mention of a significant other in the tabloids, of how at the Emmys she'd walked the red carpet alone. I'd made so many assumptions. Had she ever been in love? Ever come close to getting married? She'd turned forty in May. Had she wanted children? I couldn't recall her ever saying she did, but that was before she fell in love with Lucy.

Yes, the barbs were there, and they stung, but what hurt more was realizing how much time and energy *I'd* wasted all these months—God, all these years—imagining her as some all-powerful Oz-like character and never once considering that maybe behind the smoke screen of her rage, behind the special effects of her fame, she was just an ordinary woman whose world had also been upended sixteen years ago. At least at first, she had tried to help me, hadn't she? All those visits in the hospital, sitting with me for hours, my mom said, showing me photos of Lucy and trying to bring me back. But I was so gone, drugged on antipsychotics and antidepressants and whatever else they'd given me to blunt the truth of what I had done to my child. Kelly hadn't had that luxury, though. Her niece was on life support, her brother was broken, and maybe she was too.

It was easier to forget this. And whatever hold she had over my life now—that was all my doing. I was the one with the secrets; I was the one not being honest about my past, which was the only reason she had any power over me at all.

CHAPTER 35

I knew what flight she was on—American, number 827 from LaGuardia—and when it was due to arrive: 1:58 P.M. All morning I was hyperaware of the fact that she would be in Wisconsin by that afternoon. Moving through my routines, I felt as if I were watching myself from a distance, narrating my actions in my head. *Now I'm folding laundry; now I'm reheating my coffee.* And pushed right up against those things: *She's boarding the plane. She's somewhere over Ohio by now.*

I felt as I did when I'd had too much caffeine, my skin prickly, a buzzing in my chest.

I kept checking the flight on my computer, and finally, at 1:55, I saw "Arrived." *She's here,* I thought, and *Now it begins,* like it was some stern voice-over in a *Dateline* investigation. Standing in front of the refrigerator, picking out cashews from a container of kung pao chicken, I imagined how I'd make fun of myself to Erik later, but even then, I couldn't stop: *Now I'm in the kitchen and imagining telling Erik. . . .*

"What can I do?" my mother asked when I called her. I'd carried the phone outside into the furnace blast of mid-August heat and sat on the porch steps, the concrete warm through my running shorts.

"I don't know what I need." I laid my forehead against my

upraised knees. "I wish these two weeks were already over." Erik had phoned Kelly the day we got her letter, explaining that we'd been shocked to learn she had been chosen to teach the fellowship, that I'd planned to be out of town, that there'd been no setup. But he wasn't sure she believed him. And why would she? He'd been lying all along.

"These two weeks will be gone before you know it," my mom said.

The next afternoon, I went to Annabelle's to watch the kids until Scott got home. She and Erik were attending a dinner for Kelly, held by one of the board members. "I can't believe I'm going to be in the same room with KJ," she kept saying. I was sitting on her bed, watching her scoop her thick hair into a loose ponytail. She looked pretty, gold chandelier earrings brushing her collarbones. But after the tenth time of her prefacing whatever she was about to say with "I know you probably don't want to hear this" or "I know you dislike her," I told her to stop. "I don't dislike her, Annabelle. I don't even know her anymore."

The girls were watching the original *Grease* with Olivia Newton-John and John Travolta, and after Annabelle left, I perched on the arm of the sofa and watched for a minute. Kelly and I had been twelve when the movie came out in 1978. We must have seen it a dozen times and played the album endlessly. She was Rizzo; I was Goody Two-shoes Sandra Dee.

I was too restless to watch, so I got Spencer to bake with me. He'd decided he was going to be a meteorologist *and* a chef when he grew up. We made applesauce cookies—no flour, no butter, no sugar, so he could eat them. My job was to read the instructions while he mixed and measured with the precision of a scientist. He looked so much like his dad, all elbows as he stooped over counters too low for his gangly body.

We played chess while waiting for the timer to ring, the room filling with the smell of spices. The sound of John Travolta and Olivia Newton-John singing "You're the One That I Want" echoed from the family room. I could remember so clearly being twelve. I never questioned that my life would be any different; I didn't want it to be. I had the best friend in the world, we lived at the beach, and our parents adored us. I'd just gotten my first pair of high heels (for our seventh-grade dance) and on special occasions I was allowed to wear lip gloss, but I was still such a child. I used to arm-wrestle my dad, and on Sunday mornings when I stayed at Kelly's, we'd have pancake-eating contests. Once after we ate a dozen pancakes each, I remember her mother telling us, "You girls don't always need to eat until you're full, you know." Kelly just laughed and grabbed another pancake, but I remember feeling confused and embarrassed. Why wouldn't you eat until you were full? Wasn't that the point? I never could have fathomed then how betrayed I would one day be by my body, all the ways I would learn to not take up space in the world, not stand up for myself, not fight for what I wanted.

Ever since Kelly's letter, I'd been thinking of those dark days after the first hospital when I'd been so desperate to bond with Lucy, and though Nick was always there, he never helped me. He never got down on the carpet with us and played Duck Duck Goose with her stuffed animals, never smiled at my attempted silly antics, never showed Lucy it was okay to love me again. He'd sit nearby skimming one of his surfing magazines, but the whole time, I felt his impatience, his judgment. Maybe he couldn't join me, maybe he was doing his best, but why had I just accepted this? And where was Kelly? Or Nick's mom?

Or—and this was the most painful question—where was my mom? I don't blame her—she was desperate for me to have time with my girl—but I blame myself: Why had I never once said, "I'm failing, and I need your help"? When and where did I learn to be so silent? It wasn't just about the accident. I'd been this way my whole life.

The next day, Erik left early for the opening-night gala, his tuxedo in a garment bag. He hadn't talked much to Kelly the night before, he said; they'd been seated at opposite ends of the table, but he didn't think there was anything to worry about.

I spent the afternoon pacing and glancing at the clock in our bedroom. It seemed to move in impossibly tiny increments: two minutes, three minutes, five. I'd flat-ironed my hair and put on jewelry, but it was too early to get dressed.

In front of the large mirror over the bureau, I stared at myself, trying to see what she would see in a few hours. I was wearing one of Erik's T-shirts, and though I could take in the details—silver teardrop earrings, matching necklace, mascara—I felt I was looking at a stranger. My dress was laid out on the bed, the same dress I'd worn at my Chicago opening last week. It was the most expensive piece of clothing I'd ever bought, a navy gown so covered in beads, it was heavy. "Like those lead vests you wear at the dentist when they're doing X-rays," I'd commented as Erik zipped me up the week before. I'd felt regal in that dress, and happy and successful—the show had been amazing!—but now, I worried. Maybe the dress was too showy. I didn't want Kelly to look at me and think my life was wonderful—*How dare you!*—didn't want her to think I'd gotten over Lucy, whatever that even meant, because I hadn't.

"Stop it," I told myself. "What are you supposed to do? Wear a mourning veil, rend your sleeves?"

Yes, a small voice inside of me insisted. *Yes.*

I thought about the sumptuary laws Eva—or maybe Erik—had mentioned one Saturday night. I forget why it came up, but whoever it was—probably Eva—described how, during Shakespeare's time, there were laws restricting the "sumptuousness of dress." It was a crime to dress like someone of a higher social class, a crime to pretend to be someone you were not. We laughed—such quaint customs people had! And then the discussion devolved into Gabe and Erik ribbing Scott for being such a fastidious dresser—*ironed* jeans ("You could injure someone with those creases, dude!"). We were all laughing, but I remember thinking that behind those laws was real fear, the fear that someone wasn't who they said they were.

I felt off-balance, that feeling of stepping down to find there is no stair. I told myself that once I got through the reception, once Kelly and I saw each other and whatever was going to happen either did or didn't, I would get my equilibrium back. Except this wasn't about Kelly, was it? It was about the fact that there were two versions of me—Claire then and Claire now—and I couldn't align one with the other. Who was I?

I checked the clock again. Eva and Gabe were picking me up. I took a deep breath and glanced around the room. Everything was in its place: the bed made, clothes put away, my normally haphazard pile of books in a neat pyramid on the nightstand. I'd even dusted the photographs on the bureau: Erik and me on our wedding day; the kids on the trampoline midjump; the six of us this summer on Eva and Gabe's back deck, the sky orange with dusk. The men in Hawaiian shirts, Annabelle, Eva, and me in sundresses. I loved these photos, our happiness captured and framed, though I wished Lucy's picture were here too. I knew it wasn't possible. The girls would demand, *Who is that baby?* And I'd end up lying yet again, the lies like bright scarves pulled from a magician's hat, one after the other after the other, endlessly.

And I didn't need a photo. I had hundreds in my head: How she'd be sitting in her crib in the mornings with her wild hair swooping so preposterously in different directions that I'd burst into laughter. Or how she'd fasten her big unblinking eyes on mine when she was nursing, the damp weight of her starfish hand on my breast. Even when there weren't specific memories, I felt her presence. And I saw her. Everywhere. In the cluster of blond sixteen-year-old girls at the mall or with their boyfriends at Kopp's, getting off school buses in field hockey or track or soccer uniforms, ordering fancy coffees at Starbucks.

I paced back to the mirror and stared once more at my reflection. I was jittery but no longer filled with dread. I wanted to see Kelly. I wanted her to see me. That was as far as I could get. If she spoke to me, I had no idea what I would say. Everything sounded wrong. "It's good to see you" wasn't exactly true, and "I watched every episode of *Widows*" sounded too fawning.

Maybe just "I can't believe you're here."

CHAPTER 36

I stood outside the car and inhaled a deep breath as Gabe opened the door for Eva. The parking lot was on a hill overlooking the Program Center, visible through the full-leafed trees. *She's in there,* I thought as Gabe offered me his arm and the three of us joined the throng of people making their way down the curving path lined with solar lights. The women stepped carefully in their heels, lifting their long shimmery dresses so they wouldn't trip. I drew in another breath, grateful for Gabe's arm and Eva's chatter.

Inside the lobby, sound bounced off the high windows: piano music, laughter, people greeting each other in exaggerated voices. Eva and Gabe were immediately tugged away by her theater people. "You okay?" Gabe mouthed, and I nodded, relieved to have a moment alone. I scanned the room for Kelly, though I assumed she'd be backstage, preparing for her speech. Erik wasn't out front either, doing his usual meet and greet, which surprised me, but then Jo Balistreri, one of the docents, said, "He's here somewhere, but he hasn't stopped moving for a minute." Someone else sailed by with a "Great dress, Claire," flung out like a flower. Ken Talevi touched my arm and said, "We missed you at dinner last night."

And then we were entering the theater. Around me the

shush of gowns and rustle of programs, the creaking of seats. Nervously, I made my way to where Annabelle and Scott were sitting with the other board members.

I know Erik gave the opening remarks. I know the artistic director introduced Kelly. But I can't say I heard it. Suddenly, there was thunderous applause and she was striding onto the stage, face tilted to the rafters, arms spread, as if offering up the applause to Alfred and Lynn. She looked nothing like she had on *Widows,* where her dark hair had been straightened and she wore jeans, ballet flats, and one of her "late husband's" T-shirts. Here, her hair was big and curly and she wore a slim-fitting black gown that looked like a tuxedo—a high-necked white collar and black bow tie, and, though it was sleeveless, white cuffs at her wrists. She was stunning and elegant and taller than I remembered, and she wasn't just pretty but beautiful.

We were sitting in the front row—Erik had slipped into his seat once Kelly began talking—and though she glanced our way, Erik said the stage lights were too bright to see anything. Still, my face felt as if it were in a vise, every muscle straining to hold my expression steady. The rest of me wouldn't stop trembling. It seemed incredible and impossible that this statuesque, sophisticated, accomplished woman was the girl I'd grown up with in a Delaware beach town nine hundred miles away. This was the girl who'd accidentally knocked out one of my baby teeth while doing cartwheels and, frightened she'd get into trouble, tried to glue it with Elmer's—and I let her! The maid of honor in my first wedding and Nick's little sister and Lucy's aunt, Lucy's godmother.

But she was also KJ. She'd been on the cover of *People* and *Vanity Fair* and had starred on Broadway. And just as I couldn't make the two versions of me align, I couldn't connect the different versions of her either.

She was talking about the Lunts, but I only vaguely heard the words. Mostly, I was focused on her—her quick, fluid gestures, more contained than I remembered, and I imagined she'd been coached to not use her hands so much. We were sitting close enough to see her face, that twitch of her lips when she was about to say something humorous—she was so familiar still! It filled me with such longing—for her, yes, the her I once knew, but for me too, who I once was. That naïve girl who believed her life would work out simply because she wanted it to. That girl—because that's what I was even after I had Lucy—who never had to fight for anything, and so didn't know how when she needed to.

"I've been away from the theater for four years," Kelly said, "and the absence has not been good for my soul." *Soul.* Had the Kelly I'd known ever used that word? She was starting to wrap up her talk and I wanted more than anything for time to slow so I could hold on to this moment when she was so close and whatever else was going to happen hadn't yet.

I'm not sure why, but for the first time since that night four months ago when Erik had told me Kelly was being offered the master teacher position, the fear and grief—even my outlandish hope, which was as treacherous as anything—fell away. And in its place? Gratitude, of all things. Gratitude that Kelly had been my friend. How different I would have been without her. Her choosing me, all those years ago, over the prettier, more popular, more outgoing girls; her standing up for me when those girls didn't invite me to their parties or ignored me in the cafeteria—hadn't she shown me in a thousand ways that I was worth fighting for? Maybe I'd never learned to stand up for myself because for twenty-four years—until Lucy—she'd done it for me. But mostly, I was grateful because without Kelly there would have been no Nick, and without Nick no Lucy, and even knowing the awfulness of everything that happened, it would have been worse if I'd never had that time with Lucy at all.

Gabe handed me a vodka tonic as we watched Kelly make the rounds of the crowded lobby. Bodies angled in her direction. I saw her offer her hand to someone and heard a woman exclaim, "You do not need to introduce yourself to anyone!" Erik was with her, and he looked happy. This was his element, I thought as he bent forward to whisper something to Kelly, then nodded toward Geoff and Bunny Ellacott, who had endowed the fellowship.

"She knows you're here, right?" Gabe said.

"I think so." I couldn't stop watching her.

Around us, conversations lifted and fell: *That's what I thought . . . Apparently, she told him . . . The last time I acted in a play was the third grade. I was a tree.*

"A tree?" Gabe mouthed just as a waiter came by with mini bratwursts in puff pastry. Gabe grabbed one and plunked it in his mouth. I glanced again at Kelly, though I could only see her back. She was standing near the Steinway the foundation had rented for the event. Snippets of Noël Coward songs tendrilled through the conversations.

"There you are!" Annabelle said, edging next to us. She was wearing a high-necked backless red gown. Scott was carrying her heels in one hand, a drink in the other.

"Do you always make your husband follow two steps behind carrying your shoes?" Gabe asked, shifting sideways as someone squeezed by him.

"It's usually three steps behind, sometimes four," Scott laughed.

"It is not!" Annabelle reached over to push a strand of

hair off my shoulder. "So how are you? You look stunning, by the way. You're prettier than she is."

"I don't think so," I said. "But I love you for saying it." We glanced at Kelly again. She and Erik were talking to Dee and Joe Daly, whose restaurant group was providing the food for this event.

Another server came by, offering figs and goat cheese in phyllo dough.

"I could live on these," Annabelle said, taking one.

"That's not food," Gabe scoffed. "It's a decoration."

And then someone—another board member?—was pulling Annabelle away, and Eva was there with two of the fellows. "Claire grew up in the same town as Kelly," she gushed, and I jerked my head up: *What are you doing?*

"No kidding, so you knew her?" one of them asked.

"What was she like?"

And right then, as if she sensed we were talking about her, Kelly glanced over at our little group and our eyes met. She arched an eyebrow and smiled the barest hint of a smile, and for a second, I felt the room careen to a stop the way it would in a movie, everyone freezing in place. She'd flashed me this look a thousand times in classrooms and at parties and across our parents' dinner tables. It was a look that said, *Can you believe this?* or *You doing okay?* or *You ready to blow this Popsicle stand?* She always said that when we were leaving someplace: school, our houses, the restaurant.

You ready to blow this Popsicle stand?

And without thinking, I lifted one shoulder in a shrug and flicked my eyes, as I'd done a zillion times before too. *I can't believe this either; what the hell are we doing here?* And then she turned back to her group and I turned back to Eva, feeling as if I'd just stepped from one of those rides at the state fair that spins you around so fast the centrifugal force pins you to a wall.

I made an excuse about needing to sit down—my feet were killing me!—gave Eva's hand a quick squeeze, and wandered over to the wall of windows that faced the winding path up to the parking lot. The light was fading, although the sky held its color, a deep ultramarine blue. People were leaving, men carrying their jackets over their arms, their white shirts luminescent in the twilight. My heart was pounding. There'd been no animosity in Kelly's look. It had been warm and conspiratorial, and I had been prepared for anything except that.

The tears were there without warning then, and I was pushing my way outside, trying to keep my face composed until I was around the corner of the building, where I leaned over, hand clamped to my mouth to stop the sobs bursting out of me.

Annabelle was suddenly there, offering me a bottle of water, Gabe behind her. I was half crouching against the wall, which was nearly impossible in my gown, and I couldn't stop crying. "Do you want Erik?" Annabelle asked, and I cried harder.

"I'm fine," I kept saying between sobs, "I'm fine," until Gabe said, "You are aware that you're bawling your eyes out, right? That hardly constitutes *fine*."

Annabelle was rubbing my back. "Did something happen with KJ?"

"No." I wiped the heels of my palms over my eyes. "It was just emotional—" She'd been with me in the delivery room. She'd been there the day of the accident. How had I lost her, lost Lucy, lost my whole life?

"Can you go get us some tissues?" Annabelle said to Gabe.

"Tissues? Please. We need paper towels, we need Bounty picker-uppers."

"Stop." I tried to smile, but my face crumpled back into tears.

"Maybe a Shop-Vac," he called over his shoulder.

And then he was gone, and Annabelle was still rubbing my back. The murmur of conversation from the smokers drifted around the corner along with the smell of their cigarettes. The night was pitch-black now except for the intermittent sweep of headlights across the trees as another car left the parking lot. Finally, I stopped crying and slowly straightened up.

Annabelle gently pried my earring free of my dress where it had caught on one of the beads. "I wish you'd talk to us," she said, her hand once again moving in slow soothing circles over my back. "Whatever happened—"

"There was an accident," I choked out. "Someone we both loved . . . she was badly hurt."

Her hand stopped for a beat, then started again. "Kelly blamed you, didn't she?"

"It was my fault."

She didn't say anything for a few seconds, then turned to face me, taking both my hands in hers. I couldn't look at her.

"Even if it *was* your fault," she said, "I don't care. And Eva won't either."

I shook my head. "It's not what you—"

"I don't care," she repeated. "I just hate that you . . . that all summer . . ." Her voice wavered. "You are not going to be alone with this, okay? Do you hear me?"

I knew she didn't understand—she probably thought a car accident and maybe I'd been driving, but it was a start, wasn't it?

I have a daughter.

When I looked at her again, her eyes were filled with tears, and then she was grabbing me in a hug and whispering in my hair, "I mean it, Claire. You are not alone. You have us, and don't you ever forget it."

Before I could respond, Gabe was back with a pile of napkins, saying, "Jeez, break it up, you two," and Annabelle was snatching the napkins and saying, "Give me those," and handing some to me and dabbing at her own eyes, and suddenly, we were all laughing.

When I remember that night, I think of what comics and playwrights understand so well: that laughter is directly related to pain, that comedy and tragedy are just a hair's breadth apart. I picture the three of us—me, Annabelle, and Gabe—each of us carrying such enormous secrets, each of us terrified of all we might lose if those secrets ever came out, and I can't help but wonder if we laughed more that night, if we laughed louder, our voices echoing in the purple-black darkness, because we somehow sensed all the pain that was to follow.

CHAPTER 37

I knew I had to tell Erik what I'd told Annabelle. But not that night. He was too elated, barely finishing his sentences as we rehashed the evening: Who said what and what did I think of the fellows, of Kelly, of her speech—could it have been any more perfect? And woven into every word was his stunned disbelief that after four months of worry, the night had been . . .

"Successful?" I teased. "No, no, no. That was not success; that was magic!"

"Jesus, it was, wasn't it?"

As soon as we got in the car, I told him about the look Kelly and I had exchanged across the room. "It was so strange, but for that moment—not even a few seconds—it was like the old Kelly again, and the old me, and . . ." I shook my head. "I can't believe I'm saying this, but maybe I did need to see her."

"So, her therapist was right?"

"Maybe." Except seeing her wasn't going to help me close any doors. I wanted to fling them open even wider, ask a thousand questions: *Is living in New York as great as you imagined?* And *How is Nick?* And *Do you visit Rehoboth much? Do you ever go by my parents' restaurant?* But mostly, I wanted to ask about Lucy. Was she happy? Was she healthy? And—if I dared—did she know about me?

At home, while Erik heated the pizza—we never ate at these events—I sat in our living room and phoned my mom. "You were right," I said as soon as she picked up. "I'm glad I went."

"Tell me everything," she said. "Start at the beginning."

I settled against the couch, my dress hitched up so that I could sit with my knees tucked to my side. "Well, for one thing, she's beautiful, Mom, which I didn't remember." I pried off my earrings as I spoke, switching the phone from one ear to the other.

"Beautiful no, but definitely striking." She paused. "So how was it? Seeing her?"

"Strange, sad, surreal. She was so . . . she was just *her*; she was Kelly." I smiled into the darkened room. I could hear Erik moving up the stairs: the squeak of the floorboards, and then the sudden blast of voices from the TV in our bedroom before he muted the volume.

"Oh, Claire, I've been hoping. . . . Did you talk to her?"

"There wasn't a chance."

"No, I guess there wouldn't be." I could hear the disappointment in her voice.

"Wait. Why aren't you at the restaurant?" It was only ten her time. She was never home this early.

"I didn't go in tonight."

"What do you mean, you didn't go in? Is everything okay?" I couldn't recall her ever missing a Saturday night at the height of summer.

"Oh, everything's fine. I just . . . I didn't want to miss this call."

Something slipped in me then. "I would have phoned the

restaurant, Mom! I'm not sure why I called you at home to begin with. I wasn't thinking."

"It's okay, sweetie. Really. I just wanted to make sure I could talk to you."

But it made me ache to think of her waiting for my call.

Upstairs, a cop drama was on TV. Erik was snoring. Every light in the room was on, and his paper plate with two pizza crusts sat on the night table. I stood in the doorway watching him. Even in sleep he looked exhausted, and I felt the weight of all he'd borne these last few months because of my past. His worry about Kelly, his inability to be honest with her, that she thought him unprofessional—he deserved none of this. And I'd been too consumed with my own fears to be there for him. Even tonight, we should have been celebrating. I hated that he'd fallen asleep alone. That I'd let him. *I'm sorry,* I apologized silently.

I moved my uneaten pizza to the bureau, put on a T-shirt, then turned out the lights and climbed into bed. For a long time, I stared at the ceiling, trying to quiet my spinning thoughts, but I couldn't shake the unsettled feeling, something tugging at me that I didn't want to know.

Images from the night kept swirling past: Kelly walking onto that stage, regal and beautiful, hands upraised, and then the look we'd exchanged, and Annabelle promising me I didn't have to be alone, and how fierce she was, how protective of me. I heard myself mentioning the accident, and I felt again how much I wanted to tell her about Lucy, how much I needed to. It terrified me, and yet I knew it was the only way I'd ever be whole, the only way I'd ever stop feeling so split in two.

Finally, I gave up on sleep. Downstairs, I heated water for

hot chocolate, then drank it slowly, sitting at the kitchen table in the dark. The small light over the stove glinted off the faucet and the handle of the refrigerator. On the door was a postcard from my show the week before: *Reassembly: The Art of Collage*. My whole life, I thought—and again, felt such unease wash over me—my whole life was about reassembly. My whole life was a collage.

Outside, I stretched my T-shirt over my knees and sat on the porch steps. It was the kind of night I imagined you'd see from an observatory, staring up through the lens of a telescope into a shimmering black galaxy. Beneath the full moon, the yard had taken on a pale blue sheen, making the world seem upside down, so that I felt as if I were sitting in a frozen sky with a lake of darkness overhead. Suddenly, the grief rose up in me so strongly I felt dizzy with it. Grief for Lucy and Nick and Kelly, grief for all their pain, pain I had brought into their lives. And grief for my mom, for her terrible loneliness, and for Erik, for all the hurt I had caused him, or maybe—and I can only say this in retrospect—for all the hurt I must have sensed I was about to cause.

I'm not sure how long I sat there, my heart feeling like an empty cradle as I stared up at the dark sky, the stars winking overhead. I tried to drum up the sense of elation I'd felt driving home, the possibility that maybe I would have a chance to talk to Kelly, maybe I could ask her about Lucy. But what I felt instead was bereft.

"Why?" I spoke the word out loud, needing to hear my own voice. I had been silent for so long.

Later, I would insist that I told Annabelle about Lucy because I had no choice, and because I wanted to be honest, and because I was tired of hiding. Because I trusted her. All of this was true. But mostly, *mostly,* I told her because to not say my daughter's name felt like yet another relinquishing of the most important truth in my life.

I had loved my child. I had loved her. I had loved her. I had loved her.

I still did.

CHAPTER 38

The phone woke us the next morning: Scott asking if we could take the kids; Annabelle didn't feel well, and he had a gig at the lakefront. Sunlight pooled beneath the curtains, the glare too bright on our clock to read the numbers. Erik was lying on his back, one arm holding the phone, the other crossed over his eyes. I leaned up to pull the alarm from the night table and saw it was almost nine. Erik told Scott he'd be right over.

"Annabelle's sick?" She'd seemed so happy last night.

"A migraine." Erik sighed. "I was really looking forward to a day of nothing."

"At least we got to sleep in a little." I pushed myself up to a sitting position. My eyes burned with exhaustion. The sky had been turning light when I came to bed. Too exhausted for sleep, I lay awake, thinking, as I rarely did, about Rehoboth. The briny smell of the boardwalk; Nick surfing, the ocean fiery with sunrise; Kelly and me sitting in beach traffic after school, counting the out-of-state license plates. For the first time since I'd left, I wanted to go back. I'd been afraid of what being there would do to me, afraid of the memories, afraid of the terrible, terrible shame. But I'd had a life there for twenty-four years, a life I loved. I wanted to visit our old house a block from the ocean, and the bungalow on Fourth Street where I'd been Nick's wife and Lucy's mom. I wanted to sit in my dad's restaurant, wanted to walk the boardwalk with my mom. More than anything, that's what I pictured: the two of us walking and talking, holding our to-go coffees, the pink ball of sun popping over the horizon.

I'm ready to go home, I kept thinking, surprised I still thought of it this way. *Home.*

"I woke around two and you were nowhere to be found." Erik glanced at me, squinting one-eyed against the light. "You were up all night, weren't you?" He didn't wait for an answer, just leaned forward, kissed the top of my head, and slid out of the sheets. "You stay put. I'll bring you coffee." He stopped in the doorway. "And then I'll get the hellions while you grab another hour of sleep."

By the time he returned, I was in the kitchen, already on my second cup. Spencer was flapping his arms and pacing in a loop—kitchen, dining room, living room—his body practically vibrating with anxiety over the schedule change. "Everyone get a cooking hat!" Erik ordered as he set the keys on the table, and the kids scampered to their rooms, cheering.

"Really?" I teased as he plunked a Brewers baseball cap over my eyes. "We couldn't have a nice calm morning?"

"Good luck with that." He pulled on a knit Packers beanie with green and yellow pom-poms just as Spencer appeared wearing his foam cheesehead. I couldn't remember when Erik began this practice of everyone wearing a hat when we cooked together, but it was now tradition.

Erik started making pancakes for him and the girls—Phoebe had on her purple bike helmet, Hazel a tiara—while Spence and I made smoothies for the two of us. At one point,

Erik and I glanced at each other across the room, shaking our heads at the chaos: Spencer's shoes—he hated shoes—were kicked off, one under his stool, one by the counter; a baggie of plastic jewelry was on the table; the blender was whirring, pancake batter sizzling, and Hazel and Phoebe were arguing, first over whether a tiara was a hat, and then over whether the napkins should be folded in triangles or rectangles.

"Circles!" Erik cried. "I want circle napkins!" but Phoebe stomped off in tears, saying, "You always make fun of my desires!"

Erik looked at me wide-eyed. *"Desires?"* he mouthed.

Later, Erik took the girls shopping for school shoes, and Spencer and I went to the grocery store. He was still anxious, chewing on the collar of his T-shirt, but as we were pushing our cart across the lot, he reached for my hand. Never mind that he was thirteen now; never mind that he didn't like to be touched. I inhaled a sharp breath and felt something fierce rise up in me. Maybe I didn't deserve this life, but it had been given to me; it was mine.

At home the girls modeled their shoes—Hazel got tan bucks and Phoebe hiking boots. "Do those really count as school shoes?" I whispered to Erik as the girls pranced across the living room, pretending it was a runway.

Erik looked at me in defeat. "She's Annabelle's daughter. You try telling her no."

Annabelle phoned before dinner to say she was feeling better. The girls begged her to come over and see their new shoes, so she promised she and Scott would bring frozen custard for dessert. We ended up having it on the back deck. Scott was sunburned from being outside all afternoon, and although Annabelle looked a little blurry, her face puffy, she'd put on tiny pearl earrings and lipstick.

We talked about the kids' schedule for the week, how great the gala had been the night before, and how impossible it was that summer was almost over. Our season of perfect happiness. Color drained from the sky, and Erik flipped on the outside lights, the grass looking more indigo than green. Bugs flickered in the air.

"We should head out," Scott said, just as we heard a shout from inside the house. Gabe and Eva were hurrying through our kitchen to the deck.

"I got the part!" Eva called before she was even outside.

"You're playing Serena?" Annabelle cried. It had been Lynn Fontanne's role in *Quadrille*. Annabelle jumped up to hug her and then we all did, and Eva was telling us about the afternoon. The fellows had congregated at the lake house where Kelly was staying; a guy from Texas was playing Axel, the role Alfred had played; Kelly had been great, exacting and funny and self-deprecating.

After everyone left, we got the kids in bed and finally collapsed into our own. Erik lifted his arm for me to snuggle against him. It was the first time we'd stopped moving all day. I could have fallen asleep right there, Erik's chest rising and falling, his fingers trailing up and down my arm. Like drifting in a rowboat.

"So, tell me about your mom," he said. "You were on the phone for a while last night."

"My mom." I lifted my head from his chest and sank back into my own pillows. "My mom made me sad, Erik. Really sad."

"Let me guess. Because you and Kelly didn't talk?" He laced his fingers through mine.

"Yeah, there was that. She's so desperate for me to find out about Lucy, and of course I want that too, but . . ." I stopped. "That's not what made me sad. It's how lonely she is,

Erik. She didn't go to the restaurant last night so she wouldn't miss my call. It kills me because I came this close"—I held up my thumb and index finger—"to putting off talking to her until this morning. And then I thought, *God, there's probably been a zillion times when I* have *put it off and I didn't even realize—*" I swallowed. "Her life stopped when I left, and I'm not sure I really knew that before." I stared at our entwined hands. "This is going to sound crazy," I said quietly, "but all day I've had this sense that my mom and I somehow traded places, and I got to go out and build this whole new life in part because she stayed there, frozen in time."

Erik didn't say anything. He just squeezed my fingers tighter, making a fist of our hands.

"You think I'm nuts, don't you?"

"I think it's a lot of guilt you're carrying, but no, it's not nuts at all. Because if your mom *could* have traded places with you in order to give you a new life, she would have." He paused. "In a way, it's what you did for Lucy."

"I think I'm ready to go back," I said. "Will you come with me?"

"Are you kidding? I would love to go to Rehoboth with you."

CHAPTER 39

On Saturday afternoon the Lunt-Fontanne fellows held an open rehearsal for the public. Annabelle and I went together. The theater was only half-full. Labor Day weekend, it was too beautiful to be inside, though someone had propped open the emergency exit at the front of the room.

The actors wore shorts, T-shirts, and running shoes. Kelly looked casually beautiful in cropped black pants and a black T-shirt with a white pocket. She sat on a metal folding chair to one side of the stage, her legs crossed ankle to knee, a notebook balanced on her thigh. Now and then, she stopped the actors to offer direction.

They were rehearsing the scene where Serena (Eva) has just been handed a letter revealing that her husband has left her for another woman. She reads the letter, her face placid, then picks up her teacup and resumes chatting with her friend Harriet.

"Not quite," Kelly said when they finished. She set down her notebook and stood, cupping her face in her hands as she thought. And then, "Where do you physically feel the betrayal?" she asked Eva. "In your throat, your hands?" To the audience she said, "Truth is always absorbed and revealed in the body, before it registers in the mind."

She asked the actors to run the scene again. This time, after reading the letter, when Eva reached for her teacup, her hand trembled—barely, but the cup clinked loudly against the saucer. It was the only sound, and it was devastating. It changed the scene. I felt how we were all collectively holding our breath, willing Serena to be okay, knowing she wasn't.

The minute the scene ended, the audience burst into applause, but I felt shaken. Gabe, Erik, Annabelle, me—we'd all read the play. How had we not realized how close this came to Eva's life?

Beside me, I felt how still Annabelle was, and without wanting to, I was remembering how happy she'd been with Gabe at the gala the week before. *Truth is always revealed in the body.* I closed my eyes as if to unsee Annabelle's flushed cheeks, everything about her animated. Could she still be in love with him? I stole a glance at her, and saw Gabe leaning against the side wall, arms crossed, and I understood how much effort Annabelle was putting into the act of staring at the stage when really, all her attention was pinned on Gabe.

At the end of the rehearsal, Kelly fielded questions from the audience. Someone asked why she'd chosen *Quadrille* as the play the fellows would perform. Another asked about her plans now that the final season of *Widows* had ended.

"Funny you should ask." She paused, a mischievous look I'd seen a thousand times playing over her face. "Officially as of yesterday, I'm joining *Mamma Mia!* on Broadway. You guys are hearing it first."

A few people cheered and others clapped. "Will you miss

television?" a woman asked from a seat up front. Kelly repeated the question for the rest of us, then said, "Honestly, no. I need to be onstage. It's where I'm my best self. Better than real life." She laughed softly, and I remembered that guy who made fun of her laugh in high school and how hurt she'd been. "Think about what you just saw." She swept her hand back toward the stage. "Gesture by gesture, we figured out exactly how Serena might feel upon learning of her husband's betrayal. And what Eva ended up with felt so true, didn't it?" People were nodding. Again, I felt how still Annabelle was. "That's what I mean about being one's best self. We have the chance to get it right on the stage. We can figure out how to be and how to react, and whatever we present—grief, anger, hurt, joy—it's so real because we've drilled down past all the bullshit to what we really feel and what really matters." Kelly shook her head, almost ruefully. "So many people think acting is pretending to be something you're not, but it's the opposite. I think most people pretend to be what they're not just to get through the day."

Driving back to her house, where we would congregate for our usual Saturday night, Annabelle was quiet, idly fingering her silver cross as she stared out the passenger window. The sun was hidden behind clouds now, bands of thunderstorms gathering in the distance. Leaves twirled on the ends of branches.

"Can I ask you something?" I said.

"You can." She turned to me.

"Last week at the gala, with Gabe . . ." I glanced at her. "You looked so happy. It kind of scared me."

"It kind of scared me too." She clasped her hands in her

lap. "I don't want Gabe, Claire, if that's the question. And whatever this . . . this energy is between us, I want it to go away."

"That scene today, where Serena realizes her husband has cheated—"

"I know." A few fat raindrops splatted on the windshield. "I don't love him, Claire." She looked miserable. "That's not what this is."

"Then what?"

"I don't know."

"Would it help to take a break from our Saturday nights?"

"Probably." Her eyes filled. "It's not what I want, though."

"Me either, but maybe for a few weeks?" The rain was falling steadily, and I switched on the wipers. It was amazing how quickly the afternoon had turned, the skies an eerie green, cars with their headlights on.

"Remember when Lynn said the secret of her marriage to Alfred was that they got to be themselves during the day, but at night, they'd go to the theater and be two other people?"

I nodded.

"Well, Saturday nights are like that for me and Scott. Not that we're different people, but it's like we can just step away from the day-to-day, you know?"

"Can't you do that the weeks we have the kids?"

"Of course, but . . . Don't you feel it? That we bring out the best in each other?"

I did. I'd never been a part of a group of friends like this. We'd become each other's de facto family. I thought of how we'd spend hours together and never stop talking, of how we had spare keys to each other's homes, of how Eva and Gabe had just sauntered through our house and out to the deck last week to tell us Eva had gotten the role of Serena. I thought of how, when I had a show or Eva a play or Scott a gig, it was a given that we'd go together. I thought of Annabelle saying I didn't need them—didn't need her—and of how much I did, and of how much I *liked* that I did. *It's how friendship should be,* I thought.

As it turned out, though, that Saturday night was our last.

We were tired after a long week, and because of that and the rain, we didn't dress up. We ordered pizza and sat around the low circular coffee table in Annabelle and Scott's great room, a bamboo tray filled with flickering votives in the table's center. Spencer dragged his beanbag chair to the sliding doors, staring raptly as rain pelted the glass and lightning strobed the backyard. Echoing booms cracked open the sky and sent the girls shrieking downstairs. Phoebe snuggled with Eva on the leather recliner, Hazel curled against Annabelle, and for a while, we all just watched the storm as if it were a movie.

Once the storm passed and the kids retreated to their rooms, Annabelle, Eva, and Erik launched into Ten Chimneys gossip, and Gabe, Scott, and I had our own conversation. Scott was talking about opening for the Spin Doctors at the state fair two weeks before, and I told him what Kelly had said about being her best self on the stage. Was it like that for him with his music, I asked, was that his best self?

"You'd think so, wouldn't you?" He was sitting on the carpet, leaning against a huge cushion propped against the stone hearth. "But believe it or not . . ." He set his pizza on the paper plate next to him. "If I have a best self, whatever the hell that means, it's probably when I'm working."

"You mean painting?" I said.

He smiled. "That is what I do."

"I know, I just never imagined that . . ." *Painting houses might be fulfilling*? Jesus.

"How about a shovel for that hole you're digging?" Gabe teased.

"That came out wrong," I told Scott. "I'm just surprised it's not music."

"You and me both." He shrugged. "But I'm totally Zen when I paint. I think about all kinds of cool shit, write my best lyrics in my head. Plus, when you paint someone's house, they feel like you've transformed their life."

"Let me get this straight," Gabe said. "You're telling us that being onstage . . ." He shook his head as if to clear it. "You had women screaming for you."

"One woman. And that was my wife."

"It was a throng of women," I said.

"A *throng* of women?" Scott grinned. "Is that like a murder of crows? A conspiracy of ravens? Or is it an unkindness of ravens?" He hadn't shaved, which on someone else might have looked scruffy but on Scott looked rugged. We teased him all the time about his looks. He's downright beautiful. Blue-black hair, dark tan, and those pale green eyes. He really did have a group of women screaming for him at the state fair.

"Look, I love being onstage," he said. "I love playing music. It's the greatest ego trip in the world. But that ain't me up there."

"Even at Hattie's?" I said. "You always look like you're having so much fun!"

"I am, but the best part? It's coming home." He took a swallow of beer. "You guys, the kids, that woman right there . . ." He pointed his bottle at Annabelle, who was sitting on the other side of the coffee table. "That's all I need. Right, love?" he called to her.

"Absolutely," she said, eyes lighting on his. She'd changed into jeans and a white T-shirt that showed off her tan, and she seemed like herself again. No hint of our earlier conversation.

I pulled my feet up under me on the couch and turned to Gabe. "So, what about you?" Thunder rumbled in the distance.

"What about me?" He was sitting in the armchair next to the couch, and even in cargo shorts and flip-flops, he looked like a lawyer. Something imperious in the way he sat, legs crossed as he sipped his wine.

"Come on. Your best self."

"Who says I have one?"

"I've seen glimpses."

"Really? What does it look like?"

I sighed, wishing he didn't always need to be the funny guy, though I understood. Maybe everyone who carried a big enough secret became a magician of sorts, always distracting the audience—*look over here, look over here*—so they wouldn't notice they were being tricked.

"Okay, okay." He uncrossed and then recrossed his legs. "I guess I'd have to define *best self,* but I'm probably most on my game in the courtroom."

"But you don't even like—" I stopped. I wasn't supposed to know he hated his job.

"Shovel, madam?" he laughed.

"Hold on," Scott said. "You don't like being a lawyer?"

"Oh, I like it just fine." He glanced at Eva. "And I'm good at it." He took a sip of wine, then set it on the table next to him. "But I guess therein lies the question, or at least *a* question: Can one be one's 'best self'"—he put air quotes around the phrase—"doing something one isn't passionate about?" He nodded at Scott. "I don't know. Are you *passionate* about painting people's houses? I suppose we're back to defining *best self*."

"For Kelly, it was when she felt most . . . *real* was the word she used. Honest, maybe."

"Well, nix the courtroom, then." Gabe said. "Actually, I don't know why I said that. My best self is with Eva. Hands down."

She and Annabelle both looked up. Eva was still sprawled in the recliner, her hair piled in a messy knot. "Did I hear my name?" she asked.

"You did." Gabe smiled affectionately at her.

"Anyone need another beer?" Scott pushed himself up from the hearth.

Erik held up his empty.

"I was saying you bring out my best self," Gabe said.

"And don't you forget it, mister." A blush colored Eva's cheeks, something sweet passing between them before she turned back to Erik. "The schedule's insane," she said.

"Your turn, Claire." Gabe touched his wineglass to my wrist. "Feet to the fire. What's your best self?"

"Running," I said without thinking.

"Really?" Gabe furrowed his brow. "Not your art?"

"I know. It should be, right? Or being with Erik or the kids. What does it mean that my best self is when I'm alone, doing something that benefits absolutely no one?"

"Yeah, but is our best self really something we choose?" Scott sat down with a fresh beer. "It's like that question about what you'd wish for if you had one wish, and you know you're *supposed* to say world peace, but what you really want is to get a date with the hot barista at your coffee shop. You want what you want, right?" He glanced at Annabelle. "Bet you she says it's being a mom."

Annabelle looked up. "What will I say about being a mom?"

"That it's your best self."

"Best self? How about only self?"

"Come on . . ." Scott said. "You know that's not true."

"Don't think you're off the hook," Gabe whispered.

"What is it with you?" I whispered back. *"Feet to the fire, off the hook.* Why do you think I don't want to talk about this?"

"Oh, maybe because you're the only person who's better than me at avoiding personal questions. Which . . ." He grinned. "You're doing quite convincingly."

"Didn't I meet your best self on our third date?" Annabelle was asking Scott.

"Second date, baby. Believe me, it's etched in my memory."

"So why running?" Gabe persisted.

"Promise you won't laugh?"

"I won't even smile." But of course he smiled as he said it.

"Liar."

"Did you just call me a lawyer?" Before I could respond, he added, "Sorry. I really am listening."

I eyed him warily. "Running kind of saved me once," I said. "And now I guess it's how I process things. If I'm upset, depressed—even when I'm happy, it's like I need to run to be able to feel it." *Truth is always revealed in the body.* After I lost Lucy, running was the only thing that made me believe I could be somebody again. And those first years in Wisconsin when I had no friends because I was terrified of getting close to anyone, running was what I carried inside me all day, that tiny accomplishment. The first time I ran ten miles, I called my mom, laughing and crying because my whole life felt possible again. I took a sip of my cosmo, aware of Gabe watching me. "Go ahead," I said. "Make a joke."

"Actually, I wish I had something like that."

"Wish you had something like what?" Eva asked. "What are you two whispering about?"

"Claire's running."

"Ahhh. Your best self?" Erik said. "I should have known. Running's like prayer for you." He smiled and I smiled back. I'd never thought of running as prayer, but he was right and I loved that he understood this even when I didn't.

"So is it acting?" Gabe was asking Eva. "Your best self?"

"That, or being with you."

"Thank you," Gabe said, "but you can say acting. I promise, my feelings won't be hurt." *Feelweens,* he said, and we laughed.

The room was mostly dark now, just the flickering votives and the lamp on the end table between me and Gabe. The storm had long since passed, only the plink of raindrops hitting the metal grill on the patio. Scott had turned off the AC and opened the windows, the air almost chilly. Looking at us, I was gripped with a feeling of such specific, pointed happiness. Maybe our tiredness had loosened something in us, or maybe it was the relief of it being just the six of us again after all the events of the last month, but I liked who we were that night, liked the affectionate looks that passed between couples, liked how well we knew each other and had opinions about each other's best selves, how the answers mattered.

"So, what about you?" Eva asked Erik.

"My best self? Easy. Cooking with the kids."

"My, my, aren't you specific," Annabelle teased. "Just cooking?"

"If we're talking best, yeah. All of us in the kitchen, wearing our cooking hats."

"I love the cooking hats," Eva said. The last time she and Gabe had had dinner with us and the kids, she'd shown up wearing a Carmen Miranda turban piled with artificial fruit.

"Remind me again why you have cooking hats," Gabe said.

"*Why* we have cooking hats?" Erik shot him a bemused look. "Pure desperation." He shrugged. "Now it's just our thing. I wish I could be that dad all the time."

"Well, I wish I could say my best self was being a mom," Annabelle said. "It should be, right? I mean, if you have kids, you damn well better say that's your best self."

"You don't think being a mom is your best self?" I asked. "I do."

"It's my most important self, but you guys see how I am—total helicopter mom, like if I'm not vigilant every second, the world's going to come crashing down."

Erik flicked his eyes at me. Annabelle's vigilance really was exhausting. The constant dropping off of the high-end organic food and soap she insisted we use; the nonstop weighing in on what TV shows the kids watched and what books they read. Just that morning, she and Erik had argued about the fact that the girls would be with us for their first day of third grade. "But I'm the one who always gets them ready!" she pleaded.

"So, this is it," she said now, flinging out her arms. "My best self. With you guys on Saturday nights." Her eyes met mine, and I knew we were both remembering our conversation in the car.

We stayed much later than usual that night. Typically we wound things up by ten, but for some reason, we just kept talking—about our parents, about the fact that we were all only children, except for Eva, who might as well have been, her brother nine years older, off to college before she was ten. We'd never talked about this before. "How is that possible?" Erik kept saying. We even talked about Kelly a little. I told them how she used to say if she ever had kids, she'd name them after Shakespeare characters, and my dad always teased her that she better have girls—Juliet, Ophelia, Violet—no problem, but the poor boys: Could you imagine being named Othello or Romeo or Hamlet?

"What about Prospero?" Scott was grinning.

"Troilus," Gabe said.

Is that when Eva decided we should all go see *Mamma Mia!* on Broadway that fall? "We'll have a field trip!"

Erik and I looked at each other. No way would Annabelle ever leave the kids that long. Still, it was fun to imagine, the six of us in "the Big Apple." Scott actually called it that, and we made merciless fun of him for it.

Sometimes now I wonder if we stayed so late—it was nearly midnight when Erik pulled into our drive, the cement still damp with rain—because we somehow sensed that it would be our last time together.

I think too of how half of us would lose the very things that brought out our best selves.

PART V

HARRIET: *Are you happy?*

SERENA: *What an extraordinary question! Why shouldn't I be?*

HARRIET: *I have no way of knowing. I merely asked if you were.*

SERENA: *You are quite irrepressible, Harriet.*

HARRIET: *Is it offensive to question the happiness of those one is fond of?*

SERENA: *No, not offensive. Just a little startling perhaps.*

HARRIET: *Why startling?*

SERENA: *Because it gives a jolt to complacency, I suppose. A sudden query flung at random can pierce habitual armor.*

—Noël Coward, *Quadrille*, act 1, scene 2

CHAPTER 40

"Why doesn't Spencer have a first day too?" Hazel pushed her glasses up, leaving a smudge of powdered sugar on the lens.

"Give me those," I said, and wiped them on my running shorts. It was the first day of school for the girls. Annabelle and Scott had arrived with Dunkin' Donuts for the twins and a monstrous gluten-free muffin for Spencer. "Since Spencer has school all summer, it's just different." I held the glasses to the light before handing them back to Hazel.

"He doesn't have a first day because he doesn't go to a 'real' school." Phoebe, eight going on eighteen, put air quotes around *real*. "He doesn't even get summers off!" All four adults exchanged exasperated looks. Phoebe had on her new hiking boots with a sundress—Annabelle had stopped over the previous night to pick out the girls' clothes. After she left, Phoebe begged me to braid her damp hair so that it would be wavy. "But I thought you wanted me to do French braids," Annabelle had commented first thing that morning. "It would look so pretty, Phoebs!"

Now she said, "Spencer's school is more real than yours, missy. And I don't want to hear that from you again."

"Yeah. How would I even walk into my school if it wasn't

real?" Spencer scoffed. "It has a real door and real floors and a real ceiling and real desks and—"

"How about getting into the real van?" Scott set down his coffee mug and pulled out his keys. He was dressed in his painter's whites.

"You want a to-go cup?" I asked.

"Nope. All set."

He was driving Spencer to his bus stop in the work van, which Spencer loved because he sat up so high. As they pulled away, Spencer was grinning, waving like a homecoming queen.

Erik, Annabelle, and I walked the girls to their bus stop. A little boy with an entourage of parents and grandparents was there, along with an older girl (fourth grade? fifth?) who stood apart from her mother, ignoring her. I leaned over to Annabelle. "That's us in two years."

"Ha!" She nodded toward Phoebe. "That's us right now." She sighed. "She already looks like a teenager with that hair."

"She's fine, Annabelle." I gave her shoulder a little nudge. "Really."

And then the bus was turning into our development, and Annabelle was straightening the girls' backpacks on their shoulders, tightening Hazel's ponytail. "I can't wait to hear all about your day!" she said. "I already miss you guys so much!" She was waving and blowing kisses until the bus was out of sight. As it turned the corner, she started weeping.

"You realize they're only going to third grade," Erik said as we walked back to the house. "It's not the Orphan Train."

"But they're growing up so fast," she cried.

I gave her a ride home and promised I'd stop by with coffee when I finished running.

It was our last normal conversation.

I saw the missed call from Eva while I was waiting for Annabelle's peanut butter mochaccino, extra shot, extra whip. "You know that's dessert, not coffee," I always teased her. I figured Eva was already in rehearsal by then and I'd call her later—they had only four days until the play—so I was surprised to see her Jeep at Annabelle's. *Shoot,* I thought, wishing I'd known to get her a coffee too.

Through Annabelle's kitchen windows, I saw them sitting at the picnic table Scott had painted that glossy periwinkle at the beginning of the summer. I couldn't see Annabelle's face, but Eva looked pensive.

"I thought you had rehearsal," I said as I stepped outside and slid onto the bench next to Annabelle. I plunked her coffee down in front of her.

"I do. I just . . . I needed to talk to you." She was playing with her straw, methodically lifting it in and out of her iced tea.

My heart rate accelerated. "What's wrong?"

"I tried to weasel it out of her," Annabelle said. "But she wanted you here."

"Eves," I said. "You okay?"

She still wouldn't look at us, but everything about her felt diminished. *She knows,* I thought. *She knows about Annabelle and Gabe.* The words started a drumbeat in my head. *She knows.*

But then she was saying something about Christine and Ten Chimneys.

"Wait," I said. "You were there already? Did you see Erik?" I have no idea why I asked. *Please please please don't let her know,* I remember thinking.

She looked confused by my question. "I tried to talk to him," she said, "but he'd already left for Madison."

Of course she'd wanted to talk to Erik. He was Gabe's best friend; he'd been cheated on too. I babbled something about Erik's meeting. It was with a small theater company, or maybe it was people from the university, I couldn't remember.

"Christine and I were talking about your show in Chicago," Eva said quietly, "and I guess one of us mentioned the name Lucy Claire." She glanced up. "Kelly overheard us."

Oh, I thought, and felt the morning tilt sideways.

CHAPTER 41

When I left Christine's office," Eva was saying, "Kelly was at the copy machine—you know how it's in that alcove—and she had this . . . this look on her face. She asked why we were talking about Lucy and saying we had no right."

Annabelle scrunched up her face. "What the hell?" she laughed, then added, "Good Lord! No wonder you didn't want her here."

Eva glanced at her, then said to me, "I told Kelly there must be a misunderstanding, but before I could finish, she said something about you giving up your parental rights? And how it was unconscionable for us to mention Lucy around her?"

My mouth went dry. "What did you say?"

"That Lucy was the name you used on your art and I had no clue what she was talking about. And then I left. I was furious with her." She was playing with her straw again, dunking it in and out of her drink. When she finally looked up, her mouth was trembling. "Do you have a daughter, Claire?"

"What?" Annabelle said. "Why would you even ask her that, Eva?" She was already pissed on my behalf, and I loved her for this even as it broke me: how sure she was that I would never have kept something this big from her.

My blood was pumping so loudly in my ears I felt as if I were underwater. "I wanted to tell you," I said thickly to Annabelle. I started to lift my coffee cup, but my hands were shaking, and I set it back down.

Eva reached for my hand.

"She isn't mine anymore," I said woodenly. "Kelly was right about that." I stared at the swing set in the yard behind Eva, the empty seats swaying in the warm breeze as if a child had just abandoned them.

"Hey." Eva squeezed my fingers. "Talk to us."

"I don't know what to say." The leaves of the ginkgo moved in the breeze, their undersides turning silver like the wings of tiny birds. "Losing her is the worst thing that ever happened to me." My voice sounded hoarse.

Annabelle turned on the bench. "This is what you were talking about the other night? When you said there was an accident?"

I nodded.

"What kind of an accident?" Annabelle asked.

"She almost drowned," I said quietly. "I was giving her a bath."

"Oh my God, Claire," Eva said.

Annabelle clapped her hand over her mouth. "How old was she?"

"Seven months."

"But she was okay?"

"She was in the hospital for a while. And there was a lot of physical therapy. But now—I think she's okay."

Annabelle blew out a long breath.

"And how is Kelly connected?" Eva said. "I know you were good friends—"

"She was my sister-in-law."

Eva's eyes widened.

"I was married to her brother," I said as if it weren't clear. I traced my finger over a gouge in the painted table, then looked up. "Kelly is her godmother."

I told them everything then, my secret like a ship in a bottle. How had something this big and complicated fit all these years into the space that was my life?

I told them about the panic attacks, about seeing a psychiatrist, about taking antidepressants. I told them that I'd talked to Nick and my mom and Kelly about how scared I was, but how I also didn't really know what I was scared of. None of us did.

The afternoon of the accident came back in shards, as it always does: the glass bowl of oranges on the kitchen table, Nick's surfboard against the brick wall, the changing blue of the sky, Lucy's screaming, the roar of the lawn mower, smell of baby shampoo. And then Nick's howl, a long knife of color slicing through the silence. Later, the emergency lights washing over the house and Kelly screaming, "Let me in!" and my mom with me in the back seat of my dad's car, taking me to the hospital.

Annabelle was sitting up straight. In the stillness, all I could hear was her sniffling and the sound of my own breath, and I remembered Gabe—or was it Scott? Whoever had gone scuba diving—telling us that's all you heard underwater when you did deep-sea dives, your breathing magnified and echoing back to you, a loud whooshing.

"You're . . . you're not saying . . ." Eva looked at me with disbelief. "You let her go? You were right there?"

I nodded, feeling like some stupid bobblehead. "I didn't know what I was doing. It's—it's a severe form of postpartum that . . . it turns into psychosis."

"No." Annabelle's face was white. "This is Andrea Yates crap, Claire. This is—please *please* tell me that's not what you are saying. *Please.*"

Andrea Yates was the Texas woman who had drowned her five children in a bathtub the year I married Erik. She'd been an international horror story, her picture and her children's pictures on the covers of magazines. The journalist, Anna Quindlen, had written a column about it in *Newsweek*: *Every mother I've asked about the Yates case has the same reaction. She's appalled; she's aghast. And then she gets this look. And the look says that at some forbidden level she understands.*

"It's not Andrea Yates," I said quietly. "My daughter's alive, and she's—she's healthy. We were lucky." But I knew that's all it was. Luck.

Annabelle was crying, holding one hand across her eyes. Eva set a travel pack of tissues in front of her.

"I know this is shocking," I said.

"Why did you give her up?" Annabelle said.

"By the time I got out of the hospital . . ." I stopped. Where did I begin? With the state institution where I was incoherent, practically comatose, for months? Or with the months after that when I tried to reconnect with a child who didn't know me? Who cried as soon as she saw me? Actually, no; it wasn't a cry. It was a terrified whimper. And when she wasn't whimpering she was fixated on some task, picking up Cheerios from her high chair tray and putting them in a Tupperware container, and when I'd come close, she'd pick them up faster and faster, her little face crumpling with fear. It was devastating. And it didn't get better. Months of that, and then I'd see her toddle to Nick or Andrea or Nick's mom and I'd hear her emit that popgun shriek of joy.

"Why the hell did you give her up?" Annabelle asked again. "Were you unfit, Claire? Incapable?" Her voice rose. "I just want to understand how someone who's terminated her parental rights could think it was okay to raise another woman's children." Her voice was shaking.

"Oh my God, Annabelle. It's not like that."

"Then answer the question!"

"I gave her up because I loved her. And because while I was away, she bonded with the woman Nick got involved with. And because I was terrified, okay? Because *I* was traumatized by what happened too! You think I wasn't horrified? I didn't trust that I could be what she needed. Maybe that would have changed—I think now it would have—but at the time, I just wanted her to be okay. It's the only thing I wanted. It's the only thing I still want." I was crying now. How could I make them understand? "The accident was sixteen years ago," I sobbed. "It has nothing to do—"

"Bullshit, Claire!" Annabelle swiped her hands furiously across her face. "You should have told me this!" Her voice broke. "You were taking care of my children!"

"Annabelle, please. You *know* I love those children. You know I'm a good parent, you've told me a thousand times—"

"No—"

"I had my tubes tied. I made sure this couldn't happen again. Come on, you don't seriously think—"

But she did.

I looked at her hard eyes, arms crossed across her chest. Everything in me collapsed. "You think I could have hurt them?"

"No," Eva said. "She doesn't." She turned to Annabelle. "You're angry, and you have every right, but you don't believe that."

"The girls were toddlers, Eva! And I trusted her!" She was sobbing now. "I made you their guardian!" she shouted at me.

"Annabelle, please, this has nothing to do with that." Fear razored itself across my insides.

"It has *everything* to do with that!" she cried. "And I had the right to know!" She jerked back her side of the bench, the wooden legs scraping the cement. "I can't talk to you right now. I just—I need to go. I need you to go." At the door, though, she stopped. "Does Erik know this?"

"*What?* Of course he does." Did she really think I wouldn't tell him? "I told him the minute I realized we were getting serious." I thought this would reassure her, but everything in the hard set of her face, her stiff posture, the stone-coldness of her eyes, screamed *WRONG*.

"Do you really think he would have given me the time of day, much less *married* me, if he thought I was a danger to his children?"

"Sure, he would have, if he was thinking with his—"

"Annabelle, stop," Eva said.

"His dick," Annabelle finished.

"Don't," I said. "Please don't. You know Erik is a good father. You know—"

"A good father? Are you kidding? He's no better than you."

CHAPTER 42

The minute I got in the car, I grabbed my cell phone, thinking, *I need to call Erik*. The words tumbled over and over in my chest—*I need to call Erik*—the rhythm of them in sync with my breathing. The call went to voicemail, and I instantly redialed. Three times. Four? *I need to call Erik.*

Sweltering midday heat filled the car. I didn't turn on the air conditioner, didn't put down the windows. My tank top was drenched. I drove slowly, no radio, no sound. I felt as if I were submerged. Was it possible to cry underwater? Was this why I hadn't been able to cry more than a handful of times all these years?

A part of me had almost drowned that day too.

I moved between anger, regret, fear, and disbelief. I had believed I could tell them about my past. I had believed it right up until the moment I started speaking. What had happened to Annabelle's *I mean it, Claire. You are not alone. You have us*. It wasn't that I thought they wouldn't judge—I knew they'd be shocked and hurt, feel betrayed. But I also imagined they'd be sad for *me*. I thought they'd have questions about the hospital, about postpartum psychosis, about Lucy.

But that Annabelle would think I was a danger to our children?

No.

No.

No.

Not after sharing custody for six years, not after her telling me—how many times?—that I "get Spencer in a way no one else does." Annabelle and I were a team. If she drove Spencer to chess, could I take Phoebe to karate? Could I get the girls to Brownies if she picked them up? Just two days ago, she'd phoned and asked, "What should we do about Phoebe? All the eye-rolling and air quotes, and she's being mean to Hazel. I don't like it."

I tried Erik once more as I pulled into our drive, but it rang that odd double tone that meant he was on the line. *Annabelle,* I thought, and felt a pulse of dread in my stomach. Before I could try again, my phone rang. It was Eva.

"Hey," I said as I unlocked our front door.

"I'm so sorry," she said. "I should have spoken to you alone. I wasn't thinking."

"It's not your fault, Eves." I swallowed. "I just—how could she could think I would harm them?" My voice broke and I stopped, leaning against my office doorway. I had no idea why I'd come up here. My eyes immediately went to the photograph of Lucy, and I felt a sob bubble up in my chest.

"It's just shocking, Claire. I get why you never told us, it's just . . ."

"You think she had a right to know."

Silence. And then, "Yeah. I'm sorry. I do."

I sank abruptly into one of the armchairs. "But if we had told her from the beginning—"

"I know. She would have fought Erik for custody. You guys might not be together." She paused. "I'm about to start rehearsal. Does it help to know that Kelly feels awful?"

No, it didn't. I couldn't think about Kelly, I didn't care

about Kelly. All I cared about was Erik—and Annabelle. She was my best friend. I needed her to know I would not have harmed our children. I felt like I couldn't breathe until she knew that.

After I hung up with Eva, I tried Erik again, but just as I did, our front door opened and he was racing up the stairs to my office. "Claire?" he called. "Are you okay?"

"No," I said, and started crying.

He pulled me to his chest, but I couldn't be held, couldn't even think. "What happened?" he asked when I stepped back from him. "I could barely make sense of anything Annabelle said, beyond—"

"Beyond the fact that I'm a danger to our kids?"

He didn't respond, just lifted a stack of magazines from the armchair, set them on the floor, and sat, elbows on his knees. "I don't understand," he said after a minute. "Why now? We have five days until Kelly leaves. Five."

"I knew I should have gone away." But I also knew it wouldn't have helped. Kelly would have still overheard Eva and Christine. I explained it to Erik.

"Jesus." He looked at me bleakly.

"Tell me what Annabelle said."

"What didn't she say? We're liars, I'm reprehensible, I jeopardized the kids. . . ."

"She's livid, Erik, and I know you said she would be, but to think I would *harm* them?"

"She reacts, Claire. You know that." He held my stare. "I'm so sorry."

I stared at the magazines piled by his chair. On top was the August issue of *Delaware Beach Life,* a magazine my mom sometimes sent. An article about the Perseid meteor showers over the ocean that month. I'd saved it for Spencer. I closed my eyes against the burn of more tears. "She knows me, Erik.

She knows how much I love those kids." My voice wavered, and I waited for him to say something, to reassure me that just as he eventually came around all those years ago, so too would Annabelle.

But he only glanced at his watch and said, "I hate to do this, but I've got to get back." He stood and came to where I was sitting and leaned down to kiss me. "I wanted to make sure you were okay."

I walked him downstairs and out to the drive. The sky was overcast, leaves tossing in the sudden wind, and I crossed my arms against the chill. I was still in my running clothes. The girls would be home in a few hours, excited to celebrate their first day of school. I couldn't think or feel. I needed Erik here. I needed to talk to Annabelle.

Erik put the car in reverse. At the bottom of the drive, he stopped, leaned out the window, and said, "Why don't you give me a call when the girls get home?"

I started to respond, to say, *Come on, Erik, what's she going to do?*

But I didn't.

That was the moment I first felt the dread unfold in my chest like a paper fan. It would be there as I walked up the drive and showered and changed and pushed a cart through the grocery store, as I glanced at my phone every ten seconds, willing it to ring, willing it to be Annabelle. It felt like a blow each time another hour passed and I hadn't heard from her.

It was so quiet that day, the kids gone, the house empty. I didn't even call my mom. I was too numb and scared and ashamed, and it all felt like something that had happened before.

CHAPTER 43

Even as I walked the girls home from the bus stop, asking how they liked their new teacher, even as we waited at the diner for Spencer's bus, I was half expecting Annabelle to show up and whisk the kids away. When she didn't, the tiny ember of hope I'd been cupping my hands around all afternoon momentarily flared. Because if she *really* thought I was capable of harming the kids, she'd take them immediately, wouldn't she? That's what I kept promising myself as we made pizzas for dinner, the twins kneeling on stools at the counter, helping with the toppings, Spencer rolling dough. *Please give me a chance to explain,* I pleaded in my head.

When the clock started inching toward six and she hadn't called, my panic ratcheted back up. We tried her cell and the house phone, and Hazel left messages: "Where *are* you, Mommy? We have to tell you about our day." Her chin wobbled as she handed me the phone.

"She'll probably come for dessert and surprise us," Phoebe informed her sister nonchalantly. "I hope she brings ice cream cake."

"I'm not sure about that, Phoebs," I said, amazed at how quickly the mind creates stories to make the world feel safe.

"She'll call, though. I know she can't wait to hear about your day."

I let the twins put on the TV in the family room, which we didn't usually allow before dinner, let Spencer watch the Weather Channel in our bed. I sat beside him, staring blankly at the screen. I wanted nothing more than to watch the weather swirl in different colors across the country, wanted to be in Boston, where it was raining, or northern Montana, where there was already snow.

And then finally, Erik walked in the door, handing me pints of frozen custard, our special first-day-of-school dessert. "Has she phoned?" He draped his jacket over the banister. "I went by the house, but she wasn't there."

"She hasn't even called the girls. We left messages."

"I don't like this, Claire." He set a folder of papers on the hall table and eased out of his tasseled loafers. "Let me visit with them for a minute." He gestured toward the family room, where the girls were sprawled on the couch watching a rerun of *Full House*.

I watched as he plopped down between them. "Jeez Louise! You guys look like real third graders!"

Hazel immediately climbed onto his lap, facing him, palms on each side of his face. An eye-roll from Phoebe. He nudged her and whispered, "I heard eye-rolling starts in the third grade. Did you have a special lesson?"

Phoebe started to roll her eyes again, then stopped and let herself grin. "Daddy!"

"What about you, Haze? Have you started eye-rolling too?"

But Hazel just launched into the animated spiel I'd gotten earlier, patting her dad's cheeks as she talked: Her teacher, Mrs. Hoyer, had blue eyes and really glittery lipstick, and everyone got to choose a sticker from her big sticker book.

In the kitchen, I put away the custard and preheated the

oven, then stood at the sink and stared outside, seeing nothing. I was so relieved Erik was home. I hadn't realized how afraid I'd been.

A few minutes later, he walked into the kitchen, pulled out a stool, and sat at the counter. "I don't trust her, Claire."

"What do you mean?" I'd never heard this before. Even when he was irritated with her micromanaging, trust had never been an issue.

He stood and pulled a beer from the refrigerator, then rummaged in the utensil drawer for the bottle opener. "I was buying the custard for tonight, and I actually started second-guessing if part of her fury has to do with the fact that the kids were with us on their first day of school."

"Erik, come on. She has a reason to be upset."

"I know, believe me. It's just, how fucked up is it that I'd wonder that? And then I started thinking of how she completely runs the show when it comes to the kids and we just roll over and let her. I know that's not the issue right now, but it's not *not* the issue either." His shoulders slumped. "Do we have a bottle opener in this house?"

"Here." I reached across the counter and handed it to him, thinking of how we did give in to her—constantly. She wanted the kids to have the same bedtimes in both houses regardless of *our* schedule—fine; she wanted the kids saying prayers before meals, never mind that Erik was agnostic, but again, we figured, why not? She wanted the girls in the same class, even though we thought Hazel might do better if she weren't in Phoebe's shadow. But we gave in on that too. And had Erik not put his foot down on the first-day-of-school issue, the kids would have been at her house instead of with us. I felt again the fear I'd felt earlier. When had this gotten so out of balance? I thought of how opening gifts on Christmas morning was always at her house; ditto for Thanksgiving *and* the kids' birthdays, even when they landed during our weeks. We would have loved to celebrate in our house, but even when I offered, it never happened. It would upset Spencer to change things, Annabelle would insist, making a sad face, as if she too wished it were otherwise. And it's not as if she didn't include us in the plans, phoning weeks ahead of time to ask what we thought of an ice cream cake for the girls this year or to tell us she'd found a place that did "chocolate volcanoes with carob! Wouldn't Spencer love that?" Always, we capitulated. And okay, yes, it was easier. Or was it more than that? Was it compensation for the secret we were keeping from her?

Outside, the rain that had threatened earlier began to fall, silent under the hum of the AC. "So, will you try to go over there later? I have those articles about postpartum, and I was thinking—"

He was shaking his head.

"Why? Those articles helped you."

"I think it's too late." He took a swig of beer, then set the bottle down, not meeting my eyes. "I'm pretty sure she was at her lawyer's this afternoon." When he finally looked at me, I saw that he was frightened. "I hoped it was just her rage talking, but the fact that we haven't heard anything—"

"But what can a lawyer do?"

"She's petitioning for full custody."

And just like that, whatever anger or resentment I'd been trying desperately to muster crumbled, and the panic I'd felt earlier pounded so hard at my chest I felt sick. "Can you call Gabe? Can he—"

"I already did. He gave me the name of someone who does family law." He drained the last of his beer, set the bottle on the counter, then opened the fridge for another. "We fucked up, Claire," he said quietly, staring into the bright shelves. "The fact that we never told her—"

"Wait. What do you mean *that we never told her*? Even when I wanted to, you've been adamant that she'd never understand. And you were right!"

"Was I, though?" He let the door fall shut without turning. "I mean, I knew she'd go ballistic, but I never really considered that she had the *right* to know this." Finally, he looked at me. "It honestly never crossed my mind."

"Because there was no reason for it to! I don't care what she says, Erik. What happened with Lucy had nothing to do with her or the kids, and it still doesn't. As long as I didn't get pregnant . . ." I dropped my arms to my sides. "Why am I telling you this?"

"You're right. I'm sorry. She's got me so upside down. It just scares the hell out of me that she could use my not telling her as leverage or proof—or *something!*—that I wasn't being responsible or . . . I don't know." He set the beer on the counter but didn't move to open it. "I just don't understand why you—" He drew in a breath, then slowly blew it out. "Her biggest fear," he said, "her biggest fucking fear is that she's not a good mother—you heard her two nights ago. She's constantly afraid of messing up, not paying enough attention, and wham! You tell her this?"

"You think I had a choice today?"

"But did you have to tell them everything?"

I felt as if a line of gasoline had just been lighted. One second, the flick of a match, and I felt the world go up in flames, my own face burning with the realization of how badly I had screwed up. He was right. I could have stalled. Confirmed what Kelly said without getting into the details. Isn't that what I'd imagined countless times? What I'd wanted? To just tell them about Lucy, to acknowledge her? That was all. *I have a daughter.*

I pushed my stool away from the counter and walked to

the oven, my back to Erik as if I could block his anger. I didn't know how to explain. There was no shape to what had happened, no clear beginning, no clear end. Did it start the day she was born or that night on the Ferris wheel or the afternoon I put her in the tub? *Everything* was connected to everything else! And why bother to only tell part of it? That's what I'd been doing for six years, parceling out bits and pieces of myself and my story, and somehow it had seemed that if I kept doing this . . . what would I have left that was whole?

But even more than not knowing *how* to tell the version of the story Erik wanted me to tell, I hadn't understood *why* I needed to. Annabelle was my friend. She knew me.

I mean it, Claire. You are not alone. You have us.

The room had turned gray, and I flipped on the overhead lights, then started setting the table, pulling plates from the cabinet by the sink. Erik got up to help me. The rain was falling faster, silvery drops sluicing across the windows, turning the world blurry, like something from a cartoon. Our lives felt that way, exaggerated and out of proportion, everything in bold outlines, flattened into two dimensions.

By the time we were tucking the girls in, after again trying Annabelle's cell, then Scott's, the girls were distraught, and Spencer was agitated. How could she not call the twins on their first day of school? Moving in and out of their rooms—braiding hair, laying out clothes for the morning—Erik and I were numb and furious. I couldn't get my heart to stop racing.

Finally, Erik's phone rang. He was with Spencer; I was with the girls. Immediately they went racing into his room, screaming, "Mommy! Mommy!"

"Hey," Erik said into the phone, "I bet you want to—" He stopped. "Are you sure? They're right—" And then: "Whoa . . .

Wait, wait, give me a second." He raised his eyebrows to me in bewilderment and took the phone downstairs. Hazel started to whimper, and I scooped her up and said, "Mommy's going to talk to you in a minute, but Daddy needs to talk to her first."

"Why?" Phoebe demanded. "It wasn't his first day of school!"

Erik was standing at the kitchen counter, holding the phone, his back to me. Quietly, I sat at the table, still littered with crumbs from our pizza.

"No, no, would you—look—would you— No, Annabelle, I don't. We had a right." He turned and gave me a helpless look. "Of course, of course, you did." He nodded, mouth pinched, then said, "That's not fair." My eyes were glued to his face, nails digging into my palms, willing him to somehow get through to her.

But then he straightened his shoulders, turned around, and said, "On what grounds?" and I felt my heart spike with adrenaline. The lawyer.

A volley of broken sentences followed, their ends snapped off before he could finish: "Why would—" and "I can't believe—" and "What lawyer would even—" and "Please calm—" and "For God's sake, Annabelle, they're in bed!"

He didn't turn to face me, but I understood the entire conversation by watching his back, straight at first, then bowed over as he leaned his elbows on the counter. Early in his career, Alfred Lunt had turned his back to the audience, something never before done in American theaters, something he was told he couldn't do, something for which he was criticized. "A back can sometimes express as much or more than a face," he had insisted, and that night, watching Erik on the phone with Annabelle, I understood what Lunt had meant.

Erik's shoulders sagged and his head went down, and finally, he snapped his phone shut and turned. "She's on her way over." A muscle jumped in his clenched jaw.

"Why?"

"She doesn't . . ." He glanced at me. "She doesn't want the kids in the same house with you."

For a moment, I couldn't move, talk, swallow. When I did speak, my voice came out in a whisper. "Why are you allowing this?"

"Allowing? You think that's what I'm doing? Jesus." He pulled out the chair opposite me, sat at the table. "Her lawyer told her to file a complaint with child protection if we didn't let her take the kids tonight."

"For something that happened sixteen years ago?" I was reeling.

"Apparently, it's enough reasonable cause to say the kids are in imminent danger. Child protection would have no choice but to remove them."

"And you're taking her word for this? How do we know—"

"We don't!" He slammed his hand on the table. "We fucking don't. But she's on a rampage, and you and I both know arguing with her when she's like this is futile." He squeezed shut his eyes, his hands in fists as if it was all he could do not to throw something. After a minute, he pushed himself up. "Can you get Spencer ready? I'll get the girls."

CHAPTER 44

"It's okay," I told Spencer. I didn't know what else to say. There was no explanation I could give that would make sense to him, because it didn't make sense to me. That this was happening at all felt preposterous. "You're just going to Mom's this week instead of next week." I couldn't imagine this would last any longer.

"It's not okay! This week is Dad and Claire. Next week is Mom and Scott. Look on the calendar. This week is Dad and Claire!" He knelt on his bed and jabbed at the calendar hanging over the headboard. A weather calendar with historical weather facts for every day.

"What if we change the calendar?" I said. Sometimes this was all it took: for what was happening in Spencer's world to align with what was supposed to happen. And for the zillionth time since I'd fallen in love with this boy six years before, I thought how wise he was. Because wasn't this all most of us wanted? For the world to align with our image of it?

"We can't. We can't change it!" His voice rose in pitch. Unthinkingly, I touched his arm, his pajamas on inside out so the seams wouldn't irritate him, and he jerked away. "This week is Dad and Claire. Next week is Mom and Scott. We can't change weeks!" He hopped to the other side of his bed and, before I could stop him, started pulling things off his bookshelf—VCR tapes, a framed picture of him and Annabelle, his clock and tape recorder, books, CDs—and hurling everything to the floor.

"No, Spence, come on," I said, keeping my voice calm. I knew this boy needed a better reason for why we were changing his routine without any warning, but I didn't have it. I also knew it wasn't the dumping everything to the floor that he needed but the putting it all back later, exactly as it had been. I understood this too, desperate to return our lives to the way they'd been this morning.

Spencer started kicking and thrashing, screaming, "Not okay, not okay, not okay!" I knew to let him be, but I got down on the floor with him and kept talking, reading him facts from his calendar. "Listen to this, Spence. On this day in 1950, Hurricane Easy—that's kind of a funny name, isn't it?—Hurricane Easy produced the second-greatest twenty-four-hour rainfall in the history of US weather—thirty-eight inches in Yankeetown, Florida. That's more than three feet, kiddo." Over and over, until finally Erik rushed into the room, followed by the girls. "We're just going to Mom's, Spence," Hazel cooed, on her knees next to her brother. "No!" he screamed. "We can't go to Mom's, we can't!" Erik ended up lying next to Spencer, holding his son in a tight hug, which often calmed him in the midst of a meltdown. "It's okay, honey, it's okay." Erik's cheeks were wet with tears, but I didn't know if they were Spencer's or if Erik was crying too.

"Let's go make sure you have everything," I said to the girls.

Erik was still with Spencer when Annabelle and Scott arrived. Annabelle wouldn't acknowledge me, even as I silently begged her to please look at me. Instead, she opened her arms to the twins, who had been sitting in their nightgowns on the stairs. She was still dressed in what she must have worn to the lawyer's: tailored navy pants and a cream-colored silk blouse, her hair clipped back from her face.

Scott stayed on the porch, staring out across the yard, hands shoved into his painter's pants. The girls were bouncing up and down: "Why are we going to your house, Mom? Is it a surprise, is that why you didn't call?" and "Whose house are we going to tomorrow?"

"Come on, come on," Annabelle said, hurrying the girls along. "I'll answer your questions in the car." Hazel's glasses were askew on her face, and I crouched to straighten them, but Annabelle moved between us and ushered Hazel quickly outside. I stayed in that crouched position for a minute, then stood slowly, feeling as if I'd been kicked.

I wanted to remind Annabelle that I'd been with these kids for six years, that I knew Hazel wanted to grow up to be the Little Mermaid, that Phoebe loved going to gift shops and picking out cards for everybody she cared about, and she always chose cards with rainbows or unicorns for Annabelle. Spencer's favorite day was April Fool's and he started making lists of pranks in January (changing the clocks, filling Oreos with toothpaste). The recipe he most wanted to make was mole because it had the "most ingredients of all!" Plus, he loved the name. "Mole?" he'd laugh in his staccato giggle, clapping with excitement. Did she understand I would do anything to make that boy happy, including going to three Spanish markets to find five kinds of chilies to make mole with him? But Annabelle was already nudging Phoebe to get in the car. Scott carried Hazel, while Erik followed, awkwardly walking a screaming, kicking Spencer to Annabelle's SUV.

The echo of his howls scalded the air, and though I hated that he was so scared and confused and angry, his reaction seemed the only honest one. Shouldn't we all have been howling and screaming? Shouldn't we all have been fighting this? I wondered what would have happened if Erik had told Annabelle there was no way in hell she was taking the kids. She wouldn't have called Child Protection or involved the police—she would never traumatize her children like that—but we were too fucking scared and guilty to realize it.

CHAPTER 45

As soon as Annabelle's SUV turned the corner, Erik got on the phone. It was dark and I could barely see him, though I could hear him as he paced across our front walk. He spoke first to Gabe. "She fucking took them," he said, his voice shaking. And then Eva got on the line—"I don't think it'll help, Eves," I heard him say, and, "You couldn't have known." He paused at the steps where I was standing and said, "I'll tell her.

"Eva said she'll call in the morning," he said flatly, snapping the phone shut. The air felt thick, saturated with water. Erik's face was wrecked. Like he had aged ten years.

"Gabe's phoning the lawyer?" I asked.

"Yup." He wasn't looking at me.

"Should we go inside?"

"You can." And then the phone was ringing and he was hurrying down the drive and saying, "Mr. Dempsey? Thank you so much." Watching him walk away, I felt lightheaded with the realization that *I* had cost him his children, cost *us*. How was it even possible that this was happening again? I felt so sick with shame there wasn't room for anything else.

I kept my eyes on Erik at the end of the drive. The streetlamp cast just enough light for me to see his silhouette, his head bowed as he spoke. Except for the murmur of his voice, the neighborhood was uncharacteristically quiet: no cars passing, no music from the teenage boys across the street, nothing to interrupt the dark storyline of what had just happened.

He wasn't on the phone long. I watched him trudge up the drive, pausing once to stare up at the cloud-filled sky, not a star in sight. At the porch he seemed surprised to see me still there.

Inside, everything was as we'd left it. A glass of water on the counter, dishes stacked in the open dishwasher, the thunk of ice falling through the icemaker. I stood there, rubbing my arms. Erik opened the refrigerator, full of food I'd bought for the kids: juice boxes and string cheese, almond milk for Spencer. The room smelled of pizza. "I'm meeting the lawyer—Andy—before work tomorrow." He popped the top off another beer and took a long swallow.

I wet a cloth in the sink to wipe down the crumb-laden table, needing to do something. The house echoed with silence. "So does he think . . . did he say anything?"

"He doesn't know enough to say anything. That's why we're meeting." Anger curled the ends of his words. He leaned against the butcher block, eyes closed, holding his beer bottle against his forehead like a cold compress.

I felt stung by his anger. Was I not allowed to even ask about the lawyer? "Did you like him?" I ventured. I hated my voice, its willed cheerfulness.

"Did I like him?" He looked at me in bewilderment. "I just want my kids back, Claire."

"I know, I'm sorry. I don't know what to say."

He nodded. "I just need it to be morning." His voice sounded hollow. He downed his beer, set the empty on the counter, and opened the fridge for another.

"Are you sure you want to do that, Erik?" It was his fourth or fifth of the night.

"This," he said, flicking the cap off the bottle, "is the *only* thing I'm sure of." He paused, head bowed as if counting to ten. When he looked up, the anger was gone, but his eyes were such a wasteland, I almost wanted the anger back. "I love you, okay?" he said. "But I can't . . ." He pinched the bridge of his nose. "I've got nothing left right now." Another long draw of beer, and then, "I'm going to head on up. Can you take care of things down here?"

"Of course."

He turned to go, and I asked, "Do you want me to pack you a lunch for tomorrow?" It was a dumb thing to say, but I wanted so badly to do something, anything, to help him.

"Lunch? I guess." He said it in the same manner in which he would have responded to some homeless person asking for a buck, giving him a dollar partly out of compassion but mostly because he wanted the guy to leave him alone.

He left early to meet the lawyer. Overnight, it seemed the season had turned, fast-moving clouds racing across a leaden sky. Had the kids been with us, they would have needed sweaters.

After he was gone, I went up to my office to gather the articles on postpartum psychosis for Annabelle. I hadn't mentioned it to Erik because he would have flat-out told me not to do this, but I knew once lawyers were involved, all communication would go through them, and it seemed crazy—as long as there was a chance to appeal to Annabelle one-on-one—not to try.

I knew her as a mother. It was that simple. I knew her as a mom in a way no one else did: not Erik, not Eva, not even

Scott. And that bond felt sacred. It *was* sacred. I thought of Spencer's birthday six weeks ago and how, when we started softly singing "Happy Birthday," even that was too much, and he'd clapped his hands over his ears, shrieking, "Too loud! Too loud!" We had to sing in a whisper, and afterward, I'd watched Annabelle quietly leave the picnic table and go inside. I found her sitting on the glider out front, smoking.

"Why do I do this to him?" she sobbed. "He's never going to fit in; he's never going to be normal, and I keep trying to make him!"

I thought too of how we both indulged Spencer's plan to "grow up and be a meteorologist/chef" and live in an RV in our driveways, one week at Annabelle's house, one week at ours. "Exactly like now!" he would declare proudly, and Annabelle's face would soften with love and despair, and she'd say, "That sounds perfect, doesn't it, Claire?"

She was a great mom, the mom I wished I could have been to Lucy. I knew this in my bones. Which was why I couldn't fathom any scenario where she thought cutting the kids off from us was okay, unless she truly believed they'd been in danger. And she only believed this, I told myself as I gathered the articles into a manila envelope to leave at her house, because she didn't understand.

CHAPTER 46

Even though her car was there, the house felt empty, the doorbell echoing. As I bent to lean the envelope against the wall, I glanced in the side-panel window and nearly jumped out of my skin to see her standing in the darkened foyer. I held up the envelope, smiling out of reflex, but she turned on her heel and disappeared into the kitchen. My face felt as if it were on fire.

I'd just stepped off the porch into a drizzle so fine it was more like mist, when I heard the door open behind me. "Oh my God, thank you," I said as I spun around. "I know I'm the last—"

"What are you doing here?" She pushed open the storm door and glanced at the envelope propped against the wall. "Whatever this is, I don't want it." She nudged it with her toe.

"Please, Annabelle. Just glance at it. You don't have to talk to me. I'm not—I waited to come here until the kids were at school. I'm not trying to upset you."

She shook her head in disbelief. "You really are something, you know that? Showing up here, peering in my windows, smiling like . . . *what*? You thought I'd be glad to see you?"

"No. That's not . . ." I swallowed. "I thought these articles—"

I nodded toward the envelope. "I hoped they might help explain. I made a mess of things yesterday."

"Yesterday?" She fake-laughed. "You think I'm upset about *yesterday*? Yesterday is the only day you've been honest since you ingratiated yourself into our lives."

"That's not fair."

"Please. You are not going to talk to me about fair, are you? After keeping from me the information you did? And not just for a year, but *six*? It's unforgivable."

I stared at her incredulously. My hair was damp from the rain, and I could feel a film of it on my skin and beaded on my lashes, and it made her seem blurry and indistinct, but not so much that I couldn't feel the fury radiating from her in waves. She also looked pale, though, and tired—she was wearing baggy sweats and a faded flannel shirt of Scott's over her T-shirt—and I imagined it had been a rough night with Spencer. "I wanted to tell you about Lucy, but we both know that if I had before you got to know me, we never would have become friends."

"Correct."

"Then what would you have had me do?"

She held up a hand. "Not my problem, Claire."

"I love those children, Annabelle."

"No! You used those children!"

"Used? How? My God, Annabelle! Have you really never made a mistake, never once done anything you wish you could undo?" Tears spilled down my face, though I doubt she could tell. I was soaking from the drizzle, which was still so faint it looked like glitter, the air filled with millions of silver specks.

"Oh, here we go," she sneered, a hairpin turn in her voice. "I wondered how long before you'd try to blackmail me."

"Blackmail?" I felt like I was staring into one of those fun house mirrors, everything stretched into something else,

distorted and wrong, and all I wanted was to step away and let the world contract back into what it was before. "I know you're furious, but this is *me*. I would never use that against you. I'm just saying people mess up, horribly sometimes, and—"

"Don't you dare. Don't you *dare* try to imply there's any similarity between what you did and—" She flicked her eyes at me dismissively, her jaw hard.

"I wasn't suggesting—"

"Bullshit. That's exactly what you were doing. Do you even know what the truth looks like, Claire?"

I glanced down, a terrible neediness welling up in me. "So the last six years count for nothing?"

"Oh please. Just go away." She bent down, picked up the envelope, and flung it at me. "Take your crappy papers or whatever they are and get off my property. I don't want you anywhere near me or my kids." She stepped back, the storm door banging, though she stood there, staring at me from the other side of the glass.

I picked up the rain-soaked envelope without looking at her and walked to my car, humiliation burning in my throat. I was cold and soaked and I had trouble getting the key into the ignition, my legs shaking so uncontrollably, it took effort to steady my foot on the gas pedal.

I'd left the house without my cell, and now all I could think about was getting home and phoning Erik before she did. I needed to explain to him why I'd come here. I needed him to know how desperate I was to make this right. Although this pained me too. How could he not know this already?

There were two messages on the answering machine: Eva checking in, and Erik. The meeting with the lawyer had gone well. My taking care of the kids for the last six years pretty much nullified Annabelle's sudden claim that I was a danger to them. Erik sounded relieved, but the message only made me feel worse. How could I keep getting everything so wrong? I shoved the manila envelope into our trash and dumped coffee grounds on top.

And then I sat on a stool, took a deep breath, and called him. His phone went straight to voicemail, which meant he was talking to someone else. "Call me," I said, and then sat, shivering in my damp clothes, not knowing what to do.

I tried Erik's phone again after I changed, got the voicemail again, then called Ten Chimneys. An intern answered and told me Erik was in a meeting.

I couldn't settle. In the kitchen, I noticed the grime around the handles of the cabinets we used most and scrubbed those, and the inside of the microwave needed cleaning, and the top of the refrigerator. Something about the stillness of the air and the silvery light and waiting for whatever was going to happen next reminded me of preparing for one of the nor'easters that slammed up the coast every autumn in Rehoboth. My dad marking X's across the windows with duct tape, making sure the flashlights had new batteries. Everything eerily quiet until it was shattered by the wail of the firehouse siren that sounded for miles.

I ended up in Spencer's room, straightening the mess from the night before, righting his globe, arranging his books back on the shelf. His weather calendar was torn, and the glass covering the photo of him and Annabelle was splintered across one corner. I stared at that picture for a long moment, her huge smile, face pressed up to his. She was my best friend. I loved her. She'd taught me to be a mother, allowed me to be one. Guilt and grief slammed over me. Yes, I should have told her about Lucy, but how, *how,* could she throw away our entire friendship?

When the phone finally rang, it was our landline, and I hurried to our room to grab it.

"Do you *want* me to lose my children?" Erik's voice was so filled with rage that I thought he'd meant to call Annabelle and had mistakenly phoned me instead.

"Erik?"

"What are you doing, Claire? She got an emergency PFA against you."

"What?" I was still holding Spencer's calendar. "What do you mean she got a PFA?"

"A protection from abuse order. You went to her house this morning? You were peering in her fucking windows? What is wrong with you?"

"I went there to give her those articles! I was leaving them on the porch. I wasn't—God, Erik." I sat gingerly on the edge of the bed and stared numbly at Spencer's calendar. On this day in 1970, *a lightning bolt in St. Petersburg, Florida, struck a high school football team, knocking all thirty-eight players and four coaches off their feet.* "She actually said I was peering in her windows? Does that even sound like me?" I closed my eyes. "Why are you—"

"*No.*" His voice was steel. "Why are *you*? Stay out of this, Claire. I don't know how else to say it. They're not your kids, and all you're doing is making this worse."

I didn't answer. I didn't hang up or move or maybe even breathe. *They're not your kids.* There was so much silence on the line I thought Erik had hung up. But then, "I'll talk to you when I get home," he said, and I heard the click of the receiver. Still I sat there, holding the phone to my ear until our bedroom filled with the echo of the dial tone.

CHAPTER 47

I'd made salads with roasted vegetables and grilled lake trout, though no part of me could imagine us actually eating dinner together. I couldn't even picture the conversation where Erik filled me in on his meeting with the lawyer. It all felt beside the point after *They're not your kids*. But it also never occurred to me not to make dinner, and when I realized Erik wasn't coming home, I wrapped his meal for later, though I was tempted to toss the whole thing in the trash. Let him find it there.

I carried my salad out to the back deck. The sun had burned through the mist and clouds, leaving the sky a vivid blue that seemed to deepen once night fell. I stretched out on a chaise longue, a stadium blanket tucked around my legs, and stared up into the luminescent sky. I felt broken every time I thought of Erik's words, a huge hole in the center of my chest. But I was also angry, which surprised me. I rarely got angry, rarely let myself, as if I'd lost the right to this too. Who was I to be angry at anyone?

It felt good, though. I was angry at Erik for not coming home, angry at what he'd said on the phone, but even more, I was angry that he'd shut me out the previous night, as if I weren't also devastated. And I was angry, furious really, at myself for accepting his blame without question. Of course it was all my fault!

Except it wasn't. I wasn't the one who hauled *our* kids out of the house. I was angry at Annabelle too—or I wanted to be, though I couldn't quite summon it yet. Years of her telling not only me but the kids' teachers, doctors, other parents, Eva, Deanna—God, everyone!—that she couldn't imagine parenting without me, and in the next breath, she no longer wanted me near the kids? I didn't know what to do with that. I felt sick every time I tried to make sense of it.

I inhaled a stuttering breath and glanced at the salad I was balancing on my lap. I wasn't hungry, but I made myself eat, as if some survival instinct had kicked in, or maybe it was just a refusal to punish myself even more. I'd done that plenty in the past, refusing to eat in those months after I found out what I'd done to Lucy. I didn't think I deserved anything then, not even food.

The thermometer nailed to the railing read sixty-four degrees. I thought of Spencer and felt again the throb of grief that had been with me all afternoon. The night had grown chilly, but I couldn't go inside, couldn't sit in that too-clean, too-empty house just waiting for Erik. What would I do if he didn't come home? Twenty-four hours ago, I would have sworn by our marriage. Now I didn't know.

The phone pinged, and my hope spiked, then plummeted when I saw it wasn't Erik but Eva: *Hey, lovely! Sending you hugs!* All our betrayals of her. Tears burned my eyes as I stared at the phone. I hated how needy I was, how scared. *Please call,* I silently begged Erik, and then hated myself for that, hated that when he did deign to phone, I'd be grateful the way I always was. That was our narrative: He had given me a second chance, loved me despite what I'd done, and I was grateful and would always be grateful, was, in fact, choking on gratitude.

I was about to go in when Erik's car pulled into the drive, headlights sweeping over the cypress trees bordering the yard. I listened to the slam of his door and then his voice calling my name as the light came on in the kitchen. A minute later, light filled our bedroom window, then went off, and he was in the family room, where I watched him through the sliding glass, checking his phone. Finally, the light over the patio flicked on. "You didn't hear me?" he said, stepping outside. "Jesus. I've been looking all over the house."

"You found me." I glanced at him. "I wasn't sure you were coming home."

He sighed and sat on the edge of the chaise next to mine, elbows resting on his knees. He was wearing sweatpants cut off at the knee and the long-sleeved *We Don't Do Bivalves* T-shirt I'd made my first Thanksgiving with him. I hated those shirts. I'd been so desperate to fit in, to be the wonderful fun-loving girlfriend, and we'd broken up the next day.

"Have I ever not come home, Claire?" Erik sounded weary and put-upon.

"Well, you've never spoken to me like you did today either, so . . ." I shrugged. "I didn't know what to think."

I felt him look at me, felt his surprise that *I* was upset. Had he expected to find me curled in a ball, begging forgiveness? *Well, I'm as surprised as you,* I wanted to tell him, and almost laughed, except it wasn't funny, and I was too close to tears.

"Obviously, I was angry," he said. "You don't think I had a right to be?"

"I didn't say that. I'm just wondering if what you said is

how you really feel. I mean, obviously they're not *my* children, but I always felt like I was their parent too." I stopped, clenching my hands into fists. I could feel the anger dissolving and the hurt rushing in, and I couldn't afford that. I needed to be angry, to let myself feel what it was like.

"Of course you're their parent, Claire."

"Am I? Or was the parenting just some bone you and Annabelle tossed me so I'd keep taking care of them and worrying about them and"—my voice cracked—"helping with Spencer's tuition and putting money in the girls' college fund—"

"Stop. Jesus. You know that's not how it is."

"Don't get me wrong. I'm happy to do it. I just have to shift my thinking a little. I thought I was contributing because it's what parents *do,* Erik. They plan for their kids' futures and worry and make sacrifices. I guess it was okay for me—"

"Would you stop? Please?" He ran his hands through his hair. "You're taking this wrong."

"There's a right way to take what you said?"

For a moment we stared at each other, boxers squaring off. He glanced away first. "Look," he said. "I shouldn't have said it. It's not how I feel—at all. But it's like you were going out of your way to screw things up even more than they were." The lounge chair creaked as he shifted his weight. "I'm not saying you did it on purpose, but I have to wonder—"

"Don't." I pushed off the blanket I had tucked around me.

"*What?* I'm not allowed to wonder?"

"I don't want to hear it." I swung my legs over the side of the chair. "It's bullshit."

"You have no idea what I'm going to say."

"I know exactly what you're going to say."

He just looked at me, then said, "Can we step back for a second?"

I didn't want to fight with him. I knew he was as devastated as I was, and I wanted so badly to make things right. Because the idea that Erik and I were not as solid as I'd believed terrified me. *I can't do this again,* I thought. *I cannot lose everything.*

The only sound was the sough of wind through the trees. The silence stretched thin and somehow made the night feel chillier. I felt an ache in my shoulders. *We're both tired. I made you dinner.* The words were there and I wanted to say them, but I couldn't. It's as if we were back in those months after I first told him about Lucy, where everything was fine as long as I made no demands. Some part of us had never gotten beyond that.

"All the things you're wondering about me," I said carefully, "I've spent the day wondering: Was I trying to sabotage myself by telling them about Lucy? Like you said, why go into all that detail? Or maybe I'm just so messed up and always will be that I can't bear for my life to be good. Maybe deep down I've never believed I deserved to be happy." I glanced at him. "Is that about right?"

"Yes. That's all I was going to say. Honest to God, I'm trying—"

"Bullshit, Erik. And all of that crap I just recited? It's incredibly convenient for you, isn't it?"

He reared back as if I'd slapped him. "Convenient? Are you fucking kidding me? What part of watching my kids get hauled out of here was convenient?"

"That's not what I'm saying."

"Then what are you saying?"

"I told Annabelle about Lucy *when* I did and *how* I did because I was caught off guard. I didn't have time to figure out the perfect answer. But even if I had, Erik, I probably would have told them everything, because I believed they would understand, and I had every right to believe this—especially, *especially,* with Annabelle! She knows what it is to make an unforgivable mistake and then have to live with it. And I'm not saying our mistakes are the same—they're not, not by a long shot—but in my defense, I didn't know what I was doing the day Lucy got hurt, and Annabelle sure as hell knew what she was doing when she fucked her best friend's husband. And if that's not bad enough, we've all been running around keeping her secrets and betraying Eva at every step. So, if you want to talk about fucked up, *that's* fucked up! Not me telling them about Lucy. And yeah, maybe I was naïve, but I didn't tell them because I was *trying* to sabotage my life. I told them because I believed, and I thought Annabelle—and you!"—I jabbed my finger at his chest—"believed the same thing. That people deserve second chances. But I guess only she gets those. And that you would automatically take her side—"

"Her side? I spent the morning with a goddamn lawyer trying to clean up this mess, Claire! How the hell is that taking her side?" He stood, knocking into me, and moved toward the sliding glass door. Beyond the reach of the light, I could barely make out the shape of him. There was only his voice, which was furious. "All this drivel about you being blindsided—it's crap. You've wanted to tell Annabelle for a long time. And the happier we were, the more you couldn't bear it, the more you wanted to just raze everything. Well, bravo, Claire. You got your wish." He started to walk inside, then stopped. "You have *never* believed that you deserve to be happy—and you know what? Maybe you don't."

He stormed into the house then, and I was on his heels, shouting, "You really think the only reason to tell them about Lucy is to sabotage my life? How about telling them because she's my daughter, Erik? My *daughter*!" I was shaking I was so angry. "I am not a horrible person, I am not some monster—"

"Have I ever—"

"Yes! *Yes!* Every time you insist no one could ever understand. No one but you, of course, because what, you're such a saint? Such a martyr?"

"Was I wrong? Because I sure as hell don't see a lot of understanding coming your way." He was banging cabinets, wrenching open the refrigerator. He grabbed a beer, set it on the counter, then reached for the salad and a bottle of dressing and slammed them on the counter too. Everything was reflected in the windows, opaque with night, the blinds wide open. Erik usually closed them. It was one of those stupid things we bickered about because I liked looking out for as long as even a hint of light remained in the sky.

Now, as I watched him move from the window over the sink to the bay windows, yanking the blinds closed, it was one more thing that infuriated me.

I watched him scrape back a stool and dig into the salad. *How?* I wondered. *How the hell do you just sit there and eat?* I hated when he shoved food ravenously into his mouth like this, hated the sound of his chewing, hated the way he'd just reached into the fridge for his salad like it was his due to have a meal waiting.

"Thank you for this," he said, shoveling in another bite.

"It's what I do." I barely recognized my own voice. "Kick me in the gut, and I'll make you a sandwich."

He raised his eyes to mine, fork midair. "What does that mean?"

"You have no clue why I'm upset, do you?"

He sighed. "I already told you I shouldn't have said what I did, and I meant that, but if you need me to apologize again, I will. Gladly."

I was shaking my head.

"*What?* Is there something else? By all means, enlighten

me." He stabbed a huge forkful of salad, then stopped and held up his hand. "On second thought, don't. You're right. I don't have a clue why you're upset. All I know is that I've spent the day trying to fix the mess you've made of my life and my children's lives—"

"*Your* children. You hear yourself, right?"

"Fine. *Ours.*"

I swiped my eyes over him, then walked to the bay window by the table and opened the blinds he'd just closed. There was nothing to see outside, everything black, but I didn't care. I couldn't look at him, though I could see his reflection in the glass. "It must be nice being you, Erik." I crossed my arms over my chest to stop their shaking. "You're always right, always blameless. You never have to take responsibility."

"*I* don't take responsibility? *I* don't?" He tossed his fork into the salad and shoved the bowl away. "What do you want me to take responsibility for that I'm not, Claire?" He looked at me with contempt, got up, walked over to the trash can, and scraped the bulk of the salad into it. And then, turning and jabbing the fork in my direction, he said venomously, "I will take responsibility for a lot of things, but this is one hundred percent your doing. The fact that we're having this conversation, the fact that my children are not in this house right now, the fact that—"

"Stop confusing me with your ex-wife!" I shouted. "*Your* children are not in this house because *she* barreled in here and took them. *She* traumatized Spencer, and for you—"

"No way." He shook his head, stepping back as he did. "You will not lay this on me, and as pissed off as I am at Annabelle, you can't lay this one on her either. You want to talk about responsibility? Let's talk about the fact that all of this could have been avoided if you'd just contacted Kelly back in

March—March! She wouldn't have come, Claire. She told me that flat out today."

I don't know why that stung, but it did. Erik walked his bowl to the sink, but I could sense him watching me. I was still staring outside. After a minute, I moved to the table and lifted Spencer's chair so the legs wouldn't scrape, then sat carefully.

He turned on the faucet and began soaping his salad bowl. I stared at him, this too-tall, too-skinny man in his ridiculous cutoff sweatpants and black dress socks, and I had to remind myself that this was my husband, this was Erik, and I loved him.

"Can you just put it in the dishwasher?" I asked. Another irritation. His insistence on washing things by hand. Half the time they weren't clean and I ended up putting them in the dishwasher anyway. I don't know why I cared. I don't know why any of it mattered, except it felt like one more thing I shouldn't have had to ask for over and over and over.

He finished washing the bowl and set it in the dish rack, then stood there, hands on his hips, and said quietly, "I have had your back for six fucking years." His voice was shaking with anger. "I have kept your secret, I've compromised myself at work, I've deceived Annabelle—"

"Deceived?"

"Yes, deceived, Claire. And fine, I'll take responsibility for that choice, but she had a right to know."

"No, Erik! No, she didn't! And don't get me wrong: I wish to God I'd told her a year or two years ago, but *not* because she had a *right.* I should have told her because she was my friend and she trusted me, and there was a way to do this so it didn't have to happen how it did. But you were adamant, Erik, and I respected that. Now, though, *now* suddenly, she had the *right* to know?"

"She's their mother, Claire."

"And what? You didn't know that six years ago? Or, hell, six months ago? Why are you doing this?" He was revising our entire history. "You know what happened with Lucy could never happen again or you wouldn't have come back to me. And you know—*you know!*—that had we told her six years ago, she would have come between us. It's that simple. So, you can talk about this all you want, but maybe what you really mean and don't have the balls to say is that you wish we weren't together because it amounts to the same damn thing!"

"Fine. You want the truth so badly? My life *would* be easier if I'd never come back."

I sat against the chair, my pulse roaring in my ears. *He doesn't mean that,* I thought. *He can't.* I blinked at him, expecting he'd take it back, but when his eyes met mine, there was no give, no warmth. I felt gutted and frightened. "Why would you say that?" I finally said. "You haven't been happy?" The word came out as a croak. All the fight in me was gone.

"I'm not saying it's how I've felt all along, but it's how I feel right now. I don't know that I can get past this, Claire. The only thing I can see clearly is that I've lost my kids. And if I have to choose between you and them . . ."

"You think that's what this is about?"

"That's what it feels like." He picked a piece of lettuce off the cutting board and walked it to the sink, then stood there, hands on the counter, staring straight ahead.

"This isn't about choosing between me and the kids," I said quietly. "It's about choosing between me and Annabelle."

"Are you serious?" He barked out a laugh. "Jesus, that's what you think?"

"Do you remember the day you introduced me to them?" I stared at my hands. My wedding ring.

"Of course I remember."

"Did it ever seem odd that you didn't arrange for us to meet someplace neutral? The zoo or the park or McDonald's?"

"Considering I have a son who doesn't do well in strange places? No, Claire, it didn't seem odd at all."

"Why not your house, then? Why Annabelle's?"

"I don't know, Claire, but since you seem to have all the answers, why don't you tell me?"

"I don't think it was about meeting the kids at all, Erik. I think that day was about meeting Annabelle, getting her seal of approval. It was an audition."

"Fine." He lifted his shoulders. "So sue me. I thought it important that the mother of my children get along with the woman I was falling in love with. What is this? You're jealous of Annabelle?"

"Not in the least. I love Annabelle—" I swallowed hard. "I loved being her friend. But you have never had to choose between us. And even that was okay because it was always little shit, and I didn't care. But last night? What happened happened to both of us, Erik; it happened to *our* family, and instead of us being in it together, you tossed me aside, and I let you. Did it cross your mind even once in the last twenty-four hours that I might feel just as devastated as you? That I know what it is to have a child taken from me, and to have that happen again? I wasn't okay; I'm still not. But I've had more care and concern from Eva—who, apparently, it's fine for you to betray—than I've had from the person who's supposedly 'had my back' all these years." I pushed myself up from the table. I felt the bitterness in my voice, could taste it. "I don't know that *I* can get past this," I said quietly. "I don't know that *I* want to."

CHAPTER 48

I slept in Spencer's room. I wasn't trying to punish Erik. All I knew was that I needed to cry, and if Erik tried to comfort me, it would undo something in me I would never get back. I would have been grateful again, and I would have hated him for it.

I didn't turn on any lights, just crawled beneath Spencer's down comforter, still wearing my jeans and T-shirt. Tears leaked into Spencer's pillow as I silently cried, my chest shuddering. The pillow smelled like him, a mix of his medicinal dandruff shampoo and something else—boy funk, I called it, a smell like old pennies. I wanted to inhale that scent, I missed him so much. He was my child too. I wept, aware of the chasm of loss in me that stretched back to Lucy. How could Erik not have understood this?

As soon as the jagged peaks of my sobs flattened out, I'd picture Annabelle's look of contempt as she flung that manila envelope at me and the way I'd crept forward like a beaten dog to retrieve it, or I'd hear Erik's beleaguered sigh as he sat on the chaise, his quiet fury that *I* was angry—how dare I—and I'd be crying again, the grief like dominoes, one hurt knocking into the next and the next. I was crying for Nick because I'd loved him with everything in me and it wasn't enough, there was no such thing as *enough* after what happened to Lucy, and I was crying for Lucy, always Lucy, because there would never be a grief in my life that didn't contain her. I cried about Kelly telling Erik *flat out* that she wouldn't have come if she'd known I was here, and I cried for Eva, whom I had betrayed and would keep on betraying. I cried because I had believed Annabelle was the friend I could one day tell about Lucy, and it was unfathomable to me, even now, that she wasn't. Mostly, though, I was crying for that frightened, desperate woman Erik had brought to Annabelle's six years ago to meet his kids. That young woman who would sell her soul to be liked and accepted. I thought of our first Thanksgiving and those stupid T-shirts and how everyone must have pitied me. I cried because I had tried and tried and tried, and despite everything, she didn't want me in the same house as her kids, and he *regretted* coming back.

If there had only been anger in his voice, we could move beyond this night, I thought, but what did I do with the defeat I'd heard, as if he'd pushed those words down a dozen times before? And along with the defeat was sorrow—not sadness but something so much deeper—and I understood that Erik had been carrying this regret in him for a long time.

My life would have been easier without you.

I stared into the blackness of Spencer's room, tears streaming into my ears, and I tried to find the *when* of Erik's regret. When had he first thought it: *I wish I hadn't come back* or *My life would have been easier . . .*

But there was no such moment. Instead, I kept thinking about a morning earlier that summer when I returned from a run, elated because I'd finally figured out what to get Spencer for his thirteenth birthday. "A Cuisinart!" I said to Erik as soon as I found him. He was sitting on the bed, pulling on socks. I was bouncing with excitement.

"You want a Cuisinart?"

"For Spencer! Since he loves baking!"

Erik looked up at me, amusement radiating across his face.

"I know it's a little out-there."

"He will *love* a Cuisinart, Claire. And *I* love that you do this. You actually worry about what to get for their birthdays or Christmas. And you do this in a thousand little ways, every day. I don't tell you that enough."

I turned the soaked pillow over. Spencer's birthday was only six weeks ago. Six weeks! Had Erik regretted me then?

All night I fell in and out of sleep, the room airless, Spencer's sheets tucked so tightly under the mattress, it was a struggle to turn over. Even when I wrenched them free, I couldn't get comfortable.

I finally woke around four. The zipper of my jeans was digging into my skin, and my T-shirt was damp with sweat. I pushed myself up, my back sore from the hard mattress, and tried to remember if I had any clean running clothes in the laundry. The thought of creeping into our room and gathering my things in the dark like some fugitive—I couldn't do it.

In the laundry room, I dug out the running shorts, sports bra, and singlet I'd worn two days ago, holding them to my nose to make sure they were okay to wear. All I smelled was my vanilla body spray. For a moment I held the clothes to my face. These were the clothes I'd worn when walking the girls to the bus stop, Annabelle and me joking about Phoebe becoming a teenager; they were the clothes I'd been wearing when I told them about Lucy. *I want to go back,* I thought desperately. *I want to put on these clothes and go back to just two days ago.*

CHAPTER 49

I decided to run at the lakefront so I wouldn't see anyone I knew. The sky was dark when I got on the highway, the Milwaukee skyline, with its numerous church steeples tucked between the glass high-rises, still in silhouette. Gabe's building was one of them, and I wondered if he was on his way to work, if the lawyer was. I had no idea what he'd advised Erik to do, and felt again the stab of the word *regret*. Above me was the green sign for "Chicago and East," and I wondered where I would I go if Erik and I separated.

He was gone by the time I got home. I spent the morning in Spencer's room, scribbling notes for a collage about weather. September 11 was four days away. Thinking of that had led to Spencer's History of Weather calendar, which had led to my wondering about the weather on important dates in my own life. I read that in 1607, on the date Lucy was born (January 30), the Bristol Channel flooded, drowning both people and livestock, and in 1804, on the date I married Erik, the first tropical cyclone in modern history to produce snow toppled the steeple of North Church in Boston. I looked up my birthday, and Annabelle's, Eva's, my mom's, but the descriptions were all of tragedies, and whatever I was looking for, it wasn't that.

Finally, in *The Encyclopedia of Weather* I read: *When rocks are broken into pieces and moved by natural forces (wind, rain), it is called erosion. But when a rock is changed or broken and stays where it is, it is called weathering.* I read the words again, slowly, and then again: When a rock is changed or broken and *stays where it is* . . . Longing and grief unraveled inside me. I wanted so badly to weather this.

An officer who barely looked older than Spencer knocked on the door in the early afternoon with the court-ordered PFA. He explained it to me, making sure I understood "no contact" meant not even through a third party. He called me ma'am and was polite, but I could barely breathe, I was so humiliated. After he left, I sat on the stairs in our foyer, not sure what to do.

Eva phoned midafternoon, but I let the call go to the answering machine. "Hey, lovely. Text me that you're okay. Gabe's going to phone in a bit." Erik called to say he'd be home late, not to bother with dinner. I knew he was staying to watch the dress rehearsal, something we'd planned to do together. I realized then that I couldn't have gone. Annabelle would be there. Nor could I attend the play. I had to maintain a distance of at least fifty feet. *Even at a public event?* I wondered. How was that fair? I sat abruptly at the table, the kitchen dim and shadowy, the blinds still shut from the previous night. The microwave beeped—the coffee I'd been reheating was done—but I couldn't move. I wanted to see Eva on her big night. I wanted to see Kelly. I wasn't even sure why. Maybe because she was a part of Lucy's life, maybe because this was as close as I would get to my daughter. How could Annabelle take this from me too?

I worked on the collage half-heartedly, baking sheets of newsprint to "weather" them, googling scientific terms, jotting down ideas. The light changed from afternoon to evening.

And then someone rang the doorbell, and it was Gabe, cradling a paper bag of alcohol in one arm, a plastic bag of Chinese food in the other.

"Aren't you supposed to be at the rehearsal?" I asked as I stepped back to let him in.

"Nah. Eva says I make her too nervous."

I was mortified that he was here. I had on the too-big Walmart shorts I used as PJs, a T-shirt, and fuzzy slippers. No makeup. Hair scraped into a ponytail. "Eva sent you, didn't she?" I said as he followed me into the kitchen. I couldn't look at him. I just wanted to escape upstairs to change my clothes and brush my teeth.

"She's worried." Gabe took off his sunglasses, set the bags on the counter, and scrutinized me. "With good reason, maybe?" His voice was gentle. "Let's get you a drink."

"Let's get me looking presentable first," I said. "Give me five minutes."

Upstairs, I threw on jeans and a lightweight sweater, brushed my hair, and tried in vain to make my swollen eyes look less so with a coat of mascara. From downstairs, I could hear cabinets opening and closing, music coming on, and though I knew he meant well, I wished he hadn't come. Tears filled my eyes and I blotted them with a Kleenex, my skin raw and chapped. I imagined he'd tried to talk Eva out of this—"Come on. Claire doesn't need me to sit there and hold her hand"—and Eva, good, kind, loyal Eva, whom none of us deserved, would have said, "I know, but do it for me?"

He'd set out place mats on the counter, the plastic educational ones we hadn't used in forever. The solar system for him; dinosaurs for me. "Oh, dear," I said.

"I could have given you 'rocks and fossils,' but it looked a little chewed up. Here." He handed me a cosmo, then raised his glass: "To better days? Or maybe 'peace on earth, goodwill to all'?"

"Better days might be more doable," I said.

"Doable is good." He eyeballed me over the rim of his glass. "This is going to be okay, you know."

I didn't know, but I nodded. "It's sweet of you to do this."

He waved the comment off. "The Chinese place is right down the street, and besides, where else could I learn . . ." He lifted his container of lo mein from the place mat and read out loud: "Ninety-four moons, 3,583 comets, and a whopping 796,289 asteroids have been found in our solar system!" He set down the carton and stage-whispered: "I'm pretty sure asteroids are just rocks and pebbles."

"Yes, but . . ." I scanned my own place mat for a good fact: "Did you know ostriches are the fastest dinosaur?"

"*What?*" He leaned forward to read it for himself, then looked up. "That is an embarrassment for all dinosaurs!"

"It is, isn't it?" I laughed. And just like that, I was glad he was there. I'd often found his humor annoying—I never realized how much he used it to put people at ease.

"What?" He wiped a hand over his jaw. "I have soy sauce dribbling down my chin?"

"I was thinking that you're good at making people feel comfortable. It's a nice quality."

"Well, thank you. It bugs the shit out of Eva."

I asked if he'd come straight from work—he wasn't in a suit, but khakis and a blue oxford—and he told me Thursdays were his volunteer afternoons at the Milwaukee Boys and Girls Club. I mentioned running at the lake that morning and looking for his building, and we talked about the fifth anniversary of 9/11, which was on Monday. I complimented him on his new eyeglasses. "Very Clark Kent," I assured him.

"Is that good or bad? Eva picked them out." He took them off and looked at them, his face suddenly naked, then put them back on.

It was dark out by then and we were practically sitting in the dark ourselves, only the stove light on behind him. He rose to make me another drink, and I turned on the hanging lamp over the table, which gave the room a rosy glow. The Eagles CD he'd chosen had ended, and I put on some Lucinda. It felt odd to be alone with Gabe, and I found myself casting a series of sideways glances at him as he poured my drink from the shaker.

"You're watching me again," he said without looking up.

I smiled and sat back down. "I'm used to hanging out with you in a group."

He was concentrating on carrying my full-to-the-rim martini glass across the room without spilling. "Voilà!" he said when he finally set it in front of me, then sat down and reached for the wine bottle to fill his own glass. "I said something similar to Eva after the opening gala." He sipped his wine. "I think it was the first time I actually talked to you for real. Crazy, isn't it?" He raised his chin toward the table behind me. "What's that about?" The table was covered with the curling sheets of paper I'd baked to make them look weathered.

I glanced over my shoulder. "An idea for a collage. I'm not sure yet. Something about weather."

"Ahh, you're thinking of our boy."

Our boy. I nodded and inhaled a sharp breath. I wanted to ask Gabe what he thought about Annabelle, but I didn't want to put him on the spot. I had no idea how he felt about her. I pictured how radiant she'd been at the gala.

As if reading my mind, he said, "Her petition for custody is crap, you know."

"That's what your friend said. It's just, I'm not sure how

we're going to do this." Tears sprang to my eyes. "I'm pretty sure our friendship is over."

"And you don't want it to be? Seriously?"

"I'm not her, Gabe! I wish I could just turn off my feelings, but—" I stopped. "I'm sorry. I don't mean to jump down your throat. It's just, you saw her at the gala. She was so kind. You both were. She totally had my back. And now . . ." A fresh wave of tears streamed down my face. "I want to be angry and I'm sure I will be, but I'm just too hurt. That she really thinks I'd harm our children? What do I do with that? Or with the fact that my husband is so filled with regret for betraying her." *And regret for staying with me.* I picked up the chopsticks, set them down. My eyes, even my lips, felt swollen. "God, I am so sick of crying. I don't even know why I am—" More tears spilled down my face.

Gabe got up, disappeared into our bathroom, and came back with a roll of toilet paper, which he plunked in front of me. "You do know Erik loves you, right?"

"I do. But his allegiance is to her." I grabbed a handful of toilet paper and wiped my eyes.

"Please tell me you don't really think that."

"I do."

"Well, don't. Because it's crap. The truth is, we all kowtow to her. Even Eva." He leaned both elbows on the counter. After a moment, he said, "Look, I don't know what's gone down between you and Erik the last two days, but the reason we all bow and scrape to Annabelle is just habit. Nothing more." He took a swig of wine. "When we met freshman year, Annabelle's mom was already sick, and it was bad even then. But by the end, her mom was out of her mind with pain, and the stuff she said—screaming that Annabelle had ruined her life, that she should have aborted her—"

"My God." Why had she never told me?

"Exactly. So when Annabelle was upset about whatever—Erik didn't jump high enough or she and Eva disagreed about . . . anything—we just gave in, because Christ almighty, why wouldn't we? Why do *anything* to make Annabelle's life harder? Like I said, it became a habit."

"Why didn't Erik ever tell me this?"

"He probably doesn't realize. And look, none of this excuses what Annabelle did, but it pains me that you think Erik's making some kind of choice of her over you. She took your kids and he's scared out of his fucking mind. That's it. End of story. And if it wasn't for this play on Saturday, he'd be here and you guys would be figuring this all out."

For a moment, neither of us said anything. The Lucinda CD had ended. "So, what did you mean . . . You said you all kowtow to Annabelle, which makes sense with Erik because of the kids, but why would you? If anyone has leverage . . ."

"Leverage? Seriously?" He reached for the wine bottle sitting to the side of the counter and emptied it into his glass. "You honestly think she'd balk at using our affair against me?"

"Yes! She'd be devastated if Eva found out."

He was shaking his head. "Annabelle would chew off her own leg to get out of a trap, so if it was to her benefit to tell Eva? She'd do it in a fucking heartbeat. And somehow manage to turn herself into a victim *and* get kudos for coming clean. Look what she did to you and Erik. One mistake—and granted, it's a big one—but she takes your kids? Gets a PFA against you? It's bullshit."

"I can't go to the play because of it." My eyes filled again, and I grabbed another wad of toilet paper. "Can a person run out of tears?" I pressed the tissue to one eye. "It probably seems so stupid, crying over a play when my marriage is ending and the kids are gone."

"Your marriage isn't ending. And the kids will be back

before you know it." He took a swallow of wine. "And Kelly's connected to your daughter, so of course you want to go to the play. It's not stupid in the least." He paused. "So, let's go."

"How? She'll have me arrested! God, can you imagine that scene?"

"She'll do nothing of the sort. And I'll be happy to remind her how much she owes Eva."

"You really think—" *I can go?* I started to say, but the words slid out from under me. I had no idea why I was crying again. "I'm sorry," I sniffled. "You're being so nice and all I do is blubber."

"Shit, Claire. I'd be bawling too if I'd gone through half of what you have." He clasped his hand awkwardly over mine, gave it a quick squeeze, then let go. "I'm sorry about your daughter," he said gently. "And I'm sorry Annabelle wasn't able to handle it with more . . ." He shook his head. "Grace, I guess. Compassion."

Why couldn't Erik have said this much? I thought, another rush of tears streaming down my face. And I wondered if, despite his effort to understand my past, some part of him never really could. Had I been driving a car and hit a patch of black ice, he would have understood there was nothing I could have done, but that postpartum was a kind of black ice across my life that I never saw until I was spinning wildly out of control—he'd never made that leap. I know he wanted to, and maybe he thought he had, but I don't think he ever did.

I thought of all the times in the last six years when I'd mentioned maybe telling Annabelle about Lucy, and every single time, he'd insisted Annabelle would never understand. Was it possible, though, that his certainty wasn't because he knew Annabelle so well but because that's how *he* felt? Not that he blamed me for what had happened—he didn't. But maybe he was ashamed. Of me. And in breaking our pact of silence, by telling Annabelle and Eva, maybe I'd broken the container where he'd needed to keep that truth. My parents had a similar pact, didn't they? My dad's inability to talk about Lucy, my mom's acceptance of this. But not talking about Lucy wasn't that simple for me, no matter how much Erik might have wanted, maybe needed, this. I had tried, I wanted to tell him. Did he understand that? How hard I had tried?

"How do you do it every week?" I asked Gabe. It was too painful to think about Erik right now.

"How do I do what? Put up with Annabelle?"

"But it's more than that, right? I mean, she's Eva's best friend and you're Spencer's godfather and . . . She's kind of all over your life."

"She's all over everyone's life, Claire. But I don't dislike Annabelle. She's fun and funny and . . . It's what's so baffling. She's like two different people."

I nodded.

"I'm sure Eva's told you how, when her dad was dying, Annabelle sent care packages to Philly every day. She never missed. And look at all the crap she does to make our Saturday nights special. Plus, she's brilliant. She's handled PR for a couple of my clients, and you want someone to do damage control? She's it. But it's no accident that's her specialty. Christ, it's not even ironic. It's sad. She understands damage because she's the fucking queen of it."

"But *why*?"

"Who knows?" He was turning his glass in half circles on the counter. "Maybe because she never had a dad or because of her mom dying so young or her mom *being* so young—what was she, sixteen when she had Annabelle?" A muscle jumped in his jaw. "All I know is I've never met anyone so insecure." He looked like he was about to say more, then stopped.

"Can I ask you something?"

He swirled his wine without looking up. "About the elephant we're so expertly circling? Go for it."

"Were you in love with her?"

"Not for a second. Not even close. I wish I had been. It kills me that I betrayed Eva for something so . . . It was stupid. And I know Annabelle thinks she was in love with me, but she wasn't. We were two needy fucked-up people." He smiled, though it was one of those crooked smiles people make when they're trying not to cry. "Want to hear something truly messed up?"

"Sure."

"I envy you."

"Me?"

"Yeah, I do. Because as bad as this feels, at least the truth is out there. Whatever's going to happen is going to happen. It's out of your hands." He lined up his chopsticks, first one, then the other, so they were parallel with the edge of his place mat. "I wish to God I'd come clean with Eva from the start."

"What do you think would have happened?"

"She probably would have left me."

"Then how can you wish that?"

"Because (a) there's always the chance she wouldn't have, and I'll never know, and (b) if we had gotten through it, I'm pretty sure our lives would be very different. But even if we couldn't make it work, as badly as it would have hurt, I would have moved on. We all would have. Instead, I feel like the four of us got stuck in a holding pattern."

"I know a lot about those," I said quietly. And then, "Would you still be a lawyer?"

"Without Eva? No way. After the debacle with Annabelle, I promised myself I'd give Eva the life she wanted, no matter what. Which meant I had to make the big bucks, let her focus on acting." He smiled, and this time it was real. "You want to know what I'd be now, though? If I could do it all over again?"

"What?" I was smiling too.

"A teacher." His whole face lit up. "Kids." He held his palm out to his side. "Yea high." He shook his head. "I love being with those little fuckers at the Boys and Girls Club."

I think of that moment often. Because, of course, Gabe is a teacher. Or he will be. He just started his student teaching. Second grade. We walk by the lake every few weeks and he regales me with stories of his kids, all the wacky things they do and say. He waits until we're almost back to our cars before he asks how Eva is doing.

CHAPTER 50

After Gabe left, I crawled into bed, and whether it was the cosmos or not sleeping the night before, I slept through the alarm, waking to a still house, a ladder of sunlight on the wood floor under the window. Erik's side of the bed was untouched, though on my way downstairs, I saw Spencer's sheets in disarray, a water glass on his night table. In the kids' bathroom was the travel kit Erik kept in his briefcase, a hotel shampoo on the lip of the tub. The Conrad Chicago. We'd stayed there for my art opening. The six of us.

Downstairs, the kitchen smelled of too-strong coffee. I poured a cup, then stood at the sink to sip it. It had the consistency of mud and was about as undrinkable, and it made me ache with longing. Three days before, if someone had asked what problems Erik and I had, I actually might have said this: He can't make a decent pot of coffee to save his life.

When the phone rang, I grabbed it without thinking, then silently begged, *Please don't be my mom.* She had no clue I'd told Annabelle and Eva about Lucy, that Annabelle had taken the kids, none of it. I knew she would have said all the right things, but she would have sided with Erik, and it would have destroyed me.

It was Erik: He wouldn't be home for dinner again. "I'll probably be late; I have no idea what time."

I walked the phone over to the sliding glass door. The backyard was filled with hundreds of little birds all pecking at the lawn. "We knew this week would be crazy," I said.

"Yeah, I guess we did." I heard a softening of that hard edge, and I closed my eyes, wishing he would talk to me. "I'm going to sleep in tomorrow," he said. "I'll see you when you get back from your run."

He wasn't in bed again when I woke the next morning, but Spencer's door was closed, and Erik's keys were on the kitchen counter. Outside, the grass was wet with dew, and a single bird whose call sounded like the ding of a bicycle bell trilled over and over. Erik's car wasn't in the drive, and I felt that register. It meant he'd had a drink too many and Eva had probably driven him home. I imagined them all at Union House. Kelly would have been there. Was Gabe? Annabelle and Scott? Something wrenched in me at the thought. How quickly I would disappear from their lives.

I did my six-mile loop around the neighborhood, but my breathing was out of sync, my legs heavy. I kept picturing them—the fellows, the Ten Chimneys staff—crowded into the narrow bar, laughing and teasing in that punch-drunk giddy way of exhausted people who have been working together on a project. Raising their glasses to Kelly and Erik, maybe to Alfred and Lynn, the actors jostling to best one another with their effusive toasts. I wanted to have been included.

At least I'm going to the play, I told myself, but that was little comfort. I wasn't wanted there either. And the PFA terrified me, the thought of cops showing up. Would they walk me out in front of everyone?

But even if, as Gabe promised, nothing happened, Erik would be furious. My attending the performance would only make things worse with Annabelle. And didn't he deserve to enjoy the play without worrying about me? *My life would have been easier . . .* This was his night too. I almost owed it to him not to go. But as soon as I thought, *Okay, I won't,* something almost primal rose up in me. *I have to,* I would think, *I have to.* It wasn't a thought so much as an instinct, visceral and raw. *Why?* I kept asking myself. But I had no answer beyond the vague sense that it wasn't about Kelly or Annabelle or Eva. It wasn't even about Erik.

By the time I finished running, the sun was burning through the fog. Our newspaper wasn't in the drive, which meant Erik was already up. I sat on the porch steps to take off my damp shoes. I had no clue if he knew of my plan to attend the play, and I couldn't decide if I wanted Eva or Gabe to have mentioned it or not. Finally, I pushed myself up and went inside.

He was sitting at the counter in his Hugh Hefner robe, drinking coffee, reading the *Journal Sentinel*. Sleep lines etched his face, and his hair was sticking up in the back. "Hey," I said as I carried my shoes across the kitchen to the sliding glass door, where I set them on the mat. Sunlight streamed through the windows. "I thought you were sleeping in."

"That was the plan." He set down the paper. "Did you realize Spencer's mattress was that damn hard?"

I glanced at him over my shoulder as I poured a cup of coffee, then turned to face him. "Like sleeping on concrete. Although he does have the best sheets in the house." Eight-hundred-thread-count Egyptian cotton for our boy. Anything less "poked" him.

"Yeah, I noticed that too." Erik's tired eyes met mine, and I felt his gratitude.

"You look beat."

"I feel beat." He folded the paper in half and pushed it

aside. "Listen, Claire—" He smiled sadly. "I feel like shit for saying what I did about the kids. You're the best thing that ever happened to them, and I'm sorry. I'm really sorry."

I nodded, wanting so much, as I'm sure he did, for his words to be a salve, but all I could hear was what he wasn't saying. I was the best thing that had ever happened to his kids, but not to him. His words frightened me. I couldn't bear the thought of losing him, but what if his loving me had been contingent—without either of us understanding it—on my keeping Lucy a secret?

Outside, the sunlight was so bright I had to squint. "It's gorgeous out," I said quietly. "You couldn't have asked for better weather. Are you all set for tonight?"

I felt his confusion at my response—or lack of response, but he only lifted his mug and said, "Ready as we're going to be."

I waited for him to say more but he just extended his arms in an exaggerated facsimile of a stretch and said, "The caffeine's starting to kick in, thank God."

"That's good," I said, and opened the refrigerator, squatting down to get a yogurt on the bottom shelf. "So, it was a late night?"

"Not really."

I pushed myself up, knees creaking, and concentrated on pulling the top off the yogurt. *So, this is how it's going to be?* I thought. We answer each other's questions, but barely? I focused on rummaging in the drawer for one of my long-handled iced-tea spoons. "Did you guys go to Union House?"

"Where else?" He swallowed another gulp of coffee. "We are nothing if not predictable."

"Really, Erik?" I said. *We are nothing if not predictable*? It was his hail-fellow-well-met voice, his full-of-bonhomie voice, the one reserved for pretentious donors who treated him like the hired help. His staff teased him endlessly about this voice, and Eva did a hilarious imitation. His cheerful "fuck you very much" voice.

"I'm still your wife," I said, hating how hurt I sounded. "I'm not some asshole donor you're trying to get rid of."

His face registered surprise, then immediately fell. "You're right. I'm sorry. Honest to God, I wasn't . . . I just don't want to rub salt in the wound. I know you were looking forward to the play."

"I wanted to talk to you about that," I said. "I'm going to go tonight."

He was shaking his head. "You can't. It violates—"

"The PFA. I know."

"Then . . . I don't understand."

"I don't care about the PFA, Erik. Or I don't care enough to not go."

"Then I guess you don't care enough about me either, because if you go and Annabelle decides—"

"Well, that would be something to take up with her, wouldn't it?" I locked my eyes on his as I took a spoonful of yogurt. "Annabelle's on the board. You really think she'd do anything to sabotage the performance?"

"Are you kidding me? Annabelle doesn't think, she reacts, and when she's blindsided, she reacts badly. And how you could not know this after the other night is beyond me!" He scraped back his stool and paced to the sliding glass door, hands in fists, the sun full on his face. "I'm stunned you would even consider going."

"I have a right to be there, Erik."

"No, actually. You don't. You go to that play and you're breaking the law."

I pulled open the drawer next to the refrigerator to get a piece of Saran Wrap for the yogurt I no longer wanted. *I can't not go,* I thought, and tried to marshal my thoughts into something coherent. When I turned around, he was still standing at the sliding glass door staring out, and something—the big robe and his skinny calves and pale narrow feet—made him seem vulnerable. "I don't know why I feel like I have to be there," I said. "I'm not trying to make things more difficult."

"Really? Because I've got a knot in my gut the size of Canada. And most of it is about you and the kids and what Annabelle's going to do, if not today, then on Monday when she tells her lawyer you violated the PFA. And you can actually make things better, yet you refuse." He walked back to the counter and took a swig of coffee, his furious eyes lasered on mine.

I closed my eyes as if to deflect the heat of his anger. Who cared if I was the best thing that had ever happened to his kids if, in the end, *I* wasn't worth fighting for? *Fine, you win, I won't go,* I almost said, but I couldn't. "I want to see Eva, Erik." I didn't know what else to say. "I want to see Kelly."

"Yeah, I get that, but it's not like you haven't seen Eva in dozens of plays and won't see her in dozens more. And maybe you feel this is your only chance to see Kelly, but if it's that important, we'll go to New York; we'll see her in *Mamma Mia!*" He paused. "It's not like you'd talk to her today. She'll be backstage, and afterward, she's going to be swarmed."

We'll go to New York. I clung to that, even as I was telling him, "It's fine if I don't talk to her." Was this true? I only knew that I couldn't imagine sitting at home when she was this close.

"It's a *play,*" Erik was saying. He picked up his mug, then set it down. "It's not like I'm asking you to miss someone's birthday or anniversary or—" He looked at me, then dropped his hands to his sides. "*What?*" he demanded. "Jesus! What grave sin have I committed now?"

Someone's birthday or anniversary.

My head was so filled with noise I couldn't think. "That's it," I said, and could taste the grief. I moved to sit on the stool opposite his, one hand clapped over my mouth. "That's it."

"What's *it*?"

"I've missed everything, Erik." My voice broke. I hadn't celebrated my mom's birthday with her in thirteen years, not even the surprise sixtieth my dad had begged me to come home for. I hadn't attended their fortieth wedding celebration at the restaurant. I was too afraid to go back to Rehoboth, too afraid of my own shame.

And, most of all: I'd missed my daughter's entire life. I would continue to miss her entire life.

I felt Erik watching me, but I couldn't look at him. I knew he didn't understand what I was trying to explain, in part because I barely understood it. Helplessly, I stared past him to our kitchen table, sunlight pooling on the wood. Underneath, on Erik's chair, was Hazel's purple rabbit's-foot key chain. She did this sometimes, left things of hers—a Beanie Baby, the tiny plastic mouse from her Mouse Trap game—where Erik would find them.

I lifted my eyes to Erik's and saw the lingering anger and confusion. "Hazel left you a present." I nodded to his chair.

He swiveled to look, then got up and retrieved the rabbit's foot and just held it in his big hands. I watched him, the lines on his face, the fatigue, the love for his daughter. "What do you mean you missed everything?" he said warily.

"I never gave myself a chance, Erik. I never fought for her. I was so sure I couldn't be a good mother, I was too afraid to even try." Tears clogged my throat. "I'm not suggesting I can undo that choice, because I can't, but I've missed so many things."

He wasn't looking at me, but he nodded.

"I'm not trying to hurt you or the kids or damage our

marriage." I sat up straight, hands clasped between my knees to stop their shaking. "And I'm sorry I'm only realizing this now—I know my timing sucks—but I can't not go, Erik. I don't know what else to say. I can't keep missing my own life, which is how it feels." I pushed my lips together to keep from crying. "I'm sorry. I know I sound melodramatic."

"No," he said wearily. "No, it makes sense." He set the rabbit's foot down. Neither of us spoke. "I'm just scared," he said. "I haven't talked to the kids since Tuesday. I've called a dozen times." He was still standing, hands lying in loose fists on the counter. "I know it feels like I've never stood up to Annabelle, but it's not—I guess I always justified it because it meant the kids never got stuck in the middle. I was so grateful that you never took a stand with her, never asked me to take a stand."

"But maybe I should have, Erik. Maybe *we* should have. We've never woken with our kids on Christmas morning—not once!—and we can't ever get that back. And there's a hundred things like it. I'm not suggesting some tit for tat—I love that we all work together when it comes to the kids, and I—you know I love Annabelle, but we've relinquished too much. Or I have."

He let out a long, ragged breath. "You're right." His eyes looked bruised. "And yeah, you should be there today."

Only twenty-four hours before, I probably would have thanked him, but I hadn't been asking for his approval or permission. I'm not sure I wanted it. I got up to refill my mug, though I didn't need more coffee. I felt him waiting for me to say more. But I didn't know where to begin or if I even needed to. He understood what I'd been struggling to understand myself—or he was trying to, which felt huge. I thought of Gabe envying me because the truth about Lucy was out there. Maybe that was enough for me and Erik too. At least for now. We'd been so busy protecting the lies we'd told everyone else, we hadn't understood the lies we'd been telling each other—and the lies we'd been telling ourselves.

"I really think today will be okay," I said when I turned back around. "I'll get there right before the show starts, and I'll leave right after. I won't make things worse. And I'm not blindsiding Annabelle. I'm pretty sure she knows I'm coming."

"Wait." He jerked his head up. "She *knows*? Please, *please* tell me—"

"No, no. It's okay. I didn't talk to her." I reached across the counter for his arm. "But Gabe might have."

"Gabe? Why would—are you kidding me?" His face turned dark. "Jesus, this just gets worse and worse."

"Why? Is it really so awful for Annabelle to be reminded that we've been keeping her lousy secret for years?"

"Spare me the defense. It's his lousy secret too. And Gabe is the last person I want help from."

"Gabe got Andy for you," I said. "He was defending you the other night!"

"Ahh, yes, my good old pal Gabe to the rescue!"

"Why are you angry at him? Gabe loves you, Erik. He's your best friend."

"Yeah, well, I guess you don't ever really get over your best friend sleeping with your wife. Annabelle and I separated because of Gabe, Claire. I'm not saying we didn't have a shit-ton of problems, and I'm not saying it wouldn't have happened anyway, but forgive me if I'm a little wary about his *help*. Especially when it comes to my marriage."

Later, we would go over and over it, blaming ourselves for not hearing the door, for being so self-involved we didn't notice them standing there, Gabe holding the cardboard carrier of coffees and Eva beside him, her face leached of color. How did their presence not register? Why didn't they make a noise, call hello—*anything*! Later, I would recall how I'd thought it so wonderful, the way we just traipsed in and out of each other's houses without knocking, proof of how close we were, how we had nothing to hide.

Later still, years later, we'd wonder, actually say it out loud: *Do you think they'd still be together if they hadn't walked in that morning?* I asked Gabe once at the end of one of our walks. The wind was howling off the lake and we'd turned back early. He didn't answer at first, just shoved his hands in the pockets of his leather jacket and shook his head. "That's the million-dollar question, isn't it?"

In memory, it seems Erik and I realized in the same instant that they were there. Maybe we heard something; maybe the light shifted. My heart felt as if it were exploding.

"Jesus, how long have you—" Erik started to say.

"Oh my God," I rushed in. "That probably sounded really awful! It's not what you think."

Of course, we were making it worse.

"I'm just venting," Erik said. "I'm upside down over this Annabelle crap and I haven't slept for shit." He looked at Eva, arms limp at his sides. "Whatever you do, do not pay attention to the crazy man in the robe!"

She smiled, and I felt my breath leave and I thought, *Maybe*. Maybe she hadn't heard us. But all she said was, "It's okay, Erik. It really is. We should have called. I just wanted to see Claire before the play." She turned to me then, and whatever shred of hope I'd been clinging to dissipated. Everything about her was wooden. Her movement, face, smile. I was aware of Gabe setting the coffees on the table. I couldn't look at him.

"I figured I might not have a chance to talk to you later," she said to me. "We're headed to Door County tomorrow." I'd forgotten she and Gabe were taking off for a few days. She turned to look at him as if to confirm their trip, and she was smiling, but there was something off, the way when someone falls and breaks a leg or an arm it's still attached, but the angle is wrong. And then she just sort of sagged against the refrigerator, holding her stomach, and bent over at the waist. "So, it's true?" she said to no one in particular. "I guess I always knew, but actually hearing it out loud . . ." She was staring down. She wasn't dressed up—jeans, a UWM sweatshirt, hair in a ponytail—but she had on red suede high-heeled boots. The boots broke me. They were the kind of boots you put on when you're happy, excited about the day.

"Eva, this is all of out of context," Erik said.

"You knew too?" she said to me.

Tears rose in my eyes, and I nodded once.

"And Scott?" she asked.

"I don't think so," I said.

Behind me Gabe made a sound of disbelief.

Eva slowly pushed herself up. She tucked her hands in the back pockets of her jeans and glanced around the kitchen. "I should be mad, right?" She was staring out the window over the sink. "I should be shattered, and maybe I am, and I don't know it yet, but all I can think of is how all these years you guys have been lying to protect me, and all these years I've been lying to protect you, and for the life of me, I can't figure out what we were protecting each other from." She gave a weird little hysterical-sounding laugh. "I need to go home," she said to Gabe. She still had that awful broken smile, and her eyes wouldn't settle on any of us.

And then they were gone. Erik and I didn't move, didn't speak. We heard the thunk of the car doors. Saw the bright flash of Eva's red Jeep as it drove by. The coffees were still in the container on the table.

CHAPTER 51

When the Lunts were performing *There Shall Be No Night* during the end of the war in London, the play was often interrupted by the long whistles that preceded bomb blasts. Plaster dust fell from the ceiling onto the stage. But "the Lunts weren't afraid of death," their biographer Maurice Zolotow wrote. "They were only afraid of a scene being spoiled by a rocket exploding at the wrong time." It was one of those stupid sentences we'd all laughed about, but after Eva and Gabe drove off, it occurred to me that this was how most of us really did live: bombs exploding around us while we carried on the performances that were our lives.

Erik and I moved around the house without speaking. I urged him to lie down and at least try to rest, then sat in our sunlit kitchen, feeling sick with remorse. In that awful instant when I realized they were standing in our foyer, I saw the hurt in Gabe's eyes, and I understood that his kindnesses these last two weeks—staying close to me at the gala, bringing the Chinese food, even accompanying me to the play that night—had been for Erik.

Not for me; not even for Eva.

Eva texted Erik around noon to say she'd still pick him up and Gabe was expecting to ride with me.

"Jesus," Erik said under his breath. He was in the bathroom shaving, and he turned to me, hands falling to his sides. "How is she going to get through this?"

"The same way you and Gabe will."

"We don't have to be onstage after having our lives blasted apart."

"She's a pro, Erik. Onstage is probably the best place for her to be."

"We look like bank robbers," I said when Gabe opened the passenger door. We were both in black dress pants, a sleeveless black turtleneck for me, a black cashmere sweater for him.

"Well, you are breaking the law." He smiled wanly. "And I'm aiding and abetting."

I think I nodded. The PFA felt so completely unimportant at that point. All afternoon, I kept picturing Annabelle getting ready, being excited, having no idea that everything had changed. I'd wanted to warn her, though, of course, I couldn't.

"I feel horrible about this morning," I said as I pulled out of the circular driveway.

"Don't. It was bound to happen. That it didn't before is a miracle." He pulled the seat belt across his shoulder. I was aware of how much broader than Erik he was, though in the confined space of the car he seemed diminished. "It just sucks that it happened today." He clicked the latch into place. "Although maybe this is exactly how it should end, with a performance."

"What do you mean end? Did she say that?"

"She didn't have to." He was staring out the passenger

window. The houses on their wooded road were tucked so far back you could see only a hint of them through the trees: a roofline, a dormer widow. "Or maybe I'm the one who's done," he said quietly.

"Why?"

Sunlight strobed his face. "I realize it borders on the ridiculous to say this, because she's the one who's been betrayed, but I'm pissed. Ten years of wearing this fucking hair shirt, and for what? Don't get me wrong: I'd wear it another ten if it kept her from being hurt, but that she just *let* me? That she knew all this time?"

"But she didn't," I protested. "Not really. She suspected, but that's not the same."

"She said it was like kids who realize Santa isn't real but won't let themselves know it." He was leaning back, heels of his hands pressed to his eyes.

"Did you tell her what you told me? About how you wanted to tell her the truth all these years, and how you regret—"

"Oh, I tried." His voice was mocking, bitter. "Before I could say two sentences, my lovely wife very gently, very sweetly, put her fingers on my mouth and stopped me. She said she was glad I didn't tell her." He let out a strangled laugh. "What do I do with that? She's glad we've all lied to her for the last decade?"

"Or maybe she's glad she had ten years of believing she was happy, of *being* happy!" Is this what Erik had done for me? Pushed down the regret so we could have the life we did? Was that so awful? It didn't feel like it.

I remember almost nothing of the play. I know there were three curtain calls, and thunderous applause for Eva. Gabe and I clapped so hard our hands were sore. James Goodinson, who was on the board, slapped him on the back from the seat behind and said, "Your wife stole the show!" And then the cast was pulling Kelly onstage as the room rose in a standing ovation. Afterward, when the house lights came up and the audience filed out, their voices animated, Gabe and I stayed in our seats. People kept stopping to tell us, "You must be so proud!" and "Congratulations!" until finally, the theater was empty. Neither of us moved. I think we were numb. I couldn't believe it was over.

I thought of the roles I'd seen Eva play over the years—Mollie Malloy, the saucy prostitute in *Front Page,* or the thrice-divorced Julia in *A Delicate Balance,* or Anna Karenina standing on the edge of the stage before jumping—and in every single performance, there was a moment when she ceased being Eva, so thoroughly did she inhabit her character. Later, when she was back in the lobby, wearing her own clothes again, but with her hair still elaborately coiffed like Anna Karenina's or her eyes rimmed in dark kohl like Mollie's, I felt almost shy around her, as if she hadn't fully returned, some part of her still lingering in the world of the play. *Who are you?* I would think. Eva loved my reaction. It meant, she always said, that she'd done her job.

It never happened with *Quadrille,* though, not because she wasn't stunning as Serena—or at least I assume she was. But even with the high-collared Victorian dress and upswept hair and patrician voice, she never stopped being Eva. I heard the audience laughing uproariously at some of her lines, found myself smiling a few times, but the entire play, my heart was in my throat. Though I don't think I took my eyes from her once, I found it unbearable to see her as Serena, to see her as anyone except herself. I think some part of me knew, without fully acknowledging it—the way she'd known all those years about Gabe and Annabelle—that she would leave, slip into a new life the way she'd slipped into all those roles, becoming so quickly someone we no longer knew.

In the lobby, the audience was mostly gone. The sky was dark, small groups milling around out front, waiting for one of the passenger vans owned by Ten Chimneys that were ferrying people to the cast party at the Lunts' house up the road. Laughter and muted conversation floated inside each time someone opened the glass doors. Gabe and I stood at the back of the room, waiting for Eva.

From across the lobby, where he was chatting with the cowboy-booted actor from Texas who had played Axel, Erik nodded to me, his eyes tired. A few feet away, the theater critic from the *Tribune* was talking to the woman who'd played Charlotte. She had one of those overly dramatic, look-at-me voices, and I kept glancing at her in annoyance, as if she were the cause of the tightness in my chest. Annabelle and Scott, their backs to us, stood with Frank and Genevieve Minni.

I had no idea if Annabelle had seen me. She was waiting for Eva, and I knew she'd rush over as soon as Eva entered the lobby, bursting with excitement and happiness and pride. I'd always envied this about Annabelle, how generous she was with her praise, how she'd become almost giddy when something good happened to one of us. "This calls for ice cream!" she'd announce. "Champagne!"

The room erupted in applause then, and there was Kelly, regal and beautiful in black silk harem pants and a sleeveless blouse.

"We've started the petition to get you back next year!" Genevieve Minni called, and someone else said, "Where is it? I'll sign."

Kelly just smiled and gestured to Eva, who was suddenly beside her in a glittery silver sweater and jeans and heels. Another scattering of applause. She looked ecstatic. And then Annabelle was hugging her, the two of them rocking back and forth, Eva bending over to accommodate Annabelle, as if she were hugging a child.

"This is excruciating," Gabe whispered.

And it was—except hadn't we witnessed this a thousand times in the last few years? Eva and Annabelle hugging, laughing, making plans despite the monstrous lie between them? Shouldn't it have been excruciating all along?

And then Eva was making a beeline for us, hugging Gabe and then me, all of us speaking at once—*You were great, you were fantastic,* and *Really? Did you like it?* When Eva stepped back, her face flushed, she was squeezing both of our hands. "I wish you could come to the cast party," she said to me.

"I'm just glad I got to see you. You were stunning, Eva."

"It felt good to be up there." She looked at Gabe, brushing something from his shoulder. "You holding up okay?" she asked gently. Her eyes were filled with such tenderness and worry, not even a hint of anger or recrimination. I knew right then that she would leave him.

Four days from that night, after their return from Door County, where, Eva would tell me, she and Gabe walked and talked endlessly, she would sit at our kitchen table and tell me she'd known the marriage was over before they got home from our house that morning of the play. "Maybe if I'd been angry, there would have been hope," she said, but she wasn't. Not at him, not at us. "I was grateful," she would say. "It's as if my marriage was terminal. I probably knew at some level about their affair from the start, but the lies bought me time.

How do I regret that? Can you imagine if I'd found out right away? I wouldn't have met you and we never would have become friends. And I would have missed all those Saturday nights and watching the kids grow up, and all my good times with Gabe, my whole life with him! I wouldn't have had any of that." She'd been crying. "I didn't want it to end any more than I want a play I'm in to close."

CHAPTER 52

By the time Eva, Gabe, and I left the Program Center, Annabelle and Scott were already in the van. The *Tribune* guy was interviewing Erik. I waved, and he signaled that he'd call later. I didn't see Kelly, and though I'd suspected we probably wouldn't talk, I had hoped. I had wanted so much to know something—anything—about Lucy.

"You sure we can't walk you to your car?" Eva said as she and Gabe were about to get in the van.

"I'm fine," I lied. It was a pretty night, a little chilly, but bright with stars and a full moon. It was still officially summer, though it felt like autumn, smelled like autumn.

"You're not coming to the party?" Christine looked up from the clipboard on which she'd been checking off names as people boarded the van. "But you have to!"

"I was hoping Claire would be my ride." Kelly seemed to appear from nowhere, her hair haloed in the lights of the Program Center.

Eva squeezed my hand as she climbed on the bus.

"But there's room for you both—" Christine stopped as Kelly flashed the pack of cigarettes in her palm. "Gotcha," Christine laughed. And then, "But no playing hooky." She waved her pen at Kelly. "We need you at the party."

"You don't really have to give me a ride," Kelly said as we started up the lighted path to the parking lot. "I just wanted to apologize. When I heard Eva say Lucy's name—" She stopped, breathing heavily. "Good Lord, is this path straight uphill?"

It was. Below us through the trees, the Ten Chimneys van circled the drive, then began making its way up the narrow road.

"Anyway, Eva told me what happened and I feel awful. I meant it when I said I didn't want to make waves for you."

"I know," I said. "Thank you, I guess."

She touched my wrist. "I'm glad you came tonight." And then a sad smile crossed her face. "My big *debut* as a director." She pronounced *debut* as "day-but," a joke from high school.

I smiled. "Your big 'day-but' was a hit."

We were silent then, staring down as we picked our way over the uneven path.

"I've been remembering a lot of stuff," she said after a minute. "Like how your dad loved Frank Sinatra and always played 'New York, New York' for me. Or how when your mom came home from the restaurant, she'd go straight to the piano and start playing in the dark."

"And if you tried talking to her, she'd just smile with her eyes closed like you weren't there and keep playing. It used to bug the hell out of me."

"I loved it. It's like, that was her time and no one could fuck with it. Does she still play?"

I swallowed. "Not so much." After all the other losses my mom had endured—me, Lucy, Nick and Kelly, the house—I'm not sure why this, her no longer having a piano, felt like such a deep wound.

We reached the flat expanse of parking lot and stopped. Annabelle's SUV was a few spaces away, her mother's rosary dangling from the rearview mirror. I felt a tissue-paper-thin sadness tear inside me.

"Your artwork is amazing," Kelly said then. We were standing at my car while she finished her cigarette.

"You saw it?" But why wouldn't she have once Eva explained about Lucy Claire? Everything was on the gallery website.

"I bought *Light*."

"But that was going for—" An astronomical amount, I started to say, but it probably wasn't astronomical at all to Kelly. For some reason this made me laugh.

"Exactly." She grinned, then blew a smoke ring up to the trees. Wrinkles fanned out from her eyes. It was so strange: an older Kelly.

I crossed my arms over my chest. "Every collage is about her. But that one especially."

"That's why I bought it."

I nodded. *Ask her about Lucy,* I told myself. That's all I cared about. But just as I blurted, "I know you said you wouldn't talk about—," Kelly said, "She knows you're an artist."

"What?"

"And she knows you loved her."

Everything in me went still.

"Nick made sure of that. Andrea too." She studied me for a moment, brow furrowed, then reached into her pocket for a phone, tapped the screen, and handed it to me.

And there she was. My daughter. Lucy. Sixteen years old. My hands were shaking so badly, Kelly had to take the phone and hold it for me. I couldn't move or breathe. I wanted to memorize every detail. Her pale blue formal dress, her tanned shoulders, her dad's smile, my long brown hair. I'd always pictured her blond, like she'd been as a baby. She had freckles. A tiny gap in her teeth. She was glancing shyly at the boy next to her. "Trevor," Kelly said. "Her boyfriend. He's a nice kid."

"She's beautiful," I whispered, touching a finger to the edge of the screen.

"And funny and smart. She runs cross-country. Eva says you're a runner too."

It was a short drive to Alfred and Lynn's house. I understood without either of us saying anything that we were finished talking about Lucy. That Kelly had given me as much as she could without betraying her brother. She asked about my collages, how long I'd been doing them, and I told her what I'd told almost no one, that I'd begun them in the hospital, and working on them and running were the only things that made sense to me for years. I asked if she was eager to get home, and she was, though she was a little "spooked" about flying on the anniversary of 9/11. I told her how frightened I'd been that day for her. It was easy talking, and I wished it were a longer drive. I thought too of all the times I'd given her rides. To school and parties and my parents' restaurant. To auditions in Philly and to and from the Wilmington train station when she was at Yale. How was I now driving her to the home of Alfred Lunt and Lynn Fontanne in Genesee Depot, Wisconsin? It felt impossible. And improbable.

Without warning, my mind spun back to the morning, to Eva and Gabe, and how improbable that had been too. It was the kind of timing that belonged to a play, perfectly orchestrated and rehearsed, because just one minute either way and everything could have been different. But maybe our lives were always like this, chance upon chance upon chance. Although I couldn't know it that night, it's why we would get the kids back. Not because of the lawyers or because of anything Erik said to Annabelle or even because she had a change of heart. We'd get them back because of Eva and Gabe breaking up, and Annabelle shattering into a hundred pieces. She wouldn't have the energy or the will to keep fighting with Erik. We'd get them back because it would be easier for her to *not* have the kids as she talked endlessly with Eva and did damage control in her marriage.

At the Lunts' Swedish manor house, light spilled from the windows and across the courtyard. I pulled in behind the van, and we watched the guests disembark. Eva turned and waved to us.

"She's great," Kelly said, extracting a cigarette from her pack, then sliding it back in.

"Go ahead." I nodded at the cigarettes. "You might not get another chance for a while."

Her face opened in surprise. "I can't smoke in your car! You're a runner, for God's sake."

But I wasn't ready for her to go. "Hey, I broke the law to come see you tonight, so a little smoke . . ." I shrugged.

"You did, didn't you? Break the law?" She glanced away, tilting her head up as if to better see the stars out the passenger window. "Eva mentioned the PFA." She opened her mouth to say something else, then paused and turned to me. "I'm so so sorry about Annabelle taking your kids. I wanted to say that earlier. I'm probably one of the few people, besides my brother and your mom, who knows what that would do to you." She held up the cigarette. "You sure about this?"

I nodded.

Another van pulled up to the manor. There was something whimsical about the house, like a drawing from a children's book. A hodgepodge of additions jutted out at odd angles, and six of the estate's ten chimneys, all different heights and styles, poked up almost comically.

"I can't believe you can come here whenever you want," Kelly said. "Or is it like the beach and you just take it for granted?" We used to laugh and roll our eyes at the tourists who'd get so excited about seeing the ocean.

But Ten Chimneys wasn't like the beach at all. I thought of how Erik had brought it up on our first date, and how I'd mentioned Kelly to him that night. It felt as if this moment had somehow been preordained all those years ago. Ten Chimneys was also where I'd married Erik and, in the years after, where the six of us—me and Erik, Annabelle and Scott, Gabe and Eva—had attended dozens of dinners and parties and plays. It was where every year on May 26, we'd brought the kids with us to celebrate "Ten Chimneys Day" with a lavish Lunt-style picnic on the lawn. And now it was where Kelly and I had reconciled, if that's what this was, and where I'd seen my daughter's picture. *She knows you loved her.*

I would never take any of that for granted. But even without those things, there was something magical about this place where two people had believed they could create the life they dreamed of. And not just believed it; they'd done it. And then shared that life with all the people they loved. "If you get to go to Ten Chimneys, you must have done something right," the actress Carol Channing had remarked. Sometimes when I saw the quote, which was on everything—mugs, magnets, T-shirts, tote bags—I felt such panicked disbelief. How had *I* ended up at Ten Chimneys?

What had I done right?

"I told your husband," Kelly said, lowering the window and exhaling a long plume of smoke, "that if I'd known you were here, I never would have come."

"He told me," I said. "It was stupid not to contact you, Kel." *Kel.* The name slipped out, like a wineglass shattering on the floor.

But all she said was, "I'm glad you didn't contact me." She turned toward the window and tapped the ash from her cigarette outside. "I'm glad I came."

"Well, you did an amazing job. The show tonight, your *debut*—"

"I wasn't talking about Ten Chimneys."

And then, before I could answer, she opened the door, tossed her cigarette to the gravel, and ground it out with the toe of her shoe. "I better get in there," she said, and gave my arm a quick squeeze.

CHAPTER 53

I was too wound up to go straight home, and so I drove the long way, past Kopp's. I wanted to savor the encounter with Kelly, hold in my head that image of Lucy. My daughter. My beautiful daughter.

Beyond the darkened fields, a radio tower blinked, and an airplane pulsed across the sky like a heartbeat. I thought again of the anniversary the day after next. I'd been mystified when I looked at September 11 in Spencer's History of Weather calendar to find no mention of those perfect blue skies. Hadn't the gorgeous autumn weather been a part of what happened that day? Why was it only the damage caused by storms and lightning strikes, record-breaking days of rainfall or gale-force winds, hurricanes or droughts, that counted as history? Why not the cloudless skies, the gentle breezes, the bright September sun that had made it an ideal day for flying?

Kopp's was packed. Shadowy bands of people floated in the glare of headlights. I was tempted to get a custard, and if Erik were with me, we probably would have. *Maybe tomorrow,* I thought, and felt something in me release. We had a ton to work out—we'd both said awful things—but Kopp's had always been a good place for us, at least a place to start.

Kopp's had become one of the kids' favorite places too, where we celebrated report cards and losing a tooth, first and last days of school. Spencer couldn't eat the custard, but we brought him dessert from home, and the girls loved hearing the story of our first "date," especially the part about how it almost didn't happen. How even as Erik was suggesting we grab a frozen custard, his heart wasn't in it—he was avoiding going home to his empty house. And following him in my car, I regretted saying yes. I was tired, and now I would have to talk to this strange man.

We keep embellishing the story: how we were drenched in sweat ("She had BO," Erik loves to stage-whisper), how Erik was wearing his black "dad" socks with his gym shorts, how we were both in foul moods ("I didn't want to go to Kopp's with this skinny lady, even if she was pretty! I wanted to be with you guys, but it was past your bedtime!").

"But then you fell in love!" the girls exclaim. That's our refrain. It's also the part of the story where Spencer announces he's never falling in love because "kissing is disgusting." Phoebe has decided she'll fall in love a lot, "probably every month or so." When we ask why, she rolls her eyes: Everyone knows when you're falling in love, you buy lots of new clothes! Hazel's going to fall in love with either an astronaut or a man who drives an ice cream truck.

"Astronaut and ice cream man?" Erik laughs later when we're alone. "You think it's the white uniform?"

"*That's* what you're worried about? Not the one who wants to fall in love every month?"

Already in the rearview mirror, Kopp's was just a patch of pale light in the dark fields. It struck me that my own dreams had been just as outlandish when I met Erik. What if he was the person who could somehow, impossibly, understand who I was? What if he could believe I was more than what I had done? More than what I had lost? A thousand what-ifs, each as unlikely as marrying an astronaut. And yet, he was that man. Or at least he was trying to be.

But I wasn't that woman anymore, that wounded, frightened woman who had been desperate not just to be loved but to be rescued. Had I understood the difference? I'm not sure I had. That woman would have never insisted on attending the play that night, and she certainly wouldn't have defied a PFA order to do so. I knew this was a good thing—I was learning to stand up for myself, and because of that, I'd talked to Kelly: *She knows you loved her.* And yet, my throat suddenly felt thick with tears.

Why?

I didn't understand until I passed the darkened strip mall with the ballet studio where all those years ago Annabelle and I used to watch the girls take classes. They'd looked like little sumo wrestlers in their bunched-up tights and leotards. I'd loved being her friend, I thought. When I met Erik, I wasn't sure I could love a child again, and she had made it easy. So many exes wouldn't have. Whatever else her faults, for six years she had openheartedly shared her children with me. She, more than Erik, more than my own mom, hadn't just taught me how to be a mother; she'd let me be one.

At our house, I sat in the car, listening to the engine ticking down, our street quiet, the sky filled with a thousand ancient stars. Everything was dark but for the yellow porch light and that full, bright moon overhead. It might as well have been a stage set. In a few minutes I'd go inside, flip on the hall light, and slip out of my heels. In the kitchen, where Hazel's purple rabbit foot was still on the counter, I'd boil water for hot chocolate, then sit at the table to call my mom.

In the morning, Eva and Gabe would drive to Door County, where they would gently unravel their marriage, and the following week, the kids would start staying with us again. No big reconciliation, no fanfare, just Annabelle phoning in tears. "You win," she would sob, hiccupping and choking. It would fill me with a bottomless sorrow. How could she think we had won anything?

"It's not like that, Annabelle," I would say, but she'd only cry harder.

"I ruin everything. My whole life."

I'd want to tell her that wasn't true, want to tell her our friendship wasn't over, but I couldn't know this yet. Erik and I were too raw, and I was still too hurt. So was she. And maybe too we were both scared. Something else we had in common: We both understood how easy it is to damage what you most love.

My life would be so much quieter that fall. Eva would move to Philly to play Isabel in Tennessee Williams's Christmas play *Period of Adjustment,* which a friend of Kelly's was producing, and though Annabelle and I would resume talking, for a long time, it would only be about the kids. Still, there was a kindness to the exchanges. She'd email a recipe that Spencer and I might try, and I'd send him home with a sample of whatever we made. Or she'd offer to pick up the kids from school for me when it snowed. She never came in, but she'd beep the horn and wave. I would miss her. I would miss her insane questions and grand plans and how deeply she felt everything. Mostly, I would miss how hard she had tried to be happy, to make us happy. A few times, I'd see her car at the diner when I finished a run, and I'd want so much to go in, plunk down opposite her at our old booth, and ask how she was. But I didn't feel ready.

In January, I would drive to Rehoboth with Eva, who was moving to the East Coast for good. Erik would come the next time, but I needed to make the first trip without him. I would drive by the house where I'd grown up, sit in my dad's restaurant, and shop in Browseabout. I'd look for Lucy everywhere and think I saw her a dozen times, though, of course, it was never her. Why would she be at the beach in January? Wherever she was, she'd be in school, her junior year. I wondered if she'd started thinking about college yet, if she was still dating Trevor. My mom and I would talk constantly, walking the empty frigid boardwalk, turning backward against the wind, our eyes tearing from the cold. I told her how sorry I was for all she had given up so that I could have the life I did.

"Oh, sweet girl." She would cup her frozen hands to my face. "Who do you think I learned that from?"

On Lucy's seventeenth birthday, I'd finally go to the house on Fourth Street where I'd lived with Nick. The weather would abruptly turn overnight into one of those impossibly warm January days that are completely out of season, the air almost balmy, as if the weather itself were offering forgiveness. Nothing looked the same. The house was painted an odd mint green with lavender shutters that made me smile. Nick would have hated it. But seeing the house also made me ache. I could remember so clearly the day I brought her home, still wearing the plastic hospital bracelet with her name, *Lucy Kelly Jarrell.* I had felt like the luckiest woman in the world. I had been her mother. I still was. The tears would come then, and I would cry and cry and cry as I'd never had the chance to, as I'd never understood I had the right to.

It would feel like a kind of grace.

And not until months later—the rainy morning I showed up at Annabelle's for the first time in almost a year with a peanut butter mochaccino for her and a latte for me, and she pulled open the door, eyes welling, and said, "Get in here," and then again, the blustery afternoon when I put the finishing touches on *Weathering*—would it occur to me that theater itself, so much a part of our lives, so much a part of our own season of perfect happiness, had begun with weather. Long before the word *theater* existed, primitive man, terrified by winter, afraid he had done something to displease the gods and so was being punished, offered sacrifices to induce fertility in the spring and enacted dramatic rituals, complete with masks and costumes, to ensure the return of summer.

Theater as a kind of prayer. Like friendship. Like a marriage.

Of course I knew none of this the night of the play as I sat in our driveway, inhaling the smell of Kelly's cigarettes and staring up at the moon. But I think I sensed it: As soon as I got out of the car and unlocked our front door and walked inside, it would almost be like the opening night of a whole new play.

ACKNOWLEDGMENTS

Eighteen years ago, my twelve-year-old niece, Abby, my mom, and I sat in a diner in Genesee Depot, Wisconsin, writing to prompts chosen from the book *What If?* Abby chose the prompt that day, and it became both the title of this novel and the first page. And so, my gratitude starts there, with you, Abby. I love that this novel about families literally began with mine.

I have an amazing family. Always, our favorite subject of conversation is books. My mother, Mary Jo Balistreri, and my father, John Fischer, are the most well-read, passionate people I know. My mother worked as a docent at Ten Chimneys, and she introduced me to the magical world of the Lunts, and my brother, Mike, a dramaturge and theater critic, offered advice about plays that my characters Eva and Kelly might have acted in. I will never stop being grateful for the gift of these people in my corner.

As if having this vibrant book-loving family weren't enough, I also belong to the Rehoboth Beach Writers Guild, a community that encourages, inspires, and reminds me every day of how lucky we are, of what a luxury it is, to spend time, energy, and care on writing.

Add to all that bounty an even rarer luxury—I live in a

town with an independent bookstore. Susan Kehoe, the wildly creative owner of Browseabout Books, is both colleague and friend, whose honesty helped me decide on the beautiful cover of *A Season of Perfect Happiness*.

I wish I could name all the people who have played a role in the writing of this novel, but that would be another book. Still, Jen Epler, I will never forget our cold rainy walk on the Rehoboth Beach boardwalk a few days after I found my agent. Everyone, including me, expected I'd feel joy and excitement—and I did, but you understood the unexpected grief I didn't know what to do with. Kim Burnett, during the days of seemingly impossible deadlines, you left soup and bread on my porch. Paul Dyer, how many phone conversations did we spend talking about the only thing that mattered in this crazy publishing world? The writing. Always the writing. Judy Wood, I am grateful for the hundreds of miles we've walked after Saturday-morning Writing Boot Camp, worrying and obsessing as we debated every plot change, edit, and tweak in the cover designs of our books. And Judy Jones, you believed in me when I wasn't able to believe in myself. That belief is why I am now writing these acknowledgments.

I wrote a version of this novel in 2008, sent it out to agents, was rejected, and put it away, never thinking of it until a chance conversation ten years later with the brilliant writer Leslie Pietrzyk, who told me, "You need to revisit that book." I did because of her. And to the agent who read the manuscript and rejected it in 2008, and again in 2020, but took the time to email and explain why—thank you. The publishing world is too full of silence, and it's not okay; writers deserve a response, even if only a form letter. That agent's response was more than that, and it kept me in the game.

Which ultimately led me to my agent, Kerry D'Agostino,

who took a chance on a writer who hadn't published in fifteen years, a writer terrified of social media, a writer who had lost her way. Thank you for your belief in me and in *A Season of Perfect Happiness*. Thank you especially for getting my manuscript to my editor, Grace Layer, because Grace is . . . she *is* grace. Supersmart, generous, excited, honest. The more we worked together, the more I came to depend on Grace's keen eye. There are sections in this book that I love anew each time I read them, and many stem from a suggestion of Grace's.

Her first email to me, the day after she acquired the book for Dutton, read, "Welcome home," and indeed, it has truly been a homecoming, for Dutton published my first book in 2001. From the editor in chief, John Parsley, who has quietly weighed in at every level; to Sarah Oberrender, who designed the book cover (Sarah read the entire manuscript first, and it shows, for she captured so beautifully the feel of this novel); to Aja Pollock, without whose copyediting this book would not be the book I want so much for it to be. Aja noticed inconsistencies that I had missed through dozens of careful (or so I thought) readings. I'm in awe of—and grateful for—her skill. There are many others—Alice Dalrymple, Shannon Plunkett, Diamond Bridges, Lauren Morrow—it is daunting and humbling to realize how many resources and how much care so many people have invested.

And my husband, Victor Letonoff. At one point when I had to substantially rethink the plot, rewrite the manuscript, and do it all in ten days, I sat at our kitchen counter and looked at him with despair. "I can't," I said. "There's no way."

"What do you mean, you can't?" he said. "This is who you are, Maribeth. This is what you do. You write." I love the man who knows this about me and supports it every single day. Because the time I steal for my writing is always time stolen from him. Not once—ever—in fourteen years has he complained. *This is who you are. This is what you do.*

With that, you'd think the place of honor in these acknowledgments would go to him, my amazing husband, but as great he is, that honor has to go to my friend and writing partner—a beautiful novelist herself—Anne Colwell. For twenty years Anne and I have met once a week to discuss whatever we are working on. She has read and reread and read again every page of *Season,* and so much that is good about the book, and everything that got it to the point where I could send it out to agents, happened because of her input. I can't imagine writing without her, and I'm glad I don't have to.

ABOUT THE AUTHOR

MARIBETH FISCHER is the founder and executive director of the Rehoboth Beach Writers Guild and the author of *The Language of Good-bye* and *The Life You Longed For*. She has received three Delaware Division of the Arts fellowships and two Pushcart Prizes for her essays. She holds an MFA in creative writing from Virginia Commonwealth University.